"AND JUST WHAT *IS* 2XS?"

"It's a chip," Bent said. "A new chip."

"Just a chip?" I questioned.

He sighed. "Think of the difference—Simsense gives you the movie, but with all five senses instead of just two. BTL gives you the same, but pushes the sensory signal to the red line. Well, 2XS is the next step. It hits you at all the physiological levels: adrenaline, endorphins, *everything*. A user feels like he can rule the world."

"And of course it's addictive as hell."

He nodded. "Physically addictive and psychologically habituating. One touch of it, and you never want anything else. . . ."

SHADOWRUN 4: 2XS

PERILOUS DOMAINS

SHADOWRUN 4:

2XS

NIGEL FINDLEY

A ROC BOOK

ROC
Published by the Penguin Group
Penguin Books USA Inc., 375 Hudson Street,
New York, New York 10014, U. S. A.
Penguin Books Ltd, 27 Wrights Lane,
London W8 5TZ, England
Penguin Books Australia Ltd, Ringwood,
Victoria, Australia
Penguin Books Canada Ltd, 10 Alcorn Avenue,
Toronto, Ontario, Canada M4V 3B2
Penguin Books (N.Z.) Ltd, 182–190 Wairau Road,
Auckland 10, New Zealand

Penguin Books Ltd, Registered Offices:
Harmondsworth, Middlesex, England

First published by Roc, an imprint of New American Library,
a division of Penguin Books USA Inc.

First Printing, February, 1992
10 9 8 7 6 5 4 3 2 1

Series Editor: Donna Ippolito
Cover: John Zeleznick
Interior Illustrations: Joel Biske

RoC   Roc is a trademark of New American Library, a division of
Penguin Books USA Inc. Shadowrun, and the distinctive Shadowrun
logo, are trademarks of the FASA Corporation, 1026 W. Van Buren,
Chicago, Ill. 60507

Printed in the United States of America

To HTL
Thanks for putting up with the necessary schizophrenia
of the novelist. Reality ends here.

1

If this thing could be said to have started anywhere, I suppose it started with a woman with a gun.

It had been one of those days. I was scragged to the bone, so tired I could barely keep my eyes open as I climbed the two flights of stairs to my doss in the La Jolla Apartments. (Don't be fooled. The name may be fancy, but that's about all that can make the claim on D Street in Auburn.) Assorted lacerations and abrasions about my neck and chest were making their presence felt, and a nasty contusion on my left thigh—where my armored duster had just barely stopped a small-caliber round—throbbed dully. On the bright side, the certified credstick in my pants pocket bulged with nuyen and was like a comfortable warmth. I could never be sure when dealing with Anwar the fixer, but this time he had paid my fee in full.

I was glad to see that the corridor leading to my door was empty. Security at the La Jolla is a laugh when it comes to keeping out serious trouble, but it's generally enough to keep out the gutterpunks and chippies. Just as well, too. Scragged as I was, I wouldn't have been much good at persuading some half-drowned squatter to step aside. Reaching my door, I thumbed the lock, then stepped inside with a sigh.

The message light on my telecom was flashing, the sequence indicating the number of calls that had come in. I gave up counting at nine. What could I expect after being out of the sprawl for almost five days? For a while I'd had a portable phone, but I'd quit carrying it when the damn thing went off during a surveillance job. I'd forgotten to disable the buzzer, and almost got my head blown off. Right now I wasn't in any drekking mood to deal with phone messages, but it was possible one of the calls might be related to a case I was working on. Even better, there might be an offer to take on a new case.

Case. Why not use the word most people would for what I do? *Shadowrun.*

To me, there's a difference, that's why. Other people might not recognize it, but the distinction matters to me. Circumstances may have forced me to edge my way into the shadows, but I emphatically do not consider myself a shadowrunner. A shadowrunner will usually take on any kind of operation he's physically able to handle: extraction, datasteal, lift-out, transport, muscle, even—in some cases—out-and-out wetwork. Me, I'm selective. I'll do surveillance, I'll do recovery, I'll even do close-cover if I figure the body I'm guarding is worth keeping alive. But I've got to know the *why* before I'll take any job, and the reason has to make at least a bit of sense to me.

The world's a dark place, full of people who either enjoy making it darker or else don't give a frag if that's how it works out. I'm not so dense as to believe I can reverse that trend all by my lonesome, but I sure as drek can decide not to make it any worse. And even if I did want to make it worse, hell, I'd have too much competition.

Remember about twelve years back that revival of old—I mean *old*—pre-simsense, "hard-boiled" detective fiction? It was real period stuff, set maybe a century ago, but it seemed to really click with some people. If I'd been in business in those old days, I'd probably have had a license, an office—maybe with my name on the frosted glass door, "Derek Montgomery, Investigations"—and a gun. Now? No license, and my office is wherever I happen to be at the time. I've got the gun, though.

The throbbing in my left thigh reminded me that, unfortunately, so does everybody else. And too many people aren't afraid to use that firepower, no matter how small the provocation. Take today, for example. The guy who shot me wasn't even involved with the case I was working. He was just some wireheaded kid who'd slotted one too many "Slade the Sniper" chips and decided to unload his Streetline Special into a crowd of pedestrians. I just happened to be in the wrong place at the wrong time.

The kid's luck wasn't any better. Very calmly, very

professionally, the guy beside me handled the situation by sending a magical fireball back along the line of fire and cooking the kid where he stood. Then the mage just as calmly moved off down an alley, and that was that. Such is life (and death) in the Awakened world.

Well, at least I could turn my back on all that for the next twelve hours. Even better, I wouldn't have to worry about people pointing guns at me. And if they did, I'd be too sound asleep to know it. I kicked the door shut, made sure the maglock was engaged, and hung my duster on a hook in the corner. The drab wash of the rainy Auburn twilight leaked through the partially polarized window, giving the one-room doss a dull, tired illumination that perfectly suited my mood. I considered turning on a light, then decided against it. I could find the bed even in the dark, and that's all I really wanted to do.

For one fleeting moment I thought about food. My stomach felt like a clenched fist, but even the half-minute it would take to flash one of the packs of Soyamenu stashed in the freezer would mean a half-minute I wasn't sleeping. Easy decision. I sat on the edge of the bed, pulled off my boots, and flopped back, still fully clothed. I swear I was falling asleep even before my head hit the pillow.

I was drifting through a warm, drowsy haze when the door chimed. Probably one of my neighbors, making a courtesy call. "Frag off and die!" I shouted in my best neighborly, courteous manner.

The slag at the door didn't take my subtle hint. The chime sounded again. With another neighborly curse, I flailed around on the bedside table, creating minor havoc until I found the remote control. Thumbing a button, I opened one eye to look at the telecom screen.

The tiny security camera hidden in the wall above the door—courtesy of a chummer of mine—picked up the image of my visitor and splashed it onto the screen. I opened my other eye for a better look.

Even foreshortened by the camera angle, the visitor was definitely worth the additional effort. Tall and slim— just under a meter-eight, I judged—with short, straight coppery hair. From this perspective, it was hard to make out features, but the camera's angle of vision showed me the chrome-edged datajack I might not have immediately

spotted otherwise. Her clothes weren't quite haute cou-
ture, but they were certainly a cut above anything seen
on the street of southwest Auburn, particularly after the
sun goes down. The tailored gray synthleather suit enhanced rather than concealed the arresting curves of her
figure, but—considering the place and time—I'd have bet
that jacket was as armored as it was stylish. Mid-level
corp, I tagged her. But the look of her clothes told me
she wasn't in working-class Auburn for the rush of putting her pretty body on the line—that foolish game some
people called "sprawling." No, for that her outfit would
have been newer but would have looked older.

I hit another button on the remote. "Yeah, whaddaya
want?" I growled.

The redhead jumped at the sound of my voice, then
glanced around for the speaker. Her cool gray eyes
scanned the area around the door, seeming to pick out
the camera's location almost immediately. (Interesting, I
thought. You have to know something about tech to pick
out my toys.)

"Derek Montgomery?" she inquired. Her voice was
low and smooth, but with a touch of nervous edge. I
wondered what it would be like to hear her say my name
without that edge.

"What do you want?" I repeated, enunciating a little
better.

I knew she couldn't see me, but I had the strange sensation those eyes were fixed on mine. "I want to talk to
you," she said levelly. "It's important. It's . . ." She
hesitated.

". . . A matter of life and death?" I finished for her.

If she noticed the irony in my voice, she gave no sign.
"Yes," she shot back. "Yes, that's just what it is."

I gave her one final scan. Her clothes said money, her
manner said money. When you do what I do, the problem
isn't finding people who want your services. It's finding
people who can *pay* for your services.

"Yeah, well, maybe," I grumbled. "And just who are
you?"

I expected some kind of street handle, but she surprised me. "My name is Jocasta Yzerman," she said
matter-of-factly.

"All right," I told her, "give me a tick." I keyed up

the lights, killed the security camera, and clambered out of bed. Checking the mirror, I saw that my eyes were bloodshot and my clothes looked like I'd slept in them— no surprise there. I raked fingers through my hair, rumpling one side to erase the flat spot made by the pillow. Then I crossed to the door and swung it open.

"Come on in," I said, stepping out of her way.

In the flesh my visitor looked even better than on the screen. The thin, tight line of her mouth said she was obviously distressed about something, but I liked imagining how those lips would look in a smile. Stepping inside, she didn't spare my place even a quick glance. Just as I'd figured, she was business, all business.

"Grab a seat," I told her, shutting the door and double-checking the maglock. Then I turned back to her, giving Jocasta Yzerman my best professional poker face.

She was standing, almost quiveringly alert, in the middle of the room. But after the first millisecond I didn't even notice her bearing. That was because all my attention was focused on the weapon that had sprung into existence in her left hand.

Officially, the Colt America L36 is classed as a light pistol, barely one step up from a holdout: five mil, with an eight-centimeter barrel. But even the lightest pistol seems to have a bore like a subway tunnel when you're looking down the business end of one. From the way the barrel-top laser sight flared in my vision, I knew its ruby-red targeting point was centered between my eyes.

I gauged the distance between us. A couple of meters. If I tried to go for her gun, I'd *almost* make it before she got off a shot. It would be real close, but close only counts in horseshoes, hand grenades, and dancing. So instead I showed her my empty hands, forced a disarming smile onto my face, and put on my best let's-keep-calm-here tone of voice.

"Hey, let's keep calm here," I said somewhat lamely. "If there's a problem, we can talk about it and—"

She cut me off, her voice cold as steel. "You killed my sister," she announced.

"And now you're going to kill me? Makes perfect sense."

Again, she missed the irony. "That's right," she said. "You killed Lolita."

"Lolita . . ." That's when it hit me. It must have been my general grogginess that kept me from realizing her surname was familiar. Lolita Yzerman, a name from the past. We'd met a few years back when I'd helped her out of a real bad spot. It wasn't long before we got something hot and heavy going, but then Lolita iced me out of her life, probably figuring a chummer like me wasn't what you'd call an asset for a smart, ambitious girl like her. It had been, *frag,* almost a year since we'd spoken.

And now she was dead. Little Lolly, of the bubbly laugh and big blue eyes.

"That's right—Lolita," said Jocasta Yzerman, jolting me back to the present. "I'm glad you remember her name."

It was my turn to ignore the irony. "Hey, look," I told her, "I know Lolita . . . *knew* her, we had a thing going. You probably know that. But the last time I talked to her, the last time I saw her, was sometime early last year. I didn't kill your sister. Why would I?"

As I spoke, I watched her eyes. You can learn a lot from somebody's eyes. If nothing else, you can sometimes tell when they're about to pull the trigger. There was a shadow of . . . *something* . . . in Jocasta's gray eyes. It wasn't quite doubt, but it was enough to give me hope. No matter how steady she held that gun, her eyes told me she didn't really want to use it, not deep down. She'd steeled herself to this point, and she could probably steel herself enough to actually pull the trigger. But she didn't want to. She wanted to find some reason not to take my life. And that was a desire I could fully support.

"You had your reasons," she said.

"*What* reasons?" I asked, spreading my hands and taking a slow step backward. Noticing the move, Jocasta did the natural thing in response: she took a couple of steps forward. The distance between us was a little less. Not much, but it was a step in the right direction. "What reasons?" I repeated.

"To get out from under," Jocasta said coldly. "It was the only way to stop her from blackmailing you."

I stared at her. Blackmail . . . Sure, from what I'd seen of Lolly, she was capable of trying to carry off blackmail if the stakes were high enough. But I was safe. She hadn't known enough about me.

"Believe me," I said, becoming sincerity personified, "Lolly couldn't blackmail me because she *had* nothing on me." Again I stepped back; again Jocasta stepped forward. This time the little gavotte cut the distance between us to slightly less than two meters.

And not a moment too soon, for something changed in her eyes. When she spoke, her voice was sharper, more strained. She was working up her anger so that she'd be able to pull the trigger. "You're lying," she snapped. "You're a liar *and* a murderer. You did something bad and my sister knew about it, so you killed her. You killed my sister." She was crying now, almost hysterical.

Her finger tightened on the trigger. "Die, you motherfragger."

In that instant, I moved. I pivoted sideways, my torso and head swinging down and to the left, my right foot scything up and around. Just in time. Jocasta's silenced pistol coughed, the bullet making a whipcrack as it split the air terrifyingly close to my head, then shattered something behind me. My right foot swung on through, slamming into the inside of the woman's wrist. A perfect scythe-kick disarm. That kick would have made my instructors at Lone Star proud, though they'd probably have been sorry her bullet hadn't connected.

The charge of adrenalin must have fired me up a little more than usual. Coming around with the force of my momentum, I saw that the kick had done more than take her gun offline and break her grip. I'd literally kicked the woman off her feet. She lay huddled on the floor, whimpering, clutching her quite possibly broken right wrist to her belly.

I hesitated. It wasn't that I thought she was faking it; the impact had been hard enough to hurt my foot, even through the adrenalin. It was my emotions that were slotting me up. Part of me was glad to see my would-be murderer injured, at least to some minor degree. Had I not reacted, her little bullet would have splashed the thinking part of Derek Montgomery all over my apartment wall.

Another part of me, though, saw a woman in pain, and

I reacted in the predictable manner. She hadn't *wanted* to kill me. It was something she thought she *had* to do, something she had to work herself up to, and something that probably would have fragged up the rest of her life with guilt. I picked up her gun and slipped it into the waistband of my trousers. Then I knelt beside her.

Jocasta was curled up in fetal position, her slender shoulders shaking with the deep sobs racking her throat. I paused before tentatively reaching out to lay a hand gently on her back, taking care to make the gesture as non-sexual as possible. (That was a further complexity I just didn't want to get into.) She didn't shy away from my touch, but I could feel the muscles of her back tighten as though she might somehow pull her skin away from a loathsome contact.

I sighed. Okay, if that's the way she wanted it. I stood up, pulled the gun from my waistband, and placed it on a table within easy reach. Then I sat down in the apartment's only chair. Depending on how tough she was, it might be a while before Jocasta could pull herself together. Might as well be comfortable while I waited. I triggered the massage system, another toy courtesy of the chummer who'd done my security camera, then settled back into the armchair's warm embrace. And I watched.

It didn't take her long at all. Mentally tough, this Jocasta Yzerman. Knowing her sister, that shouldn't have surprised me. First the sobs stopped, then the shaking. Then, slowly, she unwound from her fetal ball. When I could see her face again, it seemed unmarked by a single tear nor were her eyes even red or puffy. I glanced down at her right wrist, and felt like a slotting bastard. It was already swollen and starting to discolor, though I didn't think it was broken. She seemed to pay it no mind as she rose to her feet, as though the pain wasn't worthy of her notice.

I watched her, fascinated. There was a grace, a kind of poise, to her movements that she hadn't shown before. It was as if her homicidal mission, however unsuccessful, had freed her in some way. Her eyes were steady on my face. They didn't show hatred, they didn't show fear. If anything, they showed resignation, almost fatalism. Her face was calm, any calmer and I'd have declared her dead.

"I'm sorry," she said quietly, not a trace of emotion in that voice. "I'll go now."

I was out of the chair before she'd taken a step. I reached out to grasp her shoulder, but pulled my hand back at the last moment. I'd seen emotional control before, and I'd seen what happens when it cracks. I didn't want to do anything to trigger that. Instead, I only stretched an arm out across her path like a gate. "No," I told her, "don't go."

She looked up into my eyes. "Why not?" Again, not a hint of anything in her voice, not even curiosity.

Which was ironic, because curiosity was exactly what was consuming me at the moment. There were some things about this whole slotting mess that I'd better know. I needed a better answer for the lady, though.

I tried to keep it light. "Oh, I don't know," I temporized. "Call it misplaced hospitality, but I don't feel right if somebody comes over and tries to shoot me, then leaves before I can even offer her a drink."

The response was just what I'd expected: a whole lot of nothing. At least she'd stopped walking for the door. I hesitated a moment, then grasped her shoulder. Gently, and *very* slowly I turned her around. I felt that muscle-tension reaction again, but her visible control didn't crack. I gave her a soft push toward my chair.

"Go on," I told her. "Have a seat. I'd like to talk."

She walked smoothly in the direction I'd pushed her. The grace was still there, but it had a kind of mindlessness now. Her brain was in full control of her body, but that control was below conscious level, like an autopilot. It was like a waking form of sleep-walking. She turned and plopped down into the chair.

That got a reaction out of her. I'd neglected to turn off the massage system, and it was still running full-blast. As her back and bottom touched the chair, I saw all her muscles spasm, and she virtually levitated a couple of centimeters above the seat. Then gravity reasserted itself, and she fell back into the chair's embrace. This time she didn't fight it. Her whole body seemed to go limp, and her eyelids drooped to half-mast. Her eyes were still on me, though.

I watched her for a few moments, then went to sit

down on the edge of my bed. "I'm sorry about Lolly," I told her quietly.

Again, no response. I sighed. I'd seen people strapped up this tight before. Usually they'd come out of it on their own by suddenly cracking—sometimes at the worst possible moment. A few, though, would never let themselves go. Jocasta had broken down, just for a few minutes, lying on my floor. That had been cathartic, but it obviously wasn't enough. The fact that it had happened at all gave me some hope that she could go all the way. All she needed was the right kind of push.

Why am I even thinking this? I asked myself again. It wasn't my problem. It was she who'd decided to kill me, and she could fragging well live with the consequences of that decision. I should just leave her to it, and to hell with Jocasta Yzerman. But, for various reasons, that wasn't acceptable.

I'm no idealist; an idealist couldn't last very long in the world of 2052. In fact, I'm as cold and hard as the next man when necessary. But that doesn't mean I feel good about turning my back on a situation where I might be able to help. There was another reason, too, of course. I'd known Lolita Yzerman. I think I might even have loved her. Now she was dead. It was too late to help Lolly, but I *could* help her sister Jocasta.

"Do you have a picture of Lolly?" I asked softly. Jocasta nodded. She reached into her pocket and brought out a palm-sized holo. She reached out to hand it to me. "Uh-uh," I told her, shaking my head. "*You* look at it."

She hesitated, perhaps realizing what I was doing, but then she did as I told her. She stared at the holo for a moment before her face began to twist with grief. The holo dropped from suddenly nerveless fingers. With a soft keening sound, she slumped down and forward in the chair. Her forehead was touching her knees and she was gripping the sides of her head as if to keep her skull from exploding. Once again, her body was racked with gasping sobs.

I turned away, a little embarrassed. Not wanting to intrude further on the grief of this weeping woman, I picked up the forgotten picture.

2

Lolita Yzerman. The holo was obviously an amateur job, slightly out of focus and the perspective a bit off. But it was good enough. It was unmistakably Lolly who smiled out from the holo.

On the surface, Lolly and Jocasta did not show a striking family resemblance. Jocasta was tall, where Lolly was short, with wavy blonde hair and bright blue eyes. And Jocasta was slender, somewhat sharp and austere, where Lolly was attractively rounded in all the right places. Looking closer, though, I could see the resemblance. The same cheekbones. The same mouth—a little small for the face, with good teeth. And, of course, both had datajacks high on their right temples.

Lolly Yzerman. She'd told me a little of her story. I hadn't automatically believed all of it, but some parts had the unmistakable ring of truth. Her father, David Yzerman, had been a big-rep freelance computer designer. Lolly's own brilliance in math and science had shown up early, so it was only logical that she follow in her father's footsteps. She'd entered the University of Washington's Computer Sciences program at the tender age of fifteen, graduating less than three years later, U-Dub's youngest honor grad. I suppose her father had been supplementing her training as well. Even while still a student, Lolly was doing hired-gun programming work for a drekload of local outfits, all the while building an extraordinary track record.

Predictably, she decided that she needed a datajack to really progress, but her father refused to even consider letting his daughter go under the laser until she was twenty-one. Just as predictably, Lolly didn't give a frag what her father said. She took on a few more contracts to earn enough nuyen, then ran away to get the operation done. She was still only seventeen, I think. Lolly's father had punished her when she returned home, the shiny new jack in place, but Lolly was sure he was secretly very proud. She laughed when telling me about it.

The contracts kept coming from all over: Matrix programming, system analysis, hardware design and maybe even a few shadowy Matrix runs, but she never talked about that. Until now a generalist, Lolly began to specialize. She'd always loved solving puzzles, she'd told me, and soon she found her niche in signal-enhancement and "washing." Washing was the half-art, half-science of picking out the true signal from background noise, and then cleaning it of distortion. Her goal had always been to work for UCASSA—the UCAS Space Agency—enhancing signals from deep-space probes, improving the signal-to-noise, or S/N, ratio. But she was still young, and would need to gather more experience before she could get the job she wanted. And that was why she signed on with Avatar Security Technologies, one of the Lone Star subsidiaries—to get experience.

Lone Star needs signal-enhancement specialists, too, but for a very different reason than UCASSA. When Lone Star conducts an investigation, standard procedure is to tap the telecoms of everyone even peripherally involved with the subject of the investigation. That's right, *everyone,* whether or not he or she is suspected of a crime. An infringement of personal rights? Morally and ethically speaking, you've got it, chummer. But according to the *letter* of the law, if not the spirit, it's kosher. As long, that is, as Lone Star notifies everyone whose line has been tapped . . . within four months of the tap's *removal.* But can't Lone Star get around that restriction by leaving the tap in place forever? Again, you've got it, chummer. Lone Star officers are notoriously absent-minded when it comes to notification.

Anyway, somebody has to handle all the data that comes out of the tap. In Seattle, that somebody is Avatar, and that's where Lolly ended up. Taps and bugs are notoriously noisy. The signals get fragged up by all the electronic drek just about everybody's got at home these days, and the S/N ration is fragging awful. Sure, contemporary signal-enhancement software and automatic filtering algorithms are sophisticated and wiz, but sometimes they're just not wiz enough. What's needed is that indefinable something, that purely human artistry that some people seem born with. Lolly was one of those people, and the signal-washing job might well have been created especially for her. She told me that she never listened to the contents of the taps. She didn't give a frag about what the subjects were saying. The only thing that mattered was tweaking the data stream to give that last boost to the S/N ratio.

That's how Lolly and I met. It was while doing some shadowy work for a Lone Star employee that I found out, purely by accident, that little Lolly had gotten herself into deep drek. Seems that Lolly, who was only twenty at the time, was involved in some Machiavellian political infighting, with her blackmailing some guy who was trying to block her advancement because she'd rebuffed his sexual advances. Lolly had gotten in way over her head. Because of some leverage I'd developed during my own case, I was in the perfect position to help her out, which I did, pro bono. When her opponent moved on to another company, Lolly was in the clear. Meanwhile we'd slipped into a torrid affair that lasted five exhausting weeks.

I learned a lot about Lolita Yzerman in that short time. Because of her looks, a lot of people's first impression was that Lolly was a bubble-headed blonde, with nothing weightier on her mind than getting a blast out of life. *Wrong*. That was a mask she wore, and it was a good one. If you did manage to see through it, however, you found a calculating person, someone ruthless about getting what she wanted. Part of me hurt bad when Lolly broke off our relationship, but another part recognized that perhaps it was a lucky escape.

Her tattoos probably said it best. On each ankle was a delicate tattoo that glowed baby-blue under UV light. The left one read, "Good girls go to heaven"; the right one said, "Bad girls go everywhere." Lolly Yzerman went everywhere.

And now she was dead. I set the holo down and looked over at Jocasta.

She was starting to pull herself back together. Though she still had her face down on her knees, the heaving of her shoulders had stopped. Tough woman. The second break had been bad. Some people might not come back from something like that for a couple of months—and then only if they found a good head-shrinker.

I felt the need for a drink. I didn't feel like sleeping anymore—amazing what a laser sight between the eyes will do for you—but my brain was leaden with adrenalin hangover. The bar was within easy reach of the bed (convenient), so I didn't even have to stand up. I poured myself a good clout of synthahol masquerading as scotch, hesitated, then poured a second drink for Jocasta.

When I turned back, she was sitting upright and gazing steadily at me. Those cool gray eyes were clear and focused. Still emotionless, but watchful and fully aware. That last catharsis seemed to have straightened her out, at least on the surface. (I wouldn't want to share the dreams she'd probably have, though.) Like I said, tough woman. Wordlessly I handed her the drink.

I watched her hand as she took the glass. Steady, no visible shake at all. She inclined her head minutely in what might—just—have been a nod of thanks, and took a sip. She screwed up her face a little at the taste, either because she didn't like scotch or because she liked *real* scotch, but she took another mouthful. Then she lowered the glass.

Her silence and her steady gaze, still fixed on my face, were making me uncomfortable. I took a swallow of my own drink, mainly for something to do. Then I asked, "Can you tell me what happened?"

"Lolita was shot, point-blank, in the face." Her voice wasn't the dead monotone it had been earlier, but it was dispassionate, as though describing a downturn in the stock market instead of the murder of her sister. "It happened in her apartment. The police said she apparently opened the door to someone she knew, someone she trusted. And he shot her." Her words said "he," but her eyes were still saying "you"—meaning me.

"How did you connect me?" I pressed. "How did you even know my name?"

She shrugged slightly. "I'd known about you all along," she said. "Lolita told me about your . . . involvement." For the first time Jocasta was showing a little discomfort.

"We had an affair," I told her flatly. "But you also know it lasted less than two months, and we haven't been in contact since."

"Until she started blackmailing you."

I sighed. Blackmail again. "For what? And how did you get that idea anyway?"

"She sent me an e-mail message two days ago, the day before . . . before she died." Her icy control almost slipped there. I found that somehow reassuring. Tough she might be, but she *was* human.

"And how did you know where to find me?"

She looked at me like I was an idiot. "Lolly told me."

Interesting. As far as I knew, Lolly didn't know where I lived. She had my phone number, sure, but I'd moved several times since we'd been together. "Go on about the message," I said.

"She was scared, and was just starting to realize how dangerous you were. That's why she told me all about it."

Something occurred to me. "A voice message?"

She shook her head, and her copper hair swung. "No, text only."

Even more interesting. But I'd follow up on that later. "What did she say? What was she supposedly black-mailing me for?"

"She didn't say," Jocasta said slowly. "She only told me you'd done something wrong. You'd stepped over the line—those were her words. And if she let it out, it would destroy your ongoing relationship with Lone Star."

I barked with bitter laughter, making her flinch. "Oh, drek," I almost snarled. "Do you know what my 'on-going relationship' with Lone Star is?" I didn't wait for her to answer. "They're looking for me. They're trying to track me down. I went through their training program, I was going to be a cop. Then I found out just what that meant, and I skipped. Lone Star doesn't like that. I think my continued existence offends their delicate corporate sensibilities. My 'ongoing relationship' is that they're trying to find me and I'm trying not to be found."

I swallowed back my anger—talking about Lone Star always slots me off—and took another gulp of near-scotch.

Her eyes were still on me, but now I could see the wheels turning as she thought it through. "But you worked for Lone Star," she said slowly. "That's how you met Lolita."

"Yeah, sure, I've done some work for individual Lone

Star *employees*, but it's all been shadow stuff, all out-of-the-light. For Lone Star itself? Frag, no. My only payment would be a holding cell or a nine-millimeter migraine.'' I snorted. "But I suppose you don't believe me.

"Look," I went on, a little quieter, "it's been a rough couple of days, and I feel like drek. I'm going to check my messages—now that I'm awake—but then I'm going back to bed. Feel free to finish your drink, then feel free to use the door. If you want to talk about it again, call me back in thirty-six hours or so.''

I turned my back on her, slid down the bed until I could reach the telecom, and shifted the flat screen so I could see it better. Then I keyed in Message Replay. Instantly the screen lit up with the weasel-like face of Anwar the fixer. "Dirk," he began, but I hit the hold key. I checked the time/date stamp in the bottom-right corner. Wednesday, November 13, 2052—six days ago. Probably a demand for a status report on the case. Well, I'd given him his status report a few hours ago—case closed—and picked up my payment. Frag Anwar. I hit Delete and keyed for the next message.

Anwar again, Friday, November 15. Delete. Next.

The screen lit up once more. Another weasel, not Anwar but another of his kind. "Montgomery," the weasel snarled, "the credstick you sent me is short. I'm very displeased.''

"Oh, yeah?" I snarled back at the image. The payment from Anwar would be more than enough to cover outstanding debts, including this weasel. He could wait till tomorrow. Frag him. Delete. Next.

This time the screen remained blank. Voice only. I could guess who this was. The familiar voice from the speaker just confirmed it. "Mr. Dirk," the cultured voice said smoothly, "this is Mr. . . . Johnson. I just wish to confirm that you are indeed working on . . ." I hit hold. There was no need to let Jocasta hear about biz. This particular Mr. Johnson had called a week ago from somewhere back east—Chicago, I guessed from the accent—with a simple trace job. A missing employee, and the great benevolent corporation wanted to confirm that nothing bad had happened to her (like drek). And now Johnson, like everyone else and his fragging dog, wanted a status report. Tomorrow. Save, this time. Next.

The next image, and the voice, galvanized me like a taser hit. Instinctively I glanced over my shoulder. Jocasta was bolt-upright in the chair, staring at the screen.

No wonder. The big blue eyes of Lolita Yzerman looked back at me from the telecom. In place of the familiar twinkle was a shadow I knew very well. Fear. Lolly was terrified out of her wits. I glanced at the time/date stamp: Saturday, November 16, 2052. The day before yesterday. The day before little Lolly was blown away. I leaned forward.

"Derek," Lolly's image said quietly, "if you're there, answer, please. I need to talk to you." She paused for a few moments, then her normally steady gaze dropped. When she looked up, the shadow in her eyes was darker. "I guess you're not there," she went on sadly. My heart went out to her. Poor little girl, now a dead little girl. "When you get back, call me. My number's the same. It's . . ."—she hesitated—"it's really important. I think I'm in deep drek." She forced a smile onto her face, but it was a sorry attempt. "Call me," she repeated. "I'll be waiting. Catch ya, Dirty Dirk."

I hit the key to cancel the rest of the message queue, and sat back, still staring at the blank screen. "Catch ya, Dirty Dirk." One of Lolly's phrases, words from the past. I felt the urge to bring up a freeze-frame from her message, to drown one last time in those deep blue eyes. But I resisted the temptation; I knew how much it would hurt. I remember a line from one of my old Lone Star chummers. "Some girls are like malaria, Derek m'lad," Patrick Bambra used to say, especially when he was into the whiskey. "And once you get 'em in your blood, you're never free of 'em." I wondered idly if Patrick had known Lolly.

With an effort, I pushed back at the depression that threatened to settle over me. I turned toward Jocasta.

And found myself staring down the muzzle of the L36 again, dazzled by the targeting laser. *Frag it*, I'd left the slotting thing on the table, right by the armchair. I can't have been thinking straight. If I hadn't been so bone-fragging tired, I'd never have done anything so drek-headed.

Before I could say anything, Jocasta took her finger off the trigger, and the laser died. Then she let down the pistol's hammer and snapped on the safety, all in a very businesslike manner. She extended the weapon toward me, like a gift. "I'm sorry," she said. "I was wrong. That wasn't a blackmailer talking to a victim . . . or to a murderer." I looked down at the pistol and shook my head. With a nod, she concealed the small weapon in a pouch on her belt.

Silence stretched between us for half a minute. I was feeling too emotionally drained to strike up a conversation, and she was too busy scrutinizing my face. She must have approved of her conclusions, because she gave me a tight, businesslike smile. "You said you do shadow work?" I nodded. "Will you take my nuyen?"

I was very tempted to tell her just what she could do with her money. I didn't think I particularly liked Jocasta Yzerman, but that might just have something to do with her pointing a gun at me twice in twenty minutes. But then I looked into her eyes again, and saw the hurt that was still there and would be for a long time to come. She'd lost a sister. What had I lost? An ex-girlfriend? Not even that, not even a real friend. Just a few hours' sleep and a bit of pride.

I nodded. "Sure." Neither of us had to say what the job was.

She smiled, just barely. "What's your rate?" she asked. She fumbled in another belt pouch, and pulled out a credstick. A three-ring certified credstick. I bumped Jocasta Yzerman up one notch on Montgomery's Socioeconomic Ladder and down one notch on Montgomery's Intelligence Scale. A certified credstick is pure money, no ID needed. And I've got some neighbors who'd happily geek her for a *one*-ring credstick.

I waved her off. "We'll talk about it later," I said. "I don't know if there's anything I can do."

She accepted that with a nod, returning the credstick to her pouch. Then she pulled out a card and handed it to me. "Here's my phone number," she said, smiling again with what looked almost like a real smile this time. "Call me if you get anything." She stood, smoothing the sides of her pants with her palms, and took a breath. "Now get to bed. You look like drek."

"Thanks," I said, perhaps a bit sarcastically. "Shut the door on your way out." I started to settle back onto the bed, then a thought struck me. "How did you get here?" I asked.

"By cab."

"Is he waiting for you?"

"No."

Drek. "You're expecting to flag a cab?"

"Sure," she shot back. "Why not?"

"You don't know Auburn after dark." I levered myself to my feet. "I'll drive you home." I grabbed my duster off the hook and started readying myself to go outside.

She wanted to argue, but seeing that my preparations included checking the action on my Colt Manhunter, she shut up. Smart girl. I shoved the massive chunk of metal back into the duster's built-in holster, and opened the door. "After you," I said chivalrously.

One of the only reasons I like the La Jolla Apartments is that it's about the only building in Auburn that has its own secured parking. Sure, the gate and the locks won't keep out the real pros, but at least it's some protection from the street apes who'll chew up a parked car just to pass the time. The pros wouldn't waste time on my wheels. The body's a standard 2047-vintage Chrysler-Nissan jackrabbit, beat to hell and gone and looking like a piece of drek. All the mods that make the car worth owning are well out of sight.

I thumbed the doors open, and lit up the engine as Jocasta struggled to get her long legs into the passenger side. You know what a normal petrochem Jackrabbit sounds like: a pair of boots in a tumble-dryer. Well, the engine in my baby *sings*. From the look Jocasta shot me, I knew she'd noticed the difference. I just smiled, and turned on the control systems.

Quincy, the same slag who'd done my apartment's security system, worked on the car as well. (It's a great deal Quincy and I have. Thanks to some gray contacts, he buys tech toys at wholesale price minus. I pay for them, and he installs them for free. It's symbiosis. I get some cutting-edge tech for next to nothing, and Quincy gets to play with all the neat hardware.) Jocasta just stared as I fired up the Head-Up Display and the navigation subsystem. "Where do you live?" I asked casually.

"South Fifty-sixth," she said. "The cross-street's Yakima."

I raised an eyebrow—*Tacoma, yet*—but didn't say anything as I punched the destination into the nav system. The screen flashed up a map showing the most direct route. As I'd guessed, just hop onto Route 18 over to Highway 5, then south till you smelled the "Tacoma aroma."

Jocasta watched, fascinated, as I told the nav system to transfer the waypoints to the pilot. "Amazing," she said, shaking her head. "I've only seen anything like that on a Nightsky." I just grinned, even though I'd never seen the inside of a Nightsky. "Does it have rigger controls, too?"

My turn to shake my head. "No use to me," I told her. I brushed back my hair to show a metal-free forehead. "No datajack. I'm off-the-rack."

That surprised her. "Isn't that a drawback in your . . . your occupation?"

I shook my head, and slipped the Jackrabbit into gear. It was a topic I didn't like to think about much. Sure, most of the runners I know have some kind of cyber mods. Datajacks, at the very least. I suppose there've been times when I've wished for a smartgun interface or enhanced optics. But I've always found some reason not to get myself metalled up. It just doesn't seem right. Maybe I'm just insecure, but the idea of losing even a little of myself—of Dirk Montgomery—just doesn't sit well.

We made the trip in silence. As we traveled through the apartment-blanketed hills west of Auburn, the sprawl that is Greater Seattle was glowing like fairy-lights—or maybe a convention of chipped-up fireflies—a spreading sea of light that seemed to reach to the horizons. Its brilliance leeched up into the sky, so thick with chemical smoke and its normal devil's-brew of toxins that the air itself seemed to glow with a sullen red light. The city shone on the underside of the solid cloud deck, which in turn reflected the light back to the earth. Highways were radiant rivers, and the taller buildings were pyramids, ziggurats, or talons of multicolored illumination reaching upward as though the corps wanted to own the clouds, too.

It was easy to tell when we'd entered Tacoma. The buildings were taller, the lights brighter. Even the cars on the freeway were more expensive. Toyota Elites replaced Jackrabbits, and Mitsubishi Nightskys took the place of Westwind 2000s. Even the air seemed cleaner, fresher, but I knew that was just an illusion.

Historically, Tacoma's a weird place. It used to be a sleepy little bedroom community. From pictures I've seen, it looked like small-town U.S.A. around the turn of the century. Then the money rolled in, and Seattle's poor cousin got to go to the ball.

The Taco Dome was a ways behind us on our right when the nav reminded me to take the Fifty-sixth Street exit. I hung a right, flashed around the cloverleaf, and cruised east on South Fifty-sixth, a broad, well-lit street. The buildings on both sides were tall, probably eighty-plus stories. Another difference between Auburn and Tacoma. I'd have known I was out of my neighborhood and rather out of my element even if I didn't see the rich types strolling along the sidewalks. (Strolling? At night?)

South Fifty-sixth hit Yakima, and I turned right on Jocasta's instruction. Nice neighborhood she lived in, and quite different from what we'd passed on Fifty-sixth. Tall buildings seemed to be out of fashion here. The structures flanking the road were low, no more than three or four stories, and they looked for all the world like century-old brownstones. (All make-believe, of course. The "brownstones" were construction-plastic and ferroconcrete jobs, with textured facades that probably included some kind of armor. And if they were more than ten years old, I'd be really surprised. By now, real brownstones would have been turned into piles of sand by the corrosive nasties in the air.)

"That's my place," Jocasta said, pointing. She smiled at my reaction. "Not the whole thing, just half of the top floor." I estimated the building by eye. "Just" half the top floor was maybe four times the size of my doss. Money. Definitely money.

I pulled over and hit the button to pop the door. "I'll call when I've got something," I told her.

But she wasn't paying attention. She was looking, a little dismayed, at a gunmetal-gray Westwind parked two cars up from us.

"What's up?" I asked.

She shook her head. "Tony," was all she said.

"Tony? Is that trouble?"

She shook her head again. "Not the way you mean." She was silent for a moment. "It's Tony DeGianetto. We were . . . we . . ." I let her off the hook by nodding understandingly.

"I broke it off a week ago," she said. "I thought it was amicable enough on both sides, so I didn't change the lock codes." She looked irritated but maybe a little worried, too. "I guess he's come back."

I waited for her to go on, but she didn't seem inclined. She also didn't seem inclined to get out of my car. I sighed. "Do you want me to come in with you?"

"Well . . ." She hesitated. "Tony's not dangerous. But I really don't want to talk to him. I don't want to go over it all again. Would you mind?"

I *did* mind. I was tired, and I wasn't in the mood to run cover for Jocasta Yzerman. But what the frag? "Sure," I said as sincerely as I could fake.

As we got out of the car, I looked up at the top floor of the brownstone. No lights. I pointed that out to Jocasta.

She shrugged. "Maybe he just got here."

Right on cue, a light went on in the top-right window. Followed by a much brighter light. A fireball blossomed, and the window leaped into the street. I tried to fling Jocasta to the ground, into cover, but the shockwave beat me to it. Something hard slammed into the back of my head—my car, I think it was—and out went the lights.

3

I couldn't have been out for more than a few seconds. When I opened my eyes, miscellaneous drek was still raining out of the skies onto the sidewalk and parked cars. My ears were ringing, and my head was pounding as if somebody were using the insides of my tympanic membranes as, well, as tympani. The whole front of my body felt tender, as if I'd run head-on into a wall, and the back of my head throbbed bloody blue murder. But I was still alive, and that made it all okay.

Jocasta was sprawled on her back beside me. Her eyes were open and moving, but they were glazed and definitely weren't tracking anything in the real world. I looked around, expecting to see a crowd of spectators gathering.

No crowd. Then I remembered where I was. Tacoma isn't Auburn, where people usually head *toward* trouble, just to see what's going down. Here, the pedestrians who'd been on the street only seconds before had pulled an admirable disappearing act. Besides Jocasta and me, the only person still on the sidewalk was literally *on* the sidewalk. Sprawled bonelessly on the cement. And the chunk of something that the blast had driven into his skull seemed to imply he wouldn't be moving, at least not under his own power.

Jocasta's brownstone was still standing—a testament to modern building techniques—and even the false stone facade didn't seem much worse for wear. The two windows in the top-right corner were gone, though, and a fire was blazing merrily in what had been her apartment.

Jocasta stirred and said something, but I couldn't hear it over the ringing in my ears. Then I *did* hear something else. The sound was faint but unmistakably that of approaching sirens. Logical. Not a soul on the street, but every PANICBUTTON within three blocks was probably sending out its signal.

PANICBUTTONs and sirens mean Lone Star, and that meant it was time to move. (I myself wasn't tracking all that well yet, but enough to figure that one out.) I grabbed Jocasta's shoulders, pulling her to her feet. Thumbing the passenger door open, I shoved her inside. Then I was in the driver's seat, lighting up the engine and booting out of there. (Sure, I know leaving the scene of a crime is bad news. And making a fast getaway like that could definitely start people wondering if the guy in the red Jackrabbit might be involved somehow, but I honestly didn't give a flying frag.)

My equilibrium was shot, probably because of the shock to my ears, and my depth perception kept doing strange things, neither of which helped my driving. The steering wheel kept shifting in my hands as Quincy's upgunned autopilot intervened ("More to the left, drek-head") to keep us from piling into buildings and other immovable objects. Jocasta was watching me with wide, frightened eyes, but she had the sense to keep quiet. Or maybe I just couldn't hear her.

By the time we were back on Highway 5 and heading north and east again, the ringing in my ears was starting to fade. As normal sounds began to come back, the wild panic and paranoia twisting in my chest also began to fade. Loosening my death-grip on the wheel, I let the speedo bar on the HUD creep down from outrageous to merely excessive.

As for Jocasta, she was still looking a little shell-shocked, but she had herself under control. Not knowing what to say, I tried to play it safe. "I'm sorry," I told her.

She shook her head slowly. "I should feel bad," she said softly. "Tony's dead." Her gray eyes fixed on me, silently asking for understanding. "But I can't feel bad. I'm too busy being glad it wasn't me."

I smiled comfortingly. "It's always like that," I reassured her. "You're not being cold or callous. You're still alive after somebody else didn't intend you to be. That's reason enough to feel good. You'll have time for grief later."

Jocasta nodded, but remained silent for a few minutes. As she turned to gaze toward the lights passing outside, I let the speed drop down another few klicks. Now wasn't the time to get nailed with a speeding ticket. Then I felt her eyes on me again and I glanced over.

"Why?" Her voice was quiet, but virtually crackling with tension.

I shrugged, putting off giving an answer she wouldn't like.

But she wasn't accepting that. *"Why?"* she repeated.

"Loose ends," I said with a sigh. "You don't leave your tools lying around after you've used them."

Her brow furrowed as she thought about that. It was only a couple of seconds before I saw the comprehension in her eyes. *(Smart lady,* I thought again.) "Explain what you mean," she told me.

I shrugged again. I knew she'd already figured it out by herself, but maybe she just wanted to hear somebody else say it. "Somebody killed your sister. Let's call him X," I said, then quickly corrected myself. "Or her. Anyway, X sent you an e-mail, supposedly from Lolly, and generally set things up so you'd come to my place and dust me off. Then you go home and conveniently blow yourself to pieces. I kill Lolly, you kill me, and then—poetic justice—you lose your life in an accident."

She cut me off there. "Accidents don't blow up apartments."

"Sure they do," I shot back. "Particularly since you were playing around with explosives in your kitchen—just in case you had to wire my car." She stared into my grinning face. "Oh yeah," I confirmed. "Want to bet that the forensics find evidence that you had a stash of C6 plastique or something like that in your kitchen closet?

"Anyway," I went on, "I murdered Lolly, you murdered me, and then you were hoisted by your own petard. Case closed. We're all out of the way, and X is totally in the clear."

She didn't answer for nearly a full minute. I could almost hear her brain ticking as she thought it through. "You've got to be right," she said at last. "I was programmed, then sacrificed. You were merely sacrificed." She scowled. "I can't believe it. This just doesn't happen."

"Maybe not in your world."

I could see that she wanted to ask about *my* world, but then thought better of it.

We were approaching Meridian Avenue. Time to decide where the hell I thought I was going. And then there was Jocasta to worry about, too. *Drek.* "You'd better lie low until I know what the frag's going on here," I told her. "I can find you a safe doss if you need it. Not what you're used to, but—"

"I'll handle that," she cut in. "I can stay with colleagues."

"Where?"

She thought about that a bit more. "You can drop me on One hundred-and-eighth," she said. "The south end."

Bellevue. Beaux Arts, to be exact. Even more a money neighborhood than Tacoma. Curiosity got the better of me. "What do you do?" I asked. "What corp?"

She smiled a little. "No corp. I'm a neo-ecologist at the University of Puget Sound."

I glanced at her tailored synthleathers and snorted. "UPS must have upped its salaries."

"No, they still pay drek. But KCPS pays better than scale."

KCPS. I recognized the call letters of one of the metroplex's educational trid stations. Something tickled in the back of my memory.

Then I remembered. "The Awakened World," I blurted.

Jocasta was smiling broadly now. "You watch it? I wouldn't think it was your kind of thing."

I ignored the subtle jab. "I've seen it a few times." *Mainly to watch you,* is what I didn't add. Call me narrow-minded, but I'm much more interested in mammals that look like Jocasta Yzerman than in novopossums or metapedes.

Well, that explained the money. Trid presenters, even on ratings dogs like "The Awakened World," get paid a drekload. It also explained the feeling of familiarity that had been nagging at me ever since I'd set eyes on Jocasta. Okay. Beaux Arts it was.

I cruised straight up Highway 5 to Route 99, east into the relatively quiet bedroom community of Renton, and then north on 405 through Newport Hills. As we blew toward the Intercity 90 exit, the buildings flanking the highway began to change. They were still mostly apartment blocks, except bigger, cleaner, and newer than the ones in Renton and Newport. Where the two southern districts were home to low- and mid-level wage slaves and managers, Beaux Arts was where many upper-level corp execs had their penthouses. I remembered the security rating catalog I'd scanned when I was still with Lone Star. The Star rated Beaux Arts luxury class, security rating triple-A. It doesn't come any higher.

I slowed down some more, and swung west onto Intercity 90, heading toward the East Channel Bridge, then cut right onto Bellevue Way. Right again onto 113th Avenue South East, then jog over to 108th, into deepest, darkest Beaux Arts. Bright lights rose into the sky around me. Mentally comparing the signs of the good life with my own doss in Auburn and with my final destination this evening, I let out a sigh. It was fragging hard to believe all these places were in the same city.

"Where now?" I asked Jocasta.

"You can drop me here."

I was about to protest, but caught myself. Bellevue's Bellevue, after all, and Beaux Arts is one of the few neighborhoods where someone who looks like Jocasta can walk the streets without becoming the unwilling joy-toy of some thrill-gang. It rankled a little that she didn't trust me enough to let me know exactly where she'd be staying, but only a little. There are times when *I* don't completely trust me, and I know myself a lot better than did Jocasta Yzerman.

Then I got to thinking, and realized the Beaux Arts Village was up the street from here. The Village is a little enclave, with walls and gates guarded a lot better than some banks. The houses are separated by big trees—*real* ones—most of them with a great view of the East Channel or down onto the heavily secured yacht harbor just south of the bridge. I smiled benignly at Jocasta. "The Village it is," I said mildly. She twitched slightly, and I knew I'd got her.

I didn't drive up to the Village, however. Not wanting to draw attention to either my car or myself, I just pulled over. "Remember," I told her as she swung her long legs out of the car. "Lie low, zero out. Don't let anybody know where you are or even that you're still alive. Both of us are supposed to be meat right now. X might not slot up twice."

She flinched a little, but recovered instantly. "What about Lone Star?" she asked. "They'll be looking for me after . . ."

"Frag 'em," I snarled, on basic principles. "It's safer. We don't know who X is or where he's tied in. Maybe he's got connections into the Star. Will your colleagues cover for you?"

She had to think about that one, which worried me a little. Then her expression cleared and she answered, "Yes. He owes me, big time."

Curiosity again, but I bit down on the obvious question. "Okay," I allowed. "But keep in touch. I won't ask for your number, but you take mine." I handed her a business card, the one without the street address. "Call me tomorrow. If I'm out, leave a message."

She pocketed the card without looking at it. "You're not going home?"

I snorted. "Don't worry about me," I told her. "I've done the fade before. Wherever I am, you can get me at that number. So use it, okay? Tomorrow?"

She nodded, closed the car door and started to walk away. Then turned back. I powered down the window. "I'm sorry I got you into this," she said softly. She looked upset enough that I didn't shoot back the smart-ass answer on the tip of my tongue.

"Null perspiration," I replied smoothly. "I got dragged into this when X first picked me as his shill. You just followed the script."

She bit her lip, the troubled expression only making her prettier. For a nanosecond I debated suggesting—oh so sincerely—that she'd have a better chance of making it to morning if she dossed down with me. But then I purged that thought and all the other ignoble ones tagging along with it. A quick jam with Jocasta Yzerman would be wiz, but I really *was* tired. And if I had to ditch her later, for whatever reason, any involvement would only make it harder.

"I'll call you," she said, then turned away for the second time. The ignoble thoughts returned as I watched her receding rear aspect, but I stomped on them like so many roaches. I ran the passenger window back up and pulled away from the curb.

Bellevue was a good cruise from Tacoma and from my main base in Auburn, but it was conveniently close to my secondary doss. I got back onto Intercity 90 and pointed the Jackrabbit's streamlined nose east. Hitting Route 405, I swung north, then took a right onto the old Woodinville Redmond Road, and finally onto the Woodinville-Duvall Road.

The moment I left 405, the scenery changed again, even more drastically. I was into Redmond—the Barrens—and anyone who's ever been there knows you can't miss the boundary of that district. The buildings were suddenly lower, as if the graceful giants of Bellevue had been cut off at the knees, while scattered pools of blue-white carbon arcs replaced the yellow brilliance of so-

dium street lighting. It was back in 2050 when Governor
Schultz decided that all the Barrens needed was better
lighting. At the cost of uncounted millions of nuyen, the
city engineers—with Lone Star and Metroplex Guard
units running cover—had installed high-intensity carbon
arc lights everywhere they could get to safely. The residents of the Barrens had responded in typically warm
Redmond manner by shooting most of them out. The
small hills were cut here and there by concrete-lined
drainage culverts. I couldn't see the foul and corrosive
water, which is usually liberally garnished with dead dogs
or worse, and thanks to the Jackrabbit's air filtering, I
couldn't smell it either.

As I passed Cottage Lake, I put my foot down until
the tach display flashed warning-red in the HUD. Thanks
be to Quincy, forever amen, the active suspension took
care of the speed-wobble, and the engine howled like a
banshee. Muzzle flashes split the night to my left, but
nothing unpleasant even came near me. The Crimson
Crush just weren't shooting straight tonight. Once past
Paradise Lake Road I let off on the throttle. The Crush
never played east of the intersection, knowing the Rusted
Stilettos would eat them for breakfast if they did.

Left onto High Bridge Road, then left again onto Jasmine Boulevard—no jasmine, and it sure wasn't a real
boulevard—and into the area known as Purity. A real
nasty part of the Barrens if you're an outsider, but Purity's got a kind of code you don't find many places in
Redmond. The code is simple: "Don't frag with me, I
won't frag with you (unless somebody makes it worth my
while)." If you're a local, that is.

And in a sense I was. I kept a secondary doss in Purity,
paying my protection money to the Amerindian street
gang in the area. Our deal was that I pay my nuyen, and
they get to use—but not abuse—my place when I'm not
in it. With most other gangs, you cut a deal like that and
you should have your head examined. Come back after
they've used your place and it'll be stripped to the floor-
boards. A couple of big guys will also probably be waiting to separate you from anything valuable you happen
to be carrying—or maybe the fillings in your teeth if
they're feeling militant. But this gang has a sense of
honor. Maybe it's their tribal background. In any case,

once they're bought, they *stay* bought, at least until somebody else outbids you. My secret is to pay them more than anybody who lives in the Barrens can.

I parked the Jackrabbit in what used to be a corner store until somebody took out the front wall with a grenade launcher. That's my private garage, covered under the same deal as my doss. Then I made the appropriate courtesy call to the gang's leader, a frigid-looking street samurai whose name I'd never learned, tossed him a certified credstick to cover the next couple of months, and jandered up to my apartment.

My place in Auburn is small, but my Redmond doss would fit in it with enough room left over for a pool table and clearance to make your shots. The single room was empty, like it always was when I stopped in, but I saw lots of evidence that it hadn't been for long. Again, that was situation normal. After stepping over the empty chip-carriers and used family-planning products, I powered up the telecom. As always, I checked the usage log first thing. As expected, the Amerinds had been making long-distance calls, but at least they continued to have the courtesy to charge them to another number. Governor Schultz's, I was glad to see.

I keyed in the telecom code for my Auburn apartment. When the other machine opened the line, I triggered a wiz little slave utility that I'd picked up from Buddy, a drek-hot decker of my acquaintance. The utility, which is designed to play merry hell with the local telecom corp, persuades the central switching computer that the two telecoms—one in Auburn and the other in Redmond—are actually one machine, located (electronically speaking) at my Auburn LTG number. Incoming calls ring on both machines. I can access all features of my Auburn telecom from Purity, and I can make outgoing calls from the Barrens while the grid computers would swear up and down that the calls were being placed from Third Street Southwest and D Street in Auburn. Slick, and potentially a lifesaver. With the utility running, somebody would have to be more than very good to ever trace me via telephone grid records.

While the two machines were sorting out the handshaking necessary to cooperatively dry-gulch the LTG computers, I sat back and thought about my next move.

This business with Lolly, Jocasta, and our mysterious X was understandably high on my priority list. But I had other irons in the fire as well, a couple of cases—*paying* cases—on the go. I couldn't just forget about them without doing irreparable harm to both my street rep *and* my cred balance. What I could do was back off on the intensity a little.

The telecom beeped its readiness, so I called up a listing of all incoming messages. The list couldn't tell me a caller's identity, but it *did* give me the time and date of the message and, in most cases, the LTG number from which the call was placed. That let me flip through and delete junk messages like those from Anwar the fixer. I flagged a couple more whose originating number I recognized, instructing the telecom to fire off a standard I'm-busy-I'll-call-when-I'm-not to them.

That left two messages, neither of which showed an originating LTG number. (This piqued my interest, of course. Someone with the right hardware wouldn't have too much problem suppressing the originating number, but it's not a common skill.) The fact that both were identified as voice-only gave me a good clue as to who the caller was. I highlighted the first one and hit Play.

I had guessed right. The flat, calm voice, with its trace of an accent, was unmistakable. My Mr. Johnson from (probably) Chicago. "Mr. Dirk," he said, "I assume that you are proceeding with the issue we discussed some days ago. Your binder and first week's payment have been transferred from the holding account, which, I presume, means you are still standing by our agreement. Please contact me, as per the agreed-upon arrangements, to confirm. Thank you."

Pedantic slot. I keyed up the next message.

The time/date stamp showed that it had come in earlier that evening, about the time Jocasta and I were dodging debris. "Mr. Dirk," the same voice droned, "the urgency on this issue has just increased somewhat. We believe that our . . . our asset is in physical danger. I would greatly appreciate it if you would upgrade your efforts appropriately. I would also appreciate it if you could confirm your continued interest in our arrangement. I would prefer not to have to dispatch someone to trace *your* whereabouts. Thank you."

I snarled inwardly. I don't like supervision, even remote supervision like this, and I certainly don't like
veiled threats. Sure, Mr. Corp Johnson would send another runner after me if he thought I'd skipped with his
payment. But he should respect my fragging professionalism enough not to remind me of the fact.

The slot did have a point, though. I'd been a little
dilatory with my status reports. I pulled out the alpha
keyboard and pounded in a quick note, which I dispatched to the e-mail bulletin-board system Mr. Johnson
had specified. Basically it said, "I'm on the fragging
case, and don't fragging call again," but in slightly more
cordial language.

That out of the way, I sat back and considered the case.
I'd been hired by Mr. Johnson to track down a corporate
employee named Juli Long, who had disappeared from
the company and then apparently resurfaced in Seattle.
The corporation was concerned, Mr. Johnson had told
me, that some foul play might be involved, and they
feared for young Juli's safety. My job was simply to find
her, extricate her from any dangerous entanglements in
the plex, and put her on a plane heading east.

Stripped of all the drek about the corp's concern, it
was a straightforward skip trace. For whatever reason,
Juli had tendered her unofficial resignation by running
from the corp. From the wording of Mr. Johnson's instructions, it didn't sound like a poach or an extraction
by another corp. Juli wasn't running *to* something, like
another job; she was running *from* something. I didn't
know what and I didn't have to know. I've seen what corp
life is like for a wage slave like Juli, and I'd run too.

A young woman, with little or no financial support—
Johnson had been very clear about that—coming to the
Seattle metroplex for the first time. No friends, no corporate arms around her. Raw meat for the street predators. It was almost certain that Juli Long would show up
in a couple of days, floating off the piers. There'd been
a lot of that recently.

I said as much to Johnson, but he demanded that I do
the trace anyway. If I was right, and Juli'd bought it, I
was to send him incontrovertible proof of her untimely
demise. I hadn't done much but set up a routine on my
telecom to scan all news sources and datafaxes for the

name Juli Long and her description. I'd probably have to
invest a little more effort in the matter. Eventually.

I pulled out my wallet and extracted a printout of her
dossier picture. Looked like a nice kid. Clean-cut, fluffy
blonde hair. Reminded me of Lolly.

Frag, I was getting morbid. It always happens when
I'm bagged. I thought about the early night I'd been planning, and laughed. I returned the picture to my wallet,
kicked the telecom to standby mode, and collapsed on
the bed. Images flowed over the insides of my eyelids.
Explosions, gun muzzles, targeting lasers. But mostly
young, blonde women: sometimes Lolly, sometimes Juli
Long. They followed me down into the dark pit of sleep.

4

Early morning is one of the quietest times in a jungle.
Nocturnal predators have called it a night, and their di-
urnal counterparts are only just stirring. The same thing's
true in Redmond, and for the same reasons.

I don't know what it was that woke me just after 0800
the next morning. Maybe it was the quiet. Redmond
nights are typically split by sirens, the roar of passing
Citymasters or low-flying Yellowjackets, and even sporadic gunfire. I rolled over in the relative silence, and
tried to force myself back to sleep.

But oblivion remained just beyond reach. After fifteen
minutes of trying, I gave it up as a bad job and forced
my stiff body out of bed. I was still wearing my duster,
and the armor plates had pressed into my flesh while I
slept. Running a hand under my shirt, the ridges and
depressions I encountered along my ribs felt like some
kind of bipedal armadillo. That fit: my mouth tasted like
I'd been eating ants. I cursed my way over to the sink,
ran a cup of lukewarm water, and rinsed out my mouth.
(I didn't swallow, no sir. Real Barrens-dwellers seem to
build up a resistance to amoebic dysentery and other such
pleasant diversions, but I've never hung around long
enough for my immune system to get with the program.)

Caffeine-based Wake-Ups were the only non-prescription drugs I'd allowed myself recently, except for alcohol flavored to taste. I popped out a couple and swallowed the bitter pills dry. Waiting for the concentrated caffeine to jump-start my central nervous system, I slumped in front of the telecom and flipped it back on line.

One of the best ways I've got for solving problems is to sleep on them. The truth is, my subconscious mind seems to be a couple dozen IQ points smarter than my conscious mind, and also seems to operate better when I'm not looking over its shoulder, so to speak. More often than not, if I'm trying to puzzle through something, I only need to give my conscious mind a break. I used to do this through exercise, which hurt, or through alcohol, which ultimately hurt more. Now I tend to choose sleep, and I can even justify it as resting up my body to continue fighting the good fight. When I wake up, the answer I've been seeking is often sitting at the front of my thoughts, along with a mental note that reads something like, "Here it is, drekhead."

When I'd checked out last night, the question was what to do next. The answer my hindbrain had dredged up during the night was a name: Naomi Takahashi.

I'd met Naomi while both of us were struggling through Lone Star training, undergoing the same mind-bending grind but determined *not* to get our minds bent. That was about all we had in common. She saw the Star as a way to get out from under the control of her wealthy family. I'd gone into the program as a misguided form of therapy for the guilt I felt after my parents died in some random street violence. Despite our differences, we each soon recognized that Lone Star training was an effective form of brainwashing, a program intended to turn all recruits into brutal, compassionless blunt instruments. Naomi, I, and another slag named Patrick Bambra—the chummer who equated women with malaria—swore we would never get *our* brains washed, and we clung together in a kind of mutual support group. Frag, we even called ourselves the Three Musketeers, which shows how idealistic and drek-eatingly romantic we were. Patrick got himself flushed from the program early on, mostly because even the Star's soul-killing brutality couldn't get him to see the world the way it really is. Naomi and I bore down, however, and made it through with our personalities basically intact (I like to think).

Even though the training was intended to turn us into beat cops and street monsters, it didn't destroy us enough to make us accept that fate. Naomi requested and received a transfer to data processing; I just cut out and ran for the shadows.

Naomi and I still keep in touch, but only sporadically and very carefully. She's my only remaining friend within the Lone Star system, but she'd be in deep drek if her bosses found out. I've made a few major deposits in the favor bank with Naomi over the past few years, mainly by doing some shadow work to help out friends and colleagues of hers. Now it was time to pull in a few of those markers.

I checked my watch. Just after eight-thirty; that meant she'd be at work. I selected voice-only on the telecom and punched in Naomi's direct-access code. A few seconds later, the screen lit up with her image.

Naomi Takahashi was as beautiful as the first day I saw her. Her brow furrowed slightly under her black bangs as she reacted to the fact that the call was voice-only, but her musical voice gave no hint of frustration. "Lone Star, Records Department."

I pitched my voice lower than normal and added a gravelly edge. That would be useless against a voice analyzer, of course, but probably enough to fool any supervisor who happened to be listening in. "Uh, yeah," I rumbled, "I want Joe Dar-*tag*-non. He around?"

Naomi's expression didn't change, but I saw the flash of recognition in her almond eyes. Even with my disguised voice, the brutalized pronunciation of D'Artagnon, one of the three musketeers from literature, would be the giveaway. "I'm sorry, sir," she said smoothly, "we have nobody here by that name."

"Frag," I snarled, enjoying her performance. "Later." As I cut the connection I saw her subtle wink, no more than a slight nervous twitch. Message received and understood.

I stood up from the telecom and stretched. I knew Naomi would take a break at the first opportunity to call me from a "secure" phone somewhere else. I couldn't be sure how long that would be. But knowing Naomi, not long.

To pass the time, I flipped the telecom into trideo mode and slumped down on the bed. Nothing like a little mindless trid to kill some time. Preferably something with minimal data content and scantily clad stage decorations. Something like "Nuevo Wheel of Fortune."

But I happened onto a news broadcast instead, and couldn't summon the energy to get up and flip the channel. The talking head, a bottle blonde with capped teeth and enhanced mammalian protuberances, was babbling on about the latest gang war, all the while wearing a smile that would have looked more at home in a bedroom. Oh, well, her appearance was a suitable distraction, as long as I didn't listen to what she was saying.

That was easier said than done, of course. The sound channel of news broadcasts is always electronically enhanced, with added supersonics, so that it insinuates itself into your brain. A ratings-garnering trick, of course, making it more difficult to switch off or change channels.

The video feed behind the blonde changed from the standard, pro-smooth shots of carnage and chaos to a more arresting image. We were looking down on the nighttime cityscape of Seattle. From the vibration and the way the perspective shifted, I knew the camera must be aboard a high-speed aircraft, maybe a small helicopter. It reminded me of war coverage. I started to pay more attention.

"And now, a KONG exclusive," the bottle-blonde was saying. "Last night, a KONG remote-camera crew rode along with an emergency response vehicle operated by Crashcart."

Oho. I sat up. Crashcart was a new entry on the metroplex scene, but the company had taken only a couple of months to make its presence felt with a vengeance. They were in direct competition with DocWagon, the emergency extraction and medical service, and were doing surprisingly well. Some of their success was due to wooing clients away from DocWagon with lower rates or attracting new subscribers who couldn't pay the other company's tab. But mostly it was due to their special "guerrilla marketing" tactics.

All roving Crashcart vehicles carried scanners tuned

to the same channels as DocWagon's receivers. Later, as
DocWagon started encrypting their transmissions, the
scanners were coupled with the appropriate decoding
gear. Whenever a DocWagon vehicle got a High-Threat
Response call—say, somebody went down in what some
media wags call the DMZ, or Downtown Militarized
Zone—the nearest Crashcart vehicle would tag along.
Crashcart would always let the DocWagon trauma team
make the first extraction attempt. If the DocWagon team
got themselves geeked or had to abandon a particularly
hot extraction, only then would Crashcart go in and try
to do better. In nearly a dozen cases, Crashcart had been
able to pull the victim out after DocWagon had failed.
What made it worse for DocWagon was that three of those
extractions had been top-tier corporate suits holding
DocWagon Super-Platinum contracts. Understandably,
quite a few other Super-Platinum clients were wavering
in their devotion to DocWagon. After all, if you're paying
75,000 nuyen a year, you expect the best. Some had already made the switch to Crashcart.

Sure, DocWagon mouthpieces were screaming that the
whole thing was a set-up, that Crashcart was hiring street
thugs to shoot the drek out of DocWagon vehicles and
then pull a quick fade when the Crashcart buggies arrived. But they had no proof. Crashcart didn't even bother
to deny it. They just kept blasting the airwaves with their
slogan: "Why go with the first when you can go with the
best?"

The bottle-blonde on the screen was still talking.
"Around midnight last night, the vehicle carrying the
KONG crew picked up a DocWagon High-Threat Re-
sponse call. The broadcast identified the victim as Daniel
Waters, a newsman and trideo personality with a minor
local station."

Minor local station? That was a hoot. Like just about
everyone else in the plex, I knew Waters' name, and
could easily visualize the avuncular half-smile that was
his trademark. He was the top anchorman for KOMA,
the local ABS affiliate, and definitely *not* a minor player.
In fact, most people in the sprawl seemed to rate Waters
as a source of Truth, perhaps one small step below god
almighty, and he had the ratings to prove it.

"In accordance with Crashcart's mandate," the talk-

ing head went on, "the vehicle carrying the KONG crew
stayed clear while the DocWagon trauma team made its
extraction attempt. After that, well . . ."—she smiled
almost broadly enough to swallow her ears—"the pictures tell their own story."

The video "window" that had first appeared behind
the blonde expanded until it filled the whole screen, blot-
ting out her image. Simultaneously, the metroplex night-
scape pulled back as the cameraman adjusted his zoom
lens. For the first time, I could see enough of the aircraft's interior to identify it as a Merlin, smaller cousin
of the tilt-wing Osprey II, similar in design to the Fed-
erated Boeing Commuter. I could also see that the camera was pointing out the open door on the starboard side
of the craft. There was a hulking shape to the right of
the image, but not enough light to make it out.

I wasn't interested in what was inside the Merlin, anyway. All the action was outside.

The Merlin was less than three hundred meters up,
orbiting above one of the small parks that dot the east
side of Downtown. (And that turn into killing grounds
for pedestrians after dark. If Daniel Waters had wandered
in there, he deserved everything he got.) Another craft
hung in the air over the trees and brush. It was a single-
rotor Hughes WK-2 Stallion, slightly larger than a Merlin. The flashes from the helo's anti-collision strobes
illuminated the DocWagon logo on its flanks.

The Stallion was trying to put down, but it couldn't
find a safe spot. The darkness in the park was alive with
large-caliber muzzle flashes and evanescent fire-flowers
that could only come from heavy-duty autofire weapons.
Impacting rounds struck blue-white sparks against the
Stallion's armor.

The DocWagon trauma team wasn't taking any of it
lying down. I could see the flames of answering fire from
the helo's gunports. But the targets on the ground had
concealment on their side, while the Stallion was a big
hovering target. On top of that, it was obvious that the
DocWagon team was heavily outgunned.

The final outcome wasn't in doubt, and it came quickly.
A shot from the ground must have found a vital spot,
because the helo bucked wildly and smoke poured from
its port-engine housing. The sound of the Merlin's twin

engines drowned out all else, but I could imagine the
banshee wail as the Stallion's starboard turbojet fought
to take the strain.

The DocWagon trauma team were hosed, and they
knew it. Still bucking wildly, the Stallion clawed for al-
titude, then sideslipped away from the park.

The Crashcart team responded even before the helo
was out of the area, and they did so with almost military
precision. The motor noise changed as the Merlin's wings
pivoted and the craft dropped like a stone toward the
park. The night lit up again as the gunmen on the ground
opened up on the new threat.

That was when I learned what was the hulking shape
to the right of the video image. A dazzling beam of light
split the darkness, looking for all the world like a death
ray from an old science-fiction movie. My telecom's
small speaker rattled with a noise like a giant canvas tearing or maybe King Kong farting, a colossal ripping that
went on and on. The beam swept over the ground, and I
could see trees and bushes bursting into splinters as it
touched them.

For a moment, I felt sorry for the gunmen on the
ground. The shape in the Merlin had to be a 7.62mm
minigun, probably the GE M134, a Gatling-gun style
weapon with a rate of fire up in the thousands of rounds
per minute. Typically, one out of every six or eight shots
was a "lit" round, a tracer. And even that minority was
enough to make the stream of fire look like a solid bar
of light.

There were a few muzzle-flashes as the gunmen shot
back, but not many. Nobody in his right mind engages a
minigun.

Everything jounced as the Merlin put down, hard. The
cameraman panned quickly to the other side of the vehicle, just in time to catch a squad of four armed and
armored figures leaping out the other door into the darkness. The cameraman moved, trying to follow, but another bulky figure rose up to block his way. The image
panned back to the port door.

The minigunner had stopped his continuous fire, and
was now engaging targets of opportunity. Glare from the
muzzle plume was bright enough to effectively blind the
video camera, making it impossible to discern the tar-

gets. The gunner must have had flare-compensated optics, or he'd have been flash-dazzled himself. I couldn't see any return fire. Either the gunmen were all dead, or they'd headed off for safer pastures.

There was another jolt, and the Merlin was in the air again. Belatedly, the cameraman panned over to the other side. The armed squad was back aboard, and with them was a body-shaped bundle cocooned in ballistic cloth. The image zoomed in, and the familiar face of Daniel Waters filled the screen. His short gray hair was matted with blood, and his skin looked like old parchment.

The image froze, then retreated back to become a video window behind the buxom blonde. "Another successful extraction by Crashcart," she cooed, "and another KONG exclusive." Her multi-megawatt smile faded, to be replaced by a look of concern about as authentic as her cleavage. "Good luck to you, Daniel," she said, with a slight catch in her voice. "You know we're all rooting for you." *Like drek.*

The telecom chirped, announcing an incoming call and giving me an excuse to turn off the trid. I hit the appropriate keys and the blonde vanished, to be replaced by the face of Naomi Takahashi. From the out-of-focus background, I knew she was placing the call from a public street phone. A flashing icon in the top-left of the screen confirmed she had the hush-hood down. I assumed she also had the screen polarization set so that only she could view what was on it. Seeing she'd taken the appropriate precautions, I hit the key that turned on my own video pickup.

Naomi smiled as my face appeared on her display, but it was a worried smile. So she knew what was going down, at least some of it. Her first words confirmed it. "You're in a pretty sweet frame, chummer. Got any new enemies I haven't heard about?"

I chuckled. "Just a redhead with a gun," I told her. "Nothing unusual." My smile faded; down to business. "Talk to me about Lolita Yzerman," I said. "What's the Star saying?"

Naomi sobered instantly. "Not much," she said. "They're keeping a tight lid on it. Kurtz is in charge."

That was bad news. Mark Kurtz. I remembered that miserable fragger from my training days, and I was sure he also remembered me. Kurtz had been one of the primary reasons I'd skipped out, and I'd made sure he knew it. The man was a hard-driver and as tenacious as a pit bull. Once he was onto a lead, nothing—including the facts—would distract him.

"I suppose I'm the prime suspect, right?" I asked.

"Chummer, you're the *only* suspect."

I digested that for a moment. Then I asked, "Aren't you going to ask me if I did it?"

She didn't dignify that with an answer. "I take it you're not at home."

"You take that right." So Kurtz was on the case, and they had the lid screwed down tight. "Well, thanks a lot, Naomi. I know you're sticking your neck out."

"Null perspiration," she said with a grin. "So I guess you don't want to scan the report, huh?" She waved an optical chip before the video pickup.

I goggled at it for a moment, then grinned. Friends like Naomi don't come along very often. Maybe once in a lifetime, if you're lucky. I worried for a moment about the risk she'd taken, then had to dismiss the twinges. For one thing, it was already done. For another, I think Naomi knew more about the Lone Star records computer than the designer.

"So, do you want it?" she teased.

I laughed. "Slot and run, lady. The Star's not paying you to waste cycles out of the office."

"You got that," she agreed. "Here it comes." As her video image slotted the chip into the phone's socket, I instructed my telecom to open a file to receive the data. The machine beeped and chortled happily for a couple of seconds as it digested the upload, then flashed completion. I keyed a verification routine, and telecom and chip conferred over whether the arrival corresponded to what had been sent. A second or two later, confirmation appeared on the panel.

"Got it chipped, chummer," I told her. "*Arigato gazaimashta.* I owe you."

She waved that off. "Keep your head down, Dirk," she said seriously. "Knowing Kurtz, he'll see this as a chance to clear the board where you're concerned. Geek first, then fingerprint the corpses, you know what I mean?" I nodded. "And then there's the guy that put you in the frame in the first place," she went on. "You got any idea who?"

"Maybe after I scan the report. Not now."

"Yeah, well . . ." She was looking worried again, so I gave her my best confident, roguish smile. It didn't feel convincing from my side of it, but Naomi seemed to buy it. Her brow smoothed, and her eyes sparkled again. "Okay, I'm gone. Keep in touch, *omae. Neh?*"

"You got that," I promised. "Head down." I gave her another rebel smile and cut the connection. As soon as her image vanished, so did my smile. Except for the part about Kurtz, it wasn't that Naomi had told me anything I didn't already know, but our conversation had brought home to me the reality of what was going down. X, whoever he/she/it was, had already tried once to get me out of the way. Why not a second time? And Kurtz would be glad to help him out, then arrest my corpse. Ah, well, another day in the shadows.

I pulled my chair closer to the telecom screen, bringing up the file Naomi had transferred. I recognized the standard Lone Star file-header and grinned. Naomi wasn't one to do things by halves. Instead of just scamming bits and pieces, she'd taken the whole fragging file. I started the data scrolling and began to read.

I saw immediately that Naomi was right. I was in a sweet frame.

The first part of the report dealt with the on-site investigation, which was basically just as Jocasta had described it. Lolita had been found lying face-up just inside the door of her forty-eighth-floor luxury apartment, a big nasty hole blown in her forehead. The hole was star-shaped, the report said, which equated to a contact wound: the gun barrel was touching her when the shot was fired, and the expanding gases had torn the delicate skin of her face. The door was unlocked, with no sign of forced entry. Nor did any evidence indicate that the body had been moved. The reconstruction was simple. Somebody had come to the door, someone Lolly had known and trusted enough to open the door to. The killer had stepped inside, stuck a gun up against Lolly's face, and blown the brains out the back of her pretty blonde head. Time of death was estimated at between 2000 and 2020 hours on November 17.

I stopped the scrolling and sat back. The language of
the report was factual, clinically unemotional, making it
easy for the reader to pretend that it was all an intellectual exercise. Which is just how it was intended. But
every now and then the ugly reality would squeeze its
way through the facts. A young, promising life had been
chopped short. The irreplaceable individual who had been
Lolita Yzerman now existed only in the memories of
those who'd cared for her.

I rubbed at my eyes, which were watering a little from
the strain of staring at the screen, then restarted the automatic scrolling.

The Lone Star detectives had done all the usual stuff:
accessed the call log on Lolly's telecom, reviewed the
video record of her apartment building's lobby camera,
strong-armed her financial institution into releasing her
banking records. A couple of key points caught my eye.

According to the call log, Lolly had placed a voice-and-
vid call to my LTG number on Saturday, November 16,
just short of midnight. The call hadn't been archived, but
I knew it was the message she'd left on my machine,
asking for help. Although the log did not mention my
name, nobody's better than Lone Star at tracking down
an LTG. That was the first strand that tied me to Lolly's
death.

Next, the security camera's record. At 2011, on Sunday
the 17th, a figure wearing a long duster and a hat pulled
down to screen his face, entered the lobby and took the
elevator up to the forty-eighth floor. At 2014 hours, the
figure reappeared and left the building. That was just
long enough to ride the high-speed elevator up, buzz Lolly's door, geek the blonde, and ride back down again.
But there was more. As the figure opened the front door,
a gust of wind shifted the hat-brim enough for the camera
to catch at least part of his face. I stared at a freeze-
frame of the recorded image for a few minutes. Either I
had an identical twin brother—a *murderous* twin
brother—or X the killer was magically active. The face
caught by the video camera was mine. The second strand
was in place.

Finally, Lolly's financial records. Her banking behavior was chaotic, to say the least. She made big nuyen and
spent big nuyen, and didn't seem to grasp the concept of

"minimum balance." But there was a pattern there, and the Star had quickly picked it out. Over the last nine months, she'd made twelve sporadic deposits, each one exactly 10,000 nuyen and all from the same source. And that source was . . . ? Three guesses, and the first two don't count. That was the third strand, interwoven with the other two to form a rope. And the rope formed a noose.

A *very* pretty frame.

Okay, *I* knew I wasn't guilty, and I knew how it had all been done. Illusion magic can fool cameras, which would explain my face on the security video. Bank computer systems are pretty secure, but some of the deckers running the Matrix could hack a transmission log without even breaking a sweat, especially if nobody was ever going to withdraw the "funds" I'd supposedly deposited. And the phone call to me? Well, that was legitimate, and a pure bonus for X. The way it looked Lolly had called me to put on the screws for another 10K nuyen. I'd responded by dropping over and rearranging her cranial architecture.

Sure, I could figure all this out. But my deductions were based on the fact that *I* knew I didn't flatline Lolly. Without that key datum? Lone Star would be after me with everything they had.

Time for logic. How could they track me? Some obvious ways first. Like my LTG number. Theoretically, it's a simple task for a drek-hot decker or for the telephone company itself to cross-reference an LTG number with the phone's physical location. (I'm talking plugged-into-the-wall telecoms here, not portables.) Based on that, Lone Star should already be visiting my Auburn doss.

Luckily, it's not that simple. Buddy, the decker benefactor who supplied my slave utility, also beat the location problem. As far as the LTG self-diagnostics and search routines are concerned, my LTG number doesn't exist any more. It *did* exist, but was canceled a couple of hours before the trace attempt was made . . . *whenever* the trace attempt is made. As far as the *connection* routines go, the number's perfectly on the up-and-up. Wiz, huh? And I don't even have to pay a phone bill. (Okay, okay, I know it doesn't seem to make much sense. But remember how compartmentalized big computer systems are. And how much operators—and even corporate deckers—trust the diagnostics. Ah, the wonders of our digital age . . .)

How else could the Star get a line on me? SIN, maybe? But I don't have one. Driver's license, bank accounts, medical plans? Either I don't have them or else they're associated with SINs that aren't mine.

The conclusion? It's hard to track a shadow. Lone Star would have to fall back on techniques that cops used last century.

Ah, but what about magic? Well, if I'd actually scragged Lolly, I might have to sweat a bit. A good mage or shaman could, theoretically, track me down from a fresh drop of blood, broken fingernail, maybe even a trace of exfoliated skin that I might have left behind at the crime scene. But since I *didn't* do it, any such trace should lead them to somebody else—namely, X.

The Star might *think* they had me dead to rights, of course. Anyone who enters the Lone Star training program is forced to give blood and tissue samples that remain on file. The official story is that the samples are taken to prevent problems with rejection or incompatibility of body parts in case they have to put you back together after a line-of-duty injury. I have this nasty suspicion the samples are really so a Lone Star combat mage can track someone down astrally if he or she decides to skip the force. That's why my first shadowrun, which took place even before I "unofficially resigned," was to replace my blood and tissue samples with something that wouldn't get me into trouble. If that putative combat mage tried to track me from the samples, he'd catch up with a mangy Redmond alley cat, assuming some squatter hasn't eaten it in the interim.

I let myself relax a little. As far as I could see, I was as safe as I was going to get. Lone Star hadn't tracked me down in the years since I'd bid them farewell, and I didn't think that was about to change now.

But what about Jocasta? I thought with a start. Whoever planted the bomb in her apartment might have got hold of something that would let him track her magically. Ritual magic can be even nastier than C6 plastique. Then again, if Jocasta was dossing down in Beaux Arts Village, she'd probably be okay. Most enclaves like that are protected by hermetic circles, elementals, even dual para-biologicals like piasmae or hell hounds, which can watch in astral space as easily as the mundane world. That should be enough to save Jocasta's shapely ass.

Okay, I had some breathing space. Which was good. My head hurt from the combination of too little deep sleep and too much deep thought. To take my mind off Lone Star and Lolly, I pulled up the results of the search routine I'd sent off to find references to Juli Long.

To my surprise, there was one hit. Displaying the full text, I skimmed it quickly.

Then I took the picture from my wallet and looked at it one last time. This wasn't a good week for young blondes. The fact that I'd predicted it didn't make me feel any better.

Juli Long had been found floating off Pier 23. Dead, of course.

5

I remember once reading that it's better to waste your childhood than not to do anything at all with it. I might have misspent my childhood, but I certainly didn't waste it. And I've got the wide range of contacts, acquaintances, even friends, to prove it. In my business, that's the difference between squeaking by and starving. I've never liked starving.

The contact *du jour* was a chummer named Bent Sigurdsen. Bent and I had been best buds while growing up in Renton. At ages fifteen and sixteen, we did a lot of illegal drinking together and made a lot of plans to become neoanarchists when we grew up.

So much for childhood dreams. We both followed the paths our respective fathers had chosen for us, at least for a while. Against my better judgment, I'd gone into computer sciences at U-Dub, where I stuck it out for three long, slogging years until finally getting up the courage to drop out and tell my father to go frag himself.

Bent also followed in his father's footsteps, but the difference was that he liked it. His dad was a drek-hot orthopedic surgeon, and Bent took to med school like one born to it. When it came time to specialize, he decided that orthopedics wasn't his interest, but that was okay with Sigurdsen Senior. Bent followed the pathology route instead, and when he graduated—*magna cum laude,* no fragging surprise—his old man pulled the strings to get him hired by City Health as part of the medical-examiner staff for the Seattle sprawl. (That's right, an ME, the guy who takes apart dead bodies to figure out what made them that way. I guess Bent prefers patients that don't bitch and who he's *sure* won't sue him for malpractice.)

Anyway, Bent and I kept in touch over the years. When my parents were killed, he was there to get mind-fragging drunk with me and then make sure I didn't jump in front of a bullet-train. And when I escaped from Lone Star, he immediately got word to me via Naomi Takahashi that he was *still* a friend even if I was newly SINless. We kept in touch after that. Not regularly, not often. We'd get together maybe every couple of months to pummel our cerebral cortices with alcohol. Ours was one of those solid friendships where it isn't necessary to touch base often, where you know that even after a couple of years the other person's still going to be there for you.

And so I had no second thoughts about keying in the LTG code for Bent's lab (with another one of Buddy's wiz utilities running cover for me).

Almost immediately, Bent's cherubic face appeared on the screen. "Yeah?" He frowned into what I knew was a blank screen. Bent's image was slightly blurred by the protective layer of transparent plastic that, for reasons as obvious as they are nauseating, covers the lab's telecom. Seeing him, I cut in my video pickup.

His frown instantly vanished, to be replaced with a smile that lit up his face and made his blue eyes twinkle. When Bent Sigurdsen smiles, he looks like the Cheshire cat. Any moment you expect he's going to fade from view, leaving nothing but that grin. "Hey, chummer," he beamed, "it's been a long time. How's biz?"

I was tempted to tell him, but that would only make him feel bad. And I didn't like making Bent feel bad if

I could help it. So I shrugged. "Pretty good," I told him. "Lots of stuff on the go." (Classic understatement.) "You?"

I didn't think it possible for his grin to get broader, but it did. "Wizard," he offered. "Things couldn't be better."

I could tell he was about to launch into shoptalk—no doubt a blow-by-blow rendition of how his latest customer had ended up on the slab—so I derailed that train of thought before it could get up to speed. "I've got some biz, Bent. Got a few ticks?"

"Of course," he said at once. "Anything for a chummer." (Any wonder I like Bent so much?) He gestured over his shoulder, probably at the worktable that was, mercifully, out of frame. "Jane Doe here isn't in a hurry. What can I do for you?"

"Juli Long," I said, then filled out what little I'd learned about the fluffy blonde's departure from this mortal coil. "Any chance you can pull up her file and give me a capsule review?"

Bent's smile had faded as I spoke. Now he looked sadly into the video pickup, and I could tell he was grieving for young Juli. (For the hundredth time I wondered how the frag someone as sensitive to the human tragedy as Bent could do his job.) "Null perspiration," he said. "The report should be on line. Long, Juli . . . right?"

I nodded, and he was off, attacking the telecom's keyboard with the gusto of a teenage decker. For a moment I thought I'd be treated to nothing but a view of his face as he worked, but then he remembered my existence long enough to slave my display to his. The video picture shrunk down to a quarter-size window in the upper corner of the screen, while the rest of the display revealed what was showing on his monitor. I watched as he entered the search syntax, pleasantly surprised at the speed with which two side-by-side digitized images of Juli Long flashed up on the screen. One was the same picture I had in my wallet: Juli flashed a devilish grin into the camera. The other was the identical face, but perfectly at rest. If not for the blue tinge of cyanosis about her lips, I might have been persuaded she was just asleep. The rest of the screen filled with text, but Bent quickly blanked that off my display. "Confidential," he explained, a little apol-

ogetically. "I'll tell you if there's anything interesting."
I suppressed a smirk. Bent's ability to mentally compart-
mentalize continued to amaze me, but of course now
wasn't the time to share the joke with him.

I watched his cornflower blue eyes flick back and forth
as he read the text. It took him maybe a minute, and I
was hard-pressed to keep my mouth shut and not try to
hurry him along, particularly when I saw him raise his
eyebrows and purse his lips in surprise. Finally he was
finished. "Well?" I prompted.

"Interesting case," he pronounced slowly. "I wish
she'd come across my table." Then he looked up at me
guiltily; I didn't think my telecom's microphone was sensitive enough to pick up the grinding of my teeth, but I
might have been wrong. "Heart failure," he stated.
"Apparently brought on by the chip she was using."

It was my turn to raise my eyebrows and purse my lips.
"Simsense good enough to kill?"

He shook his head. "There's more to it than that."

I waited, then realized he wasn't going to continue
without prodding. "Oh?" I said.

Bent looked uncomfortable, and I knew I was pushing
the limits of what he felt easy about doing. Friendship's
a big thing to Bent, but he's got his own somewhat con-
voluted sense of ethics. I watched as friendship fought
with principles, and was relieved when friendship won.
"There's another file reference here," he told me. "File-
spec L-S-S."

"Which means?" I asked, though I could guess.

"Lone Star Secure," Bent confirmed. "Lone Star's
put a security hold on the appended file for some reason."

"Can you get past it?"

He looked almost affronted for a moment, then his
smile returned. "Of *course* I can. The question is . . ."

"Will you?" I finished for him. "It could be interesting, chummer. Something even you haven't seen before.
Simsense to die for . . ."

As I'd expected, he took the bait. "Yeah," he mused,
"yeah, could be interesting." Then he looked up and his
gaze met mine. Deep in those intense blue eyes was a
gleam that told me he knew perfectly well what I was
doing, but he didn't care. "Your LTG number's the

same?" I nodded. "Then I'll get back to you. Hang easy, chummer." And with that he broke the connection.

I sat back, fingers laced behind my head. If Bent Sigurdsen said he'd get back to me, he would. Good thing, too. The Star doesn't lock the file on a stiff unless it's something *really* out of the ordinary. I considered getting on the line to my eastern Mr. Johnson with a status report, then thought better of it. He could wait until I had the answers to a few more questions. Juli Long sure wasn't going anywhere.

The next day dawned cold and gray. No rain, but the clouds were like dirty lead, and the air had a chilling damp that made my head hurt. (Or maybe it was the half-bottle of ersatz scotch I'd drunk to kill the dreams.)

Lolita Yzerman had been very much with me as I'd tried to get to sleep last night. Little Lolly's memorial service was scheduled for today, Thursday, November 21. But how could I go? Null perspiration. I had a bucketful of fragging good reasons why not. It wasn't until I climbed into bed on Wednesday night and then couldn't turn off my brain that I realized how much Lolly's death was slotting me up.

I tried for more than an hour, but my brain wouldn't cooperate. Sleep? Null program, cobber. I would just start to get that warm, floating feeling when some image of Lolly would flash into my brain—a smile, a turn of phrase, or something more intimate—and I'd be awake again, lying there tingling. The worst moments were when I saw the shadowy stranger with my face raising the gun and pressing it against little Lolly's forehead . . .

I gave it about ninety minutes before I conceded and reached for the bottle of synthahol. Only that eventually managed to push Lolly, and everything else, out of my brain, so that finally I slept.

This morning, of course, I was paying the price. A dull headache had taken up residence behind my left eyebrow, and seemed disinclined to leave. I accepted the pain as partial penance for missing Lolly's memorial. As further penance, I decided now was the time to do something that I'd been putting off as rather unpleasant. I had to go to see Buddy.

Don't get me wrong, Buddy the decker is a good

friend. I respect her, trust her, even like her. But not face to face, and *definitely* not when I'm feeling under the weather.

Everyone has a history, but Buddy's is more interesting than most. In my experience, most drek-hot deckers start off as the stereotypical computer nerd. Often they get into decking simply because they get along better with machines than with people. But Buddy came at decking from the other side. She was originally into neurological research at U-Dub, where she made some major breakthroughs in monitoring. Like any researcher, she had to learn about computers, over time becoming especially intrigued by techniques of interfacing electronics and the brain. The logical next step for her was research in that area.

That was a while back, sometime about 2027, before decking became what it is today. Buddy was right out on the cutting edge, with a background that set her apart from other computer researchers. Not only did she understand the hardware and software, she also knew a lot about the "wetware."

When the axe fell during the Crash of '29, her qualifications weren't lost on the government. One of the first people to be recruited for the "enhanced" Echo Mirage program, Buddy later became a member of the cadre that led the major assault against the computer virus that lobotomized the world's datanets. Everybody in Echo Mirage was a volunteer, and Buddy wouldn't have missed it for the world. But she paid a steep price for that experience.

The cyberdecks the Echo Mirage team used were barbaric compared to the toys you can pick up at any Radio Shack today. The software was even worse. From the little I understand of it, the persona programs were really kludges, just as likely to hang as to work right. And without the persona program to run interference, it's the decker's naked psyche that confronts the alien world of the computer Matrix. Most people know that four of the Echo Mirage team died, while others came out mind-shattered and vegetative. Buddy survived and even remained functional, but she didn't make it totally unscathed.

Perhaps she'd always had the tendency, or maybe it was

purely a result of her experiences. Whichever, she came
out of Echo Mirage with what the shrinks call a "bipolar
disorder." In English, that means she's manic-depressive,
but with a twist. At the highest point of her cycle, she's
about as down as I am on a bad day. At the bottom, she's
out-and-out paranoid. Apparently this hasn't stopped her
from pulling in some major contracts over the years. I
guess the corporations don't really care how fragged up
a decker is as long as he or she can perform. (In any
case, paranoid isn't a bad way to be in the sprawl.)

The personal significance of all this was that I had no
way of knowing in what stage of the cycle Buddy might
be at the moment. Calling wouldn't help: she never answered her phone. You just leave a message and hope.

So that's what I did. I punched in her code and waited
for her outgoing message—a very informative five seconds of dead air, followed by a beep—and told her I was
coming over. That being all the preparation possible, I
jumped in the car and headed south on 405. I tuned my
radio to the traffic station, just in case something was
going down that I ought to know about.

And hit the jackpot the first time. It seemed that something big and tentacled had slobbered its way out of Lake
Washington and onto the deck of the Route 520 bridge,
the floating one connecting Bellevue and Downtown. After eating a couple of cars, the thing had slobbered its
way back into the water. The traffic advisory was rec-
ommending that drivers select an alternate route. No
drek. Ah, the wonders of the Awakened world.

I took the advisory to heart, of course, my alternate
route taking me down 405 until it cut west, then up Am-
baum Boulevard into White Center. Buddy had a place
on Roxbury Street. It was a good-sized flat near the top
of the tallest building in the area. With the apartment's
western exposure, she also had a great view out over
Puget Sound toward Vashon Island.

The view meant nothing to Buddy, however, other than
a reminder of how vast and threatening was the outside
world. Within days of moving in, she'd covered up the
big, beautiful windows with sheets of reinforced construction plastic. She'd also reinforced the door, the
walls, the ceiling, even the floor, and rigged every possible entrance with security devices. (While making all

these modifications, Buddy had asked me to recommend an air-conditioner mechanic who also knew high-voltage electricity. Jumping to the obvious conclusion, I assumed she wanted him to rig unpleasant surprises for anyone who tries to break in through an air vent.) At the same time, she was beefing up the apartment's sound insulation. Which was just as well, considering Buddy's other obsession.

That other obsession is percussion. From the way I put it together, she'd always loved percussion-heavy music, stuff with lots of polyrhythms. Her tastes became even more arcane and twisted after her Echo Mirage days, until no commercially available music would suit her. That was when she built herself a computerized drum machine, programming it to write and play its own intersecting polyrhythms, using insanely complex weighting algorithms to make it stay with the stuff she finds pleasing. And that's the crux of the matter. To anyone else, Buddy's "music" sounds like street repairs or like driving around with rocks in your hubcaps. To make it worse, she plays it so loud I'm surprised Sea-Tac Airport hasn't threatened to move.

(As a trivial footnote, a while back I thought I'd figured out that Buddy took her street name from Buddy Rich, a drek-hot jazz drummer from the previous century. Buddy didn't confirm or deny my speculation, but only pointed out scornfully that even if Rich's music weren't woefully simplistic, it was slotted up anyway by all those horns and drek playing over it.)

So that was why I looked on a visit to Buddy as penance of a sort. A paranoid, depressed drum addict certainly wasn't my company of choice on a Thursday morning.

I parked on Twenty-eighth Avenue Southwest, just around the corner from Buddy's place, then tried vainly to run between the heavy—and probably acidic—raindrops that had begun to fall. I gave my name to the doorman/guard in his booth of bulletproof glass, and was reassured when he buzzed me in. At least Buddy was enough with the program to put me on the guard's "okay" list. I rode the elevator to the fortieth floor, where I got off and turned left down the hall.

Buddy must have scoped me out with her security sys-

tems, decided I was really me, and that I posed no immediate threat. Mechanical locks, bolts, and chains
rattled; maglocks snapped open. The door opened a
crack. I put on my best reassuring smile. "Hoi, Buddy,"
I called. "Can I come in?"

The door opened wider, releasing a sound like multiple epileptic drummers trading chops. Trying not to let
my smile slip, I gritted my teeth and stepped into the
apartment.

Buddy was so quick in buttoning up behind me that she
gave my shoulder a hefty clip with the door. Then she busied
herself locking the dozen or so fastenings that she'd unlocked
to let me in. Her preoccupation gave me a chance to look her
over.

She was a small woman, short and thin-boned. I knew
she was in her early fifties, but she could have passed for
at least twice that. When we'd first met, I thought she
looked like someone on her deathbed, and she'd looked
worse every time after that. Buddy had no muscle tone
whatsoever, simply because she never did anything even
vaguely physical. And the only reason she wasn't a tub
of lard was because she ate only when she remembered
to . . . which was rarely. The corpse-like pallor of her
skin didn't help, either, but what else could be expected
for someone who probably hadn't stepped out of the
house in years?

The walking-dead look was completed by her costume,
consisting of several meters of gray cloth wrapped sari-
like around her form. Although this get-up looked like a
burial shawl, I knew the gray fabric was actually ballistic
cloth. Buddy's paranoia at work again. Her gray hair was
chopped brutally short, and the entire right side of her
head was depilated so that nothing got in the way of the
three chrome datajacks in her temple.

The last lock secured, she glanced up at me with
bright, bird-like eyes. Then she flashed me the lengthiest
smile I've ever seen on her sharp face: a millisecond at
least. I breathed easier; she had to be pretty near the top
of her cycle.

With that worry out of the way, other concerns flooded
back, chief among them an intense aural discomfort.
"Hey, Buddy!" I shouted over the background din. "Can
you turn the drums down a notch?"

She scowled. "They *are* down," she snapped. But then she relented. From the recesses of her ballistic-cloth sari she pulled out a remote-control unit, and thumbed a key. The deranged, spastic percussion dropped in volume from painful to merely irritating. I knew enough not to ask again; this was as good as it was going to get.

I followed Buddy as she picked her way through the hallway and into the living room. The floor, like every other available horizontal surface, was covered with piles of printouts, chips in chipcases, experimental breadboard rigs spewing medusa-heads of optical fibers (and even, here and there, real-and-for-true metal wires), tools and instruments, and all the other drek you'd find in any electronics lab or gadget store. In the center of the room, in pride of place, was Buddy's baby: a custom Fairlight Excalibur cyberdeck. It was sitting on the floor, surrounded by a bewildering array of peripheral garbage wired into the deck in some totally incomprehensible way. With a fluidity that belied her appearance, Buddy dropped into a perfect lotus beside the deck, then turned to stare up at me, waiting.

I glanced around for a place to sit down, but Buddy seemed to hold to her old belief that furniture was redundant when you had floors. There was a small table and a single chair, but both were covered in junk. The floor, then.

Even before I could begin to sit, Buddy scowled with impatience, reached over and shoved everything on the chair to the floor. I nodded my thanks and sat down.

"Well?" Buddy demanded. Even an "up" Buddy was an abrasive Buddy.

"Datasteal," I answered curtly. I knew the best way to deal with her, and had prepared my spiel on the driver over. "Avatar Security Technologies. I want you to crack into their work logs—"

"Avatar's Lone Star. Why them?"

"Did I ever mention someone called Lolita Yzerman?" Buddy shook her head. "She was"—I hesitated—"a friend. Now somebody's geeked her. I want to find out why."

"She was Avatar?" I nodded. "Tap work," Buddy pronounced. "Heard something she shouldn't."

Buddy may be strange, but she sure isn't dumb. Based

on just one or two of my remarks, it took her something
like two seconds to figure out what had cost me several
minutes of skull-sweat. "You've got it," I said. "I want
to find out what it was she shouldn't have heard. Can you
do it?"

She just snorted at that. Of *course* she could do it.
Paranoid or not, she had the same overblown ego of any
decker worth the name.

"*Will* you do it?"

She thought about that for a moment—a long time for
Buddy. "Standard rates?"

I thought about my credit balance and sighed. "Standard rates."

She flashed me another millisecond smile. "Worth the
nuyen," she announced. "You ride along."

"Sorry, Buddy," I reminded her. "No datajack, remember?"

She scowled again. "Still a coward?"

I smiled. "Still a coward."

"Doesn't matter. Picked up something just for you.
Trode rig." She pointed to the high-tech junk piled
around her Excalibur. "You can ride along, jack or no
jack."

I looked askance, surprised that she'd actually gone
out of her way to pick up the electrode net. It was more
than likely a commercially available set-up intended for
use by those who wanted the full experience of simsense
without having to spring for a datajack implant. I'd used
one occasionally, and probably still had one for my old
Atari simdeck buried in the back of the closet, but I'd
never thought about using one to ride the Matrix. It made
sense, though. The cyberdeck's internal systems were really just simsense circuitry designated to translate the
quasi-reality of computer data into a multi-sensory sym-
bolic form that could easily be understood.

I must have been thinking for too long—maybe a second or two. Even on her best day, Buddy's patience
doesn't last that long. "Come on," she said. "See the
Matrix."

And that, of course, was the fascination. Everywhere
you turn, you read or hear something about the "virtual
reality" that is the Matrix. But if you haven't got a datajack in your skull, you can never experience it directly,

or so I'd thought. And if what they say is true, you're missing out on as rich an experience as if you'd been born without eyes. (In fact, the second-best decker I know is blind, and she'd be ecstatic if she never had to jack out. In the Matrix she can see.)

So the temptation was major. But so was the fear, cowardice, or call it what you will. I'd never had a datajack installed because I didn't like the idea of anyone messing with my mind. I wasn't sure I liked the idea any better if the messing came from the outside via electric currents. The brain's delicate. Induce a current in the wrong place and Dirk Montgomery spends the rest of his life believing he's an orange.

"Did you build the rig, Buddy?" I asked, trying to keep my voice casual.

Buddy shook her head. "Got it from VRI in Cheyenne," she shot back. "One of their latest. Beta test model."

VRI and Cheyenne set some of my fears to rest. The firm's one of the best in the world, and Cheyenne is the source of most of the cutting-edge decker technology going. But "beta test model" didn't inspire confidence. "They've got you looking for bugs?" I asked.

"No bugs," Buddy said with the kind of certainty usually associated with natural laws or stone tablets replete with commandments. "It's the best yet, but too expensive to be commercial. I'm showing them how to make it cheaper."

"So it's safe?"

She snorted. "I tried it," she said flatly. "Didn't slot me up any."

I looked into her death's-head face, saw the impatience building in her eyes, and sighed. I knew the signs. If I didn't go along with her, she'd just close up and I'd get no help from her. The choice facing me was easy to state, but harder to make. Did I risk getting my brain scrambled by Buddy's trode rig, or up and leave and wait for our mysterious X to blow that same brain out the back of my head? Decision, decisions . . .

It was the thought of actually running the Matrix that made up my mind, I think. I'm a sucker for new experiences. It'll probably kill me one day, but maybe this wasn't the day. I sighed again and nodded. "I'm in," I told her.

Buddy flashed me another millisecond smile, an approving one. I think Buddy likes me, at least as much as she's able to like anybody, and she obviously thought I'd made the right choice. She leaned over and scrabbled around in the pile of techno-drek beside her Excalibur. Within moments she pulled out something that looked like a crown of thorns with a few dozen hair-thin optic fibers trailing out of it. The contraption sported some straps and bands to hold it in the right place on the subject's *(victim's)* head, including a chin strap. Yeah, it was a beta test model; it had none of the ergonomics of current commercial rigs. Buddy held it carefully, almost with reverence, like it was the crown of the kingdom. She got up onto her knees and approached me, ready to place it on my head.

If I was going to back out, now was the time. Frag, of *course* I wanted to. But I kept my jaw clamped shut. Buddy gently set the rig in place on my head. It was like some horrible parody of a coronation. The tiny, thorn-like electrodes pricked my scalp, and the straps felt cold and alien against my skin as Buddy tightened them. The rig was a little heavier than a lightly armored helmet, and the balance was different, making me feel top-heavy.

As I got used to the sensation of having this *thing* on my head, and struggled to quell the acidic churning in my stomach, Buddy settled herself back into full lotus, the soles of her scrawny feet toward the ceiling. She picked up the cyberdeck and settled it comfortably in her lap. Then she took the jack by the end of its optic fiber, and slipped it into one of the three sockets in her right temple. The jack settled home with a metallic snick that I found profoundly disturbing. Buddy's fingers flew across the keyboard, running some kind of diagnostic, I suppose.

After a few seconds that seemed like hours, she looked over at me. "Ready?" I didn't trust myself to speak, so I just nodded. "Okay," she said, "Phase one." She hit a key.

6

And I was struck blind. Frag, what a freaky, terrifying sensation. I'd always imagined that blindness must be like an engulfing blackness, but this wasn't like that at all. Blackness is an attribute of *something;* blindness is *nothing.* I hated it, and I feared it. I heard a mewling sound, and realized it was my own voice.

"Stay frosty," Buddy told me, her voice as crystal clear and reassuring as I'd ever heard it. "That's just clearing the stage. Now it's show time." I heard the faint click of a key-press, and the reality of the Matrix burst into my brain.

How to describe the Matrix? Scientists call it a "consensual reality," a virtual reality. I'd experienced a diluted form of "virtual reality" during Lone Star training; anyone who's been in a flight simulator or even played some of the better trideo games has. I thought I was prepared for the Matrix. I thought it would be like a simulator, but more so: different in degree, but not in kind.

Wrong! My belief that a simulator had prepared me for the Matrix was as naive as the kid who thinks that seeing a soft-core movie lets him know what a romp in the hay would be like. In even the best simulator, you know deep down inside that you're in a simulator and not where your senses are saying you are. But in the Matrix, you're *there,* and you fragging well know it. To hell with the fact that my meat body was still sitting in Buddy's doss. I—the *I* that matters, the *I* that usually inhabits that meat body— was in the Matrix, and that's all there was to it.

My first impression was of size. The Matrix is big. As big as a world, as big as a universe. There's a horizon, but it's a *long* was out, and it's an artifact of perspective, like the "vanishing point" of art and not of curvature, as in the "real" world. (In fact, the distance has the strangest sensation of non-linearity, if that makes any sense. It's like—and here I really feel the inadequacy of words—the further away something is, the faster distance increases. Like the Matrix is mapped onto some non-Euclidean space. Or maybe not.)

My second impression? The Matrix is *beautiful!* The pitch-black sky is crisscrossed by intermittent beams of light in more colors than have names, each looking solid as steel. The "ground" is black, too, with the same kind of network of intersecting lines. And scattered throughout the space between are big glowing icons that represent nodes within the Matrix. I could pick out the shapes of the ones nearby—a perfectly mirrored sphere, a ruby-red pyramid, an image of the Space Needle, a pagoda glaring in eye-piercing green—but the ones more distant were just specks of light. Toward the electron horizons, the discrete icons blurred together until they looked like an impressionist cityscape shining into a starless sky.

And that was when I realized exactly where I was. If the image of the Space Needle was to scale, I was way the frag up in that black sky, maybe a few thousand meters up, with nothing below but a dizzying fall to whatever ground there was. My first impulse was to look around for Buddy, and that's when I got my second major shock. I couldn't control my body (if I even had a body here; I certainly couldn't see it). My mind was sending out the orders to turn my head, but my angle of vision didn't move. It was as if I was paralyzed.

I'll freely admit it: I panicked. I called out, "Buddy!" and was only slightly reassured when I heard my own voice.

Then Buddy's voice sounded in my ears, as close and immediate as if she were standing right behind me. "Null perspiration, chummer," she said. "I'm here." There was something different about her voice, but at first I wasn't sure what. No matter what phase of her cycle Buddy was in, her voice always had an edge of tension. Not now. For the first time since I'd known her, Buddy sounded relaxed.

Good for her. *I* was far from relaxed. "I can't move," I almost shouted. "And where are you?"

She chuckled. (The Buddy I know does *not* chuckle.) "Stay frosty," she told me again. "Course you can't move. I've got the stick, you know what I mean? You're just a passenger. See?" To prove her point, my field of vision shifted as though I were turning my head from side to side, up and down. "And where am I? I'm *here*, and—if we're being precise—you're *not*. You're just kind of tapping into my senses. Got that?"

I didn't answer for a moment as I struggled to bend my mind around the concept. Then, out of the blue, I picked out an image that did the job for me. In Lone Star training I'd operated a surveillance drone, the kind usually designed to be run by riggers—another datajack connection—but the Star had manual-control systems as well. You put on a headset, complete with vid-screen "goggles" and stereo speakers, that connects you with the drone's "senses." As you drive it around with a little hand-held control until, you see and hear everything the drone does. That's basically the situation I had here, except the control unit was in Buddy's hands, not mine. I could live with that.

"Got that?" The repeated question had Buddy's familiar impatient edge to it.

"Got it," I replied.

"Okay, so here we go." She chuckled again. "Hang onto your brain cells, and enjoy the ride."

It was like being strapped to the nose of a missile. We tipped over and accelerated straight downward at a speed that was absolutely ludicrous. Just as we were about to plow into the ground, we pulled up, then dived headfirst into a glowing light-beam. As the bright blue brilliance engulfed us, we accelerated even more. Though I knew my body was sitting, safe and sound, in Buddy's apartment, it felt as though the speed was tearing the breath from my lungs.

The speed run lasted only seconds before we burst out of the glowing data pipe. Immediately before us was a huge Matrix construct that I recognized instantly. It was the box-like Lone Star building, with the enormous five-pointed star on its side and its gold mirror finish reflecting all the lights of the electron world.

"We're here," Buddy informed me unnecessarily.

"Welcome home," I muttered.

We drifted closer to the Lone Star construct, and for the first time, I could see "my" body reflected in the gleaming surface of the star. It was really Buddy's body, of course, or more precisely the icon she'd chosen for herself. What I saw was a beautiful woman in her early twenties. Her body was slender, almost perfect, her expression warm and caring, her flowing hair the color of polished ebony. The woman was dressed in an elegant evening gown that glowed the brilliant green of laser light.

Was this how Buddy pictured herself? The idea was grotesque, ludicrous, until I realized how tragic it was. Of *course* this was how she saw herself. It was probably how she'd looked when young, when still a rising-star researcher. And probably still did in her mind's eye. What about the walking-dead body the rest of the world saw? That was just a prison, chummer, a prison of flesh that young girl'd got herself trapped in. No wonder Buddy spend most of her time in the Matrix. It was the only place she could be herself.

The shining gold star opened in front of us like a curtain drawing back. I'd been too busy with my thoughts to see what Buddy had done. I mentally shook myself, forcing my attention back to what was going on around me. When we stepped through the wall, we came into a corridor lined with doors that seemed to stretch away to infinity. With the institutional gray of its walls, ceiling, and floor, it might have been a real hallway in a real office building except that the ''doors'' were actually barriers of shimmering light. We cruised down that hall at a comfortable walking speed.

''Where are we?'' I asked.

''The Avatar directory in Lone Star's datastore,'' Buddy said. ''When stuff gets transferred from Avatar, this is where it ends up.''

I wanted to look around nervously, but of course I couldn't. I knew I wasn't really there, yet the sense of being inside the Star's facilities was decidedly uncomfortable. ''What about security?''

''We came in the back door,'' she explained. ''There's heavy security on the front end, but once we're inside, it's only trivial drek.''

''Why? That doesn't make sense.''

''Sure it does,'' she said. ''If you've got a really hot security system on your office door, are you going to load your desk drawers with alarms too? Too much security degrades system responsiveness.''

I knew I was distracting Buddy with my questions, but I couldn't let it go. "Then how did we get in here so easily?"

"Back door," she repeated, her tone impatient. "I know the chummer who did the security for this part of the system. I taught him all he knows, and he's an unimaginative little slot. Always uses the same tricks." As she spoke, we continued down the corridor, looking from side to side at the many doors as we went. Suddenly Buddy muttered, "Aha," and we stopped in front of one doorway that was, as far as I could see, identical to all the others. I considered asking Buddy how she knew this was it, but decided against it.

"Okay," Buddy murmured, more to herself than to me, "this is where things get interesting." The alabaster-skinned arm of Buddy's icon reached into my field of vision. The slender hand held a scalpel whose blade glittered like diamond. With great delicacy, Buddy ran the scalpel down the shimmering barrier that blocked the door, from the top of the frame all the way down to the floor. The barrier sizzled and parted like a curtain as the scalpel blade passed. When the scalpel reached the ground, the barrier vanished totally.

What came next happened so fast that I could barely grasp it at the time. At the instant the barrier blinked out of existence, a shadowy figure leaped out into the hallway right past us. As it sprinted away, I thought my sanity had cracked: the figure was a vintage, Wild West-era U.S. sheriff, spurs and hat and badge and all.

Buddy responded instantly. My field of vision snapped around, and Buddy's arm again came into view. But this time it was clutching a huge, fragging hogleg of a six-shooter revolver. She steadied the brutal piece of ordnance with her other hand, and squeezed off a single shot, taking the "sheriff" in the back of the neck. The slug knocked him clean off his feet, and when he hit the ground, the figure flickered and vanished. His dusty-brimmed hat, which the impact had knocked off his head, lasted an instant longer, then it too flickered into nonexistence. Buddy opened her hand, and the six-shooter was gone.

"What the frag was *that?*" I demanded breathlessly.

"Life and death in the Matrix, cobber," she said jauntily. "There was white ice on the doorway. When I broke through, it tried to trigger a trace program, but I unofficially canceled it. No strain."

If I could have shaken my head, I would have. "Are you sure it wasn't another decker?" I asked.

"No way," she shot back. "Any decker worthy of the name would have stayed to duke it out." I remembered the hogleg roaring in Buddy's icon's hand, and was silently grateful that we hadn't gotten involved in any decker dogfights.

When we stepped through the open door and into the space beyond, I think I gasped out loud in amazement. From the scale of the corridor, I'd expected the typical three-meter-square wage-slave office. The Matrix had done it to me again. We were in a space that could only just be called a room. The walls were slightly farther apart than the width of the doorway, but they extended away ahead of us and upward until they merged at infinity. And those walls were like something out of tequila-fueled nightmare. They seemed to be made of different-sized rectangular blocks, each filled with a swirling cloud of glowing characters, some just zeroes and ones, some alphanumeric, and some Greek symbols and happy-faces and other drek (encrypted files maybe?).

Buddy, predictably, didn't waste a moment rubbernecking, which meant I couldn't see as much of this strange space as I wanted to. She just walked along slowly, running the palms of her perfect hands along the surfaces of those infinite walls. "Lolita Yzerman, right?" she asked.

I tried to nod, vainly, of course. "You got it," I told her.

We stopped, and turned our merged perceptions to face one wall. Buddy laid both palms against it, and the two blocks she touched glowed brightly. "Getting warm," she murmured. With no warning, as though it were the most natural thing in the world—and in *this* world, it might well be—we lifted from the ground and floated straight upward. As we climbed, Buddy touched one block after the other, coaxing each to a brilliant glow under her fingers.

Finally we stopped. "Lolita Yzerman," Buddy announced. She reached out to touch one particular block in front of us, and it flared ruby red. Then she extended her hands *though* the wall of the block, and the characters within swirled like a data dust-storm around her fingers.

"Can you download the files?" I asked.

"No chance. That would trigger drek like you've never seen. We can browse, though."

"Do it," I told her.

It was as if somebody had placed a transparent computer display in front of my eyes. I could still see the wall and Buddy's hands, but superimposed over it was brilliant amber text scrolling by so fast I could make no sense of it. "Can you slow it down?" I asked.

Buddy snorted, but the text *did* slow its frenetic scrolling. Not enough for me to read it, though. I debated asking again, but decided against it. Buddy knew what we were looking for as well as I did, and she'd be more likely than me to spot paydata anyway. I kept my silence.

"Your chummer wasn't high up in the hierarchy, was she?" Buddy asked.

I tried to shrug. "I don't know. Why do you ask that?"

"This is all petty drek she was assigned to," Buddy said. "Acquaintances of suspected tax evaders. Nothing worth getting flatlined over. It's all small, sordid stuff."

I remembered the efforts that my mysterious X had gone to. Nothing small, sordid, or petty there. "There's something else," I said firmly. "If you dig deeper, it'll be there."

Buddy didn't answer, but her silence was a rebuke in itself. The scrolling text picked up speed again, and I knew better than to complain. The text blurred by for several more seconds, then stopped abruptly. I heard breath hiss through Buddy's teeth in surprise and frustration.

"What's up?" I asked.

"Shut up," was all she would say, in true Buddy style. She pulled one hand out from the wall and inserted it into another block. More text flashed in front of my eyes, this time jade green and laid out in the format of a directory listing, but still scrolling too fast for me to read. She pulled her other hand out, drove it into another block. Another blurred directory listing, another hiss of anger from Buddy. Then she drew both hands out of the wall and all the blocks went dull again. *"Frag!"* she spat out.

A big red push-button appeared in the air in front of us. Buddy stabbed it with a slender finger.

And we were back in the real world. I was sitting on the chair in Buddy's apartment, my hands locked in a death-grip on the seat. Buddy—the real, walking-dead Buddy—squatted on the floor in front of me, her cadaverous face in a frown. She pulled the jack out of her temple and set her cyberdeck aside.

"What the frag happened?" I demanded. Buddy didn't answer, just went about neatly coiling the jack's optical fiber. I undid the chin strap and pulled the crown-of-thorns contraption off my head, dumped it unceremoniously on the floor. "What happened?" I insisted.

Buddy shot to her feet and began to pace jerkily about the apartment. Out of the Matrix and in her meat body, the old familiar paranoid Buddy was back. "Dead-ended," she said at last.

"What do you mean?"

She dropped to the floor again, sinking back into lotus, clutching her knees with both hands and rocking back and forth with barely restrained anger. "Records are gone," she said. "Not deleted. *Gone.*"

That didn't make any sense, of course. I bit back on my own frustration, struggled to keep my voice calming. "Buddy," I murmured, "I need you, chummer. You've got to tell me what you mean. What did you find? Use simple words, *omae*, like you're talking to a baby. Okay?"

Buddy continued her rocking for a few moments, and I was afraid I hadn't got through. But then I saw the tension go out of her body. She looked up and flashed me another strobe-light smile. "You know what your chummer did at Avatar, right?" she asked, and her voice was almost as relaxed as it had been in the Matrix.

"She washed dataline taps."

"Signal enhancement," Buddy confirmed. "They keep two copies of everything. The original tap record and the enhanced version. Okay?" I nodded. "They also keep records of who worked on what tap and what the case was."

"And . . . ?" I prompted.

"And most of those records are gone," Buddy said.

"The original tap data she was working on *and* her enhanced version."

"Deleted?"

"*Not* deleted," she said firmly. "When a file's deleted normally, there's a Delete flag set to show that a file was there and to record who authorized the deletion. No flags, no flags anywhere. The records are just *gone*. As far as the system's concerned, they were never present at all."

"But they were?" I said, confused.

"Of *course* they fragging were. On the file level, there's no record. Down at the level of the storage media, there's a number of clusters that used to be allocated to those files, and now those clusters are free. Understand?"

Clusters didn't mean a thing to me unless maybe you're talking about grapes—but I nodded encouragingly. "And what does that mean?"

The set of Buddy's jaw told me that she was done talking baby-talk. "*You* figure it," she snapped.

"Okay," I sighed. "So the files *were* there, but aren't any more. Two options. Option one: somebody decked into the system and blew away the files. But to do that he'd have to be pretty hot, right?"

"*Nova* hot," Buddy confirmed.

"Option two, then," I continued. "Lone Star blew the files away themselves. They can do that?" A curt nod from Buddy. "Which means they're covering up . . . something. Either way, it means this *isn't* small stuff. Which I already knew." I got wearily to my feet. "Thanks, Buddy. I'll transfer the credit when I get home." I headed for the door.

"William Sutcliffe."

I turned back. Buddy was still sitting on the floor, watching me. "What?" I asked.

"William Sutcliffe," she repeated. "It was his dataline. A chummer of his was under investigation, so they tapped Sutcliffe's dataline."

"And who's William Sutcliffe?" I asked.

"Fragged if I know," Buddy snapped back. "*You're* the fragging investigator."

I got out of there fast, and damn near flew back to my doss in the Barrens. All the way home I wracked my brain for some kind of line on this William Sutcliffe. Null program, cobber. I'd never heard of him in my life. But Buddy was right, I *am* an investigator, and I could put out various feelers to track down our Mr. Sutcliffe. The supposed dead end wasn't quite as dead as it seemed.

The message light was flashing on my telecom, so I let myself down in front of the screen and hit the appropriate combination of keys. The screen lit up, and when I saw who it was, the whole room seemed to light up as well.

The young woman smiling out of the screen was attractive rather than beautiful, the lines of her face were utilitarian at best. But her brown eyes sparkled with life, and her smile was as bright as the sun.

"Hoi, bro," my sister Theresa said. "Sorry I missed you. Just checking in to let you know I'm still breathing. Hope things are rolling well for you, and"—she shrugged lightly—"and I guess that's about it. Catch you later, Derek."

After the image vanished, I sat staring at the screen for a few moments, a lump in my throat. Theresa has that effect on me, always has. Part of it is that she's my baby sister—at twenty-five, six years younger than me—the other part is that she's the only living family I've got left. But there's more to it than that.

I remembered her back in the old days, when we were growing up. Theresa was tall and gangly as a kid, all freckles and skinned knees, sudden enthusiasms and innocent laughter. She was the one with the imagination, but it was strong enough for both of us. Even when I was in my rebellious mid-teens, Theresa was one of the few calming influences in my life. I think she kept me sane.

But then we started to grow apart. It's during the teens that you've got to learn one of the most important lessons in life: the world's a dark and dangerous place, and you've got to deal with that if you want to get by. Theresa learned the first part, but not the second. Instead, she'd tried to isolate herself from the world around her. She immersed herself in books, the trideo, and whatever the frag else she could to keep the big bad world from infringing on her reality.

Infringe it did, of course—big time—the year I turned twenty-two and Theresa was sweet sixteen. I'd just had

one of the all-time great fights with my old man. It was
the night I told him I'd dropped out of computer science—dropped out of the whole University of Washington system, in fact. He blew his top, like I knew he
would, but didn't quite take a swing at me—which I *hoped*
he would, because then I'd have been justified in pushing
his teeth down his throat. Instead, he kept the violence
on the verbal and emotional level. That only made it
worse, of course. I stormed out of the house, wishing
him dead in my heart.

It was the next morning that I got the news. The stupid
fragger had obliged me. After I'd left he'd taken my
mother out for a drive, probably to calm her down after
the ugly scene with her son. Whatever the reason, he
drove into a patch of turf claimed by a particularly militant go-gang calling themselves the Junk Yard Dogs. And
then—*goddamn him to hell!*—my old man stopped the
car, and the two of them got out for some fresh fragging
air. The Dogs were out to play that night, and my parents
were just raw meat. The police report said they had died
quickly, and I want to believe that.

I took it hard enough, but it damn near blew Theresa
apart. She stayed with me while I tried to put her back
together as much as I could. It was obvious from the start
she wasn't coping, but I lied to myself that she'd pull it
out and get back in control.

Then one night she just vanished, no message, no
nothing. I fragging near went mad, but I couldn't track
her down. She showed up a week or so later, acting as if
she'd only stepped out for an hour or so. I went up one
side of her and down the other, but she just stood there
and took it, giving me this inane smile. And that's when
I saw the shiny-new datajack and the optical fiber trailing
down to the simsense-chip player on her belt. Theresa
had found a better way to escape from the world.

She stayed with me for another couple of months. During that time, I tried to monitor—and moderate—her chip
usage. For the first few weeks, she spent most of her
waking hours with simsense drek pouring directly into
her brain. After that, though, she started to pull back.
She was still a user, but at least she wasn't the full-blown
addict chiphead I feared she'd become.

I guess I was hard on her. Like a self-righteous teetotaler, I ground her for using chips at all, for using them to dilute and escape reality. (And, at the same time, I was almost single-handedly supporting the synthahol industry.) I ground her too much. A few weeks before I was to enter Lone Star basic training, I came home and found her gone. The note she left made it abundantly and painfully clear that she could do without my lectures and my posturing. She'd found somewhere else to crash, with people who weren't so fragging tight-assed. The note was scrawled longhand on a scrap of paper, and was wrapped around her credstick. My baby sister had dropped out for real.

I tried to track her down, both then and after I was into training. But even with the Star's resources, it's slotting near impossible to get a line on a member of the SINless understrata. Maybe six months later I was *still* looking, but growing ever more convinced she'd gone the same way as our parents.

Then, out of the blue, she called me. From a public phone, of course, so I couldn't put a trace on her that way. I screamed at her for a while, and she just listened until I calmed down. And then we talked and came to a kind of rapprochement. Neither one of us was going to change our world view to suit the other. But what was wrong with that? We'd each found what we needed at the moment. I had the Star, she had her chummers—chipheads or BTLers, some of them, but still her chummers. We talked, and something strange happened.

We became friends. Not siblings, not big brother-little sister, but friends. We weren't the same, we had different views—I thought she'd funked out, she thought I was lying to myself—but that was okay, really. It was a strange revelation.

Since then we'd kept in touch every few weeks. She won't tell me where she is, so it's always Theresa who makes contact. Probably afraid I'd do something stupid like try to send her credit or such drek, and she's right. Twice she called for help after getting into some drek over her head, but it's never been anything too serious. I look forward to her calls, and wish we could get together face-to-face. But that's beyond the scope of what she'll allow, and since she's the one in control I've got to live with it.

I was glad of her call now. It was good to see the face
of at least one blonde who wasn't on a slab.

7

How do you track down someone if all you know is
his name—William Sutcliffe, for example? Various ways,
chummer. Some legal, most not. Predictably, of course,
the chances of success increase with the illegality of the
means. (Call that Montgomery's Law. Copyright is with-
held, royalties are appropriate.) Nevertheless, I decided
to try the law-abiding ways first.

There are a couple of database-retrieval services tailor-
made for just this kind of thing. It's like flipping through
a "phone book" for the whole of North America—or
beyond, if you let the search routine run on. One simply
churns through the LTG and RTG subscriber records in
case Mr. Sutcliffe consented to have his LTG number
posted in the open listenings. In the more likely situation
that he didn't, there are similar services that search corporate employment records—though the number of corps
that consent to release the information is pretty fragging
small—and even electronic publications, newsfaxes, and
screamsheets.

From what Buddy told me, the good Mr. Sutcliffe
would seem to be a pretty small fish who only came to
the attention of Lone Star and Avatar because he was the
chummer of a tax evader. The odds were pretty good,
then, that this superficial kind of search would turn up
something.

Like drek. Appearances to the contrary, Sutcliffe
wasn't a small fish. People don't get killed for listening
in on a small fish. So I expected that the legal searches
would be merely the first round, and that I'd have to get
into some serious and hideously illegal digital tap-
dancing. I had to go through the motions, though. Who
knows? I might get lucky.

I was sweating away, writing the most efficient search
syntax, when the telecom beeped with an incoming call.

I considered letting the machine take it, but then reconsidered. I hit the key for voice-only, and growled, "Yeah?"

The screen lit up with the image of Jocasta Yzerman. Her hair shone like burnished copper, set off perfectly by her ivory jacket and jade-green eye make-up. She looked like a million nuyen. Her brow furrowed as she stared into what I knew was a blank screen. I hurriedly cut in my video pickup, and she looked relieved. "Mr. Montgomery," she said formally.

"Call me Derek," I suggested. "Or Dirk."

She hesitated. I could see her trying to decide between being too informal or too rude. She solved the problem by doing neither. "Have you found out anything?"

My turn to hesitate. William Sutcliffe's name *was* a lead, but I didn't know if it would pan out. "Not really," I told her. She clouded up instantly. An impatient woman, Ms. Yzerman. "I'm checking out some possibilities," I added quickly.

But she wasn't listening. "*I've* got something," she said irritably. "But I don't know if I should bother telling you."

Great. I ground my teeth, but kept my voice disinterested. "Your call. If you want to run with it alone," I said with a shrug, "tell me where to send flowers."

She bit her lip. I could tell she'd shaken off the shock of the bombing as fast as she'd shaken off Lolly's death, and she was ice-cold in control of herself. She didn't want me involved: didn't trust me and she didn't like me (there's no accounting for taste). On the other hand, she needed help. Otherwise she wouldn't have called in the first place. I forced myself to keep still and waited her out. Finally the hard line of her body relented. "Somebody's been trying to reach me," she began. "I don't know who, but he's been leaving messages all over—"

"Where?" I cut in.

She shrugged. "At work, at the university. Don't worry," she snapped. "I haven't been there. I retrieved the messages remotely. I'm not that dumb."

I was about to tell her about the various trace routines you pick up at just about any deckers' hangout, then remembered she was in the communications biz, if only peripherally. Maybe she had done it right after all. "Okay," I allowed. "Go on."

"He wants to meet with me," she continued. "He said he knows what Lolita was working on before she was killed. He says he's got a copy of the tap record."

A copy of the tap Lolly was "washing"? That would give us a lot of background, if it wasn't a set-up . . . which it was, of course. "So he set a time and a nice safe place for the meet, right?" I said sarcastically.

"No, drekhead," she snapped back. "I said I never talked to him, and he didn't say anything about a meet. I'm supposed to phone him tonight so we can discuss it."

Now *that* made me sit up and take notice. "He left an LTG number?"

"If I'm supposed to call him, he'd have to, wouldn't he?"

I ignored the sarcasm in her voice. "Give it to me."

She thought about it for a moment, then yielded. I opened a data window on the telecom and keyed in the digits as she recited them. She opened her mouth to say something else, but I cut her off. "Give me a few ticks." I put her on hold and expanded the data window to fill the screen. This could be something big. I fired up one of my grossly illegal search utilities and fed in the LTG number. The utility chewed on it for ten seconds, then spat up a wad of text onto my screen. "Paydata!" I crowed. I stashed my find in memory, and brought Jocasta back from electronic limbo.

"Okay," I told her briskly. "I'm going to meet with your mysterious benefactor. What time are you supposed to call him?"

"Midnight," she said. "But I told you, we haven't set up a meet—"

"He doesn't think so," I gloated, and stuffed the data my search routine had retrieved down the line to Jocasta's telecom. "See that address? The LTG number he gave you is for a hard-wired phone, and *that's* where it's jacked into the wall. At midnight tonight, there's a good chance your nameless friend's going to be sitting at that phone waiting for you to call. And I'll be paying him a visit."

Her gaze was steady. Those gray eyes showed some grudging approval, but they showed steel-hard determination as well. I knew what she was going to say before she opened her mouth. *"We'll* be paying him a visit," she said flatly. "It was my sister who was killed."

And it's my neck that's on the block for it, I wanted to shoot back. But I'd already decided to let her win this one. If she wanted to put her shapely body at risk, so be it. I wasn't responsible for her safety. On the other hand, if tonight's phone call was intended to lead Jocasta into a trap—which I figured was close to a certainty—then our surprise party was a reversal of that trap, and it made sense to bring along an extra body and an extra gun. So, "Okay, *omae,"* I told her. "You're coming. Where do I pick you up?"

She shook her head. "We'll take my car. Somebody might have seen yours outside my place in Tacoma."

I blinked. "You've got a car?"

"Of course. I didn't take it when . . . on that first night . . ."—When I came to kill you, is what she meant—"so nobody could trace me."

So you took a cab instead, I thought. Real smart, Jocasta. I didn't let any of that show on my face, of course. I just nodded agreeably. "You drive, then. Pick me up at the Redmond Center Mall at twenty-three fifteen. I'll be wearing a white carnation."

She snorted. Humor-impaired, I decided. "Where are we going?" she asked.

I grinned. "Downtown."

I let myself sink into the upholstery of the passenger seat, and smiled. I'd been playing guess-the-car with myself while waiting, and felt smug that I'd pegged it right on. Jocasta drove a Hyundai-AMC Harmony, a good entry-level exec luxury car. I'd blown out on the color, though. I'd figured a stolid corporate black, not candy-apple red. Maybe there was some spark to Jocasta's personality that I hadn't seen yet. Or maybe it was just that the red model was on sale.

Jocasta herself was wearing another slate-gray tailored suit in synthleather, accessorized in brushed steel and hematite, and she looked like something out of *Corporate Woman* magazine. Her matching purse was at my feet, and I'd already confirmed that her Colt America

L36—the laser-sighted pistol with which I'd become personally acquainted—was inside.

My own garb was a marked contrast to hers: a black "business suit" consisting of close-fitting roll-neck shirt and black pants that could almost qualify as tights, topped with my trusty duster. The only accessory I carried was my Colt Manhunter, and it wasn't color-coordinated with the rest of my outfit, so sorry. As she pulled to a stop to let me in, I noted Jocasta's look of distaste. Well, okay, sure, I looked like some piece of street drek the rat dragged in. But my duster could stop a round that would core Jocasta front-to-back, and I was also fragging sure that jangling jewelry wouldn't give me away or get caught in a door or some other such drek.

I'd told Jocasta we were going downtown, so she'd immediately navigated us onto Route 520 heading west. Now she glanced over at me and asked, "Where are we going?"

"Deepest darkest downtown," I told her. "Westlake Center. Suite 4210."

The traffic was almost nonexistent as we hummed over the floating bridge and into the sky-raking lights of central Seattle. Jocasta knew downtown, I was glad to see, so I didn't have to direct her onto the fastest routes. We followed I-5 south, then swung off the freeway and cruised along Fifth Avenue toward Seattle Center.

Westlake Center has been around for over sixty years, but it's undergone some significant changes during that time. When it was built in the late 1980s, it replaced the old south terminus of the monorail line. (This was back when the monorail ran only from the corner of Westlake Avenue and Olive Way to Seattle Center and back, before being extended into the circle route it is today.) It was originally a three-story shopping complex, with the monorail terminal incorporated into its upper floor.

Things have changed since then. At about the same time that the monorail route was extended and the obsolete Alweg wheel-driven monorail replaced by state-of-the-art maglev technology, some developer realized how inefficient was the use of space at Westlake Center. Only three stories? In downtown Seattle? Give me a fragging break.

And that's when Westlake Tower began its rise into the

smoggy sky. With the newly renovated Westlake Center as its base, the Tower became a sixty-story magnet for members of the mid-to-upper corporate executive strata. For a yuk, I dressed up in my best and showed up at the rental office when the Tower first opened. They wouldn't even let me in to see the show suite unless I could prove my credstick had the credit balance to make it worth their while—which I declined to do, of course. As I was leaving, though, I heard some bona fide customers yakking about the rates. A small suite on the fourth floor—the one right above the monorail station and obviously in the low-rent district—was renting for *thirty-K* nuyen per month. Jocasta's mysterious "benefactor" was on the forty-second floor, high enough to have a view, and no doubt also with a rent high enough to bankrupt many a small company. Kinda makes you think, doesn't it?

Jocasta tooled her Symphony around onto Stewart Street and down into the parking lot underneath the Tower. The security guard looked into the car, his face showing some doubt when he scanned me. But he opened the gate and let us head down. Jocasta and I exchanged a quick grin over the guard's geeky-looking black gloves and Zorro-style hat, but my amusement was tempered by the word on Westlake Center security. Death on two legs, is what I'd heard, dorky outfit notwithstanding. And those effete black gloves were actually shock-gloves with enough juice to make even a troll lose interest in the proceedings.

It was a little after 2330 hours, and all the stores in the Center above would be closed. Some of the restaurants and the brew-pub called Noggins would be open for another hour or two yet, and a number of cars were still in the transient parking levels. (The residents' cars were, I knew, nice and secure a couple of levels down.) Jocasta followed the glowing signs reading Elevator To Westlake Tower Lobby, and parked as near to the elevator block as she could.

She killed the engine. "We're here," she said, "but how are we going to get upstairs? There's got to be security in the lobby."

I smiled to cover the fact that I didn't have the answer . . . yet. I was pretty confident we'd somehow find a way past any kind of security. Maybe it's my air of childlike

innocence (like drek). "Trust me," I said ingenuously.
She didn't even dignify that with a snort of derision.

We were out of the car and Jocasta was just setting the
alarm when I first heard it: the explosive roar of large-
bike engines, ricocheting around the concrete confines
of the underground lot. *Multiple* engines, which didn't
make me feel particularly comfortable. A full-on go-gang
wouldn't waste their time cruising Westlake Center's underground lot, but I wasn't in the mood to deal with even
some wannabes. I grabbed Jocasta's right elbow and hus-
tled her toward the elevator block.

We didn't make it in time. The big blocks were still
concussing their way closer when the first of the bikes
glided to a stop in front of us. With the noise of the hogs
in my ears, there was no way I could have heard this
bike. It was one of the newest-generation Japanese crotch-
rockets, driven by a turbine engine that even when
cracked wide open didn't get much louder than an electric fan. The bike looked fast and mean and had a rider
to match.

He was the classic elf phenotype—tall and slender,
high cheekbones, slightly pointed ears—and wore mahogany leathers a shade lighter than his skin. Around his
right wrist was some kind of bulky bracelet. I didn't recognize it, but it looked vaguely familiar. His tight curls
were cropped short, forming a red-dyed skullcap. When
he grinned at us, at first I didn't get why he seemed to
radiate such a palpable sense of menace . . . then I saw
that his teeth had been filed to sharp points. Charming
gentleman. I tried to spot the colors on the back of his
jacket, but his stance hid it from view.

The rider released the throttle and flexed his hand as
if to work cramps out of his fingers. The razor-studs on
his fingerless gloves caught the light perfectly. It was
almost theatrical, but I was feeling a little too overly
stressed to enjoy his performance.

"Good evening, worthies," the elf said in a voice like
velvet. "Going upstairs, are we? Well, perhaps you'd like
to, er, *chat* with my friends and me before you depart."

On cue, the other bikes arrived. Three of them, two
Harley hogs and another quiet rice-rocket. The hog-riders
were human; the guy on the Suzuki Aurora was an ork
running for troll. All three wore the same mahogany

leathers as their leader. The roar of the Harleys was a physical pain in my ears and a thudding concussion in my chest. When one of the hog-riders revved his engine just for the frag of it, I felt Jocasta flinch beside me. My ears rang like gongs.

The leader was talking again. At least, his mouth was moving, but I couldn't hear word one over the blast still echoing around the confined area. I shook my head to clear it . . .

And my gaze fell on the ork riding the Aurora. He had something cupped in the palm of his hand, and his eyes flicked back and forth between it and us. Then he nodded almost imperceptibly to the leader.

Fear was suddenly in my belly, like a ball of dirty ice. Even though I couldn't see it, I knew what the ork had in his hand: a holo of one or both of us. Setup!

With all my strength, I shoved Jocasta to her left, between two parked cars, then flung myself after her. As I did, I saw the elf's machine pistol clearing his holster. Time seemed to kick into overdrive, and everything suddenly seemed to move at a slow crawl. I saw the machine pistol barrel coming up, saw the elf clamp down on the trigger. The first rounds spattered off the floor as he let the recoil drag the barrel up toward me.

Then I was behind the car, slamming into Jocasta, bringing us both to the ground. Bullets tore into the car's bodywork, but none penetrated. I grabbed Jocasta and scrabbled my way under the next car in line, dragging her after me. Her eyes were wide and her face pale, but she seemed to be holding it together. I judged that she wasn't likely to fall apart and get us both geeked. Then came an echoing concussion that I felt down to my bones, and the first car that had sheltered us depreciated in resale value somewhat drastically. One of the bikers was packing heavy ordnance or—pray it wasn't true—was magically active. Well, one thing at a time. While fragments of car were still rattling to the ground, covering the sound of our movements, I dragged Jocasta another car down and one car over. The tactical decision was simple: put as much distance—and heavy metal—between us and the bikers as fast as possible.

Of course, the bikers knew that just as well as I did, and they had the edge when it came to speed. The ad-

vantage was with us only so long as we could keep between or under the parked cars, where they couldn't easily
follow. Unfortunately, that meant we were more or less
pinned down. The double row of cars we were sheltering
among was maybe twenty cars long, but we'd be cut down
as soon as we left their cover, to head for the elevator,
for example, or to cut across to Jocasta's car, which was
in another row. I had to find a way of evening things up
a bit. Darkness, maybe. I looked up, considering shooting out the overhead lights. But there were too many of
them, I saw immediately. I didn't have enough ammu-
nition to get them all, and the bikers wouldn't give me
enough time. As soon as I revealed our location, they'd
be on us.

The concrete space echoed with engine noise. The
bikes were moving, no doubt splitting up to flank or sur-
round us. I let go of Jocasta and drew my pistol, thumbing off the safety. The two-and-a-quarter kilos of heavy
metal were reassuring in my hand. I clutched the weapon
like a talisman and rose to a crouch, ready to sneak a
quick peek over the hood of the car beside me. The bikes
were moving, and the noise gave me some clue as to their
disposition. But the echoes were deceptive enough that I
had to check by eye. I gripped my pistol tighter and
psyched myself up.

Just as I started to raise my head, I caught a flash of
movement out the corner of my eye. I turned.

It was the ork on his turbine-driven Aurora. With the
Harley hogs revving their engines, I could never have
heard his approach, which, of course, was exactly what
the ork had counted on. He was grinning nastily, one
hand on his bike's throttle, the other cocked back as
though ready to throw a baseball. But that wasn't a baseball in his hand. It was a ball of twisting, glowing energy, some kind of spell, and he was all ready to hurl it
at us. I spun as fast as I could, bringing my big Manhunter around to bear. My time sense was still in turbo
mode, so I had plenty of time to see the ork's filthy grin
get even wider. We both knew I wasn't going to make it.
His muscles tensed as he prepared to throw the spell.

And that's when the tiny spot of red blinked on between his eyes. His eyes widened as a neat hole punched
itself into his brow-line and his head snapped back. The

spell—whatever it was—discharged, rocketing up and away, then glancing back down off the low ceiling to explode a car two rows over. Ork plus bike toppled over and landed with a thud.

I looked down at Jocasta. She still had her Colt America lined up on where the ork's face had been, her finger on the trigger with enough pressure to keep the sighting laser burning. She was rock-steady, as if carved out of marble. Then I saw her hand begin to shake. The pistol wavered and the laser cut out. I grabbed her shoulder, felt her jump from my touch. She looked at me, her eyes dazed. I knew what was going on in her mind. First kill: she was comfortable with her weapon, and she was probably a hot damn at blowing away targets on the pistol range. But she'd never shot anything that was alive, had never seen up close and personal what her little pistol could do to flesh and bone. I squeezed her shoulder and gave her my best reassuring, frag-the-world smile, all the time railing mentally at her to shake it off and get with the program. I was much relieved when her lips curled in the faintest of smiles. "Stay here," I said, then moved forward in a knee-cracking duck walk, keeping my head below the level of the car.

I moved over one car and popped my head up to see what was happening with the other bikers. As I'd guessed from the sounds, the Harleys were buzzing around the car—still burning happily—that the ork's spell had demolished. It was the leader who really worried me, though. With that bloody quiet bike of his, he could be anywhere and I wouldn't know it until he cut me in half with his machine pistol. I looked around quickly.

And there he was, one row over and moving our way at walking speed. Like a good general, he'd sent his troops off to check on the commotion while he cruised elsewhere, in case the toasted car was a diversion. (Which it was, albeit not a purposeful one.) I ducked back down and considered my options. The downed ork's bike was a tempting option, but I discarded it after a moment's thought. I can ride a bike but I'm not the best, nowhere near in the same class as the typical go-gang jockey.

That was when Jocasta grabbed my ankle. I was so keyed up, my reflexes didn't know whether to blow her

away or scream out loud. I solved the problem by having
a slight childish accident. I glared at her.

But she wasn't looking my way. She was pointing
across the open aisle. I followed the angle of her finger,
and broke into a grin.

It was another elevator block, this one leading not to
the lobby of Westlake Tower, but to the Westlake Center
shopping mall instead. The elevators themselves were no
use; I could just see us standing there, waiting for the
car to arrive, all the while absorbing a couple of kilos of
high-velocity lead. No thanks. But next to the elevator
was a red-painted door marked Fire Exit. Since we were
underground, that had to mean stairs leading up into the
mall. Just the ticket. Unless the stairs were unusually
wide or the bikers unusually good, there was no way they
could take their mounts up with them. Which meant we
were on even footing again as far as mobility, but *we'd*
have the advantage of high ground as we high-tailed it
up those stairs. Perfect.

Perfect, that is, if we could get to the stairs without
getting scragged in the process. The hog-riders were out
of the picture for the few precious seconds we needed.
But the leader on his rice-rocket would see us the moment we broke cover, and stitch us crotch to crown. I
grabbed another glance, hoping he'd turned back or was
taking another turning. No luck. Time was running out,
I knew. We probably had only seconds before the hog-
riders decided there was nothing of interest around the
blazing car and came back to join their boss.

"The stairs," I hissed at Jocasta. "Get ready." She
nodded, and tensed herself to run.

I tensed myself, too, but not to run. Not yet: I had to
distract the elf, and subtlety wouldn't do it. I raised my
head over the hood-line of the car once more, and
squeezed my pistol to stop my hand from shaking. The
elf's head was scanning left and right as he cruised down
the row of cars. I waited until he was looking the wrong
way . . .

Now. I popped to my feet and brought my weapon to
bear. I squeezed the trigger four times, and the big Manhunter roared in response. The recoil punished my hand
and wrist, and the reports were like blows to my already-
abused ears. I know I hit him with my first shot, and

maybe with my second. I was more concerned with squeezing the rounds off fast than with fighting the recoil to keep the barrel on line, so the third and fourth shots were off the mark. But they were probably close enough for him to hear them (and if you've ever heard the whip-crack of a Manhunter round passing close by, you know how distracting it can be). Anyway, he lurched backward as if he'd been kicked in the shoulder, and he ditched his bike. I don't think I hurt him bad—those leathers were almost certainly plated—but at least he was down.

"*Go.*" I yelled to Jocasta. She was off like a hare, sprinting for the fire exit, and I was close on her heels. She flung open the door and darted through. I was following her as automatic fire exploded off the wall and doorframe around me. I didn't hang around to check, but I was sure it was friend elf sending us a farewell gift. Slamming the door behind me, I looked around for some way of securing it. But this was, after all, a fire escape, which meant the door was designed so it *couldn't* be secured. I gave it up as useless, and took off up the concrete stairs after Jocasta. *Wide* stairs, frag it, easily wide enough for the rice-rocket, although too tight for the Harleys.

One flight, two flights, and the blood was pounding in my ears even louder than our running footsteps. We were halfway up the third when I heard the metal fire door crash open, accompanied by the ripping discharge of a machine pistol. The bikers had figured we might be trying an ambush, and weren't taking any chances. I wished for a grenade or something equally unpleasant to send down the stairs to keep the kids occupied, but of course I never carry the gift that's appropriate to the occasion.

Another half-flight, and I heard the sound I'd been dreading: the whine of a high-revving turbine. Friend elf had brought his bike and was assaulting the stairs. We didn't have long.

Jocasta flung open the door at the top of this flight and stopped. I joined her. A short hallway lay ahead of us. To our immediate right was another fire door with panic bar, probably leading outside. At the other end of the hallway was a brightly painted door labeled To the Mall.

Decision time—*again*—and quick. Outside, and hit the streets? Or into the mall, with (hopefully) lots of people and the dorky security boys. Put that way, the choice was easy. "Come on," I yelled, and nearly dragged Jocasta off her feet as I charged for the door to the mall. From the sound, I could tell the elf was almost on our butts. I had a bad moment when the doorknob—no panic bar here—didn't turn immediately. But then I twisted it the other way and it opened easily. I remembered only at the last minute to stash my pistol, then we stepped through the door, shutting it after us.

We stood there a moment, overwhelmed at the transition. From the life-and-death world of the street, we'd stepped straight into the business-as-usual operation of a flashy corporate mall. Bright lights, tastefully riveting shop-window displays, even a few premature Christmas decorations hung here and there. There weren't many people, as most of the shops were closed, but the few patrons still coming and going to and from the restaurants and bars were dressed in much the same style—or at least the same quality—as Jocasta. I was very much out of place.

Who gave a frag? One of the Westlake security guards, a troll who looked like a *real* geek in his Zorro hat, was giving me the baleful eye. If we moved out of the area fast enough, maybe Zorro and crew and the bikers would keep each other busy while we bugged out.

I could hear the elf's turbine bike even through the shut door. We didn't have time. I grabbed Jocasta's elbow again, and dragged her further from the door. Zorro the troll was up on the mezzanine level, looking down at us over the glass guardrail. Better get him into the action now rather than later, I figured.

"Hey, security," I shouted up to him, waving. "We need help down here. There's something going down in the underground."

He scowled down at us, and I saw him mutter into his radio headset. Then he started down the escalator toward us. He locked his black-gloved hands together and squeezed, and the shoulders of his uniform almost tore apart at the seams as his musculature shifted. All right, already, I was impressed. Jocasta and I moved further from the door toward the foot of the up escalator. A corporate-looking couple were on their way up. As they

passed the troll, he glanced at them, touching the brim
of his hat in a sketchy salute.

That was why he was distracted when the fire door
burst open and the elf howled out into the mall. The troll
spun, and his bloodshot eyes bugged wide open. He
reached for his weapon, reached fast.

But the elf already had his machine pistol out and
ready. He tightened down on the trigger, emptying the
whole clip into the security guard before the troll's piece
had even cleared its holster. The troll just stood there,
and I thought for a moment his armored uniform had
done the trick. But then the blood burst forth from multiple head wounds and he pitched forward—crash, bang—
down the escalator. The corp woman screamed, and her
partner very bravely flung himself prone, leaving her
alone up there to absorb any lead coming their way. I
charged up the elevator at a full run, dragging Jocasta
with me. I knocked the corp broad aside, and I think
trod on her swain's neck. Jocasta's high-heeled boot must
have come down on some more sensitive part of his anatomy, because he howled in treble.

I risked a glance back over my shoulder. The elf had
jammed another clip into his weapon, and was cutting
loose. Bullets sparked and sang off the metal steps of the
escalator. The bullets tore a scream from the corp broad
and threw her to the steps in a bloody heap. The elf was
using his favorite trick again, letting the recoil walk the
fire up to his target—us. We had maybe a second. But
we were at the top of the escalator. I flung myself forward, dragging Jocasta down with me. Before I hit the
ground, something slammed into my left elbow with the
impact of a baseball bat. It felt as though the flesh on my
hand and forearm had burst into flame. I bit back a
howled obscenity, and rolled away from the top of the
elevator.

I looked around quickly. No security up here. *Why?*
Hadn't the drekheads heard the gunfire and the bike?

The bike . . . I crouched low and risked a glance down
the escalator. Corp broad and corp guy were still lying
on the escalator, perfect obstacles. (Obstacles? *Yes.* A
good rider can run over a prone body on flat terrain without undue risk of ditching. But not while riding up a
staircase. The elf *might* make it, but better odds were

that he'd be over the guardrail before he knew what happened.) The elf recognized the situation, too. He was at the foot of the escalator, revving his bike angrily, glaring at the bodies. Which meant he wasn't looking at me. I pulled out the Manhunter, and drew a bead on his dark face. As they'd taught us at Lone Star, and as the troll security guard had discovered to his terminal detriment, even the best body armor in the world won't protect you from a through-and-through head shot. I triggered the sighting laser to check my aim—yep, center-head—and brushed the reactive trigger twice.

But the fragger must have seen the flare of my laser. Flinging himself aside just as the big pistol boomed, he triggered off a quick burst that sent me rolling for cover. Frag, *almost*. I all-foured it over to Jocasta, who'd hunkered down behind a synthetic marble bench. Her pistol was out, leveled at the top of the escalator. Good thinking. I joined her and chose the same aiming point. When the elf came up the escalator—which he would, I knew it—we'd blow him off that fancy bike. Hopefully by then Westlake security would have arrived to deal with the two foot soldiers.

The corp-chick's body reached the top of the escalator, followed by the corp-guy. He was still alive, and the moment he hit the top he vaulted over his erstwhile date and headed off for parts unknown. I wiped cold sweat from my brow and steadied my gun hand. The elf'd be coming any moment.

A booming gunshot and a scream sounded behind us. I turned. The corp-guy was collapsing to the floor, cut damn near in half. A dozen meters further on, a mahogany-clad figure had emerged from a hallway between two storefronts. He jacked another shell into the chamber of the big fragging shotgun he carried, and swung the muzzle around toward us. I rolled and sent a couple of slugs his way. No chance I hit him, but he was so busy ducking back that his own shot went way wide. A store window exploded into fragments, and the well-dressed mannequins within came apart.

I sent another round his way, yelled, "Let's go!" at Jocasta, and took off in the other direction. Jocasta hesitated—I think she still wanted to ambush the biker—but discretion took over. As we ran, she demanded, "Where did *he* come from?"

I shrugged, then mentally kicked myself. The elf on the bike had come up the same stairs as we did. But the other two guys could have taken any other route, including the elevators. The second human could be anywhere, even just around the next corner. We hung a hard right, down one of the "arms" of the cruciform mall.

And the other biker *was* just around the corner. *Just* around, like maybe a meter. With us coming round that corner like a bullet train, he had just enough time to bug his eyes before I plowed into him. He went one way, his gun went the other, so I pumped a round into his chest at point-blank range, and we kept on going. Another store window detonated behind us, this time blown to bits by automatic fire. That meant friend elf had mounted the escalator and was after us big-time.

We took another hard right, and skidded to a stop. A couple of meters ahead of us were two Zorro-type security guards, weapons drawn, ready to geek us on the spot. I essayed an ingenuous smile, but it's hard to look non-threatening when you've got two-and-a-quarter kilos of laster-sighted iron in your fist.

"Turn into ice," one of the Zorro-cops snapped. "Drop it, *now!*" his partner added. I turned into ice, and was about to drop the Manhunter.

That's when Jocasta stepped forward. Her hands were empty; her Colt had vanished miraculously. Her posture was erect, her expression aloof, and she looked every bit the high corporate official. "He's my bodyguard, you drekhead," she snapped. "The killers are behind us." Her delivery was impeccable. The Zorro-cops thought so too. The two guns wavered.

Friend elf chose that moment to come around the corner, machine pistol blazing. One Zorro-cop went over backward, spouting blood from his throat, and I felt something hammer into the back of my duster. The other security boy switched his point of aim away from the bridge of my nose, and squeezed off a quick burst. This close, I could feel the overpressure from the submachine gun like slaps to my face. I sent another heavy slug the elf's way for good measure.

The biker had started to turn our way, but the sudden

fusillade of lead changed his mind. He unloaded from
the turn, and kept going clear across the intersection. Our
security man gabbled something about "motorcycle
gangs" into his radio headset, and took off in hot pursuit.
(A classic case of brave like hero, smart like streetcar, if
you ask me.) He rounded the corner, and the mall echoed
with the chatter of automatic fire. There was the high-
pitched scream of the elf's grease-gun and the deeper-
throated roar of the Zorro-cop's SMG. No, more than
one deeper-pitched weapon. The Zorro-cops were finally
arriving in more force.

Which was all to the good. While security and biker
were busy blazing away at each other, Jocasta and I could
make ourselves scarce. I turned my back on the fracas
and started to run again, grabbing Jocasta's arm as I went
by. She shook me off with a curse, but followed.

We were in one of the shorter "sub-arms" of the mall,
and there was a wall of glass in front of us. The lights
of nighttime Seattle shone through, a little blurred and
given a greenish tinge by the bulletproof transparency.
Were we in a dead end?

No. There was a door, another fire exit. I hit the panic
bar at a dead run, Jocasta on my heels, and we burst out
into the cold night air. A concrete staircase was to our
right, a wheelchair ramp to our left. I found myself curs-
ing the concept of wheelchair access. If the elf got
through the gauntlet of security guards, he'd be able to
blast his bike down the ramp without any problem. We
sprinted down the stairs; two flights and we were at road
level. When I skidded to a stop, Jocasta just avoided rear-
ending me. I hesitated, my sense of direction totally
wasted by our flight through the mall. It took a moment
to get my bearings. Looking around, I saw the big illuminated billboards shining down on us: one for the Universal Brotherhood ("Be All You Can Be!"), the other
for Fiberwear Disposable Clothing ("The Future Is Disposable"). That told me we were on Olive Way, facing
roughly southeast. The area directly around Westlake
Center is wide open, kind of a paved park, and astonish-
ingly well-lit. This time of night, the place was deserted.

Well, almost. I saw one of my erstwhile colleagues—
a Lone Star bike cop, brave soul—cruising away from us
along Fifth. I felt very exposed.

I reached out to grab Jocasta, but thought better of it at the last moment. "Let's get out of here," I said breathlessly.

"What about my car?" she demanded.

I bit back on my suggestion as to exactly what she could do with her car. "Pick it up in the morning," I told her. "I'll even pay the parking."

She glared, but at least she followed as I cut across Olive. I could see an alley between Fourth and Fifth, its entrance looking dark and safe and inviting. I felt like sprinting, but I didn't have a sprint left in me so I settled for a painful jog. As I trotted along, I checked my watch. Still short of midnight. We'd packed a lot into the last five minutes or so. Well, that's life in the big city.

We were halfway across Olive, perfectly illuminated by streetlights, when I heard another burst of gunfire from behind us, the sound of something fragile shattering and a frenetic whine that was becoming almost familiar. I glanced back, knowing what I'd see. The blue-white of a high-intensity halogen light zigzagging its way down the illuminated glass wall of Westlake Center. The elf was still with us and was, in fact, soon to join us. Jocasta saw it, too, and we picked up our pace. Into the alley, and we couldn't see Westlake Center anymore.

Alleys are very much alike, whether they're out in Redmond or downtown behind the Mayflower Park Hotel, which was where we were. Same blue-painted dumpsters, same scavengers, both four- and two-legged, waiting for you to do something dumb. We legged it down this one as though the devil were at our heels. We were a couple of dozen meters from the street when I put on the brakes. The alley was narrowed down to maybe six meters by two dumpsters facing each other across empty space. I pointed to the dumpster on our left, and tried to gasp out instructions to Jocasta.

She picked up immediately on what I meant, which was good because I was sucking wind too intensely to speak coherently. Her pistol was back in her hand as she ducked around the back of the huge metal container. Her slate-gray synthleathers merged with the shadows, and she fragging near disappeared. Perfect.

I ducked into the cover of the other dumpster, and heard the scrabbling of either a big rat or a small squatter getting out of my way. I crouched down, gun in hand, and stuck my head around the dumpster's corner to watch the entry to the alley. For a moment I considered the elf biker's options, of which he had several. From watching the slag operate in the mall, however, I thought I had him pegged as the direct-action, in-your-face type. Odds were he'd seen us duck into the alley, and those same odds said he'd come after us with a mittful of throttle in one hand and his grease-gun in the other. I heard the approaching whine of a high-revving turbine, and tensed.

One thing I'll say for that elf, he had guts. No brains, but serious guts. He came in hot, leaning into the turn so low that his bike's pipes sprayed sparks from the road surface. His headlight dazzled me so much I couldn't see the muzzle flash from his weapon. I could hear and feel the slugs slamming into my dumpster, though, and knew very well he was hosing down the alleyway. I squatted lower so my face was at knee-level, and brought the Manhunter to bear.

It was Jocasta who opened up first, despite my readiness. Her small Colt spat once, and the bike's headlight exploded. Exceptional shot, or else extremely lucky. Either way I wasn't going to argue. Through the swimming red afterimages, I could see him silhouetted against the lights outside the alleyway. I put my sighting dot on his chest, a head shot being way too uncertain right now, and squeezed the trigger six times, maybe seven. The big gun clicked empty.

Jocasta was blazing away, too, but she was using the trick the movie cowboys never figured out: she aimed for the horse. Her rounds smashed sparks from the body-work of the bike, slammed into the gas tank. Something burst into flame. Elf and bike parted company. He skidded, flopped bonelessly into the alley wall, struck Jocasta's dumpster with a meaty thud.

Jocasta got the elf. I got the bike. Flaming and kicking up sparks, it slammed into my dumpster. Laws of inertia being what they were, that kicked the wheeled container back my way, and the metal smashed into my shoulder. I did half of a half-gainer and landed on my head. For the next few moments I did what one normally does in such a situation: I went "duh" and watched the pretty lights.

A shrill squeal penetrated what was left of consciousness, that and Joscasta calling my name. I forced myself to my knees, which was as far as I could get. She grabbed my arm—now I knew how irritating that was—and half-dragged me to my feet. I swayed there for a second, then shook my head to clear it. It hurt like hell, but it *did* bring back some clarity.

The squeal was still in my ears; surprising, since I'd figured it was an artifact of my occipital impact. I looked around for the source.

It was the elf. For a horrid moment I thought he was screaming, lying there with his broken back, but then realization dawned. It was his bracelet. No wonder it had looked familiar: I'd seen something like it in my Lone Star training, although I'd never had one. It was one of the life-function monitors that DocWagon issues to its Super-Platinum clients. As soon as something critical goes wrong with the client—and I guess a broken back fits that category—the monitor immediately calls a roving DocWagon team, all the while letting forth a teeth-hurting scream to let everyone know that someone's gone down.

My shock-numbed cranium chewed on that for a moment. Super-Platinum service runs seventy-five-K per year. Serious nuyen, and *not* a sum you'd expect a go-ganger—even the gang boss—to be good for. And DocWagon is *very* careful with their credit checks.

Well, worry about it later. Jocasta was tugging on my arm, making let's-get-out-of-here noises. Seemed like a good idea. I broke into a shambling run, and we got out of there.

We stuck to the alleyways, cutting across Pine Street. We'd just hit Pike, another block on, when we heard the siren, and ducked back into the shadows. It was an emergency-response team vehicle, like I'd expected, sirens and warning strobes working overtime. Surprise, surprise, it was Crashcart, *not* DocWagon. I watched around the corner as the van hung a screeching left onto Fifth and roared out of sight. Curiouser and curiouser.

8

After flagging down one of the new autocabs, we were heading back toward Bellevue. Jocasta had jammed a credstick—*not* a personalized one—into the foul machine's maw, and pointed out our destination on the touchscreen. Then she'd settled back into the seat and withdrawn from further intercourse with anything, flesh or otherwise. From the set of her jawline, I could tell she had "a good mad on," as my old chummer Patrick Bambra would have put it.

It wasn't a normal anger, though. That I could tell. It had an edgy, unstable feel to it, almost like her brain was using the anger to keep itself from thinking about what we'd just been through. I could understand the attraction of that. Frag, I kind of wished for a similar defense mechanism. We were approaching the bridge across Lake Washington when I saw the shakes start, saw her lips press together so hard they almost disappeared. The trauma was starting to burn through the facade of anger. No matter how hard her subconscious tried to keep a lid on it, her forebrain wasn't going to be able to hold back the nasties too much longer.

I could justify it as a therapeutic move, helping her maintain the defense mechanism she was choosing to hold herself together. In reality, of course, I did it for the entirely selfish reason that I didn't want to be in a closed cab with Jocasta when she fell apart. I said something I figured would re-ignite the anger in full force. "We were set up," I remarked.

She picked up on it immediately and turned on me, eyes flashing. "You fragged up," she spat out. "It might *not* have been a set-up if we'd played it straight." I started to say something, but she cut me off. "I'm not finished. If I'd called, the way I was supposed to, I might have got another location for a meet. A *safe* meet."

I got three words in: "But the bikers—"

And she was off again. "They were there to protect

the contact, in case we did something drekheaded like
track the phone number. If we'd played it straight, we'd
never have met the fragging bikers.''

"You don't know that,'' I protested.

"I know that we hosed the meet,'' she shot back, "and
I know we've lost the contact. He's not going to trust me
twice.'' And that was all she said, on that subject or any
other.

She was still blazing mad—the shaking of fear over-
powered by the trembling of anger—when she bailed out
in Beaux Arts. I redirected the cab toward Purity, and
immediately began to feel like a piece of drek for letting
her go like that. I looked out the rear window, but she
was already out of sight. The sullen clouds started to rain
about then, which suited my mood perfectly.

I slept late the next morning, Saturday, November 23,
and the denizens of Purity were already about the business of stealing lunch by the time I rejoined the world.
The bruises on my elbow, back, shoulder, and head—
caused, respectively, by impacts from bullet, bullet,
dumpster, and alley—were turning all the colors of the
rainbow, and I felt like an old, old man. I considered
calling Jocasta to apologize for last night, but realized I
didn't have her number.

I was putting together the day's first pot of soykaf when
the telecom beeped. Seeing the grinning face of Bent
Sigurdsen, I cut in my video pickup.

His grin faded somewhat when he saw me. "Hoi,
Dirk," he said, a tinge of concern in his voice. "Are you
okay, chummer?"

I ran a hand through my hair, more out of form than
any belief it would actually help, and shrugged. "How
could anybody *not* be on such a fine November morning?"

"Afternoon," he corrected me.

"Whatever. Got something for me?"

He nodded. "What do you know about 2XS?"

"To excess?"

"Uh-uh," he corrected me. "Digit and letters: Two
X-ray Sierra. Do you know anything about it?"

I shook my head. "Never even heard of it."

Bent scowled, an expression for which his face is ill-suited. "I wish I could say the same," he said sadly. "It's a real scourge on the street at the moment. Lone Star, even the FBI, are turning the heat up as high as it'll go to stamp it out or just to get a line on where it's coming from. I shouldn't be telling you this, but the story is 'no joy' from all over. Nobody seems able to touch it."

I nodded sagely. "And just what *is* 2XS?"

"It's a chip," he said, obviously keeping it brief. "A new chip."

"Just a chip?"

He sighed. "A chip, like simsense is a chip and BTL is a chip. Okay?"

I chafed a little under his keep-the-words-short-for-the-moron approach, but nodded. "Okay."

"Think of the difference between a simsense and a BTL chip. Simsense gives you the movie, but with all five senses instead of just two. BTL gives you the same, but pushes the sensory signal to the red line." He paused to see if I was following. "Now take a BTL chip—"

"Okay, okay," I put in. "I scan it."

"Well, 2XS is the next step. Like BTL, but it hits you at the physiological level as well: adrenalin, endorphins, *everything*. Apparently, a user feels like he can rule the world while he's running it. But it works at such a basic level that you can't run it on standard simsense gear. You've got to feed it right into a datajack, so it hits the brain directly."

"And of course it's addictive as all hell."

He nodded. "Of course. Physically addictive *and* psychologically habituating. One touch of it, and you never want anything else."

"And of course it degrades, so it's fragged after you've slotted it a couple of times?"

"Yeah," Bent confirmed. "It's nasty."

"Yeah," I echoed. It sounded nasty. BTL chips—"Better Than Life"—were bad enough. Unlike normal simsense, BTL chips had no governor, no limitation on the intensity of the sensory record. When you slot a BTL chip, you feel and experience *exactly* what the person who recorded the chip was feeling and experiencing, just as if it was all happening to you. Everything and anything: orgasm, life-risk, fear, exaltation, even—for that once-in-a-lifetime thrill—death agony. While the chip's feeding the sensory data into your brain, you *are* the subject of the recording.

Which is plenty wild enough to wreck the sanity of regular users. (I recalled the punk kid who'd taken a potshot at me just hours before Jocasta showed up in my life. He'd probably slotted a BTL chip that put him into the mind of a sniper so many times that he'd finally decided he *was* the sniper.) But at least BTL chips don't have a direct effect on the body. Sure, you get somebody scared, and adrenalin pumps into his body. But stuff like endorphins and the natural "energizers" that allow forty-kilo mothers to lift cars off their infants don't get triggered by BTLs. (Otherwise the weird cobber "auditing" the death experience on BTL would kick off for real.) According to what Bent was telling me, that limitation *did not* apply to 2XS. Scary. Scary as hell.

My disturbing thoughts must have shown in my expression. Bent's face was equally serious. "There's more. It also seems to be very debilitating, even over the short term."

"I guess it would be," I said, thinking out loud. "You take a car engine and rev it from dead-stop to redline, just like *that*"—I snapped my fingers—"Do that a couple of times, it'll be kind of debilitating to the engine."

A smile appeared briefly on Bent's face. "That's a good analogy. Would you mind if I used it?" I waved that off. "Please keep all this to yourself," he said. "I'll be in deep drek if it gets around I told you."

I raised an eyebrow. "Why? Isn't this common knowledge?"

He snorted. "Not hardly. This comes from Lone Star Secured data files."

LSS, that twigged a memory. "Juli Long?" I asked.

"Of course," he said. "You asked me to look into it."

"This was all in that secured file?"

Bent looked uncomfortable. "Nooo. That file led me to some others . . ."

"Which were also secured," I finished. "Null perspiration, Bent chummer. Locked and encrypted. Nobody learns it from me.'' I paused. ''So what you're telling me is . . .'' I let it trail off.

Bent nodded firmly. ''Juli Long was addicted to 2XS,'' he confirmed. ''She died from it.''

A rough week on blondes.

I had no reason to stall any longer, so I followed through on the conditions of my employment concerning Long, Juli Carole (deceased). Going through standard channels, I electronically claimed the body, using the employment and personal data my Chicago-based Mr. Johnson had given me. Then I arranged for Juli's mortal remains to be shipped back to the welcoming arms of her former corporate home.

To spare my own feelings, I struggled to blot out the human dimension, concentrating on my task as merely a shipping transaction. Null program, of course. Juli's holo was still in my wallet, and I didn't want to take it out to destroy it because then I'd have to look at it. The question that kept running through my head was whether she'd gotten into 2XS chips before or after hitting Seattle. Sometimes I really enjoy my chosen career; this was not one of those times.

I'd just blanked the screen and sat back to rest when the telecom beeped again. Frag it. I wanted to go back to bed, but it could be something important. Jocasta, maybe?

I hit the key to answer the incoming call, but the screen stayed blank. Okay, two could play voice-only; I didn't cut in my video. ''Yeah?'' I said.

''Is that you, Derek old son?'' The voice was musical, somewhat high-pitched though definitely male, and brought to mind smiling Irish eyes.

I couldn't help but grin. ''Patrick, you fragging reprobate,'' I roared. ''Keep your hands off my daughter!''

It took him a moment, then he came back, his voice reason itself, ''Ah, but Derek, you know I wouldn't be messing about with your daughter, seeing as how I'm sleeping with your mother.'' He laughed then. ''It's a pleasure to be hearing your voice, boyo,'' he went on. ''Humor has been sadly lacking in my life for the past days.''

''Oh? Is that why I don't get to see your face?''

"One of the patrons of this fine establishment seems to have taken a bite out of the video pickup." The humor faded from his voice. "I'm in trouble, Derek. I need to talk it out with someone."

"So I got the short straw?"

He was silent for long enough that I wondered if he'd been cut off. Then he said quietly, "No, it's not like that, not like that at all. You're better at all this than I am, Derek." I heard a grim chuckle. "I think you're what I want to be when I grow up, if you didn't frighten me a little."

I sighed. Melodramatic, but that was Patrick. "What's going down?" I asked.

"Not over this contraption," he said quickly. "Meet me."

"Why?"

"I can't," he said. And for the first time I could hear what was behind his facade of humor: a healthy dose of fear. "I'm at a place called Superdad's, if you can believe it. It's in Kingsgate."

"I know it," I said. "I can be there tonight, call it twenty—"

"*No*," he almost shouted, then more calmly, "No. Can you make it sooner? Now?"

I sighed again. I had enough on my mind already without worrying about pulling Patrick's fat out of another fire. But, frag it, he was a friend, and I wasn't quite cynical enough to write off friendship. Not yet, at least. "Okay," I conceded. "Give me an hour." And I broke the connection before he could thank me.

I sat back in my chair, considered what was left of the bottle of synth-scotch—the sun was, after all, over the yardarm somewhere—but discarded the concept. I guess the thought of diving into a bottle to hide had been prompted by hearing from Patrick.

Patrick Bambra has that effect on a lot of people: he drives them to drink, then keeps them company. It had been a while since we'd been in touch. The last time we'd talked was some months after I'd bailed out of Lone Star, when he called me, all in a lather, asking me to talk some rather large "debt-management consultants" out of re-modeling the architecture of his knee joints. It sounded like something similar had happened again.

Which didn't surprise me one iota. Patrick's comment about wanting to be me when he grew up had a germ of truth to it. After he'd been flushed from Lone Star training, he'd rattled around for almost a year, doing odd jobs here and there. Then I quit and went into the investigation racket. Almost immediately, the way I heard it, Patrick decided that was the career for him. So, in a back-door kind of way, I felt responsible for him. Just what I needed right now.

Kingsgate is one of the less appetizing areas of the Redmond Barrens, and that's saying something. It's just east of Highway 405, opposite the Juanita district of Bellevue, and to say it's seen better days is a cosmic understatement. Soon after the turn of the century, before Seattle really began to fall apart, Kingsgate was being touted as "the next Bellevue." Developers expected the high-tech businesses that were taking up residence in Bellevue to leak across 405 into Kingsgate, bringing their money with them. It seemed to be working for a few years, then something went very wrong. The successful tenants started pulling out of the flashy industrial parks and downtown-style office buildings, and their less-successful competition couldn't afford the astronomical rentals. If the building owners had reacted by dropping their rates, they might have pulled it out. But they hung tough, expecting things to turn around.

Things never did, of course. Commercial vacancy rates spiraled up, income for the property-owners dropped. People defaulted on loans, and the banks ended up with vacant buildings they didn't know what to do with. There was some brief hope that the rest of Redmond would somehow be able to pull Kingsgate out of the drek, but of course Kingsgate was an omen of what was in store for the rest of the area.

And that's how the Kingsgate of today came into existence. Lots of flashy office buildings, empty except for squatters and other unofficial residents. Overgrown industrial parks that all too often serve as battlegrounds for rival go-gangs. Though the rest of the Barrens area slid rather quickly down into oblivion and chaos, remember that Kingsgate did it first and did it best.

Superdad's was a sleazy dive located on the ground

floor of what used to be the Seattle Silicon building, with a sputtering neon sign outside advertising GI LS—LIVE G RLS. I pushed open the door and walked into the relative darkness. Rhythmic music pulsed from cheap speakers, but it was almost drowned out by the sound of a trideo tuned to the sports network. My nose was assaulted by the reek of stale beer and other, even more unpleasant odors. In a moment my eyes had adapted to the lighting, or lack thereof, and I looked around the place.

The room wasn't large for a watering hole, maybe twenty meters square. Dominating the place was a large U-shaped bar, manned by a scrawny young kid who looked chipped so high he almost vibrated. Behind the bar was the stage, where a massively endowed teen-age ork danced topless. I watched her for a moment, somewhat impressed by her skill: it's tough to dance as completely and consistently off the beat as she did. Her eyes were rolled up so only the red-shot whites showed, and she seemed to be totally oblivious to her surroundings, dancing for herself alone.

Which was just as well, because nobody was paying her the slightest attention. Two burly orks sat at the bar, one watching the Urban Brawl game on the trideo mounted over the stage. The other had his face planted on the dirty bar-top and was blowing bubbles in a puddle of spilled beer. The only two other patrons were at a table as far as possible from the stage, lean and mean street weasels engaged in an intense business discussion. I guess the lunchtime trade wasn't what kept Superdad's going.

I jandered over to the bar. The chipped bartender was playing with a bottle of whiskey, spinning it high into the air and catching it. As he juggled it with his right hand, he shot out his left, pointing a dirty index finger at my chest. "You?" he barked. "Drink?"

I shook my head. "I'm meeting someone," I told him.

He thudded the bottle down on the bar, and looked me over quickly. Then he nodded. "In the back," he said, hooking a thumb over his shoulder.

I thanked him, and went through the door he'd indicated to the left of the bar. I found myself in a short hallway, lit by a single naked bulb on the ceiling. There were two other doors, the one directly in front of me marked Dressing Room (complete with a star, clumsily cut out of gold mylar), the other marked Office. I pulled my armored duster closed across my chest—paranoia, I know, but even paranoids have enemies—and felt the weight of the Manhunter in my holster.

As I stood there, the door to the dressing room opened, and a diminutive girl came out. She wore nothing but a couple of kilos of silver chain, and her hair had the same sheen as her "clothing." She shot me a saucy smile as she squeezed by me—totally unnecessary, as I wasn't blocking the doorway—then vanished through the door into the bar proper. I had to smile. Sometimes this job offers the most interesting rewards.

I went down the hallway and knocked on the office door. I heard movement from inside, and then a tentative, "Yeah?"

"It's me, Patrick," I told him.

The door opened, and there was Patrick Bambra, smiling awkwardly down at me. "Ah, Derek," he said, "you're a sight for sore eyes. Come on in." There was whiskey on his breath, I noticed. He stepped back, and I followed him into the office, a small room crammed with crates of beer, a desk, and a rusty metal cot. He sat down on the cot, which creaked alarmingly, and gestured to the desk chair. I shut the door behind me, then also sat.

For a few moments, I just looked him over. Well over two meters tall and thin as a rake, Bambra looked ridiculous sitting on the low cot, arms and legs akimbo and seemingly all joints. He didn't seem to have aged a day since our time together at the Star. I knew he was three years younger than me, but with his boyish, freckle-spattered face and mop of bright red hair, he looked ten years younger than that. He still wore the string tie and silver collar tabs that had always been his trademark. I waited a few moments, but he didn't seem to want to start the conversation. "What's going down, Patrick?" I said as last.

He hesitated, unable or unwilling to make eye contact. He shifted uncomfortably. The embarrassed act might have fooled anyone else, but I knew he was sifting through what he did and did not want to tell me. I sighed, and reconciled myself to hearing less than the whole story. "I'm into something that's a little too deep for me, I think," he said finally. "Some people seem to want me dead."

"You're working on a case?" He nodded. "What is it?"

He looked away again. "Would you be liking a drink?" he asked suddenly. He reached under the bed and pulled out a half-empty bottle of synthetic Irish whiskey. He examined the label for a moment. "It's not too bad, really." I shook my head. "Well, I think I'll be having one. I need it." He reached under the cot again and retrieved a grimy glass. He poured a hefty shot, thought about it, then doubled the amount. He looked at me again, holding out the open bottle. "Sure?"

"What's the case, Patrick?"

Patrick put down the bottle, took a mouthful of whiskey. His prominent adam's apple bobbed as he swallowed. "I don't know as I can tell you that, Derek m'lad," he said slowly. "You know how it is, the code of honor and confidentiality we have to operate under . . ."

I tuned him out, knowing he could be going for a while. (At Lone Star, one of our classmates had once suggested that Patrick Bambra must have kissed the Blarney Stone. Another had decided that instead the Blarney Stone had kissed *Patrick.*) When his steam finally ran down, I fixed him with a cold stare. "You said you needed my help," I reminded him.

It was as if he'd been pumped up with hot air, and somebody had stuck a pin in hm. He seemed to visibly deflate. He nodded and lowered his eyes. "I'll tell you what I can," he said quietly. "A woman hired me to follow her husband. Not a particularly noble cause, but I needed the money. In any case, I've been on the case for a while. Then, a few days ago, things took a bit of a twist, and it became more personal." I drew breath to ask for clarification, but he hurried on. "I can't be telling you about that, Derek, and don't ask. It's not only my life I'd be putting at risk, do you understand?" I nodded grudging acceptance. "I found that I had to track down somebody else," he continued, "someone who's a mem-

ber of the Universal Brotherhood. You know about the
Brotherhood?''

"Of course," I said. Hell, you couldn't go more than
a couple of blocks without seeing a Brotherhood billboard
or some slag standing on a street corner handing out pro-
paganda. "Go on.''

"So I went to the Brotherhood to track her . . . the
person.'' He examined me closely to see if I'd noticed
his slip, but I controlled my expression even though I
was chuckling inwardly. I thought I scanned at least part
of this: friend Bambra, who claimed to have sworn off
women before he turned twenty, had fallen in love with
someone he shouldn't have. *Cherchez la femme,* for sure.

"I lied my way up the hierarchy," he proceeded, "until I hit somebody at a high enough level that he'd have
to know the person I was after. But he stonewalled me,
shut me down for good and all.'' Patrick's flashing eyes,
uncharacteristically serious, locked with mine. "He also
put me out of sanction, Derek.''

I stared at him. "Out of sanction" was an old espionage term that one of our Lone Star classmates had dug
up, and that we'd started using any chance we got. What
it meant, in essence, was shoot first and then fingerprint
the corpse. "Echo that," I said. "Are we talking about
the same Universal Brotherhood here?'' The Brotherhood I knew was some kind of flaky love-cult, some
touchy-feely organization that suckered in the hard-luck
stories that were all too common in the sprawl. A death
order and a peace-be-upon-you-brother show like the
Universal Brotherhood didn't go together.

Patrick smiled wanly. "That's how I was feeling at
first," he admitted, "but my word on it. I'm after talking
to this fine gentleman, and the next thing I know I'm
dodging bullets. I don't like that, Derek. I've never been
liking it.''

I made a T with my hands. "Time out," I said. "I've
got to know more about all this. You can't tell me who
you were looking for, right?'' He shook his head quickly.
"How about the guy in the Brotherhood?''

"Sure, and I can tell you that," Patrick said. "His
name will always be emblazoned in my brain. He was a
Mr. William Sutcliffe.''

9

I shook my head to clear it. They say it's a small world, but this was utterly ridiculous. Maybe I should start re-examining my disbelief in synchronicity.

Patrick was watching me, and those bright eyes didn't miss much. "Would you be knowing the gentleman?" he asked.

I wasn't in the mood to discuss Lolly or the fact that it was Sutcliffe's tap she'd been washing when she bought it. "I've heard the name," I answered guardedly. "When did you meet with him?"

"This was yesterday."

"Oh."

Patrick waited for me to say something else. "Well," he said slowly, when it was obvious I had nothing to add. "I guess this is what it comes to. I need you to help me."

"How?" I asked. "I can't bodyguard you. I don't know if you've heard, but I've got people after my own hide."

"Yes, I had heard that."

"But you're doing the right thing," I went on. "Find a place to belly up for a while. Maybe hook up with some other runners, some muscle."

He nodded. "I had figured that much out," he said. "But the thing is, that way I won't be having any free-dom of movement."

I smiled and shook my head. "If you won't tell me who it is you're looking for, I can't help you much there, can I?" He looked down, avoiding my gaze. "There's one thing I *can* do, though," I said. "I've got reasons of my own to dig up dirt on William Sutcliffe. If I find something you might use, I'll get it to you immediately. As long as you agree to do the same: anything *you* learn, you tell me. *Karimasu-ka?*"

"I understand, Derek," he said quickly, and his voice sounded sincere. Patrick Bambra was frightened for his

life, and he'd do whatever it took to protect that life.
"I'm in your debt."

I waved that off. "Where did you find Sutcliffe?"

"He's at the Brotherhood chapterhouse in Redmond.
The corner of Belmont and Waveland." Then his expression changed to genuine concern. "But I wouldn't be
going there in person, boyo. Ask the wrong questions,
and they might decide *you're* out of sanction, too. And
I wouldn't be knowing what the wrong questions are."

I shook my head. "I'm not that dumb," I told him.
He looked mildly offended—as though I'd added "even
though *you* are"—but said nothing. I got to my feet.
"You've got my number," I said. "Check in with me
from time to time, I'll tell you what I've found. And you
call me the moment you find out something." I opened
the door and was halfway into the corridor when I thought
of something else and turned back.

"If I were you, I'd set up some kind of security with
the bartender. Have him warn you if anyone out of the
ordinary comes snooping around. He didn't know who
the frag I was, but told me right away where you were.
For all he knew, I could be the one who put you out of
sanction." I left him there, sitting on the bed, turning
pale and chewing on that disturbing thought.

As I drove homeward, my mind kept turning back to
Patrick. He'd always been something of an enigma, or,
to be more precise, an anachronism. As though he'd been
born maybe a century too late. He loved the literature of
the 1930s and 1940s, particularly the "hard-boiled"
genre of detective fiction, and could immerse himself for
days in the *film noir* classics based on those books. When
there was a minor revival of that kind of stuff a dozen
years back, Patrick was in heaven. He even got me
hooked on the same drek for a while, but not for long.
It's tough enough to survive in the sprawl even when
you're paying full attention to *today*.

But nobody could say Patrick Bambra wasn't a survivor, albeit sometimes by default. He'd been flushed out
of Lone Star training, but had managed to keep body and
soul together until deciding on a new career. In the years
since, he'd found enough cases to keep himself going.
Though some were the knight-in-shining-armor kind of

thing he dreamed of, the work was mostly sleazy divorce jobs. He still deserved credit for somehow managing to do that and keep his skin unpunctured. I knew people far more competent than Patrick who couldn't say the same.

Still, Patrick is a romantic through and through, and the sprawl is not kind to romantics. His latest problems were a case in point. I was pretty sure I could scan how things had developed, no matter how secretive Patrick tried to be. A woman had hired him to track her husband—he'd admitted as much—which meant a classic slimy divorce case. The way I reconstructed it from here was that while following the guy, Patrick had seen the correspondent, in other words, the sweet young thing with whom the subject was two-timing on his wife. What would a thorough-going romantic do in a case like that? Bingo! Fall in love with said sweet young thing and try to track her down for his own purposes. She happens to be a member of the Universal Brotherhood, so friend Bambra seeks her there. Which is where he meets William Sutcliffe . . .

And Sutcliffe takes out a contract on him. Serious overkill for matters of the heart, no matter how sleazy. Obviously Sutcliffe or people associated with him got worried that Patrick might find out something more important than the whereabouts of his putative lady-love, and decided to remove the risk. Just the way they'd removed the risk with Lolly. The difference being that Patrick was still breathing.

So one thing hadn't changed, Mr. William Sutcliffe was still the lead of choice. What *had* changed was that I had a reasonable place to start tracking him down.

I remembered Patrick saying that the Universal Brotherhood's chapterhouse was in Kingsgate and not too far from Superdad's. I turned onto Belmont. The chapterhouse was right on the corner of Belmont and Waveland. It had once been a four-plex movie theater, built back when going to the movies was something people in Redmond did. (Now simsense, armed assault, and civil insurrection seem to have overtaken movies as the major pastimes.) The building had a clean, attractive facade, and the two floors of offices above the "theater level" were notable in that all windows were intact. The marquee that used to advertise the films playing was still in place, but now carried quite a different message: "The Universal Brotherhood—Come in and find the power of Belonging." As I cruised by, I saw maybe a dozen people coming or going through the big front doors.

I hung a left onto Belmont, drove slowly past the entrance to the alley behind the chapterhouse. Seeing a scrum of squatter-types pushing and shoving to get in through a doorway in the rear of the building, I figured this had to be one of the Brotherhood's well-known charity soup kitchens. I wondered if the building also had a free clinic.

As I drove away, heading back to Purity, I thought it through. The Universal Brotherhood was one of the few rays of light that shone into this part of the sprawl. They gave food to the hungry, shelter to the homeless, and medical aid to the sick or damaged. Sounded pretty good to me. Oh sure, I'd heard rumors that they'd managed to cut themselves a sweet deal when it came to dodging taxes, but what organized religion hadn't? The Brotherhood seemed to be on the up and up, as much as any organization could be in the twisted world of 2052.

That didn't mean individual members of the Brotherhood hierarchy—William Sutcliffe, in particular—couldn't be dirty in some way. That's the way it seemed to scan. Sutcliffe was involved in something deep and dark, which Lolly learned about accidentally from the line tap. Then Sutcliffe found out that she was on to him, so scratch Lolly. A couple of days later, Patrick comes around asking questions about his love interest. I had no idea whether the woman Patrick was tracking had anything to do with whatever drek Lolly had turned up, or whether Sutcliffe was simply paranoid about *anyone* asking *any* strange questions. One way or the other, he'd reacted according to type, so scratch Patrick . . . almost. Either Bambra was luckier than Lolly, or else Sutcliffe hadn't put the same time and effort into removing him.

So William Sutcliffe was still the key. That conclusion was firm and clear in my mind as I parked my car and went upstairs to my Redmond doss. I sat down at the telecom, saw the message light was blinking. I hit the keys, and Jocasta's face filled the screen.

She was looking tired, definitely the worse for wear, but her expression seemed to be some mixture of embarrassment and determination to get through whatever was on her mind. "I'm sorry about the way I reacted last night," she said without preamble. "I didn't expect things to work out the way they did, and I wasn't ready for it. I wanted to blame you for everything because then I'd be too busy hating you to know what was going on in my own feelings. Well, that's it." She smiled wearily. "I hope you slept better than I did. I'll call you later." And her image vanished.

I sat back and mused for a moment. She'd talked fast, and her words had sounded stilted and rehearsed, which they probably were. But I sensed the sincerity. Good. Jocasta was a valuable source of information. I preferred not to be cut off from what she could tell me.

The search utility I'd sent after William Sutcliffe had been running for almost twenty-four hours. If his name appeared in any of the standard public databases anywhere in North America, the utility would have found it by now. I terminated the search and called up a summary of its results.

Nothing. The utility had flashed through every UCAS public database, then started on the Native American nations, Cal Free, CAS, Québec, and even Atzlan. As I'd half expected, all attempts to search the Tir Tairngire network had come up Access Denied, but the odds were low that a Seattle operator like Sutcliffe would have connections with the elven land. After coming up empty on this continent, the utility had gone on to have its way with the Caribbean League, then jumped the Atlantic to Europe. (Fragging good thing I wasn't going to have to pay the connect fees.)

I can't say I was surprised by the results. Very few of my chummers would have shown up on such a superficial scan; neither would major underworld operators or corporate heavy hitters, albeit for different reasons. It didn't really matter anyway, now that I knew Sutcliffe had a connection with the Universal Brotherhood. I'd heard from a couple of shadow deckers that the Brotherhood kept its membership roster confidential, which probably meant its officers were even deeper in the shadows. That meant it would be impossible for me to get a line on Sutcliffe myself. I'd have to use the services of a good decker.

Buddy. I called her number, waited for the beep, and described what I wanted: a full-scale, damn-the-torpedoes, don't-spare-the-nuyen search for a William Sutcliffe, starting with the Universal Brotherhood. As fast as possible, standard rates with—and this hurt—a 20-percent bonus for next-day service.

I hung up feeling I was making some kind of progress. Unfortunately, I couldn't do much personally to advance matters over the next few hours. I reviewed in my head ways I could go about tracking Sutcliffe. Buddy was covering all the bureaucratic avenues. Magic? I'm no mage, but even the drek-hot practitioners out there wouldn't be much help. As far as I knew, you couldn't track somebody magically with nothing to go on but a name. *(Could you?* If somebody had figured out how to do it, that meant Lone Star's combat mages might someday track me down, no matter where I went. It would definitely be in my best interest, I realized, to stay a little bit more in touch with magical research.)

How about the personal touch? I could show up at the Brotherhood chapterhouse and try to track Sutcliffe the old-fashioned way. But that didn't seem like a good option, considering that I'd be operating on his home turf and that I had no idea how far the corruption—if that's what it was—spread throughout the Brotherhood organization. Unless I was extremely good or extremely lucky, neither of which I wanted to depend on, I'd end up with a price on my head just like Patrick.

No, no matter how difficult it might be, the best I could do right then was wait.

I think it was Karl Marx who described religion as the "opiate of the masses." Of course, old Karl didn't have trideo. It was with a kind of perverse satisfaction that I lost myself in the cultural wasteland that afternoon. Let's face it, who *couldn't* enjoy gems like "Under the Stars," a sitcom about a beautiful but naive rock groupie, or that potboiler about a family with somewhat unusual intergenerational relationships, "Up the Auntie"? I could feel my brain turning to oatmeal.

It was a little after 1800 hours that I found myself zapping through the evening news shows. Computer-animated talking head on KORO, two *very* erudite political analysts on KSTS, very mammalian blonde on KONG (zap back to that channel a couple of times), gonzo journalist doing a high-speed rap on pirate FOAD. And Daniel Waters on KOMA.

Yes, Daniel Waters, the same guy I'd seen pulled out of the downtown park on Tuesday. Today was Sunday and the slag was already back on the air. Sure, he looked like pure drek: sunken eyes, a serious bulge under one shoulder of his tailored jacket that could only be a dressing or a cast, and a sallow complexion that made him look half-dead. (Couldn't they fix that with makeup? I wondered idly. But then I realized why they'd probably let it be or even augmented it. "Journalist nearly dies but *insists* on returning to his anchorchair as soon as he's off the respirator." Gets you right *here,* doesn't it?) I remembered the image of Waters' face from that news broadcast: skin white as bone, short hair caked with blood. Now? He looked slotted out, that was for sure, but he was functioning. As for the aura of almost-godlike wisdom he usually emanated, it hadn't diminished a wit. If anything, it seemed greater than usual. I suppose people also paid Lazarus a little more attention after his time off. His co-anchor wasn't immune to the change, either. Every time the camera cut over to her, she had her brilliant blue eyes fixed on Waters, an expression of unconditional adulation on her cheerleader-cute face.

If Waters noticed her attention, he didn't show it. Like a true professional he focused all his concentration on the job. I could tell it was costing him, though. Every few seconds, his eyes would narrow a little as though he was fighting off a jolt of pain. For the first time I felt sorry for the poor sod: he wasn't ready to go back to work yet, but his producers were no doubt using the restrictive clauses of his contract to force him.

The telecom beeped, announcing an incoming call. For some reason I didn't want to turn off Daniel Waters, so I shrank the trideo image to a small inset in the top-right corner of the screen, and killed the audio. Then I answered the call.

It was Jocasta, so I cut in my video feed immediately and said hello.

She smiled, a little uncomfortably. Still concerned about the night before, I figured. Her first words confirmed it. "Two things," she said briskly, jumping right in. "First, I apologize again for last night. Second, it took me a while, but I understand what you were doing in the cab when you were slotting me off so badly. I just wanted to say thanks."

I could read in her face that an apology was about as easy for her as it is for me. And I could also read, as clear as anything, that she was uncomfortable about what she perceived as her lack of coolness under fire. (Why, I don't know. I'd guess that nine out of ten people on the street think they could open fire at living targets and kill people who wanted to kill them, and not choke up about it afterward. All but the very rare exceptions are dead fragging wrong.) But telling that to Jocasta right then would sound patronizing, so I just shrugged.

Her expression softened as though she'd gotten some painful obligation out of the way. "Where do we stand?" she asked.

"William Sutcliffe," I replied. "It was his line tap that Lolly was working on." Her face lit up, and I could literally feel her enthusiasm. "Whoa," I said. "I don't have anything more on him at the moment. Just his name. He's not in any of the public databases, but I've got a decker checking out some shadow sources. Depending on how deep he's buried, that could take some time. Days, maybe a week."

She sobered quickly, and I could see her thinking. After a few moments, she nodded. "What can I do to speed things up?"

I was about to mention the Universal Brotherhood connection, just in case she had some line into the group that was inaccessible to me. But then my attention was drawn to the trideo window in the corner of the screen.

Daniel Waters was still doing his newsman shtick, but it was obviously heavy going. He was twitching like he had the DTs or St. Vitus' Dance, and it looked like he was losing control of the left side of his face.

"What is it?" Jocasta asked sharply.

"Trideo channel four," I said. "Something's fragged." And with that I put her on hold, swapping windows so Daniel Waters filled the entire screen, with Jocasta up in the corner. I turned up the volume.

Waters was in serious trouble. The twitching was even

more pronounced in the larger image, and his familiar, perfectly enunciated baritone was coming apart at the seams. One moment he'd be the old Daniel Waters, ratings king, the next he sounded like a brain-fried chip abuser. I watched, frozen in sick fascination.

". . . And the visiting representatives met with the Secretary of the Treasury," Waters was saying, "to discuss the advisability of extending further credit to the Third World War." He stopped, blinked for a moment, confused. Then his avuncular smile returned and he went on, "I'm sorry, that should be 'further credit to the Third World War.'" He looked around him, as though responding to some strange sound, then looked back directly into the camera. There was something different about his eyes, and I realized that they were focused on infinity, as though he were actually looking at his audience, rather than the teleprompter.

He frowned in puzzlement. "You know," he said, his tone casual, conversational. "I'll be fragged if I know what's going on here." He twitched, a spasm that jerked his entire body like a puppet being controlled by an epileptic puppeteer. The left half of his face was sagging, that side of his mouth turned down in a scowl. His eyes rolled. "I'll be dipped in *drek*," he suddenly roared.

Until now, the producer must have been as frozen by this spectacle as I was. Now, however, he must have suddenly realized he had to do *something*. The camera cut away to the nubile co-anchor. No help there. She was staring at Waters, her mouth hanging open. Cut back to Waters. His eyes were rolling wildly, and half his face hung like raw meat, no muscle tone at all. His perfect enunciation had degenerated to an unintelligible mumble, something like, "Ah wugga wah ah wugga wugga." His hands, in fact his whole body, shook violently like a flag in a high wind. He clutched at his jacket, tugging in a frenzy at the fabric. His microphone flew free from where it was clipped to his lapel, then clattered to the floor. Waters' right eye opened wide, almost bulging from his chalk-white face. He clutched again at his jacket—no, at his chest. He jerked spasmodically again, then pitched forward. His face hit the desk with a crunch.

The screen went blank for a moment, then was filled with an innocuous cityscape, a KOMA logo in the bottom corner. Seemed that the evening news was over for the time being.

I reexpanded Jocasta's image to fill the screen. "Did you see that?" I asked.

She shrugged. "I'm surprised it hasn't happened before. You know how prevalent drug and chip use is in the entertainment industry."

"Sure," I said, "but they know not to overdose before they go on the air. This is KOMA, remember, the big leagues. It's not one of the pirates, where it doesn't matter how brain-fried the talent gets. Anyway, there's more to it than that." I went on to tell her about Waters' extraction from the park. "Crashcart again," I said.

Jocasta was umimpressed. "He'll show up in drug rehab next week," she predicted.

10

He didn't, of course. On Wednesday, November 27, the official announcement came that Daniel Waters, anchor extraordinaire, had died. No more details on what happened, just that he was flatlined. No memorial service, send donations to the Daniel Waters KOMA Memorial Scholarship Fund etcetera etcetera drek etcetera.

I'd had lots of time to think over the past few days. Buddy had sent me a brusque message that she was on the electronic hunt for William Sutcliffe. I called back to ask that she give me regular status reports, but asking that of Buddy was like asking a fish to whistle. I'd tried my own resources, but soon realized that Mr. Sutcliffe was buried too deep for my limited capabilities. Jocasta had called each day to check up on my progress. Though I didn't mind talking to her, it irritated me that I had nothing positive to report.

The rest of the time I did almost nothing. I'd put my other cases on hold so I could hang around the apartment. For one thing, I didn't want to miss a call from Buddy. For another, I didn't care to attract the attention of the mysterious X or anyone else who wanted to terminate my existence.

In other words, I had lots of time to think. I went over the incident with the bikers a hundred times, and each time the Crashcart life-signs monitor the elf was wearing seemed to take on more importance and to raise more questions. I'd made a quick call directly to Crashcart, pretending to be a corporate expediter exploring the advantages of Crashcart as opposed to DocWagon. They'd almost fallen over themselves giving me all the information I needed to make a decision.

It seemed that you get a life-signs monitor only if you subscribe to the Executive Diamond service, which is very much like a DocWagon Super-Platinum contract: unlimited free resuscitations, free High-Threat Response service (although the client is liable for death benefits for Crashcart employees geeked during a hot extraction), a 60 percent discount on extended care, and 10 percent off on cyber-replacement technology. All for the bargain price of 65,000 nuyen per year. Compared to DocWagon's Super-Platinum fee of seventy-five K per year, it *was* a bargain. But sixty-five K annually is well beyond the reach of your average biker, unless . . .

Well, unless somebody else is paying the tab (why?), or unless the biker is actually more than he appears to be (what?), or unless there's a connection between said biker and Crashcart itself (huh?). The first two possibilities got me thinking paranoid again: was friend elf somehow associated with the mysterious X? I had no data and no immediate way of getting any, so I put that question on the back burner. The third possibility didn't seem at all likely, but it did keep Crashcart near the forefront of my thoughts.

Then Daniel Waters kicked off, after losing it in a very spectacular manner on national trideo. Interesting, but seemingly unrelated—except for the fact that it was Crashcart that had pulled him out of the park. That was two strange events, both involving Crashcart in one way or another. It wasn't a strong link, and any other time I would have written the whole thing off to coincidence. But right now I had some idle cycles.

No, let's be honest, I was getting stir-crazy just waiting for Buddy to dig up the dirt on Sutcliffe. I was ready to chase down *any* lead, no matter how strange, just to do *something*.

So I called up Bent Sigurdsen again. He was glad to hear from me, which was almost worth the effort right there. "Hoi, Dirk," he grinned. "We've got to stop meeting like this." He was obviously in his lab, wearing gloves up to his elbows and a green coverall. Fortunately for my digestion, he either hadn't actually started for the day or had taken a break between clients and had changed into unspattered gear.

"Echo that," I told him.

"What can I do for you this time? Or is this a social call?"

"When this is all out of the way, I owe you a dinner," I said. "My treat, your choice of location and menu."

He crowed at that. "Done and done," he laughed. "Make sure your credstick's healthy." I winced inwardly. Bent is something of a gourmet, and the last time I'd stood him to a dinner he'd chosen McDuff's. That's right, *the* McDuff's, and the bill had come to over three hundred nuyen for the two of us.

"I suppose you're going to make me earn my meal," Bent went on. "What do you need this time?"

"Daniel Waters," I said simply. "What happened to him?"

"Damned if I know," he shot back. "Ratings wars getting a little nasty? Just kidding." His grin faded. "That's actually a good question, you know. You'd think he'd have come across my table, but he's not in the queue. Why is that, I wonder?" Bent's mouth twisted into a frown, as though he was personally offended that he wouldn't be dealing with Waters. Who knows, maybe he was. He turned away from the screen to check another terminal. As he rattled away on the keyboard, his frown deepened.

Finally he turned back. "They did him last night," he mused. "Definitely counter to SOP." That surprised me a little, although I suppose it shouldn't have: coroners can have Standard Operating Procedures, too. "They used Lab One—that's *my* lab—but they brought in one of their own people to do the post."

Any other time I'd have been amused by Bent's pettish

reaction. I had other things on my mind. "Who's they?" I asked.

He blinked. "Lone Star. Just like you suspected—you wouldn't be calling about just another stiff."

I let a (wholly feigned) self-satisfied smirk spread across my face. If Bent wanted to give me credit for intuition I didn't have, let him. "Tell me what happened," I said.

He shrugged. "It doesn't say much here. He broke down Sunday night, then immediately slipped into a coma, as you know." As I *didn't* know, but I stayed mum. "He was showing no cerebral functioning when the wagon arrived to pick him up."

"Crashcart, right?"

Bent shook his head. "No, all KOMA employees are still covered by DocWagon. Why?"

"Nothing," I said. "Go on."

Bent glanced back to the other terminal. "There's not much else. Admitted to Harborview at seventeen-oh-three, 24 November 2052. Life support terminated twenty-two-fifteen, 26 November—last night. Post-mortem begun twenty-two-fifty-one—that's fast—completed oh-one-ten this morning." He frowned again, but it was an expression of puzzlement, not affront. "Waters flatlines at twenty-two-fifteen, and the Lone Star doc starts cutting thirty-six minutes later," he said slowly. "And transit from Harborview to here is twenty minutes, give or take." He looked at me expectantly.

It took a moment, then I got it. "Sounds like they were waiting for him to die," I said. "This *is* Lone Star we're talking about?"

Bent grinned. "Not an organization renowned for their humanitarianism, but I think we can safely assume that Lone Star doesn't routinely geek newsreaders. What does that leave us with?"

I was tracking him better now. "The Star is *real* interested in why he croaked," I said. "So why *did* he croak?" I laughed humorlessly. "The file's Lone Star Secured and encrypted, right?"

"With bells and whistles," Bent told me. "You want me to dredge it up, I assume." I started to nod, then hesitated. It must have been the doubt showing in my expression that made him chuckle. "Chill, Dirk," he told me, "This is just routine department politics. Null perspiration."

That's probably what Lolly said. I nodded, but I wasn't easy about it. "You'll get back to me?"

"As soon as I've got something," he reassured me. "Later." And he broke the connection. Leaving me with less to do, and more to worry about.

One thing about Bent Sigurdsen: when he says he'll call back, you *know* he'll call back. By the clock it wasn't much more than an hour later—although it felt like several times that—when the telecom beeped. I hit the appropriate key, and Bent's face filled the screen. He was out of the lab, virtually the only time I'd ever been on the phone with him when he was elsewhere. The background looked to be a window-wall with a view of the Sound and Bainbridge Island in the distance.

"I've got something," he said, "but I don't know what the frag to make of it." He paused, fixing me with those blue eyes. "What exactly are you working on, Dirk?"

My turn to pause. My first reaction was to clam up, to give Bent some palatable line about it being better that he didn't know. But then I had to ask myself, better for who? Not knowing what was going down, Bent would be much more likely to stumble into something that might attract the attention of our mysterious X. How can you avoid your enemy if you don't know who he is? Add to this my desire to tell *someone*.

To make it short, I spilled my guts. Starting with Jocasta's arrival at my Auburn apartment, I took him through the whole chronology up to the present moment. If I missed anything, it was a simple slip.

When I was done, his penetrating stare had softened. I could see that in his heart he was mourning Lolly and the others who had died. "Thanks for telling me the truth," he said simply. "It's good to know. I guess I'd started to worry . . ." He trailed off.

"That I wasn't working the right side of the street?" He nodded, a little embarrassed. "Don't grind it, chummer," I told him. "That's what the shadows are like. Sometimes *I* don't know. So, what can you tell me?"

"It's twisted," he admitted. "According to the post, Waters shows many of the same symptoms as Juli Long."

I paused for a moment. "You mean Daniel Waters was addicted to 2XS?"

"That's what's twisted. The report describes the same kind of neurophysiological aspects as appeared in Juli Long. It certainly seems that similar processes occurred."

"What's so twisted about that?" I said, then echoed Jocasta's comment about how prevalent was drug and chip use in the entertainment industry.

Bent smiled grimly. "Maybe," he said, "but Daniel Waters didn't have a datajack."

I shrugged. "So maybe you were wrong. Maybe you *can* run it through a standard simsense deck."

He was shaking his head before I'd finished. "Not a chance. I've done some checking. The signal degradation on a headset would make 2XS useless. You wouldn't get much more effect than from a regular simsense chip. Certainly not enough to cause what happened to Waters."

When Bent Sigurdsen sounds that emphatic, you don't argue with him. I'd learned that he knows whereof he speaks. "Okay," I said, "so what happened?"

"I don't know. But that's not the only strange thing in the report. Look at this."

He leaned forward to pound on his telecom keyboard, and my screen split in two. Half showed Bent; the other showed a Lone Star file header with a body of text below it. I skimmed the text quickly: it was medical language describing the condition of the late Daniel Waters.

"That's the report," Bent said, confirming what I'd already figured out. "It was encrypted, but I decoded it. Now look."

Bent hit a key, and the report started to scroll up my screen. Too fast for me to read it, but I could see it was standard text. And then suddenly it wasn't. Instead of standard alphanumeric characters, I saw a great wad of weird, graphic-like characters, Greek letters, mathematical symbols, and so on. My telecom beeped arrhythmically as the mass of drek scrolled by. Then it was over, and we were back into standard text. Bent hit another key. The report vanished, and his earnest face filled the screen again.

"What was that?" The words came out of my mouth even though I thought I already knew.

"There's a section that's been encrypted using a different algorithm," Bent said, corroborating my guess. "I tried to break it, but not a chance. If the rest of the report is like a locked door, that section's like a vault."

I thought for a moment. "Can you send it to me? Maybe I can find someone who can break it."

He grinned. "I'm all ready to send. Ready to receive?" I entered the appropriate commands. "Go ahead," I said. The transfer took only seconds, and my telecom beeped to acknowledge receipt. "Received and verified," I announced. "Anything else I should know?"

"That's it for now," Bent said with a chuckle. "But when you get it cracked, you'll probably need me to interpret it for you."

"I kinda figured as much. Thanks, chummer."

"*De nada.* Talk to you soon. Hang easy, Dirk." He broke the connection.

I sat back. I felt like I'd tuned into a mystery vid after it was thirty minutes into the story, making me miss all the important background clues. Nothing seemed to connect in a logical and obvious way. But I felt a sick certainty that just about everything that had happened over the last week *was* somehow connected. It was paranoia in the extreme—like there was this Grand Plan that They had set up, and I was just a pawn unlucky enough to start to sense that I *was* just a pawn. I didn't like it at all.

I did my best to shake off the feeling, to blot out the images of hideous truths behind the façade of reality. It would all make sense if I could put the pieces of the puzzle together in the right way, or so I told myself. And the biggest puzzle piece was the double-encrypted section of the Lone Star medical examiner's report.

If Bent couldn't break it, there wasn't a hope in hell I could. I needed a pro—Buddy? But that would mean distracting her from the search for William Sutcliffe, which I still believed was the key lead. Buddy was the best there was, but maybe I didn't need such a heavy-hitter to bust the Lone Star encryption. Surely there were other deckers who were capable, available, and cheaper. I brought up my contacts database and started scanning.

She called herself Rosebud, and she was a dwarf. We met at a bar called The Mad Woman on Northeast Fifty-first. Rosebud was squat and muscular, with short legs and arms. Her build reminded me of a fireplug. When I entered the bar, she was sitting in a shadowed booth toward the back. As she waved me over, I picked up a pitcher of beer and two glasses at the bar.

She grinned at me from under her unruly thatch of chestnut hair and stuck out her hand. I took it, feeling fingers as thick as bratwurst grip mine painfully tight. I tried to give as good as I got, but not a chance. Rosebud poured herself a tall glass of beer, tossed off half of it, and refilled the glass, then filled mine as an afterthought. Then and only then did she speak.

"Long time," she rumbled in a voice much too low and gravelly for anyone named Rosebud. "Biz is good. Manager now."

I remembered my first run-in with Rosebud, which took place soon after I'd cut loose from the Star. After graduating in Matrix programming from U-Dub, she'd been suckered in by the urban folklore that running the shadows is an easy way to make major nuyen and get your rep splattered around the sprawl as some kind of hero. That may be true for the top echelon, but the income of most shadowrunners, when averaged out over the year, comes out to something like minimum hourly wage, with the added chance of getting geeked. As to the rep thing, unless a runner is tops, and unless his rep is limited to the right circles, the last thing he wants is to get a name for himself.

Rosebud had found that out the hard way. Her first job should have been as straightforward as it gets: Matrix cover on a corporate lift-out. Rosebud never did figure out exactly what went wrong, which happens all the time. All she knew for sure was that the corp scientist stopped a few slugs before he could be pulled out. On top of that, his records were missing, and those records were the thing her employer wanted even more than the scientist. This put Rosebud in the unenviable position of being hunted by both sides: her employers *and* the corp who employed the scientist. She got my name from somewhere and hired me, pure and simple, to save her butt. Just a little matter of tracking down which one of her partners had double-crossed Rosebud's employer, *then* double-crossed the corp who'd turned him, proving to

both sides that the scientist's records had been destroyed,
with no copies made. Just a walk in the park. Yeah, right.

Anyway, her close call was enough to convince Rosebud to turn away from the shadows. She applied for a
SIN and rejoined the ranks of the working stiffs, but on
her terms. She found herself a job at a computer store
and decker hangout called Siliconnections, where she was
apparently now a manager. But she also chummed around
with a group of shadow technomancers who called themselves the Dead Deckers Society. That seemed to provide
her the perfect balance of security and excitement. Rosebud was happy.

"Glad to hear it's working out," I told her, and it was
true.

She nodded. "You?"

"Keeping busy."

She raised a bushy eyebrow. "Street buzz says you're
in trouble."

"*Sukochi,*" I admitted. "Some trouble. I'm looking
for technical talent if you're looking for work."

"Matrix run?"

I shook my head. "Just a simple decrypt job." I pulled
out an optical chip. "I've got the file here. I give it to
you encrypted, you give it back to me in clear. I transfer
credit, that's it. If you had your deck with you and you
had the time, you could do it now."

"Don't need no deck," she said, taking the chip from
me. "And time I got." She brushed her thick hair back
from her forehead. For the first time I saw her hardware:
two datajacks and some unusual kind of chip receptacle
in her right temple. The skin around the chip socket was
pink and looked very tender.

"New toy?" I asked.

Rosebud smiled broadly, and for the first time she
looked almost pretty. "Got tired of depending on out-
board hardware," she said, tapping her head with a
knuckle. "Now I got what I need with me all the time."
She socketed my chip into her receptacle. The faint click
as it seated gave me a shiver. "You know what kind of
encrypt?"

"Not for sure," I told her. "Some kind of Lone Star
secondary algorithm, I think."

"No-brainer," she announced. "Back in a while."

Her eyes closed and she settled back against the padded booth.

I watched, fascinated. This was all new to me. I'd seen deckers jack in before, of course; it was freaky enough seeing them interface their brains directly with computers through plugs inserted into their datajacks, but this was one step further up the scale. Rosebud had apparently installed enough computing power right inside her skull that she could handle my decrypt job on her own. Intellectually, I understood that the interface was the same no matter where a decker's hardware was located. But as far as my emotions were concerned, Rosebud had virtually *become* a computer. It's a frightening world we live in.

I drank beer and watched her as seconds stretched into minutes. My attention eventually drifted away to the rest of the bar, and I watched the comings and goings of the rough-looking clientele. I must have watched one slag—an edgy-looking samurai wannabe—too long. He glared at me, and about fifteen centimeters of polished steel extended with a hiss from his forearm. I very obviously changed the focus of my attention to the wall beside me.

"Not so easy," Rosebud said at last, startling me. She extracted the chip from her head socket and tossed it on the table in front of me. "Lone Star seven-cycle code. Serious drek." She tapped the chip with a meaty finger. "Pretty hot, huh?"

"Didn't you scan it?" I asked.

The dwarf snorted. "Not my fragging business," she snapped.

I poured her a beer to placate her. It seemed to work. She tipped it down her gullet and held her glass out for a refill. "Wizzer stuff, Rosebud," I told her. I pulled out my credstick. "What's the going rate?"

"For a chummer, two hundred," she told me. She pulled out a pocket computer—a bargain-basement model—and opened the stick slot. (I was glad I wasn't going to have to shove my credstick into her head . . .) "Slot it," she said with a smile, "then drink up. Or you in a hurry?"

Actually, I *was* in a bit of a hurry, but it would have been rude to slot and run. Especially after Rosebud had charged me only two hundred when I'd been expecting about a K. So it was with a slightly foggy head and dry mouth that I drove on home.

Bent answered immediately when I called him. "Did you get it?" he asked, then smiled broadly as I held the chip up to my video pickup. "That was quick work."

I slotted the chip into the telecom and fired the de-crypted file over the line to Bent's machine. "Take a look at it as soon as you can," I said.

"First free cycle I get, chummer," he assured me. "Did you scan it yourself?"

I shook my head. "I figured it wouldn't mean anything to me. Call me when you know something?"

"Echo that," he smiled. "Later, Dirk."

I broke the connection, leaned back in my chair and rubbed my aching eyes. Then I looked around the squalid little apartment. The last thing I wanted to do was sit around here, but I figured I'd better stay close to the phone. Frag it. Waiting is always the hardest part.

11

I ended up doing what I usually do when it's necessary to wait. I slept. Frag, I can even justify the habit. Back in Lone Star training, they used to tell us "Rest is a weapon"—a great line, and one I'm convinced they stole from somewhere else. So what I was doing that Wednesday evening was honing a weapon.

In fact, I almost slept through the telecom's beep. When it finally penetrated my numb brain, I rolled over fuzzy-headed and blurry-eyed to check the time display. Oh-five-thirty. It had to be Bent.

Right in one. Predictably, he looked disgustingly cheerful—fresh, well-rested, and ready to face the day. My mouth tasted like something had died in it, and for a moment I hated him. "*Good* morning, Dirk," he en-thused.

"Blaargh," said I, or something to that effect.

"I thought you'd want to hear this as soon as possible,'' he continued. Then his smile faded a little as he noticed my remarkable lack of coherence. "Do you want to get a soykaf or something before we start?" he asked.

I nodded wordlessly and stumbled into the apartment's kitchen nook. The process of nuking up a mug of soykaf gave me the time I needed to pull my mind back from the edge of sleep. And the first gulp of soykaf—too hot, on purpose—finished the job. By the time I sat back down at the telecom, I was feeling almost myself. "What have you got for me?" I asked.

Bent's expression grew serious. "More than I think you want to hear," he said. "You're into something pretty deep and dark, chummer. No wonder Lone Star put a lid on it."

From anyone else (Patrick Bambra, for example) I'd have written that off as melodrama or incipient paranoia. Bent isn't given to that kind of mental indulgence. I felt the acidic churning of anxiety in my belly as I told him, "Go on."

Bent's eyes flicked away from my face to look at a spot apparently over my right shoulder. For an instant I felt the urge to look behind me—true paranoia—but then I realized Bent must have split his screen so he could view the report while he was talking to me. I forced myself to relax as much as I could.

"This is the dope that Lone Star locked up tight," Bent began. "You'll understand why. When Crashcart picked up Waters from the Hubbell Street park, he was messed up pretty bad. Entry wound left posterior, super to scapula . . ."

I stopped him. "In English, Bent."

He nodded. "In English, someone almost blew half his body away. Waters took a shotgun blast in the back of his left shoulder, up high over the shoulder blade. It tore out his clavicle—his collar bone—and basically pulverized much of the skeletal support for his left shoulder joint. Significant nerve trunk damage, massive blood loss, bone fragments driven into his lungs . . . He should have died then and there, from shock if not from blood loss."

"But he didn't."

Bent smiled. "He was a tough bugger, no doubt about that."

"From what you say, he should still be in a hospital bed."

"He should," Bent agreed, "and I'll get to that. Actually, though, the nature of the injury was such that the treatment was pretty clear-cut. Twenty years ago, there'd have been nothing anyone could do for him. But today—"

"Cyber replacement."

"You got it, chummer. An interesting job, too. They didn't give him a full arm, just part of a shoulder. The installation was easy enough, but the fact that there were two major interfaces . . ."

I held up a hand to stop him. "Sounds pretty fragging major. But he was up and around, what, three days later?"

"He was up," Bent said. "But he shouldn't have been. They hadn't even fully enabled the cyberware. Even the partial activation they gave him was too much too soon."

"Then why?"

"You know as well as I do. Contractual obligations. KOMA Corporation needed him back on the air as soon as possible, and being a good little wage slave, he went, ready or not." Bent looked sour. "If I had anything to do with his case, he wouldn't be out of bed for another month."

I refrained from pointing out that—officially—if Bent had anything to do with the case, it meant that Waters was already dead. "So what killed him?" I asked. "It sure wasn't post-operative shock or drek like that."

"Of course not," Bent said, "and this is where it gets scary. Daniel Waters died of neurophysiological reaction to some circuitry in the cyber-replacement hardware."

I shook my head; this didn't make sense. "Some kind of rejection, then?" I proposed. "But I thought you said . . ."

"I know what I said," Bent interrupted. "Hear me out. He died because of a very negative reaction to some circuitry in the cyber hardware. But that circuitry had no business being there in the first place. It was a neurological link-up that had no connection to either motor functions or sensory nerves. It's like opening up your car's engine and finding a coffee grinder attached to the transmission. It simply shouldn't be there. And it was that"—

he searched for the right word—"foreign circuitry that killed Waters. It fed some kind of signals into his brain stem that really fragged with his central nervous system. It's possible the effect might not have been lethal if they hadn't activated the hardware while he was in such a weakened condition. I tend to think not."

"Just what the frag *was* this hardware?" I asked.

"Part of what Lone Star wanted to cover up is that they didn't know," Bent said. "Their ME described the circuitry, but when it came to function, he used a politically acceptable phrase meaning 'Fragged if I know.' "

I felt a chill work its insidious way up my spine. "But *you* know, don't you, Bent?"

He nodded slowly. "Yes, but only because you had me look into the Juli Long case. The circuitry uses almost exactly the same technology as 2XS chips."

I stared at the screen. I didn't know what to say. "So it was like he was perpetually slotting a 2XS chip?" I said.

"Not exactly," Bent corrected. "The intensity would be much lower."

"But in principle . . ."

"In principle, yes," he allowed.

I shook my head. Too much, too strange. "Who did the work?" I searched my memory for the name of the hospital to which Waters had been taken when he crashed. "Harborview?"

"No hospital," Bent said. "Crashcart picked him up, so they took him to the Crashcart central clinic and body shop. That's who did the work."

"So *Crashcart* installed the 2XS circuitry?"

"If that's really what it was."

"Look," I said, "if 2XS is that lethal, what are the symptoms?"

"I'd only be guessing."

"Well, *guess*," I snapped.

He blinked, but nodded. "I'd *guess*"—he stressed the word—"you'd see disorientation, physical and mental. Memory lapses. Massive mood swings. Loss of motor control, apparent palsy. On the finer level, arrhythmia, maybe loss of homeostasis . . ."

"And death would be caused by . . ?"

"Progressive cessation of neural functioning," he said.

"Higher cerebral functions first, so probably irreversible coma, followed by eventual cessation of the entire autonomic nervous system."

I fixed Bent with my hardest stare. "Chummer," I told him, "you know *nothing* about any of this, *karimasu-ka?* Maybe you pulled the files, but you never decrypted them, you never scanned them. You just passed them to me. You know *nothing* about this. Scan me, *omae?"*

He nodded slowly. "I wish that was true," Bent said.

How the frag did I get myself into this? I found myself wondering. I lay back on the bed, staring at the ceiling. Not even six in the morning, and already it was one of those days.

Something pretty bad was going down. (No surprise, this was the sprawl after all.) While looking for one conspiracy—our murderous X—I'd found something that sure as frag looked like another. Was there any connection?

My first response was a resounding No, and a desire to purge Daniel Waters, Juli Long, and 2XS from my mind like erroneous data. But, on closer inspection, there did seem to be some tenuous connection—and it was none other than the elf biker. He seemed to be the pivotal figure at the moment. He was connected to whoever had phoned Jocasta with the claim of information about Lolly. It was simply too much of a coincidence for him and his ork lieutenant to come out shooting in the Westlake Center underground. He was also connected to Crashcart, which was the best explanation for his Executive Diamond contract with the company, something he shouldn't have been able to afford. And Crashcart was connected with 2XS, as illustrated by the premature demise of Daniel Waters.

Though I had no evidence—real or even imagined—to support it, I had the undeniable feeling that there was another linkage tying everything together. A was related to B, which was related to C and D. What if D were somehow connected with A? And, further, what if the whole alphabet soup was somehow connected to X? Say, for example, a link between William Sutcliffe and Crashcart?

I shook my head. Sheer paranoia, part of my mind told me. But another part wondered if I was being paranoid enough. A paranoid is someone in possession of all the facts . . .

So what I needed were all the facts. Specifically, I needed to know more about Crashcart, the company that ran the medical service and the corporation that owned it (if any). That kind of information was available via the Matrix, but the kind of deep-background dirt I really wanted would be hidden in the furthest shadows. Again I had need of a decker. Rosebud? No, I decided, the varsity for this one. It had to be Buddy.

I drank another mug of soykaf to fortify myself, then called her number. She'd changed her outgoing message, in that there was one: "Frag off and die *[beep]*." I cursed silently at Buddy's non-real-time communication paradigm, and left a message. In essence, "Dig up all the dirt on Crashcart, and be particularly aware of connections with Sutcliffe." I hung up, visions of depleted credit balances running through my brain. When you use the best—which Buddy was—you pay through the snout. And one of the major disadvantages of being a SINless shadow is that you can't just throw up your hands and declare bankruptcy. No credit, no life. And bodyleggers—"purveyors of gray-market transplants"—were always around to take any debts out of your hide, quite literally.

So what was I going to do now? Buddy would get back to me in her own sweet time. Bent had given me everything he could, and I didn't want to drag him in any deeper. Ditto Naomi. Jocasta I could talk to, but she still hadn't given me her number. I could probably get her a message through KSTS or the university, but that wasn't what I wanted right then.

I looked over at the bed, thinking it was still early enough to justify going back to sleep. But my brain was awake, and I decided I'd honed that weapon enough.

I should have thought about it earlier. You want the phone to ring, you take a shower. It was buck-naked and dripping lather that I bolted across the room and hit the Receive key, but only after being sure the video pickup was off, for reasons of discretion as well as security.

I didn't recognize the face that appeared on the screen. It was a young ork, maybe in his early twenties, the sides of his head depilated and his hair built up into a multicolored, Iroquois-style crest. He wore biker-style leathers, none too clean but showing a collar lined with synthetic leopard skin. I knew the combination of collar and crest identified the gang he ran with, but I couldn't place it at the moment, and besides, couldn't have cared less. From the slight breakup of the image, I guessed he was using a public phone somewhere.

"Yeah?" I barked.

He frowned into what I knew was a blank screen. "You Dirk Montgomery?"

I hesitated. I guess my paranoid reflections had gotten to me. "I can take a message," I told him.

His turn to hesitate. "Teri gave me this number."

Teri . . . *"Theresa?"* I snapped.

"Yeah, Theresa Montgomery," he said. "I got to talk to her brother."

"You are," I told him. "Why?"

"She crashed, pretty bad it looks like. Maybe she slotted a bad chip, maybe too many, I don't know."

I closed my eyes. I'd feared this phone call, but expected it in equal measure. I don't think I ever really believed my sister wouldn't turn into a chiphead. "What happened?" I asked quietly.

"I don't know," he babbled defensively. "I wasn't there when it happened. She—I don't know—she got twitchy. She forgot who we were, she started screaming—"

"How is she now?"

"She's not here . . ."

"Where is she?" I shouted. I could see the ork considering cutting the connection, so I forced myself to sound more reasonable. "Sorry," I said. "But she *is* my sister. When you saw she was in trouble, you took her somewhere, right?"

He hesitated, his belligerent expression softening a little. "To a clinic," he said. "We took her to a street clinic."

I ground my teeth. Since our parents had died, I'd maintained a DocWagon basic contract for Theresa. I still had her card in my wallet. But she refused to take it or register herself with the DocWagon organization. That would have involved putting her residence on file, and she probably feared—with justification, I suppose—that

I'd use the data to track her down somehow. I'd maintained the contract in the vain hope that Theresa would call me if something happened to her, giving me a chance to dispatch the DocWagon trauma team if necessary. I wanted to scream at this gutter-boy ork, abuse him to hell and back for taking my sister to some squatter clinic when she could be in a reputable DocWagon trauma ward right now.

But of course the ork had no way of knowing that Theresa had DocWagon coverage, and it sounded as though she'd been in no condition to tell anyone about it. No matter how much I wanted to blame the ork, how could I? What if he hadn't called me at all, totally washing his hands of Theresa?

I struggled to keep my voice even and non-threatening. "Okay, you took her to a street clinic. Where? Which clinic?"

"I didn't take her," the ork said. "The way she was . . . No way I could manage her on a bike. Fitz took her in his car."

"*Where* did Fitz take her?"

"The UB," he said. "The Universal Brotherhood, they've got free clinics, and . . ."

"Which chapterhouse?"

"Meridian and Twenty-third. It's nearest."

Meridian and Twenty-third. That was in Puyallup, the Wildwood Park region to be exact. With that jog to my memory, the ork's gang affiliation fell into place. The leopard skin and Iroquois cut meant the ork ran with the Night Prowlers. Compared to real social deviants like the Tigers and the Ancients, the Prowlers are wussies— or "mabels"—to use the pejorative currently in vogue— generally limiting themselves to the less terminal forms of aggravated assault and armed robbery. But they're still not people you'd want to meet in a dark alley. It worried me more than a little to think of Theresa hanging with them.

"When did this go down?" I asked him.

"Last night, late." He shrugged. "Three, maybe four when she started to lose it."

"Thanks for the buzz," I said, and I meant it.

The ork almost smiled, but of course smiling would have been much too uncool. "Null," he said. "I like

Teri. She's stone, you know? If you see her before I do, tell her Pud says hoi.'' And with that Pud the ork ganger broke the connection.

I called up the directory, scanned for the Brotherhood's Puyallup chapterhouse, and hit the key to place the call. I was pleased to get a real receptionist—cleavage, frizzed blonde hair, capped teeth, and all. Not only is a real one usually better-looking than the video-construct voice-mail systems that are proliferating in the corporate world, but you can actually argue with her.

''Thank you for calling the Universal Brotherhood,'' she said, sounding like she meant it. ''How may I help you?''

''You've got a clinic there?''

She nodded. ''We sure do,'' she said proudly. ''A free clinic, for those unfortunates who can't afford insurance or normal health care. Just another way we're contributing to the fabric of life in the sprawl.''

I waited for her to finish the sales pitch, but it took all the self-control I had. ''I need to find out about one of your patients,'' I told her.

She frowned, a pretty little *moué* that, in my present mood, made me want to strangle her. ''I'm very sorry,'' she began predictably, ''but we can't give out information on—''

''She's my sister,'' I barked. ''Her name's Theresa Montgomery, or maybe Teri. She was brought in early this morning. At least tell me if she's all right.'' I meant to say, ''tell me if she's alive,'' but at the last moment the words wouldn't come out.

A look of real concern appeared on the receptionist's face. ''I'm *so* sorry,'' she said. ''You must be very worried. I'll check the records for you.'' Her face vanished, to be replaced by a recorded talking-head blathering on about the Brotherhood's philanthropic projects. I muted the volume and chewed my nails.

Cleavage-frizz-and-teeth was back quickly, looking puzzled. ''. . . very sorry, Mr. Montgomery,'' she said, as I brought the volume back up, ''we have no record of a Theresa or Teri Montgomery, or any name phonetically similar.''

''Maybe she couldn't give her name,'' I suggested,

"or maybe she gave a fake one. She's in her late twenties, tall with short blonde hair—"

"I'm sorry," the receptionist told me firmly, "but your sister's not here."

"How do you know that?"

She bit her lip. "I shouldn't be telling you this, but the records show we've had no admissions at all since about twenty-two-thirty last night. Are you sure your sister was brought *here?* There are other free clinics, you know."

I hesitated. Pud the ork had said so, but it was Fitz who'd taken her, and Pud hadn't gone along. "No," I told the receptionist, "I'm not sure. Thanks for your time."

I keyed the telecom off before she could give me a no doubt insipid farewell. I grabbed my duster, made sure my pistol was securely in the holster. I had a gang to visit.

12

In general, Puyallup is about on a par with Purity, except that it seems to be trying to crawl up out of the ashes while Redmond seems totally oblivious to its condition. The Meridian region looks to be a little better off. No burned-out cars on the sidewalk and most of the buildings still have doors and windows. Nevertheless, the air carries that same scent of barely repressed violence, and Lone Star patrols are always well-armed and on the jump after dark.

I parked my car in the secured lot on Seventeenth Street, across from Wildwood Park. I contracted with the guard for a nonexistent second car as well to make sure he found it more to his best interests to keep the car intact for me than to give it up to the local chop-shop artists. Then I strolled along Twenty-third Avenue into the heart of Night Prowlers territory.

Shaikujin are always amazed at how easy it is to track people down once you know their neighborhood, but

that's the reason it's so important to make sure your enemies don't know where you hang. For thrill-gangers,
that's not easy, of course. Your colors mark you, and
anyone who's seen them knows the likely places to find
you. To avoid being found, you've got to hole up somewhere else. With a gang, that means ducking into another
gang's territory. Which, in turn, means doffing your colors—which no self-respecting ganger is going to do will-
ingly—so that the gang whose territory you've entered
won't serve you up as an object lesson to anyone with
territorial ambitions.

What that meant to me now was that I could be confident of getting a line on Pud the Prowler. It didn't cost
me too much in time or nuyen. It was just a matter of
strolling Twenty-third, overtipping blatantly for an indi-
gestible breakfast from the local soykaf stand, then paying for five packs of Js but "neglecting" to take them,
and finally buying another breakfast at another spot—a
meal I donated to a couple of squatters in an alley. And,
all the time, talking to *everyone*, asking about the Prowlers in general and a young ork named Pud in particular.

As Rosebud might have put it, it was a "no-brainer."
Within an hour, I had enough background that I could
probably have written a pamphlet called, "A Day in the
Life of Pud and his Chummer Fitz." Pud and Fitz—a
troll, natch—were given to greeting the day with a round
of red-eyes at The Mill, a neighborhood watering hole.
After that, their schedule took them to an assortment of
pool halls and simsense arcades, punctuated by cruises
around their turf. Then they'd cap the day off with massive substance-abuse sessions near the reservoir, and
maybe a nice, diverting little rumble (or whatever) with
the Ladies from Hades, an all-female gang who claimed
the territory on the other side of Shaw Road. Sounded
like a fulfilling life to me.

It was only the early portion of Pud's busy day that
concerned me, of course. I checked my watch. Just short
of ten, which meant The Mill was the best bet.

The Mill had once been home to Jimbo's One-Hour
Dry Cleaning; you could still see where the old neon
tubing had been torn from the wall. The single window
of the narrow frontage was tinted so you couldn't see in

from the street. The establishment's sole identification was a small rusted sign on the door.

Breakfast wasn't The Mill's best time. As I stepped through the door, I saw only two customers sitting at the bar, a rummy drinking his first meal of the day and Pud the ork. Pud was working on his second red-eye—a mixture of beer and tomato juice that I personally find repugnant—but wasn't so engrossed in breakfast not to look up and give me the evil eye as I came in. I twitched as his gaze passed over me, but then the logical portion of my brain reminded me I hadn't turned on the video pickup during our phone conversation. I settled myself at the end of the bar, five stools away to Pud's right, and quietly ordered a bloody mary from the bored bartender. As she mixed my drink, I considered how I would make my approach to Pud.

The drink arrived and I took a sip. Not enough dill, predictably, and I think the gin was watered. I half-turned toward Pud and raised my glass. He glanced over, curled his lip. "Teri says thanks," I said, loud and clear enough so he could recognize my voice.

I was watching his eyes for that initial reaction. It's the eyes that always give it away when you've achieved tactical surprise. And I saw that I had.

If I was expecting a guilty response, I didn't get it. The young ork's eyes opened a little wider in surprise, then his face split in a grin. Totally sincere, I'd bet on it. "She's doing okay?" he asked. "That's wiz." Then he remembered who and where he was and the role he should be playing. He schooled his expression back to its normal scowl. "You her brother, huh?"

I nodded. "Teri told me where you might be, so I came down to say thanks personally." I went through that fast so he wouldn't catch any holes in my story. Then I hit him with something that might distract him, at least a little. "Can I buy you another breakfast?"

He glanced at the depleted red-eye on the bar in front of him, grinned in spite of himself. "Yeah, why not?" He rang the glass with a fingernail to get the bartender's attention, then pointed at his drink. "Another," he told her. "Egg in it, this time."

My gorge rose at the thought, but I kept the half-smile

fixed on my face. "Breakfast of champions," I remarked.

"Fragging A," my newfound companion agreed.

I looked around casually. "Where's Fitz? I wanted to buy him breakfast, too."

"Dunno." Pud shrugged. "He came back after dropping Teri, then he faded. Haven't seen him since."

I filed that away for future reference. Then I just sipped my drink in comradely silence for a few minutes, trying to ignore the grotesque slurping noises coming from my left.

"I'm trying to figure out exactly what happened to Teri," I said finally. "I think the medics want to know, too. How did it all go down?" Pud glanced over at me, and I saw incipient doubt in his eyes. "Teri doesn't remember dick about it," I added hastily.

He nodded at that, and the doubt went away. "Teri likes to run a couple of chips at the end of the day," he told me. "Last few weeks she's been doing something new."

"Do you know what?"

He shrugged expressively. "Nah, not my business. I stay away from that drek. I prefer real life, you know?" He smiled, showing his discolored fangs.

"So she was chipping last night . . ." I prompted.

"Yeah, like I said. I was drinking pretty good, so I'm kinda fuzzy about the time. I think it was about one that she started getting flaky."

"Flaky like how?"

He scowled a little, obviously slotted off that I kept interrupting him. "Like forgetting what she was saying," he said. "Like starting to say one thing, then half-way through kinda switching programs and saying something else. She knew it was happening, and it slotted her off at first, then she got drek-scared about it. Next thing I knew she was shaking. I thought maybe she was on a bad chip, but I looked and she didn't have anything slotted." He grinned crookedly and showed me an egg-sized contusion behind his right ear. "Teri didn't like me checking, so she clipped me up-side the head with a fragging brick. Not her style."

I nodded. "You're right. It's not."

"Then the shaking got so bad she couldn't stand. Every

time she'd try, she just fell down. That's when we figured
we had to do something. Like, we all think Teri's stone,
even drekheads like Random. We didn't know where to
take her. I think it was Fitz came up with the Brotherhood. Those love-junky guys are flaky, but word on the
street is their clinic's the best.''

"So Fitz took her in his car?"

"Not his really," Pud confided. "He kinda borrowed
it for the evening, you know?" I knew. "Teri seemed to
be shaking it off a little toward the end there, Fitz told
me. But he didn't want nothing to happen to her so he
took her anyway."

"Did he just drop her off at the door?"

"Nah, he went inside. Picked up some souvenirs,
too." He reached into his pocket and pulled out a small
object, which he tossed onto the bar. I leaned closer for
a better look. It was a polished silver name tag on a
velcro backing. Etched into the surface was the Universal
Brotherhood's pyramid logo and the name "J. Bailey,
R.N."

Pud chuckled. "Don't know how he got it. That Fitz,
he cracks me up."

After leaving The Mill, I looped the conversation
through my mind again and again. But no matter how
many times I ran it, it shook out only two ways.

First, Pud's troll chummer Fitz did actually deliver a
strung-out Theresa to the Universal Brotherhood free
clinic sometime early in the morning. While there, he'd
succumbed to a propensity for petty larceny and lifted
Registered Nurse J. Bailey's name tag. Corroborating evidence was the tag and the fact that Pud seemed to gen-
uinely care about Theresa.

The other possibility was that Fitz took Theresa
somewhere else, and for some reason went to a lot of
trouble to convince Pud that she was in the Brotherhood
clinic. Corroborating evidence for that theory came
from Ms. Frizz-and-Cleavage on the chapterhouse
switchboard. Nothing else, really; Fitz's absence this
morning wouldn't even qualify as circumstantial.

What it came down to was, who did I believe? The
Brotherhood's receptionist or a troll ganger? At the mo-

ment it was a toss-up. So the first thing to do was track down Fitz.

No, the *very* first thing was to eliminate the possibility of an innocent error. I found a public phone booth, stuck chewing gum over the video pickup, and called the Brotherhood again.

I got another receptionist, this one dark-haired and dark-skinned, but with the same flashing smile. "Thank you for calling the Universal Brotherhood," she said, echoing the party line. "How may I help you?"

I smiled back. "Can you tell me the name of the person in charge of your free clinic?"

"Why, sure," she replied. "That would be Dr. Phyllis Dempsey. She just replaced Dr. Boris Chernekhov, and—"

"Could I speak to Dr. Dempsey, please?" I said.

She hesitated. "May I ask what this is in reference to?"

I shook my head. "Sorry, it's personal."

"I am very sorry," she said, "but I'm afraid it's against policy to transfer personal calls. I *can* connect you to Dr. Dempsey's voice-mail system and you can leave a message."

"I'll just leave a message with you," I told her. "Tell Phyllis that my wife found out, and the drek really hit the fan . . ."

The receptionist's eyes opened wide. "I . . . I'll c . . . connect you right away," she stuttered. "Hold a moment." She left me grinning at the same recorded sales pitch for the Brotherhood. I'd read about that gambit in one of the hard-boiled detective stories Patrick Bambra had loaned me years ago. It's good to know that some things never change.

Dr. Phyllis Dempsey wasn't long coming onto the line. She was a statuesque black elf, with tightly curled hair cut into a businesslike flattop. She had a full, mobile mouth that looked as though it would smile easily, but right now her lips formed a flat line and her chestnut eyes sparked with anger. "All right," she snapped, "you've played your little game with Glory, and probably started some gossip—which I *don't* need. So you can just tell me why the frag I shouldn't have Lone Star trace your nasty ass for phone intimidation."

I had to grin. Good, honest anger was refreshing, even though it was directed at me. I was thinking that under different circumstances I could get to like Phyllis Dempsey. "I'm sorry for the subterfuge, Doctor," I said placatingly. "It was a cheap trick. But I really needed to speak to you. Live, not just by message." I had my momentum up and kept on rolling, right over her attempt to reply. "I got a phone call this morning that something happened to my sister and that a friend delivered her to your clinic."

The hard line of the doctor's mouth softened incrementally. "You called earlier, didn't you?" she said. "Candy said some doting brother was asking about a nonexistent patient."

"I thought it might be a mistake," I told her. "File fr . . . *screw*-ups happen, even in the best of organizations."

That raised a minimal smile. "Yes," she agreed, "file *frag*-ups do occur. But I can promise you, not this time. I've been here since midnight last night—thank god I'm back on regular evenings starting tomorrow. Plus, I checked the oh-four-hundred shift report. So I can personally vouch for the fact that we've admitted *nobody* new. Rare, but there it is."

I sighed. "Thanks, doctor," I said. "I believe you."

A real smile now, tired but sincere. She was silent for a moment. "If what you say is true, I can imagine what you must be going through and I honestly hope you find your sister." Then her voice and face hardened again. "And if you're some kind of scam artist, I hope you get geeked in an alley." The screen went blank.

I chuckled as I continued my stroll along Twenty-third. I always claimed to like women with strong personalities, with fire. Phyllis Dempsey definitely qualified. I made a mental note to track her down when this was all over— if I lived that long.

But aside from all that, where did her story leave me? If I believed the good doctor—and I did—then it led me right back to Fitz the Night Prowler. So it was back to the same business as before—talk to everyone, being as loose with my credit as I could, but this time with the focus on the troll. It wasn't so easy this time because I didn't want Pud to find out I was tracking Fitz, or worse yet, run into the young ork while I was nosing about. We'd parted on friendly enough terms. But dogging his chummer's tracks wasn't a particularly friendly thing to do, and three red-eyes—even *with* egg—don't buy as much good will as they used to.

I spent the morning walking the streets of the Wildwood Park district of Puyallup. Lots of leads—a three-meter-tall troll with an Iroquois and an attitude isn't easy to overlook or forget—but none led anywhere useful. During my wanderings, I saw Pud a couple of times, but he was always alone and, luckily, he didn't see me. (In fact, I got the idea that he was as interested as I was in locating his big chummer.)

It was almost 1400 when I discovered I had a shadow. Maybe I'd have spotted her sooner if I hadn't been so tired; maybe not. She was a young ork, probably in her early teens, which meant she had the physical development of a twenty-year-old human—a *big* twenty-year-old human. I'd never seen her before, but I did recognize the meaning of her brightly dyed crest of hair and the fake leopard skin collar on her bike jacket. Why was a Night Prowler trailing me?

I watched her for a few minutes, never letting on I'd spotted her. For an amateur, she was a good shadow. Seemed to have a natural talent for it. I remembered the Surveillance Tradecraft instructor I'd suffered under at the Star. He'd have killed for a student like this girl.

Of course, that still didn't answer the question of why she was watching me. I mentally reviewed my conversation with Pud once more, and finished even more convinced that he'd told me what he believed was the truth. This shadow, then . . . Did it mean there were different factions within the Night Prowlers? Not unheard of. Gangs breed politics and infighting almost as much as do corporations. Still not letting on I'd spotted the tail, I continued westbound on Twenty-third, all the while considering my options.

I think it was memories of Dr. Dempsey's directness that made up my mind for me. All right, then. The straightforward approach it would be.

Feigning an intense interest in a window display of Fiberwear clothing ("The Future is Disposable"), I casually scanned the street up ahead. Maybe twenty-five meters in front of me was the entrance to a commercial alley, flanked by two tall buildings. Perfect. I picked up my pace a little. Not enough to appear suspicious, but sufficiently to extend the distance between me and the ork girl. My plan was simplicity itself: duck into the alley and find cover, luring my shadow in after me. Then I'd take her—non-violently if possible, and definitely non-lethally—and play a quick game of twenty questions.

The alley was ten meters away, then five, then . . . I darted around the corner, flattened myself against the wall. I took in the alley with a quick glance. Couldn't have been better, a dead end with a dumpster and piles of drek. Long enough that I could be confident of no interference from the street, and with no way out other than the street. Perfect. I trotted further in, looking for a good spot to hide.

Movement up ahead. I guess my mind was operating in "combat mode." Out the corner of my eye I saw something move in a pile of trash, and without thinking I spun to the side. The report of the heavy pistol and the *spang* of the round ricocheting off the alley wall were simultaneous. An ambush. I should, by all rights, be dead, but somebody was either clumsy or impatient. I dragged out my Manhunter and sent a slug down the alley, more to keep my would-be assassin's head down than with any hope of hitting anything. Then I turned and bolted. Gunfire erupted from behind me—more than one barrel, that was for sure—and lethal wasps buzzed past my ears.

I sprinted out of the alley, taking a hard left back onto Twenty-third. I looked over my shoulder as I ran. Pursuit hadn't emerged from the alley yet, but my original shadow—little miss ork—was legging it my way, brandishing a hogleg as long as her arm. Without slowing, I half-turned and slammed a bullet into the parked car beside her. She shrieked and flung herself into the cover of said punctured car. That's when I heard the heavy, booted running footsteps of my ambushers echoing out of the alley. Thank god, should she exist, that the Prowlers were mainly a thrill-gang. If they'd been a go-gang, I'd have had to contend with bikes as well as guns.

Of course, it doesn't pay to overgeneralize; the scream of a high-revving engine reminded me of that. I couldn't see the bike yet, but I knew it was coming. Okay, change in tactics. A few moments before, the sidewalks were fairly busy when I'd ducked into the alley. Now? Deserted, chummer. It seems the people of Puyallup rival Barrens-dwellers in their ability to pull the quick fade. With no mobile cover—read "pedestrians"—off the street was better. Another alley, maybe?

No, up ahead was something even better. It used to be a bike dealership, but like many establishments it had succumbed to the negative effects of an economic downturn and all that drek. An up-and-over door, no doubt leading to the workbays, a single human-sized door for customers, and a small, painted-over display window. I flung myself through that window, arms up to protect my head and face, already tucked for a rolling recovery. The glass shattered into a million fragments. I landed on my shoulder, the momentum taking me into a graceful roll that brought me up into a squat. It would have been perfect except for the service desk that I butted into with a mighty lick, splitting open my forehead and exploding a bunch of fireworks behind my eyelids. I forced back the darkness that wanted to take me, and struggling to my feet, made my weaving way into the darkened service-bay area.

I looked around me, the last firework stars still drifting through my vision. The place was perfect: dark, with a high ceiling, and only two doors. One to the service counter (with the forehead-shaped dent in it), the other presumably to the back alley. I considered simply bolting out the back right now, but I couldn't be sure more Prowlers weren't waiting out that way. Besides, if I hung tough here and played it right, I might still get my game of twenty questions . . .

I picked my position carefully, behind one of the big metal posts that supported the ceiling crane that hung overhead. I squatted down, switching my attention and my aiming point between the two doors. After my experience in Westlake Center, *nobody* was going to sneak up behind me again.

Hushed voices from the front of the shop, broken glass grinding under boots. I steadied my gun against the pillar, at the last moment remembering to turn off my sighting laser. For this range, open sights should be good

enough, and the laser would give away my position in the dark.

A small figure darted into the doorway, perfectly back-lit so he looked like a pistol-range silhouette target. I brushed the Manhunter's reactive trigger twice. The heavy slugs slammed into the center of the figure's chest, probably right into his body armor. That was fine; I wasn't after fatalities here. The figure stumbled back and disappeared. Another figure, another two shots, and the doorway was clear again. Time to change positions. I triggered another four rounds, this time pumping them *through* the thin walls on either side of the door. Confusion was what I wanted, and judging by the yells and curses, confusion is what I got. I darted across the open space and squatted down behind another pillar, closer to the back door.

There were lots of shushing sounds from the service area, then nothing. In the sudden silence I heard a faint, metallic creaking.

Above me. I looked up. It was little miss ork, crawling along one of the rails that mounted the crane to the ceiling. Needing both hands to keep her on the rail, she had her gun clenched between her teeth. Jesus, she's a wraith, I thought. The amateur tradecraft on the street had been all a put-on. *This* was what she could really do. She'd somehow sneaked into the building, and climbed up there—again, *somehow*—and was getting into perfect position to put a round down through the top of my cranium. Eat that, body armor.

My pistol came up instinctively, leveled at the bridge of her nose. Our gazes locked, and I saw her eyes grow wide. There was no way she could get to her gun in time, and she knew it. I saw the realization of inescapable death burst into her consciousness.

Of course I couldn't pull the trigger. I spun aside, took two running steps toward the back door. Four heavy rounds followed by my boot slammed into the lock, and the door burst open. I sprinted through and into the alley.

If there'd been any Prowlers there, I'd have been meat. I was expecting some kind of impact as I turned left and took off down the alley. Another alleyway—no, more a narrow accessway—opened to my right. I took it without thinking. There was a wall ahead, a rusted ladder bolted to it. I went up that ladder like I had a rocket pack.

I was on the roof of a low building, the expanse broken only by an elevator block and a couple of small, cylindrical ventilators. I stopped for a moment to get my bearings. Seventeenth Street. That meant my car should be that way. I turned to my right and jogged across the roof.

I'd just passed the first of the ventilators when a figure stepped out from behind the elevator block. It was Pud the Prowler, a cold expression on his face and a Beretta 200ST in his fist. Its muzzle was steady, point of aim apparently my upper lip. I turned to ice. The Manhunter was back in my holster. I'd never have managed the ladder without two hands free. And not a chance I could draw it before Pud squeezed the trigger. (The irony in the similarity of my position with little miss ork's wasn't lost on me; I just wasn't in the mood to appreciate it.)

"Tell me one thing," Pud said quietly. "Why'd you do it?"

Slowly—very slowly—I extended my open hands at waist level. "If I knew what you were talking about, I might have an answer for you," I told him.

"Why did you kill Fitz?" he demanded. "He was my chummer." Tears glistened in the ork's eyes, and I knocked half a decade off my estimate of his age. Young or not, the gun was rock-steady, and his finger was tense on the trigger. Another few grams of pressure and that'd be it.

"I'm sorry," I said, trying to pour sincerity into my voice. "I didn't even know he was dead."

"Yeah, right," Pud spat out. "The other Prowlers say you've been looking for Fitz all day. Looks like you found him, huh?"

I started to feel a little hope. Pud's gun hadn't moved a millimeter, but the fact that he hadn't pulled the trigger yet was something. I remembered how much faster orks reach physical maturity. Pud looked to be in his early twenties, but he was probably only fifteen or so. He'd probably never geeked anyone before, or if he had, only in the heat of a rumble. Shooting me down in cold blood was different. Was he hoping I'd talk him out of it? With my peripheral vision I checked out my options. The cylindrical ventilator was close, but it wouldn't offer me more than a moment's cover. If I wanted to live, I had to talk fast. And no bulldrek, the truth and nothing but, hoping Pud could tell the difference.

"I was looking for Fitz, yes," I told him calmly. "Like I was looking for you earlier. I wanted to talk to him."

"About your sister?" he snarled. "That doesn't scan. Go to all that trouble just to say thanks?"

"No," I took a deep breath and took a risk. "I lied to you. The Brotherhood clinic says my sister never arrived. I want to find out what happened. *That's* why I'm looking for Fitz." I paused, gave him a moment to think. "What happened to your friend?" I asked.

For the first time the gun trembled a little. "Got his throat ripped out," Pud said harshly, "over in the park. The other Prowlers, they heard you been looking for Fitz, they think you did it."

"But you don't," I said softly. "If I'd geeked him, why would I still be looking? That's what I was doing when they tried to dry-gulch me."

Pud shook his head, hard. "I don't know," he almost cried. "You're confusing me."

"I just wanted to find Teri," I pressed. "I just wanted to find my sister."

Pud snarled. The gun barrel shifted, and he clamped down on the trigger. The little autofire pistol spat, the bullets shredding the construction plastic of the ventilator beside me. Fragments lacerated my cheek and my hands, but I didn't move. The Beretta clicked empty, and Pud glared into my face.

"Get the frag out of here," he hissed.

I got.

13

I managed to hold it together until I got to my car, and *then* I got the shakes. Close calls, too many and too close. Just a few seconds difference in the timing and little miss ork would have drilled an extra set of nostrils into the top of my head. And if Pud had been a tad more hard-assed, he'd have emptied his Beretta clip into my face. I was getting too old for this drek.

As I cruised home, the question on my mind was, of course, who killed Fitz? It wasn't me, and I didn't think it was Pud—or was it? Now there was a paranoid thought, but it still didn't narrow it down much. And that led to the next question: was the troll's death connected with Theresa's disappearance? Maybe Fitz hadn't taken her to the Brotherhood clinic after all, and somebody had offed him to make sure her true destination never came to light. The questions seemed only to create more murk and shadows.

It was a relief to return to the familiarity of my own front door. The beeping of the telecom greeted me as I stepped in. I dashed over to it, almost punting an empty whiskey bottle through the window in my haste. I hit the Receive key. "Hello," I gasped.

A wizened face appeared on the screen. "About fragging time," Buddy grumbled.

I sat down at the telecom and keyed on my video pickup. "Thanks for calling back, Buddy," I said. "Got anything?"

She looked pained at my lack of faith. "*Course* I got something," she snapped. "I got you a line on Crashcart. Want the file?"

"In a minute," I told her. "Just give me the highlights."

Buddy scowled. "Scan the file, then ask questions." Her image disappeared, and the screen filled with text. I scrambled to open a capture file and store the incoming data.

There wasn't that much to it. Either Buddy hadn't managed to find much, or else she'd edited it down to show only the important drek. (That worried me a little. Who could be sure from one day to the next just what Buddy was going to consider important?) But I couldn't do anything about that now, so I started reading.

The first section dealt with management and ownership of Crashcart Medical Services Corporation and its wholly owned subsidiary, Crashcart Clinics Inc., both headquartered here in Seattle. Buddy had done a good job, listing the boards of both corporations—identical lists—and the members of the management team. I skimmed through the names, looking for one I recognized—William Sutcliffe, perhaps?—but came up dry.

Ownership was detailed similarly. Apparently, Crashcart MSC, the parent company, was a privately held corporation, owned by five individuals who sat on the boards of both it and the subsidiary company. On the surface, totally normal, and not even the Infernal Revenue could take issue. But Buddy had dug deeper, prying into the way credit flowed through the organization. When looked at this way, it became obvious that four of the five "owners" were actually fronts. Oh sure, they existed, sat on the boards, and voted, but they were just stage-dressing. The real power was the fifth shareholder, an elf called Dennison Harkness. According to Buddy's analysis, his was the only decision that counted. The other four shareholders voted with him, or one or two voted against him when he wanted it to look like real democracy was at work. But they were, in fact, only puppets, with Harkness pulling their strings. Play-acting aside, the large and growing Crashcart medical empire was owned and run by one man.

Or so it seemed. Buddy had taken the saga one step further. As it turned out, *Harkness* wasn't his own elf either. He was in the pocket of a multinational conglomerate called Yamatetsu Corporation (head office in Kyoto, branch offices everywhere from Adelaide to Zurich), and he danced to *their* tune. Interesting, yes. But was it relevant?

I asked Buddy what kinds of things Yamatetsu was involved with in Seattle.

She didn't answer directly, but the text on my screen scrolled without me touching the keyboard, and a small section appeared in inverse video. "Thanks," I said, and scanned the section.

Yamatetsu was a typical diversified multinational, in that it didn't manufacture any products or market any services. Instead, it bought and sold, raped and pillaged, other firms that did manufacture products ranging from diapers to nerve gas or else marketed services as diverse as interior design and corporate security.

No, that wasn't quite true. According to Buddy's research, the company did have one division that developed products for the military market. It was called ISP, for

Integrated System Products, and was not a subsidiary but actually a part of the parent company. ISP was located in the sprawl. Somewhere. No specific location was given. I re-read the section, trying to make sense of what ISP did. They didn't develop weapons, as I'd assumed at first. Instead, they were working on something called Sympathetic-Parasympathetic Integrated Suprarenal Excitation Systems (SPISES), or "booster technology." I skimmed forward and backward through Buddy's report looking for further explanation of just what booster technology did, but found nothing.

"What's this booster stuff?" I asked.

Buddy's sour face appeared in a small window in one corner of my screen. "SPISES," she replied, pronouncing it "SPY-seas." "Circuitry in cyberware, or just jacked in." She tapped her datajack. "Heightens sensory acuity, concentration, strength, reaction, all that drek. They say," she added.

It sounded like wired reflexes, maybe combined with skillwires. I said as much to Buddy.

"Drek," she shot back. "That's invasive, artificial. SPISES does it naturally. Doesn't just trigger adrenalin, but jacks your endorphins, too."

An "idea" light flashed through my brain, but I put the thought on hold. I'd have to talk it out with someone whose knowledge base was different from Buddy's before I could tell if it made any sense. "You did great," I told her. "Thanks. You're going to keep looking for William Sutcliffe, right?"

Buddy snorted. "Already found him." I did my gaffed fish imitation, and she grinned fleetingly. "Tough job. Fragging tough. It's gonna cost you." Of course it was going to cost me, but I'd worry about that later. "Here he is," she said.

A dossier-style picture appeared on-screen. The guy looked totally neutral: apparently mid-height, hair midbrown, nothing distinguishing about his face. Looked like a nonentity or an accountant. "So who is he," I said, "what is he, where is he?"

"Tough job," she repeated. "UCAS military, that's why it took so long."

"He's army?"

She shrugged. "Guess so. But no uniform, no rank."

"Civilian consultant, maybe?" I mused. Then I saw the impatience on Buddy's face. "Okay, okay, got it. So what's he do?"

"Something with evaluation and procurement, personnel-enhancement systems." She looked at me expectantly, apparently waiting for me to say something. To make some connection. I didn't answer at once, and second by second I could see her frustration and disdain building. Buddy waits faster than anyone else I know.

Personnel-enhancement systems . . . And then I saw the connection Buddy had picked up on. "He's dealing with Yamatetsu," I blurted. "Buddy, you amaze me."

That mollified her, I was glad to see. She nodded. "He brought them in to demo SPISES for the agency," she confirmed. "Full evaluation's scheduled for spring and summer."

I shook my head. This was getting way the frag too heavy and complex. Pieces of the puzzle led to more jig-saw pieces, and those pieces fit together, but I still didn't have the first clue what kind of picture they made up. Then I mentally shook the pieces, and two of them shifted, fitting together to form a different pattern. I suddenly had a hypothesis that made some sense.

I knew that military procurement, particularly anything involving cutting-edge systems, is a megamillion-nuyen business. If Yamatetsu could get its booster drek picked up by the UCAS army, what would their profit picture look like? Pretty fragging good, I expected. And any corp worthy of the name would do whatever it took to land that kind of contract. Up to and definitely including corruption, such as kickbacks of some serious nuyen to someone in the evaluation and procurement infrastructure. Someone like, say, William Sutcliffe. How sensitive would *either* party—Yamatetsu or Sutcliffe—be if they found out that Sutcliffe's line had been tapped and that Lone Star might have a record of them discussing this diversion of funds? Pretty fragging sensitive. Sensitive enough to geek the person washing the tap—Lolly—and anyone else with the slightest chance of finding out the dirt? To quote Pud the Prowler, fragging A.

I grinned. It hung together, and it answered a lot of questions. Maybe the connection with Crashcart and the possible tie-in to 2XS weren't relevant at all. Like, one hand doesn't know what the other hand's doing? Possible. The Lolly-Sutcliffe angle might involve Yamatetsu's ISP division, while the Crashcart-Waters-2XS angle involved Crashcart Medical Services Corporation, and never the twain shall meet.

And what about the apparent contract out on Patrick Bambra? I focused again on the screen, which showed me a very slotted-off Buddy. "What's the connection with the Universal Brotherhood?" I asked her.

"Sutcliffe's a member," she said. "Joined three years back. Now he does volunteer work for them. Helps manage their counselors." She fixed me with a killer glare. "That's it," she declared. "Slot and clear."

"Thanks, Buddy," I said again as I slotted my credstick and transferred credit. A *lot* of credit. "I really appreciate it." But there was nobody there to hear my last sentence. Buddy had broken the connection the moment the transaction was complete, and I was left thanking a blank screen.

I sat back. My glance fell on an almost-full bottle of synthahol I'd picked up the day before. What the frag? I deserved a drink, and maybe it would help turbocharge the old brain cells. I poured a decent slug of indecent pseudo-whiskey, and settled back on the bed to cogitate.

The closer I examined my hypothesis, looking for holes, the stronger it seemed to hang together. The corruption-kickback aspect and the under-the-counter relationship between Sutcliffe and Yamatetsu *felt* right; I'd lay money on having that part of it pegged. As to that being the reason for Lolly's death, I still wasn't 100 percent convinced, but anything else seemed too coincidental. Call that 95 percent. The link between Crashcart and 2XS? The Waters case implied it strongly, but didn't prove it. Call that one 80 percent. And assign nominal 70 percent odds of *no* links between Sutcliffe and Crashcart.

What about Patrick? Maybe Sutcliffe was getting twitchy, and had overreacted when Patrick started nosing around. Patrick knew nothing and cared less about Yamatetsu and the UCAS military, but Sutcliffe might not believe it. I wasn't confident at all about that part: call it 30-percent confidence.

Theresa and the deceased Fitz? No data. Probably an

indirect link, in that Pud's description of Theresa's symptoms sounded uncomfortably like 2XS addiction. (Frag Theresa for becoming a chiphead.) No firm link at all with Fitz's death. That was okay: coincidences do happen, and only a paranoid believes everything's connected to everything else.

Satisfied, I took a good swallow of my whiskey. I had it chipped.

Except for one little, niggling idea, the one that flashed into mind when Buddy was describing booster technology. SPISES didn't sound too unlike 2XS, *neh?* Of course, even if that was true, it didn't necessarily mean anything. "Convergent evolution" happens with technology as well as with life forms, and damaging developments frequently spin off from beneficial discoveries. But it nagged at me, and I had to confirm or deny it.

That meant Bent, of course. I felt guilty for a moment about how much of his time I was burning, but then I remembered the dinner I owed him. He'd even the ledger, I was sure of that.

"Hoi, Bent," I said as his face appeared on the screen. "Long time."

"All of eight hours," he chuckled. "What's buzzing?"

I'd called Bent at the lab, but I saw from the out-of-focus background that he was at home. Must have forwarded his calls from one phone to the other. Obviously he didn't want to miss out on anything interesting. "I won't take up too many cycles," I promised, "but this may be important. Have you ever heard of SPISES?"

He blinked, then shook his head. "No bells," he said.

"How about booster technology?"

"In what context?"

"Military," I said. "Jazzing physical reactions, that kind of drek."

He started to shake his head again, then hesitated. "What does SPISES stand for?"

I racked my brain to remember. "Sympathetic-Para-something Something-renal Excitation System," I burbled. "Okay, so I'm no expert," I threw in when Bent smirked.

"No drek, but *now* we've got bells," he said. "I've read something about it in medical journals, but I don't know many of the details. The way I scan it, SPISES is, theoretically, the next logical development after boosted reflexes." His eyes half-closed and his voice became less animated, almost monotone, as he switched into lecture mode. I struggled to stay with him.

"With standard boosted reflexes, you've got to drop tiny little devices called 'initiators' right into the cortex of the adrenal glands—the suprarenals—and other glands. When you want to kick into overdrive, a neuro-electrical interface picks up the appropriate neural activity—the 'go-code,' as it were—and triggers control chips implanted in the brain, which then activate the initiators. Your suprarenals pour out adrenalin, and you get jazzed. Follow me?" I nodded slowly. "Installing standard 'wired' or boosted reflexes is an enormously invasive procedure," he continued, "as you can imagine. Interface, control chips, and initiators, plus all the support technology, 'glue chips,' and wiring to get them to hang together. It's even more invasive than skillwires or even muscle replacement—and that's saying a lot. Are you still with me?"

I nodded again. "And SPISES booster-technology is less invasive, right?" I ventured.

He smiled broadly. "Right. Orders of magnitude less, in theory. The way I scan it, this is how it works. When a non-wired person needs a jolt of adrenalin—say when he's scared or angry—the nervous system sends an activation impulse to the suprarenals." He hesitated. "I'm really simplifying here, maybe too much."

"I'm not going to have to install the drek," I told him with a grin. "Simplify it, use the Easter Bunny as an analogy if you have to, just so I know what this stuff does. Okay?"

Bent laughed out loud. "No Easter Bunny, but I'm giving you the real high-level-of-abstraction overview here." He paused, recalling his train of thought. "Anyway, the guys experimenting with second-generation booster technology asked, why do we have to put in our own wiring and initiators, when the body's got its own? In other words, the brain and the nerves. All they had to do, they figured, was give the subject conscious control of the neural mechanism the body already uses to dispense adrenalin and even some neurochemical substances. Theoretically, you could hook the little booster box into a subject's datajack. When the guy wants a jolt of warp-speed, he thinks the mental command. The booster box picks up the command, then sends a jolt to the right part of the brain to trigger a massive signal to the adrenals. If you've already got the datajack, getting boosted is just a matter of jacking in the box. Or, if you've got a cyberlimb or eye or anything, you just hook the booster circuitry into the cyberware, and use the neural interface that's already in place. And—again theoretically—the boost is completely natural because it uses the body's own mechanisms to deliver it.''

"Sounds incredible," I said. "Why isn't it on the streets?"

Bent looked thoughtful. "It's never that simple. Remember your analogy about 2XS? Like goosing your car's engine from zero revs to red line in a split-second? That's what booster technology does. According to the literature, nobody's ever tried it on humans or metahumans. Just dogs, and they got a lot of *really* fast, *really* mean dogs who died *really* soon. I think a lot of people believe they'll never get it safe, and it's a dead-end technology."

I thought that over for a few moments, then said, "What would you say if I told you somebody out there is marketing it?"

"Booster technology?" I nodded. "I'd say somebody's going to end up with a lot of really fast, really dead clients," Bent said, "unless someone else has made a major breakthrough but hasn't yet published in the literature."

He leaned forward. "Who's marketing," he said, "and who's buying?"

"Yamatetsu Corporation's selling."

He shook his head. "Never heard of them. And the client?"

"Potentially, the UCAS military."

"I suppose that makes a horrible kind of sense," he said slowly. "How did you stumble onto this, Dirk?"

"I honestly think you're better off not knowing," I told him. He accepted that with a nod. "Now I've got one more question for you. Is there any similarity at all between this, what did you call it, second-generation booster technology and 2XS?"

Bent was silent for a moment. "Sometimes I despair

of the scientific mindset," he said finally. "We learn to pigeonhole things, and because of that we miss connections and correlations that are obvious to other people." He looked me square in the eyes. "In answer to your question, yes: the two technologies could be very much alike. *Could* be," he stressed again. "The effects are very similar. Until now, it hadn't occurred to me just how similar. The actual *technologies* might be light years apart, you understand."

I nodded. "I understand," I told him.

He paused again, then asked very quietly, "What have you been working on, Dirk?"

I hesitated. "Look, Bent, I don't think you'd better phone me anymore, chummer. When I'm out the other end of this, I'll get back in touch with you. Do you understand what I'm saying?"

His smile vanished instantly. He nodded slowly. "I understand. Don't worry. I can take care of myself." He paused. "But if things get really hairy, call me, no matter what, okay? You can't slay all the dragons yourself, *neh?*"

"Thanks, Bent. I'll talk to you soon."

"Keep your head down. Later, chummer."

I broke the connection and sat back. I felt very much alone. If I was right about Yamatetsu's business arrangement with Sutcliffe, I was in a game with some very big players. Frag, they don't get much bigger than a major multinational and the slotting UCAS military complex. If our mysterious and murderous X was a member of either group, I was in deep drek.

The telecom beeped again, and I thumbed the Receive key. I expected it to be Bent, back with something he'd forgotten, and was pleasantly surprised to see Jocasta instead. "Hoi," she said. "I thought I'd check in and see if you'd found out anything."

I hesitated, debating. My first reaction was to brush her off, much as I'd done with Bent, and for the same reasons. But she was already involved, in as deep as me, simply because X had targeted her for removal as well. Given that, wouldn't I be doing her a disservice by withholding important information? I was forced to answer yes. (A wave of relief washed over me as I reached this conclusion. It was selfish and unworthy, but I was feeling

very alone and very overwhelmed, and I desperately
wanted to talk to *somebody*.)

She'd sat silently, watching me, as I went through the
brief moment of soul-searching. Now it almost looked
like concern in her eyes as she asked, "What is it?"

"The game just got a lot bigger," I began, then went
on to tell her what I'd learned about Sutcliffe's position
with the military, Yamatetsu's booster technology and its
ownership of Crashcart, the possible similarities between
SPISES and 2XS . . . Everything, no punches pulled. I
even told her about my sister's disappearance. And I finished off with my suspicions about why Lolly had been
killed.

I have to admit it, it felt good. I'd always heard about
the power of catharsis, but I guess I'd never really tried
it. The weight was still on my shoulders, the tension still
in my chest, but now it seemed a little more bearable.

Jocasta was silent awhile after I finished, obviously
running it through her own mind. "Thanks for telling
me about your sister," she said quietly. "I appreciate
your honesty, and I'm sorry." She paused again. "Maybe
the troll took her to another clinic. Or maybe she transferred herself for some reason. She could be lying in a
bed right now waiting for you to get in touch. Have you
checked elsewhere? Maybe it's all something innocent."

I nodded. "You could be right."

Her voice and expression had softened while we'd been
talking about Theresa, but now her familiar businesslike
mien returned. "You think the connection between 2XS
and this booster drek is significant, don't you?" she
asked.

"It feels that way, but I still don't have any evidence."

"Trust your gut," she said, then hesitated again. "You
realize you're implying that Yamatetsu's putting 2XS on
the street."

"It makes sense," I said, a little defensively. "Assuming it *is* the same technology, what corp's going to turn
away from another profit center?"

She shook her head. "I don't buy that. It's too much
of a risk. There's got to be some other reason."

"What?" I challenged.

"Your doctor friend"—I'd disguised Bent's identify, at
least to that degree—"said there were no records of any-

one testing booster tech on humans, right?'' I nodded. ''But Yamatetsu had to run human tests before they could even consider selling it to the army.''

I could see where she was leading. ''You're saying they're using 2XS as a field test for SPISES?''

''Could be.''

I grunted. It made a kind of sense, but still didn't ring totally true for some reason. Like part of my brain was saying, ''Close but no banana.'' ''We're missing something,'' I mumbled.

''But what?''

''I wish I knew.''

''And how does Crashcart tie into all this?''

''A Crashcart clinic plugged 2XS circuitry into Daniel Waters.''

''Your friend *thinks*,'' Jocasta amended.

I jumped to Bent's defense. ''The symptoms are the same, the circuitry's similar.''

''Similar,'' she stressed, ''not identical. If you're right about the 2XS-SPISES connection, maybe they meant to put a booster into him and it fragged up.''

''Why would they do that?'' I demanded.

''Competitive advantage, maybe? God knows they're in a major marketing war with DocWagon.'' She paused. ''Or, more likely, it's another case of putting beta-test SPISES on the street for field testing.'' Her voice and face became more animated as she followed that through to its conclusion. ''Maybe that's why Yamatetsu created Crashcart in the first place . . . As a way of disseminating SPISES . . .''

''And of evaluating its effectiveness,'' I said. ''They install it in someone who gets trashed, then bring him back for follow-up exams to see how the tech's working.''

''That's why they're gunning so hard for DocWagon,'' Jocasta said. ''If they can drive DocWagon out of business, there's less risk of anyone finding out what they've been doing.''

For a few moments I'd been carried along by Jocasta's enthusiasm. But suddenly the rush totally evaporated. The logical structure we'd built just didn't hang together. Again, I had the inescapable feeling we were missing something crucial. We had most of the pieces of the jig-saw puzzle, and we'd put them together to form a picture. But it felt like we'd hosed it by forcing a couple of pieces into spots where they just didn't fit. I shook my head.

"What?" Jocasta demanded.

"I don't buy it," I told her simply.

"Why not?"

"You said trust my gut," I reminded her. "It doesn't feel right."

"Why not?" she insisted.

"I just don't buy it." I looked at her steadily. "Do you?"

She looked ready to shoot back some angry retort, then suddenly seemed to deflate. She smiled, embarrassed. "Not really," she said quietly. "I feel . . . I feel *overwhelmed*. The scope of this, it's just too big. It seems like the only logical thing to do is jump into a hole and pull the hole in after me. You know what I mean? But you're probably used to this."

"Save me space in your hole," I said.

She laughed at that. "Maybe." She sobered again. "What are you going to do now?"

"See if I can find the missing pieces. But first try and get a line on my sister."

"Let me know how that goes," she said. "Call me at this number." An LTG number appeared on-screen. Jocasta smiled. "I hope you find her."

"Thanks."

She cut the connection before I could say anything else.

14

Hospitals in the sprawl are very careful about patient confidentiality and protecting their patients from scam artists or worse. But this caution has to be balanced with some accessibility, some means by which worried relatives and friends can find out if old Uncle Ted is lying critically injured in intensive care or if he simply ran off with that waitress he'd been eyeing.

Improved communication technology has managed to

solve that problem, while creating many others. All registered hospitals and the vast majority of private clinics now offer an LTG number giving access to a kind of limited bulletin-board system. Call in on your telecom and transmit the name—the true and complete name—of the person you're interested in. The bulletin-board system will tell you whether said person is currently registered at the clinic or hospital, but only a yes or no answer, no further information available. Then you've got the option of leaving your own name, relationship to the patient, contact information, and any message. From there on it's up to the hospital staff and/or the patient to decide whether to get in touch with you. It makes it simple for the hospital to screen out the majority of scam artists, while providing a quick and efficient way to track down a missing person.

Of course, as the Seattle Tourist Board is proud to point out, there are fifty-four hospitals and clinics in the sprawl. Checking them all out would take a lot of time.

If I did it manually, that is. Let us give thanks once more to modern technology. It was a job of maybe two minutes to whip up a simple exec program to instruct the telecom to phone all the possibilities, submit the name Theresa Mary Montgomery, and notify me of any hits. I could even download the exec to my telecom back in Auburn and have *it* run the program, leaving my phone in Purity free for other calls. I figured it would take maybe half an hour for the program to run through the whole list.

While it was doing its electronic thing, I called up Naomi Takahashi. At home, this time, since it was early evening by now.

She picked up almost at once. As usual, I had my video pickup turned off. "Yes?" she said.

"Yeah," I grunted, "I, uh, I gotta call you want an exterminator. Gotta bug problem, huh?"

Naomi smiled. "No bugs here, *omae,*" she laughed. "I'm very careful about that."

I cut in the video. "You can never be too careful," I told her. "How's it going, girl?"

"Busy. I'm carrying extra load because people are being diverted to track some deviant called Derek Montgomery."

That sobered me somewhat—about as much as a bucket of ice water. "They're taking it that seriously, are they?"

"And then some," Naomi confirmed. "I don't know exactly why. You must be mixed up in something pretty heavy."

She hadn't asked the question, not right out, but I answered it anyway. "I am, Naomi, but I can't tell you about it."

She nodded. "Do you need any support from my end?" she asked.

"Two things," I told her. "First, promise me you'll be real careful, okay? No exposure, no risk. If you have to stick out your neck one millimeter, I can do without it. Do you understand?" I might have been laying it on a little thick, but I was still very scared.

Naomi took it in stride. "No strain, chummer, just tell me what it is. I know how to cover myself."

"I want whatever you can get me on a corp called Yamatetsu. Particularly their operations in Seattle, and particularly anything that's raised flags at the Star."

"Yametetsu, got it. Null perspiration. What's the second thing?"

I hesitated. The idea had come to me as I was placing the call. And in a way it seemed to make sense. The question was, did I have the balls to go through with it?

"Dirk?" she prompted.

I took a deep breath. "Where can I buy an 2XS chip?" I asked.

Maybe I live a sheltered life, but I'd never made a chip deal before. The only idea I had of how it worked came from cheap trideo shows. You know the kind I mean— shady neighborhoods and rat-infested chip-houses, gun-toting dealers who look like the scum of the earth and who'd be as happy to blow you away as look at you.

Probably there are places like that. But when I finally managed to persuade Naomi I was serious, she directed me to a place about as far from my mental image as you could get. No run-down chip-house in some squatter neighborhood. The address was—believe it, chip-truth— a Trideo Depot store in a shopping mall. A fragging mall! What *is* the world etcetera?

As soon as I was off the line with Naomi, I checked

the search program. It had completed the list and terminated, with no hits. In other words, Theresa Montgomery hadn't been officially admitted to any healthcare provider in the Greater Seattle area. Frag it.

Of course, the key was "officially." Every system has back doors. It was conceivable that Theresa had been admitted somewhere *un*officially, or under another name. Neither of which I was equipped to explore at the moment. Much as it hurt to do so, I had to put the issue on the back burner. Lacking the least idea of how to proceed further in Theresa's direction, the best thing seemed to be getting on with something else and hoping for a flash of inspiration.

The Trideo Depot was in the Overlake Mall, down near the Touristville region of Redmond. Not too bad as Redmond facilities go: most windows and doors still intact, few bullet holes in the walls, and a vacancy rate of under 50 percent. The Depot was a typical trideo-rental facility. There were two terminals—"industrially hardened," of course—running directory search software, and a half-dozen screens showing selected scenes from the top-renting chips. For a few moments I was distracted by a wall-sized array alternating between clips from *Neil the Ork Barbarian XIV* (dialogue sample: "Die, scum-sucker!") and *Behind You All the Way* (dialogue sample: "Oh, oh *yes* . . . "), but shook myself free of the trideo spell and made my way to the counter.

On duty was a guy about my own age, whose job was probably dealing with unreasonable requests that the directory terminals couldn't handle. He looked clean-cut—almost abnormally so, considering the locale—and smiled politely as I approached. "Anything I can help you with?" he asked.

"Yeah, uh, maybe," I said uncomfortably. I recalled the key phrases Naomi had mentioned. "I, uh, I'm looking for a new chip. Something really hot, you know?"

His polite expression didn't change. He just handed me a hard-copy list about half a page long. "These are our new titles," he said. "See anything that appeals to you?"

I didn't even look at the listing. "Not really," I told him. "I guess I'm looking for something . . . heavier. Something . . . excessive?"

He took back the listing. "I'm afraid I don't know what you mean," he said mildly.

I knew what was going on, of course. He didn't know who I was; I could be a Lone Star undercover cop. So of course he wasn't going to volunteer information. If I was legitimate, I'd ask for what I wanted. If I was a narc, I couldn't because that would be entrapment. Of course, *I* didn't know *him,* and *he* could be a narc. I wasn't sure, but I assumed trying to *buy* 2XS was also a crime. I hesitated, then decided I'd take the risk.

I leaned forward so that our faces were just centimeters apart. "Look," I told him, "I want 2XS, and I'm tired of slotting around." I slipped a certified credstick across the counter. "Do you want my business or not?"

Still his expression didn't change, but the credstick vanished. He moved back to a more normal distance, and said, "We aim to please. Just wait here." He vanished into the back.

I looked around the empty store nervously, regretting I'd ever come up with this fool idea. He was back quickly, with a garishly colored chip box. He handed it to me and said, "I think this will satisfy."

I glanced down at the box. The chip's title was apparently *Space for Rent,* and the cover picture made it abundantly and anatomically clear exactly what space was being referred to. The box appeared professionally shrink-wrapped. I looked up again and raised an eyebrow. If I'd paid five hundred nuyen—the going price, according to Naomi—and received nothing more than a hard-core porn chip, I'd definitely be back to speak to the salesclerk. He nodded almost imperceptibly, and I decided not to press the issue now. I thanked him and left.

What the frag was I doing? According to Bent, 2XS was a killer mind-bender that could only be used through a datajack. I had neither death wish nor datajack. So what did I think I was up to?

I suppose it was a perverted version of the old know-your-enemy rationale. Partially, at least. Whatever was going down, 2XS seemed to be at the heart of it, and maybe knowing exactly what the chip did would give me some insight into events.

I also had to know what it was that my kid sister had

been feeding into her brain. Why? Morbid curiosity, a desire to understand, again the possibility of insight. Take your pick. Those reasons made up the acceptable party line, but maybe there was another reason. The need to prove that I could handle something that had slotted up my sister? Could I really be that petty? I forced that uncomfortable possibility from my mind.

That was the why, but what about the how? The question had a nice one-word answer: Buddy.

I didn't call ahead this time—I just showed up. For one thing, I wanted to do it *now,* while I had my courage up. The other thing was that if Buddy decided not to let me in, I'd have an excuse to bag out. I gave my name to the guard at the door, and suffered seriously mixed feelings as he nodded me through.

I rode the elevator to the fortieth floor, walked down the hall and pounded on Buddy's door. Then I shifted uncomfortably for about a minute, trying to decide whether to knock again, wait longer, or just bug out. I was leaning more and more toward option three when the multiple locks snapped free and the door swung open.

Buddy was apparently going through a particularly quiet phase of her cycle. The rhythm synthesizer was still churning out its frenetic licks, but the volume was way down—somewhere just below the sound-pressure level of an idling Harley. She stood in the doorway, hands on her hips, and looked me up and down, the movements of her head quick and bird-like. Then she flashed a momentary smile and stepped back to let me in. "Hoi, Dirk," she said, for once actually giving me enough time to step inside before slamming the door behind me.

"Hoi, Buddy." I intended to go right into my spiel, but my dry mouth seemed to seize up on me.

She examined me again. "You're wound," she remarked. "Wound tight."

If my level of stress was such that even Buddy could sense it, I was *definitely* wound tight. "I need your help, Buddy," I told her.

She shot me another smile. "I figured. Come through." I followed her into the living room, watched in surprise as she pulled a remote from the folds of her ballistic-cloth sarong and cut back the percussion effects by a few decibels. Then she sank down into full lotus, and stared up at me. "What?"

I looked around, saw that the inductance headset still seemed to be connected to her cyberdeck. Part of my brain cursed: another excuse shot to hell. I pulled out the 2XS chip—I'd turfed the garish packaging on the way over—and held it out to her. "It's like a simsense chip," I said. In my nervousness, I found myself slipping into her own curt speech pattern. "I want to slot it."

She looked at the chip but didn't take it. "Why?"

I didn't want to get into that. I'd asked myself the question too many times already. "I want to use the headset. Can you do it?"

"Simsense, sure." She stared into my eyes. "It's more than simsense, isn't it? BTL?"

"More than BTL," I told her. "It's important, Buddy. Can you do it?"

"*Course* I can do it."

"Will you?"

She thought about it a long time. Two, maybe three seconds. Then she shrugged and pointed to the chair. "Sit down."

I sat. She took the chip, turned it over and over in her fingers. Then she met my gaze again. "More than BTL?"

I nodded, swallowing a fist-sized lump that had inexplicably lodged itself in my throat. "I want to put some conditions on this," I said. "I want you to run this for"—I hesitated—"for one minute. Sixty seconds only. Then I want you to cut it off. And I want you to destroy the chip. Destroy it. Got me?"

She looked down at the chip, then back into my eyes. "You're scared of this," she said. Damn fragging right I was scared of it. "It's going to slot you up?"

"I don't know," I said honestly.

"*Thirty* seconds," she corrected. She tapped her Excalibur with a scrawny knuckle. "I'll watch you."

"Don't ride along, Buddy," I warned her, not even knowing if that was possible.

"You kidding?" she snorted. "Don't want to frag *my* brain. I'll watch your brain waves." And then she busied herself with the connections between the crown-of-thorns headset and her cyberdeck.

I thought about that. I didn't have the first idea about

the average deck's standard equipment, but if Buddy had an electroencephalogram or some other thing that monitored brainwaves built into her cyberdeck I'd feel a lot more comfortable. I took off my duster, put it—and my holstered Manhunter—well out of reach. Then I tried to find a comfortable position on the hard chair.

Buddy's adjustments were quick. Much too soon she was settling the inductance headset onto my cranium. "Buddy . . ." I began.

"I'll watch you." Her words were brusque, but I thought I heard something like real concern in her voice. Or was I just imagining it? She snugged down the last strap, sank back into lotus, and settled her Excalibur across her knees. I watched as she seated the chip into one of the deck's sockets. She looked up at me and smiled. "Show time," she said quietly.

I think I started to say something, to tell her I'd changed my mind. But before I could utter the first syllable, her skeletal finger hit a key . . .

I stand on the hill, looking down over the battle plain. My helmet and my armor catch the golden light of the rising sun, and the many encrusted gems throw back spears of brilliance. I wear a king's ransom, but it is fit and it is meet that I do so. My position as king is mine through right of birth, but reinforced through achievement. No man has yet to best me in single combat, though some two score have tried. I heft my axe, feel its comfortable weight in my hands, run a callused thumb over the ritual notches in the shaft. I have taken life, I will do so again. Such is my right, my honor, and my responsibility.

I see movement on the plains below. It is the foe. The prey. Soon we will descend this hill, fall upon them like wolves upon sheep. Soon my body will tremble with the battle rage, my ears sing with the song of warfare. Soon my axe will taste blood. Soon will victory come to me once more. Another victory added to all that have gone before. Another verse in the saga that will praise me as the greatest warrior of this or any age.

The disk of the sun clears the horizon. A bow-shot distant behind me, I hear the sounds of my army girding themselves for battle. The smoke of the cookfires is pungent-sweet in my nostrils; the beat of sword against shield, the clarion call of the trumpets ring in my ears. My heart swells, ready to burst, with the joy of the impending fight. I wonder momentarily how it would feel to be other than I am, to feel fragile, to feel mortal. Subject to fears and to the vagaries of chance. I cannot conceive of it. And why should I even try? I am as I am, and I would have it no other way. I turn, to rejoin my followers.

A sound from the trees to my right. I spin, my axe comes up. Eight of the foe burst from the thicket, swords gleaming in the morning light, howling their battlecries. They sought to ambush me, to foully slay me here. But my foes know not who they face, to have sent only eight.

I charge to meet them. My axe keens as it swings, seemingly eager to hew, to slay. I bellow my joy to the heavens, and my voice is a terrible cry to rival the massed trumpets. The axe bites home. Hot blood showers over me . . .

I was lying on the floor. Somewhere.

Buddy's apartment, I thought. I rolled over. A figure stood above me, a dead woman wrapped in a burial shroud. I reached for my axe.

No! No axe. Who was I? *What* was I?

"Dirk?" the dead woman asked.

Yes, Dirk. Derek Montgomery, born and raised in Seattle. Mortal, vulnerable. For a moment I wanted to kill her, peel the skin of that oh-so-concerned face from the bones of her skull. How the frag could she have taken from me what I had? What I was? Where was my axe?

My . . . my what? The vision of the axe, the armor, faded from my mind, became the memory of a dream, or the memory of a memory. It had no intensity, none of the passion that just moments ago had flooded through me.

"Dirk?" Buddy said again. Yes, Buddy. I knew her. I knew me, I knew where I was. And then the sense of loss washed over me like an ocean wave. I could have howled. I could have wept. My eyes flicked to the cyberdeck resting on the floor. Something glittered. The chip was still in its socket. I tried to reach for the deck, but my muscles wouldn't obey.

Buddy saw what I was trying to do. With a speed that belied her cadaverous appearance, she bent and snatched the chip from its socket. Threw it to the floor. Brought her heel down on it, and it shattered into myriad fragments.

And then I howled, and the darkness washed over and consumed me.

I came back to myself, and I knew who "myself" was . . . is . . . whatever. I was still lying on the floor. I opened my eyes.

No more than a couple of moments could have passed. Buddy crouched beside me, her cool hand on my cheek. I looked up into her face, saw the fear and the concern. "Dirk?" she said once more. And from the tone of her voice I knew how she intended the question.

"Yes," I told her. "Yes, Dirk." I ran a quick inventory of my feelings, a kind of mental self-test. There was still sadness and black depression in my heart, but overlaying it was a terrible fear. I forced myself to sit up, looked down at the floor. Yes, there were the fragments of the chip. It really was destroyed; she really had crushed it. I found that more reassuring than I'd have believed possible.

"You okay?" she asked.

I thought about it for a moment. "I am now," I replied. I ran a hand through my hair, rubbed my eyes. Tried to wipe away what remained of that memory. "What happened?"

"I watched your cerebral activity," she said. "It went"—she searched for words, obviously deeply disturbed—"it *changed*. Abnormal. Looked like a psychotic episode. Delusions, more than delusions. I jacked you out." She pointed to the optical lead attached to the crown-of-thorns I still wore on my head. The jack lay on the floor, pulled free from the cyberdeck. She fixed me with her bright eyes. "What did you experience?"

I tried to remember. But the memory was too painful— or, more correctly, the knowledge that that's all it would remain—so I tried instead to forget. "Another world," I told her.

"What was that chip?" She stirred the crystalline fragments with her toe.

"They call it 2XS."

"More than BTL?"

I nodded. "How long was it running?"

She shrugged. "Ten, twenty seconds."

Subjective time had seemed much longer than that. I'd already inventoried my emotions. Now I tried to feel my body, check out *its* status.

I was bone-fragging tired, like I'd run a marathon, played a game of Urban Brawl, and then gone best-of-three-falls with Neil the Ork Barbarian. I settled two fingers on the opposite wrist—difficult, the way both my hands were shaking—and timed ten seconds on my watch while counting my pulse. I lost count at about thirty-five beats, and it was still short of ten seconds. I recalled Bent's comments on how debilitating 2XS was to the body, and decided he'd underestimated by a few orders of magnitude.

Then a terrible thought struck me. "Buddy," I asked, "how efficient is this thing?" I pulled the inductance rig from my head.

She shook her head. "Not," she answered simply. "Twenty or thirty percent. Maybe."

That seemed to make the shivering worse. "So," I said, trying in vain to keep my voice calm, "if you run something straight through a datajack it's going to seem more intense?"

"Infinitely," she said.

Oh, frag. Theresa . . .

15

On the drive home, the crushing sense of depression, of devastating loss, kept hitting me with an impact so fierce it made me gasp. The episodes came without warning and when least expected. Just when I thought I'd forced the 2XS experience from my mind and that I was totally back to normal, it would all come rushing back. The memory of knowing my destiny was absolutely under the control of my own indomitable will, knowing that whatever I wished to do was right and just simply because I wished it. And, worse, the realization that I would never feel that almost-godlike certainty and power again. Never again.

Each time it struck, my hands quivered so hard that I almost lost control of the car—I *would* have lost control if not for Quincy's modified piloting circuits. Also fleeting, flitting around the edges of my mind the question, So what if I lost control? Now that I'd lost forever that mighty warrior in his gem-encrusted armor, what matter if I died? Death would be the only sure way to erase the memory of that loss . . .

Like most people, I've thought about suicide, but merely as a kind of intellectual exercise. Always in my head, never in my heart, and I'd always dismissed it out of hand as the last resort of an utter coward. But now, during the drive back to Purity, suicide was not a thought, but an option I considered deep in my heart. And that scared me profoundly.

What if Buddy *hadn't* destroyed the 2XS chip? I wondered. What if I had it in my hand now, knowing that all I needed to recapture those awesome sensations was to slot the chip into a player and plug the connection into my datajack (presuming I had one)? The answer was as simple as it was chilling. I'd be running that chip again right now. Even knowing that it was fragging up my brain waves, giving me psychotic delusions, killing me by millimeters. Of *course* I'd be running it, if only to escape the depressive episodes. Bent had been oh so right that once you got a touch of 2XS you'd never want anything else. Frag, you don't even want real life.

And it was that horror my baby sister had taken into her life—or so I assumed. She'd been a chiphead years ago so she had that tendency toward electronic escapism—and she had the datajack. Even if she'd slotted only a single 2XS chip, as an experiment, perhaps, she'd be well and truly hooked, addicted and habituated, forever. How much worse would be the depressive aftereffects for someone who'd been using the chips for days or weeks? How much greater the attraction of suicide?

That was one possible explanation for Theresa's disappearance, and one I couldn't discount, no matter how painful the thought. I reviewed my conversation with the good Dr. Dempsey from the Brotherhood clinic, trying to remember her exact words. She'd said that nobody had *been admitted* last night. That meant officially. Now, would the head of the clinic be working the admitting desk? Hardly. She'd be in the wards or the operating room or whatever they had there, while the admitting desk was being run by lower-level drones.

I was seeing another scenario. Fitz takes Theresa into the clinic's lobby, lifts the name-tag souvenir, and hits the road so as not to get officially involved. Theresa, suffering from 2XS overload and postchip depression, wanders out into the streets, maybe geeks herself or gets geeked, or just crashes in an alley. The drone on the admitting desk hasn't filled out any of the appropriate forms, so Theresa hasn't been officially admitted. Would the drone report such an occurrence to Dr. Dempsey? Probably not. That was one way of reconciling both Dempsey's and Pud's stories. If it had happened that way, as well it might, I'd have to broaden the parameters of my search.

By the time I reached my doss, the frequency of the depressive episodes had decreased, and their impact had abated drastically. Thanks to whatever gods there be. Shagged to the bone, I tossed my duster onto a chair. The bed looked warm and enticing, but I had something to do before I could sleep. (Also, I had to admit, the thought of sleep—and dreams—terrified me at the moment.) I checked my watch—just past twenty-three hundred hours—sat down at the telecom and keyed Naomi's home number.

As expected, I got her voice-mail system, please-leave-your-message-after-the-fragging-beep. So I left my message. "Naomi," I told her recorded image, "I need something else, and please make this higher priority than"—I hesitated, just in case Naomi was wrong about having a clean line—"the other issue we discussed. My sister's gone missing, Naomi. I think she did a bad chip-trip. Crashed and burned. Can you check the files to see if she's turned up? MVA records, crime victims. Hell, you know the drill. She's SINless, which won't help. First name's Theresa Mary. Call me soonest, okay? Thanks much, *omae*. I owe you, big time."

I killed the phone line, programmed a wake-up alarm

for nine the next morning and hit the sack. Though I needed sleep bad, it steadfastly refused to come as I tossed and turned. Part of me was glad; I was still scared of the dreams I might have. I decided I may as well put the time to good use, and mentally reviewed any options I might have missed, any other ways to track Theresa. Magic, maybe?

I'm mundane, and the circles I move in are almost exclusively so. It's not that I'm a magophobe like some people I've met. It's just the way it's worked out. The main disadvantage to this is that I tend to think in mundane terms. It's not that I forget about magic—impossible to do in the Sixth World—but it's rarely in the forefront of my mind. When a problem crops up, I always approach it from a mundane mindset and come up with mundane ways to solve it, thinking of the magic option only when nothing else has worked—if then.

So, could a mage or shaman track Theresa for me? Theoretically, yes, but from what I know of the magic involved, he or she would need something that had been part of Theresa—a lock of hair, a skin sample, some blood, or maybe something that had been important to her emotionally. Needless to say, I was fresh out of such items. If she'd been hanging with the Night Prowlers, maybe they'd have something that might serve. But that would involve enlisting the cooperation of at least one Prowler. Considering they'd tried to geek me just hours before, that didn't seem overly likely. How about Pud? Not a chance, I thought. He'd do me no favors on top of the one he already had done by letting me live.

Magic seemed to be a dead end, at least based on my limited knowledge. I switched my focus back to mundane lines of inquiry, and that was when sleep engulfed me like a black wave and I went bye-bye.

I woke to the insistent beeping of the telecom. I checked the time display. Nine o'clock.

I shook my head to clear out the cobwebs. The dreams hadn't been as bad as I'd expected, but they'd certainly been no picnic. Fortunately, they were fading fast in the gray morning light leaking through the partially polarized windows. I got up and nuked up a full pot of soykaf, drank my first cup black and as hot as I could take it to shock me into full wakefulness.

What to do today? I had the urge to call Naomi, to ask her if she'd got a line on Theresa. Or to badger her, I suppose. That was neither reasonable nor fair, of course. Assuming she was on the same shift, she'd have started work at oh-eight-thirty, meaning she'd have risen about an hour earlier. That was probably when she'd received my message about tracking Theresa. No matter how good Naomi was, chances were she hadn't made much significant progress, particularly since she'd have to conceal her unofficial research. No, I had to give her more time, no matter how hard it was to wait.

What else? Not much. I could try and get a line on Yamatetsu, but Naomi was a lot more skilled and better-equipped than I was. I could pound the pavement in and around Puyallup, looking for some kind of clue to Theresa's whereabouts. But that was a low-odds proposition at best. The odds were much better that all I'd find would be a militant Night Prowler just itching to geek me in the street.

I debated whether to stop by the Puyallup Universal Brotherhood chapterhouse for a conversation with the clinic admitting-drone, but discarded it. The person on duty at nine in the morning wouldn't be the same one who'd manned the desk a couple of hours past midnight. Dead end there.

But I needed to do *something*. No, I amended quickly, I needed to talk to someone. I retrieved the number Jocasta had given me and placed the call.

The call was picked up almost immediately, but the screen stayed blank. "Yes?" It was Jocasta's voice.

"It's me," I told the empty screen.

On came the video, and Jocasta appeared. She was wearing a terry cloth robe, and her hair was a little disheveled. I had to grin. This was the first time I'd seen her when not the perfectly groomed corporate. And, to be honest, I thought she looked a lot better this way. More vulnerable and more human. I kicked in my own video.

"Morning," I said.

She looked down at her robe, plucked at the lapel, a

little embarrassed. "Yes, it is." Then she looked back into my eyes. "Any word on your sister?" she asked.

I was surprised—and warmed—that this was her first question. "Nothing good," I said, then gave her a brief rundown of my busy day yesterday. The only thing I left out was my run-in with the Prowlers.

When I was finished, she looked at me in shock. "That 2XS sounds like serious drek," she said. She shook her head, and seemed to shudder. "I wouldn't have had the guts to try it." I shrugged. "I can understand why you're so worried about your sister, though," she went on. "What else are you doing to track her down?"

I told her about Naomi, but didn't give her name, of course, implying that my contact at the Star was male. "That sounds good," she said. "What about magic?"

"I don't know any mages personally," I said. "And I don't know if one could help anyway. You've got to have something connected to the person, don't you?"

"That's just for ritual magic, I think," said Jocasta, after a moment's thought. "Certain spirits can track a person astrally. All it takes is for the mage to have a mental image of the person."

"I didn't know that," I said quietly. That scared me; it meant I wasn't anywhere near as safe as I believed. "Is there anything else I should know?"

She shrugged. "I'm not an expert. Just a dabbler at best. You should talk to Harold."

"Hold the phone," I said. "You're a dabbler? You're telling me you're a mage?"

She looked embarrassed again. "No," she said, "I'm on the shamanic side. But I'm not a shaman. I've . . . I've got a touch of the Power, no more, and I'm not schooled in it."

"Why didn't you say something before?"

"It never came up," she shrugged.

"Tell me about it. What *can* you do? It might be important."

She shrugged again. "I can't do much," she said slowly. "But sometimes I can feel things. It . . ." She hesitated, and I could tell she was uncomfortable discussing it.

"Go on," I said reassuringly. "I'm interested. Really."

She was silent, and the flickering of her eyes told me she was conducting an internal debate. Finally she nodded, and began, "You know how most kids have invisible friends? I had one, too. Lolita always had lots of friends, but . . ." She shook her head, stopping that train of thought. For an instant I could see Jocasta as a young girl, with the same vulnerable expression now in her eyes.

"I was more comfortable by myself, I think," she said. "I was ten when I first realized that . . ." She hesitated again, and tried another tack. "We grew up in Arbor Heights. I was out walking—it was safer to walk then than it is now—and I was pretending that Sarah was walking with me." She blushed and lowered her gaze. "Sarah was my invisible friend." I nodded, but didn't say anything.

"I was walking along a main street. Marine View, it was. I can remember it as clearly as yesterday. It was a Sunday morning, I think, the first really warm day of the summer, and there wasn't much traffic. I was crossing the road at the corner. Crossing with the lights," she added with a quick grin. "There was a man crossing with me. He reminded me a lot of my father. He smiled at me, and said it was a nice day to be out walking. We were halfway across the street when I heard it." Her voice trailed off.

"Go on," I prompted.

"We were halfway across," she said again, "and I heard a voice right beside me. 'Jocasta,' it said. I could hear it as clearly as, well, as anything. I thought it was the man at first, but it wasn't a man's voice. It wasn't a girl's voice, either, not really. Then it spoke again: 'Jocasta.' I looked up at the man, but he didn't seem to have heard it. He just walked on.

"And suddenly I knew—I mean, I really *knew*—it was Sarah who'd said it." She shrugged. "I know it doesn't make sense, and it made even less at the time. But I was sure it was Sarah. I was scared, but I knew I had to get off the street. I turned and ran back to the curb. The man looked over his shoulder. He was puzzled, and he was going to say something . . ."

I thought I knew what was coming next.

"The car came round the corner fast," she said. Her voice was almost a whisper, and I could see the remembered terror in her eyes. "A black Acura Turbo convertible. I can still see it. Low to the ground, it would have looked fast even if it had been standing still. It hit the man, he had no time to react. It hit him full on, so hard it knocked his body twenty meters, and I knew he was dead. The driver started to slow down like he was going to stop. But then he accelerated again and just sped away. I couldn't move for I don't know how long, as the crowds gathered and the police arrived. I knew if I'd kept walking, if Sarah hadn't called my name, I'd be as dead as that man. That scared me more than anything."

I was silent for a few moments after she'd finished. I could easily picture the young Jocasta, probably quite prim and proper with her copper hair *just so,* standing on the curb, her gray eyes filled with an understanding beyond her years. "Did you ever figure out what happened?" I asked finally.

"I never learned for sure," she answered. "I can only guess. I think somehow, without knowing it, I'd summoned a spirit. Maybe it was my need for a friend that called it, the strength of my desire that Sarah be real. But . . . I don't know."

"What happened later?" I asked.

She shrugged. "I grew up," she said simply. "And of course I didn't let myself think about Sarah anymore. When I remembered that day, I had all kinds of eminently logical explanations for what happened. You know the kind of thing: I'd subliminally heard the approaching car, and Sarah's 'voice' was just a manifestation of my own instincts. That kind of drek." She grinned. "I'm always amazed at how good we are at lying to ourselves.

"Over the next ten years, I changed," she went on. "I started feeling this . . . this *kinship* with the land, that's the best way I can explain it. Like we were . . . connected, my soul and the land." She chuckled. "Once I get an idea sometimes I become obsessed with it. I guess I did with this one. Lolita started calling me 'pinkskin,' and Dad . . . Well, Dad got disgusted over the interest I showed in biology and those other 'fuzzy' subjects at school.

"And that's what led me into neo-ecology at UPS. I got my bachelor's degree, and then went on for a Master's. That's when I met Harold."

She'd mentioned that name before. "Who's Harold?"

"Harold Moves-in-Shadows," she said. "Makah, Dog shaman, and one of the best neo-ecologists around. He was my thesis advisor." From the tone of her voice and the look in her eye, I'd have laid odds that he'd been more than that. But of course I didn't say anything. "He recognized something in me," she continued, "something in my aura. He said I had a touch of the Power and that I had the potential to become a shaman."

"Did you?"

"I tried to follow the path," she said slowly. "More to please Harold, I think, than because I really wanted it for myself. I took his totem, Dog, and I tried to learn what he wanted to teach me." She shrugged. "I never got far. Probably because it's a road you can walk only if you're driven by the desire, and I never was. I was always more interested in the intellectual demands of neo-ecology than I was in . . . well, in magical mumbo-jumbo. And I suppose I eventually resented Harold for trying to make me into someone I wasn't."

"You broke up over that," I ventured.

She looked up at me. For a moment her eyes flashed, then the anger was replaced by wry amusement. "Am I so transparent?" she said. "You're right, of course. We *did* break up over that. But we continued to work together, and we still do on occasion, and we're still close friends."

"What did you learn about magic?" I asked.

"What can I do, you mean?" She chuckled softly. "Not a whole hell of a lot. Sometimes I can assense astrally. Not always, and usually when I least want to. And that's about it. Once I summoned a spirit, though Harold probably helped me more than he let on. But it stayed around only long enough to scare the drek out of me." She thought for a moment. "Do you want me to talk to Harold?"

I considered it. "Not now, but thanks for the offer. Maybe if the mundane way comes up dry. I'd rather not involve anybody I don't have to."

Jocasta accepted that with a nod. "What are you going to do in the meantime?"

"Wait," I said, shrugging.

"What about—what did you call him?—X?"

"The same thing. My Lone Star contact's checking into Yamatetsu as well. When I learn more, maybe I'll know better what we can do."

"I'm a good researcher," she pointed out. "I can do some digging, too."

I thought about that for a moment. "Maybe," I said slowly. "You'll have to be very, *very* careful. If Yamatetsu really is involved in this drek, they'll have watchdog programs on everything even slightly relevant, with ice and maybe deckers guarding the real paydata."

"I won't touch anything to do with Yamatetsu itself," she said sharply. "I'm not stupid. But it's a tenet of scientific research that you can learn a lot about an unknown process by studying how it affects processes you *do* understand."

I held up my hands placatingly. "You're the expert," I told her. "Just don't get yourself killed." I hesitated, then added, "That would be a waste."

Her hard expression softened. "That's not in my immediate plans," she told me. Her lips curved in a smile that was both tired and warm. "I suggest you take your own advice. Good luck with Theresa." And with that she was gone.

16

They say still waters run deep. I'd never really bought into that saying, knowing that still waters are more often stagnant, but it was definitely true of Jocasta Yzerman. She was almost the exact opposite of Lolly, and not just in appearance. The face Lolly had always showed to the world was soft and vulnerable, but the real woman had been as cold and sharp as a scalpel. Jocasta, on the other hand, had shown me a cold and brittle edge when we'd first met over her targeting laser. I'd labeled her a tough

corp bitch without much trace of humanity. But now I'd
seen behind the mask—no, now she'd *shown* me what
was behind the mask. I saw that she was more human
and caring—vulnerable—than Lolly had ever been. Curiouser and curiouser, said Alice.

I was lying on the bed, staring at the ceiling, willing
the clock to run faster. It had been a long morning and
an even longer early afternoon. I'd promised myself I
wouldn't call Naomi until 1530. Now it was 1500 hours
and had been for the past half hour—or so it felt. I finally
gave up—frag promises—and rolled to my feet. I keyed
in Naomi's direct line, and spent the seconds while the
connection was being made scripting my approach. No
D'Artagnon this time, just in case somebody had realized the significance.

The screen lit up, but not with Naomi's image. The
woman whose image appeared was a decade older, wearing a Lone Star uniform. Naomi's department were non-
uniform employees. What the frag?

The woman's face could have been carved from stone.
When she opened her mouth to speak, it looked like her
jaw was on hinges. The movement wasn't communicated
to any other part of her face. Her eyes were like flint.
"Lone Star Public Relations," she said.

I broke the connection immediately, rechecked the
number I'd entered. Yes, it was Naomi's number. Maybe
the Lone Star phone exchange was having a seizure, I
told myself. But I didn't believe it.

I threw on my duster, fragging near ran down to the
street to find a pay phone that worked, no easy job in the
Barrens. The one I finally located had a functioning video
pickup, so I smashed it with my gun-butt, much to the
amusement of two gutterpunks watching the show. Then
I re-entered Naomi's number.

And got stone-face again, plus her "Lone Star Public
Relations."

"Yeah, uh, hoi," I said, roughening my voice. "I'm,
uh, I want Naomi Takahashi."

"I'm sorry," stone-face said in a voice that wasn't
sorry at all. "Ms. Takahashi is unavailable. Who is this
speaking?"

"A chummer of hers." I searched for a name from the
past that wouldn't raise any flags. "Gerry Moore," I

said, naming a contemporary of ours who'd transferred to D.C. a couple of years back. "I'm in town for a few days and I wanted to see her. Can you connect me?"

"Please turn on your video," stone-face ordered.

"I'm at a pay phone," I told her. "Somebody's smashed the pick-up."

The woman reached out of frame, no doubt to trigger a trace on my location. I felt a cold knot of fear in my belly.

"Look," I said, struggling to keep the tension out of my voice, "can I talk to Takahashi or not?"

She glanced down, probably reading my LTG number from a hidden display. She'd know I was telling the truth about the pay phone. All public phones in the Seattle region have a nine as their third digit. "I'm sorry," she lied again. "Ms. Takahashi was killed in the line of duty."

The world seemed to go dark around me. I slumped slowly until my forehead rested against the cool plastic of the booth.

"Are you still there?" stone-face said. I saw her reaching to break the connection.

I willed myself back into some semblance of control. "When?"

"I'm not free to divulge that information at this time."

I wanted to strike out, to reach down the phone and strangle the fragging tight-lipped bitch. I wanted the battleaxe I'd wielded yesterday. "What the frag happened?" I yelled. "She works in fragging *Records*. How can you get killed in the line of duty in *Records*? Killed in a fragging disk crash? In a typing accident?"

Stone-face was totally unmoved by my anger. "There have recently been terrorist incidents directed against Lone Star and its employees," she explained coldly. "Ms. Takahashi lost her life in such an incident. The memorial service will be on Tuesday, but since you're not a member of the immediate family . . ."

I slammed my fist down on the Disconnect button, hard enough to crack the hardened plastic. She was dead, Naomi of the flashing almond eyes and quick laugh. And I'd killed her, I was sure of it.

I left the booth, and walked the afternoon streets of Purity. I didn't know where I was going, nor did I really

care. My mind was ablaze with a churning mixture of
anger, sadness, and guilt. My teeth ground together so
hard I could feel the muscles of my jaw almost cramping.
Walking alone in the Barrens, I knew I presented a temptation for street drek that would be glad to kill me for
my boots or my duster. In a way I wished someone would
make a move against me. Not out of a death wish, though
I suppose my own death would have been a form of ex-
piation. No. I hoped somebody would jump me so I could
take out my anger on another, kill someone, just as
somebody—X—had killed Naomi.

It could only be X. Sure, there might have been some
terrorist incidents against Lone Star people, and there
probably *had* been deaths. But it was much too coincidental. I send Naomi out to dig up the dirt on Yamatetsu,
and *coincidentally* she gets taken down by random terrorist violence? No. She'd dug too deep, come too close
to something important.

Of course she'd dug too deep. I should have known it.
Naomi was a good researcher, the best I'd ever known.
She'd have dug as deep as discretion allowed, then gone
even deeper, warnings or no warnings. She'd have kept
on digging until she hit paydata, or until somebody or
some*thing*—IC, maybe—stopped her. Stopped her dead.
It might have been X who pulled the trigger or initiated
whatever ended her life, but it was me who killed her.
Frag!

Without being consciously aware of where my steps
were taking me, I was back on the stairs leading up to
my doss. I had to do *something,* but what?

Maybe Naomi had found something, I thought, as I
shut the door behind me, dropped my duster in a heap
on the floor. She might have kept a record of her results,
or at least the leads she'd been following. No way she'd
have kept records like that on her machine at work; she'd
have stored them on her home telecom. Maybe she'd even
slaved her home system to the one at work—much the
way my telecom here was slaved to the one in Auburn.
It was worth a try.

I sat down at my own telecom, entered Buddy's number. After the beep, I started yelling into the microphone. ''Buddy! Buddy, frag it. If you're there, pick up.
It's fragging important.''

Nothing, no response at all. If she was decking at the moment, she might not even be aware of the incoming call. What the hell could I do to attract her attention? Nothing came to mind. *"Buddy!"* I yelled again, feeling an awful sense of futility. Yelling at a blank telecom screen, what could be more pointless?

Then suddenly the screen wasn't blank anymore. There was an image on it, not a normal video image but something that resembled medium-resolution computer animation and three-dimensional rendering. I saw a beautiful young woman with ebony hair, wearing an elegant laser-green gown. I recognized it immediately: Buddy's icon from the Matrix. What the frag . . . ?

It took me a moment, then I realized what was going down. Buddy *had* been jacked in, but somehow she'd become aware of my call. She'd decided for her own reasons to answer it, but why go to the trouble of jacking out, then moving her meat body to the telecom? Why do anything so gauche when all she had to do was divert a few electrons here and there along the lines that connected her telecom to the greater Matrix? A neat trick.

"What is it?" Buddy's voice snapped from the speaker. The icon's mouth didn't move. I guess Buddy decided not to waste computer cycles on animating the image more than was necessary. "I'm busy."

"Naomi's dead," I said. The words almost caught in my throat.

"Naomi?"

Then I remembered, Buddy had never met Naomi. "A close friend," I told her. "Somebody who meant a lot to me." Buddy didn't answer; she just waited for what she must have known would come next. "I need your help."

"What?"

"I need to know how she died. The data will be in the Lone Star system."

"Lone Star again," Buddy almost snarled. "You don't ask for much, do you?"

"It won't be that tough," I said almost pleadingly. "I want to know about the cover-up, because there's certainly going to be one. And what's the good of covering up if you bury your lies so deep nobody can get to them?"

She thought about that for a split-second. "Maybe," she allowed.

"The stuff I want will be in the Public Relations Department files," I hurried on. "Minimal ice there, if any, right?"

"Maybe," she repeated. Another split-second pause. "Standard rates?"

"*Double,*" I told her on impulse. "But I want it fast."

The glowing icon didn't move, but I could imagine Buddy shrugging. "Your nuyen."

"There's something else."

She snorted. "Of course there's something else."

"There's a telecom connected to this line." I keyed in Naomi's home number and transmitted it to Buddy. "Can you penetrate the telecom and upload the data files?"

"Naomi's telecom?" Buddy asked.

"That's right."

Yet another pause, even longer—almost two seconds, an eternity for Buddy. "She was helping you out." It wasn't a question.

My eyes burned. Probably from looking at Buddy's high-intensity image, I told myself. "Yes," I said quietly.

"I'll do it," she answered at once. "Double rate for Lone Star, no charge for the telecom. I'll call." The glowing image vanished.

I wanted to go hide in the bottom of a bottle and not come out until the world was a better place. I wanted to ride forth on my fragging white horse and run a sword through a few gullets. I wanted to cry on Jocasta's shoulder like a child. I wanted to find some poor sod who would look at me the wrong way so I could pound his miserable bones to powder. And most intensely—and frighteningly—of all, I wanted to lose myself in the pseudo-reality of the 2XS chip.

Of course I did none of those things. (Not really, except for a solid hit of whiskey to settle my nerves.) I just sat and waited for Buddy to get back to me. It was difficult, but I even refrained from calling Jocasta just to talk. Like just about everyone else, I've got call-waiting on my phone, but I didn't want to risk an impatient Buddy hanging up rather than waiting for me to change lines.

It was just after eighteen-hundred hours when the
telecom beeped. Fast turnaround, but those two hours
had felt like years. I pounded the Receive key before
the first beep had even finished.

Buddy appeared on the screen. The real-flesh Buddy,
not the laserlight-clad icon. "What have you got for
me?" I asked immediately.

"The report on your friend's death," she replied.
"Ready to receive?"

I opened a capture file and told her, "Send ahead."
The report wasn't long, much less than a megapulse of
data, and took only a second or two to transmit. I wanted
to scan it immediately, but could sense Buddy's impatience. She wanted to have this over with and get back
to her own biz, whatever that was. "Thanks," I told her.
I slotted my credstick, waited while she made the appropriate—that is, large—deduction. "And her telecom?"

"Nothing."

I frowned. "I don't know what exactly I should be
looking for," I said slowly. "Maybe you should just
transmit everything that was there and—"

"There was nothing," she snapped again. "The telecom's storage was empty. Totally empty. No programs,
no data. Just like a new unit waiting to be loaded with
the software. Somebody beat me to it."

"Somebody deleted everything?"

"That's what I said."

"Would you have to do that in person," I asked, "or
could you do it over the phone line?"

"Over the line."

"How difficult is that?"

"Not," she said. "Once you've penetrated the telecom's security, just issue a global delete."

"And how tough is that security?"

"Not," she repeated. "Any decker worthy of the name
could do it."

I slammed my fist down on the table so hard the telecom jumped. "*Frag* it," I snarled. "She *had* found
something, then."

"Probably that's what killed her," Buddy said, echoing the thought in my own mind.

"Yeah, well," I mumbled, not wanting to dwell on
either that or my own guilt. "Thanks, Buddy."

''Yeah. Sorry about your friend.''

''So am I, Buddy.''

I broke the connection, brought up the file that Buddy had transmitted. As I'd expected, she'd copied the whole record, Lone Star file header and all. Buddy was never one to do a job by halves, particularly if she was getting double rate for it. The report was very simple, the incident it described horrible in the extreme. Naomi had come to work early, purportedly to catch up on some departmental backlog. At about nine-thirty she'd ridden the elevator down to the staff cafeteria on the tenth floor, and fifteen minutes later caught the elevator back up to the thirtieth floor. Sounded like a standard Lone Star soy-kaf break. There were two other workers riding the car with Naomi, and their testimony made up much of the report.

They were just passing floor twenty when *something* materialized in the elevator car. The two reports varied drastically—predictably—but some features corresponded. First, the *thing* was a bipedal creature, definitely not human or metahuman, and second, it was terrifying. It paid no attention to either of the witnesses, but lashed out with an arm and quite literally tore Naomi's head off. Then it vanished. End of show. Nobody knew what the frag it was or where it came from, or—more important for Lone Star—how it made it through the arcane defenses of the headquarters building. The official conclusion was that some terrorist group had decided to slot up the Star by sending in some magical nasty—a city spirit, the report surmised—to cause terror. Naomi Takahashi died simply because she was unlucky enough to be near at hand.

Like fragging drek. If you're a terrorist with a city spirit and you want to kill somebody, just anybody, why go to the bother of sending the monster into a fragging elevator on the fragging twentieth floor? Much better to send the nasty into the lobby or the word-processor pool or maybe the executive suite. And if you *are* drek-headed enough to pick an elevator, why not maximize the effect by geeking *everyone* there, hmm? No. Naomi's death was an execution. A particularly unusual and messy one, but an execution nonetheless. She'd queried the wrong data-

base or accessed the wrong file, and some hit mage at
Yamatetsu had sent forth his pet to silence her.

Take it a step further. This putative "hit mage" was
probably X himself. I already knew X was magically active; my face on the security camera in Lolly's building
had proved that. Why hypothesize more than one murderous mage? Occam's razor (with which I would glee-
fully and with relish slit X's throat).

Yamatetsu. That had to be the key. I had to find out
more about the company. The whys and the hows as well
as the whats. There was something there, something important enough to kill—and keep killing—to protect. I
had to find out what it was. And then I had to find a way
to bring X down—and the whole of Yamatetsu, if that's
what it took.

And I had to do it myself. No more sending friends to
do the dirty work, risking their necks for me.

But how? I wrestled with that question the rest of that
evening and late into the night, but didn't come up with
a totally satisfactory answer. I woke the next morning
feeling like drek—too little sleep, too much stress—but
forced myself out of bed and back to the telecom.

First things first. I knew next to nothing about Yamatetsu Corporation, other than the quick thumbnail sketch
Buddy had given me. Time to remedy that. Starting point,
the public datanets.

Most of the datanet entries talked about Yamatetsu's
international operations. God, it was a monster. From its
headquarters in Kyoto, its influence spread virtually everywhere in the world: Atzlan, Europe, the Soviet
(dis)Union, even, reputedly, Tir Tairngire. It owned or
controlled several hundred smaller corps in virtually
every industry—automotive, food processing, electronics, hospitality, armaments, travel, and so on and so
forth—and had at least some financial participation in a
thousand more. Its revenue figures were unavailable (no
fragging surprise), but judging by what information I
could lay my hands on, I figured its annual profit figures
exceeded the GNP of quite a few small countries. (I'll
admit it, that doesn't mean much to me, financial matters
not being my strong suit. A more meaningful comparison
was that Yamatetsu appeared to be almost *twice as large*

as Mitsuhama. And I'd never even heard of it before a couple of days ago. That was terrifying.)

Yamatetsu had limited investments in Seattle, relatively speaking. It owned the City Center Building at Pike and Fifth, and that's where it had its local headquarters. From there, its management team, led by Senior Veep Jacques Barnard, controlled the destinies of only a dozen or so local companies and some three thousand employees. Small potatoes, petty cash, a mere bagatelle.

The corp also had a secondary facility in Fort Lewis. In fact, from the datanet description it sounded like Yamatetsu had its own little industrial park hidden away in the trees. Predictably, none of the public databases offered any indication of what kind of work was done at this outlying facility, but I could make a good guess. In general, what are you going to find in the Fort Lewis District? The military, that's what, chummer. Fort Lewis is home to the Seattle Metroplex Guard, McChord Airbase, and training facilities and accommodation for almost twenty corporate security forces (read "private armies"). Add to this the fact that any corp loves to be as close to its potential market as possible. I figured I'd found Yamatetsu's ISP division, developer and marketer of SPISES booster technology.

I tried to do a little digging into the background of Senior Veep Jacques Barnard. Know your enemy and all that drek. But—no surprise—there was nothing on him in any of the databases to which I had access. No mailing address, no LTG number. Presumably, anybody who wanted to contact Barnard either already knew how to do it or did it care of Yamatetsu's Seattle HQ.

Okay. So I'd exhausted that source of information. What was the next step?

I sat back and thought it through once more. What exactly was I looking for?

X, part of my mind yammered. X, so I can kill him.

But how did I expect to track him down? the more logical portion of my brain demanded. Assuming X was a part of Yamatetsu—still an assumption, even though a very fragging good one—where was he or she in the hierarchy? Or, to ask the same question another way, where did the sweetheart deal with Sutcliffe originate? Veep level, meaning that the whole Seattle structure would be

backing his actions? Or—at the other end of the scale—
an ambitious product manager willing to do anything to
advance his career? Maybe it was wishful thinking, but
I tended to favor the lower end of the scale. If someone
at veep level, or even Barnard himself, had ordered it,
there wouldn't have been any frag-ups, and I wouldn't be
around to worry about it.

So the question remained, how to track X? I knew
nothing about him or her . . . But X knew all too much
about me.

I wanted to shy away from that line of thought, but if
I really intended to track down X, was I willing to put
my own neck on the line to do it? (Like I'd been so
willing to do with Naomi's? a perverse voice within me
mocked.) The truth of the matter was, I simply couldn't
think of a better way of going about it.

Okay, then, down to tactics. I fired up the telecom
again, checked the status of Naomi Takahashi's apartment. According to the leasing records, on her death the
lease devolved upon her parents. If they didn't do anything to renew it, the lease would expire on December
31. Whether they renewed it or not, the apartment would
be empty for about a month. That would make a perfect
killing ground. All I had to do was drop a few clues that
I was crashing there, then take X when he came to kill
me. Simple.

Simple—*maybe*—if X was a mundane, just another
street gun. The problem was I knew X was magically
active. And you've got to fight fire with fire.

17

Like most denizens of the shadows, I've always considered fixers to be a necessary evil. I don't like dealing
with middlemen, and I strongly resent paying a percent-
age to someone who plays people like me off against one
another while staying out of the shadows himself. My
especial disdain was generally reserved for weasels like
Anwar, regardless of the fact that he'd brokered most of

my best-paying jobs over the last year and a half. Now, however, I was glad for the fact of his existence.

Except for Jocasta Yzerman, who I wasn't counting, I knew no magicians. But I needed one, and fast. If I was seriously considering luring X into a trap, I mustn't forget the decidedly unnatural way Naomi had died. If another monstrous horror like that should rear its ugly head again, I'd better be ready to meet such a threat. And that meant I needed a mage.

Anwar must have been in a particularly benevolent mood: he only soaked me three hundred nuyen for the name and contact data, and an extra seventy-five for a preliminary phone call from him to establish my bona fides. What a deal.

The name I got was one Rodney Greybriar, located at Suite 5, 1766 Galer, in the Capitol Hill district. No LTG number; apparently Greybriar preferred doing business in person. I wasn't too happy about that, but had to admit that Anwar would never have enjoyed such a long and profitable career if he'd been selling out his clients on a regular basis.

Capitol Hill has an anachronistic, almost bohemian, feel to it, a total contrast with the rest of the sprawl. In fact, as I cruised Galer looking for a parking place, I might almost have believed I was somewhere very far from downtown Seattle. The buildings were a schizoid mix of 1980s-vintage structures and contemporary apartment complexes ranging from soulless lower-class housing to middle-class buildings with some semblance of security. Greybriar's building, 1766 Galer, was one of the former. Designated a heritage building, its lower floor boasted some lovingly restored neon-work that identified it as the Fitness Connection Aerobics Center. The signs were still in place, but the exercise gym had long ago been broken up into four economy-size apartments. Suite 5 was on the second—and top—floor, apparently taking up half the floor space. Pretty good, I thought. There must be nuyen in the magic biz.

A car pulled out of a space across the road from me, so I darted over the center line and took it, earning a one-fingered salute from a middle-aged woman whose eye had been on the same spot. Then I walked the half-block back to Greybriar's building. Suite 5 had a private entrance, it seemed, a narrow staircase leading up from the street. As I climbed the steep stairway, I loosened my Manhunter in its holster. No sense taking any chances.

The door to Suite 5 had no viewport or buzzer. I scanned the frame around the door, the ceiling above it, even the floor, but saw no sign of any kind of security gear. No cameras, no sensors, no nothing. Maybe mages don't need drek like that, I thought, suddenly feeling very cold. I reached out to knock on the door.

And a voice in my ear froze me where I stood. "You must be Mr. Dirk," the voice said. A warm contralto, definitely feminine, the kind I'd normally love to have murmuring in my ear.

But not right now. I spun, looking for the source, my hand reaching for my weapon. I spun so fast I almost catapulted myself back down those steep stairs. All to no avail. No one was there.

Which made it even more unsettling when that same inviting voice chuckled beside me. Slot it all, now I knew why I didn't hang with magicians. "Enough of the games," I snapped.

The voice answered at once, its tone contrite. "I'm sorry, Mr. Montgomery. I didn't mean to startle you. Please enter. Rodney is expecting you."

The door swung open with no preliminary clicking of locks and latches being released. My heart still felt like it was lodged in my throat, so I forced it back where it belonged and stepped into the entryway. The door shut behind me as soon as I was through it. I spun again.

This time someone was there. A striking, willowy blonde dressed in a floor-length gown—robe?—of jade green that perfectly set off the luster of her waist-length hair. She stood with her hands demurely behind her back, which only served to exaggerate her magnificent figure. She was tall, the top of her head level with my forehead, and she regarded me with large eyes, almost impossibly green. A trace of a smile played around her lips. "I really am sorry," she said, and it was the same luscious contralto from before. (Like hell you are, I wanted to say, but refrained.) Her eyes twinkled with amusement; for the first time I realized they matched her gown. "But you *did*

jump nicely," she added quietly. "Please go on through."
She gestured with a slender hand.

The front door of Suite 5 opened into a small hallway,
more like an antechamber. I strode forward, leaving the
blonde to lock the door—if that was necessary—and entered the main area of the apartment.

I suppose I'd expected the apartment to be something
on a par with Buddy's, dark and claustrophobic, filled
with disorder bordering on devastation, but with magical
gizmos replacing the high-tech gizmos. Fetishes or am-
ulets or such drek, I suppose. Jars containing eye of newt
and toe of frog. And books, books, books everywhere:
dusty grimoires showing cabalistic symbols on their covers and with ornate ritual daggers as bookmarks.

Wrong. Suite 5 was light and airy, decorated in
an open plan that maximized the sense of space. Furniture was sparse but attractive—and expensive—in a
Scandinavian-retro kind of way. It was also positioned
just so, making the place look like a plate out of an interior decorating rag. Several pieces of art hung on the
walls, mostly geometric abstracts. The place was im-
maculate, nothing out of place and not a piece of newt
or frog anatomy anywhere in sight.

The room I was in was L-shaped, and I stood at the
top of the long side. The rest of the room went around a
corner to the right. And it was from around that corner
that I heard a voice—male, this time—"Mr. Dirk, I assume. Please, join me."

Walking toward the voice, I rounded the corner.
Though no less artistically arranged than the rest, this
"wing" was more like an office. Bookshelves lined two
walls, though I saw nary a mildewed grimoire. A top-of-
the-line telecom was against the third. In the center of
the room was a desk, in the same clean-lined style as the
rest of the furniture, atop which was another computer.
From this angle I couldn't see exactly what appeared on
the screen, but it looked something like my conception
of a pentacle.

Behind the desk sat an elf, and behind him stood the
green-clad blonde. I looked around. There was no other
door leading into the office area, and no physical way she
could have beaten me here from the entry hall. I glared

at the blonde, gritted my teeth, and vowed never to deal
with mages again.

The elf's polite smile faded as he saw the expression
on my face. He glanced over his shoulder, seemingly
unaware that the blonde was there. "Amanda," he
scolded, "I'll ask you to stop tormenting our guest."

Amanda hung her head, looking remorseful as a
naughty child. Initially I'd judged her to be about my
own age, but now had to admit I could easily be off by a
dozen years. "I was only having fun, Rodney," she
whispered.

The elf softened. "I know that," he said. "But fun
and business rarely mix well. Now run along. We'll talk
later."

Amanda nodded, flashed me a megawatt smile, then
vanished into thin air. Now you see her, now you don't.

Before I could comment, the elf smiled wryly. "I do
apologize for Amanda," he said. "Her, um, high spirits
sometimes interfere with her good manners." He stood
and walked around the desk to join me, extending his
hand. "My name is Rodney Greybriar, Mr. Montgomery."

I shook his hand and looked the elf over. He was short
and stocky for an elf, standing a couple of centimeters
less than me, but with shoulders almost as broad. He had
thick, chestnut-brown hair. Unlike most elves, his hair
was curly and he wore it shoulder-length at the back and
shorter at the sides, highlighting the points of his ears.
His face was broader than the average elf's, too, with a
strong jaw. He wore black trousers and boots, a white
shirt buttoned to the neck, and a well-tailored black
jacket. Silver flashed on both lapels, stickpins bearing
unfamiliar—and probably arcane—symbols.

"Our mutual friend Anwar says you're in need of my
services," Greybriar went on. "And, I might add, he
gives you a solid referral. Now, how may I be of assistance?"

For the first time, I paid attention to the elf's voice.
Slightly higher-pitched than I'd have expected from one
of his build, with a distinct English accent. (Real or assumed? I wondered.) The overall effect was somewhat
foppish, almost effeminate.

I didn't speak for a moment, taking the time to phrase my requirement in the best way. Greybriar seemed to misunderstand my hesitation. "I do hope Amanda didn't, um, disturb you too deeply," he said with genuine concern.

"She didn't *disturb* me," I corrected. "She scared the drek out of me. Who is she anyway?"

The elf turned away, perhaps a little disturbed himself, or maybe embarrassed was a better word. "Amanda is, um, is a companion of mine." He glanced back at me from under his curly mop of hair, and his almond eyes twinkled with wry humor. "Not one always and entirely of my choice, I might add." I raised an eyebrow at that, but he shook his head. "Not because of sexual orientation on either of our parts," he hurriedly explained. "Things would be very different if Amanda were a human or a metahuman."

That was the last thing I'd expected him to say. "What is she, then?" I asked.

Greybriar grinned, then chuckled dryly. Despite myself, I found myself liking the British-sounding elf. "A very good question, that," he admitted, "one that it took me some time to answer. Shall we?" He gestured to the living room section of the L-shaped room, waved me over toward the couch. "Please, have a seat." As I did, he settled himself in an armchair. "Some refreshment?" he offered.

I couldn't resist. "Tea?" I asked innocently.

The elf grinned again, and I found his grin infectious. "Actually, I prefer beer at this time of day."

I shook my head. "Nothing for me," I said. "You were talking about Amanda."

"Yes, yes I was, wasn't I?" He settled himself more comfortably in his chair. "Amanda is what is known in some circles as an anima, a free spirit," he said slowly. "I believe her to be a city spirit of some variety, although she never talks about such things."

"So how," I began, then just kind of trailed off. "How . . . ?" I waved a hand vaguely.

"Quite," Greybriar smiled. "I'm not exactly sure myself about the whys and wherefores of it. Again, Amanda is very . . . careful . . . about what she will and what she won't talk about. She started, um, hanging about, you might say, just over a year ago. At first I suspected

she might be a summoning gone wrong, but I found myself at first unable, and then unwilling, to banish her. She's
a harmless sort, really, although her sense of humor leans
somewhat toward the embarrassing on occasion. But she
has never done anything that's brought me harm. I think
of her somewhat like an undisciplined child . . .''

"I heard that!" Amanda's contralto sang out, though
she was nowhere visible.

The elf's smile broadened. "You see," he said softly,
then raised his voice and continued, ". . . albeit a rather
charming one."

"That's better," the anima replied.

I shook my head. "Does she live here?"

"Not as such," Greybriar responded. "She comes and
goes pretty much as she wishes. Although she does always seem to put in an appearance when I have guests,
whether business or social. On occasion a touch awk-
ward, that."

I had to chuckle. "Is Amanda her real name?"

"Not her True Name, no. She suggested I call her that,
and it seems to suit her, wouldn't you say?" The elf
rubbed his hands together briskly and said, "Well, down
to business. What is it, exactly, that I can do for you?"

"I need magical protection," I told him bluntly.
"Some kind of"—I hesitated, not knowing the correct
terms—"some kind of magical burglar alarm. I'll be
staying in an apartment. I need something to keep things
out."

"I see." Greybriar nodded, steepling his fingers and
touching them to his lips. "And exactly what is it that
you expect to be coming to call?"

"A city spirit, I think."

He raised an eyebrow. "Oh? You've got on the wrong
side of a shaman, have you?"

"Not that I know of."

"Then why a city spirit?"

I hadn't intended to raise the topic, but now it seemed
sensible to give the elf more information. I quickly sum-
marized the events that led to Naomi's death, leaving out
her name, of course.

Greybriar listened without interruption, his brows
drawing closer and closer together as I continued. When

I finished, he was silent for a moment. Then he asked slowly, "The official conclusion was a city spirit, is that true?" I nodded, and the elf's frown deepened. "It *might* have been a city spirit," he went on, "but from the description I tend to doubt it."

"What was it, then?"

He shrugged. "It could have been many things." He leaned forward, resting his elbows on his knees, still watching me keenly from either side of his steepled fingers. "Actually, though, the nature of the culprit disturbs me less than other matters. Are you familiar with the magical protections that Lone Star uses?"

"No," I answered.

"In specific terms, neither am I," Greybriar admitted. "But I know very well how *I'd* go about it, and I can't imagine that an organization like Lone Star would cut corners when it came to astral security." He fixed me with a cool and steady gaze. "That thing, whatever it is, simply should not have been able to do what it did."

"Hold it," I said. "I always thought that if something's powerful enough, it could break through *any* kind of protection. Or is that drek?"

"No, it's not drek. Magic is like anything else: there is no such thing as an unbreakable barrier. Just like the bulletproof windows in a corporate office won't stop an artillery shell. But, think of this, what would happen if you *were* to fire an artillery shell through a corp office's window? Would you then be free to climb in and go about your nefarious business?" I snorted, and Greybriar nodded in agreement. "Precisely," he said. "You'd have set off who knows how many alarms, and alerted everyone not deaf.

"The same would be true with crashing through the magical protection," he went on. "Lone Star probably has magical barriers, wards, and doubtless spirits or elementals patrolling astrally. An attempted penetration, in the middle of the day, would certainly trigger alarms and alert every magically active employee in the building. Did either of these happen? No." He paused. "So much more to this than meets the eye."

Just like everything else. I nodded slowly. "I'll keep that in mind," I told him.

"Do that." He sat back in his chair. "As to your defense problems, I can help you, but it will be expensive." I nodded in agreement. "Wards as primary defense, I think, with a fire elemental on patrol. And perhaps a watcher spirit to alert you if anything engages the elemental. Does that sound adequate?"

"You're the mage," I told him.

"All right, then. How long will you need the protection?"

I thought about that. "A week," I said. "To start with."

"Hmmm," the elf murmured, "that *will* be expensive. My standard rate for a week would be seven thousand nuyen."

"Cut him a deal." Amanda's thrilling contralto sounded from nowhere.

Greybriar rolled his eyes in apparent disgust, but the half-smile playing about his lips seemed more indulgent than anything else. *Interesting.* "Considering the fact that Amanda likes you," he continued smoothly, "I think . . . five thousand?" He waited for an answer from the empty air, but none came. "Five thousand," he confirmed. "Is that acceptable?"

I sighed. It wasn't acceptable, but it was better than getting my head ripped off. "Deal," I told him. I made the appropriate credit transfer, and gave him the address of Naomi's apartment.

As I was leaving, Amanda's disembodied voice whispered in my ear, "See you around, Derek." I hoped not.

Another fragging angle, I grouched to myself as I drove southwest into deepest darkest downtown—corruption in Lone Star itself. How else could the *thing* have got through to geek Naomi?

Then I remembered I'd already found evidence of nasty drek at the Star: the missing-but-not-deleted files in the Avatar directory. *Frag* this multi-conspiracy biz. It was much too easy to forget something. I was definitely getting much too old for this drek.

I wasn't looking forward to the next step in my plan, but I saw no better option at the moment. Following my assumption that X was some kind of middle-manager at Yamatetsu and that he (or she) was the one who handled the contact with Sutcliffe in Fort Lewis, I had to figure a way of attracting the murderer's attention without giving him any reason to suspect a trap. Not easy. Even harder would be finding a way of closing that trap.

What the frag did I think I was doing? part of my mind nattered. Did I really think I could bring down X? *Yes*, another part answered forcefully. I was mad as hell. Cranked up and ready to rock.

I still didn't have the solution to how I'd draw X out of his shell. But I understand enough about the way my mind works to know how to provide it with the background it needs. One of the things it needed was a better feel for the Yamatetsu Corporation.

I parked my car in the Seattle Hilton parking lot at Sixth and University, leaving my Manhunter locked in the glove box, then walked the three blocks to the City Center Building at Fifth and Pike. Yamatetsu's Seattle headquarters was another heritage building, built in the late 1980s, I'd guess, and restored to its turn-of-the-century retro opulence maybe a decade ago. I walked in through the revolving doors—how long since those were in common use?—knowing very well that hidden electronics were scanning my body for offensive weaponry.

Then I was into the marble-tiled lobby. I looked up. The lobby was double-height, more than ten meters from floor to ceiling, with a mezzanine looking down into the entranceway. Suspended from the high ceiling were two huge inverted bowls of what had to be real glass; turquoise and aquamarine swirled together in artful artlessness, like "end-of-day" glass. The bowls glowed with internal light, creating a deeply peaceful ambience throughout the space. I rode the escalator up to the mezzanine, which was carpeted in rich, dark hues rather than floored with polished marble. Antique 1990-vintage furniture formed cozy and inviting "conversation groupings," and here and there glowing glass cases displayed turn-of-the-century and contemporary works of art in ceramic, crystal, and light sculpture. Anywhere else, I'd have been sure without a doubt that the art objects and antiques were copies. Here, though, in this elegant environment, I was convinced they were authentic.

I strolled toward the elevator core. To my right was a small, oh-so-trendy wine bar, already doing brisk trade from well-dressed corporators getting a jump on the cocktail hour. To my left, a row of little boutiques, the kind where you've got to show a triple-A credit rating to even get past the front door. Directly in front of me was the inevitable security desk, situated between casual visitors like me and the elevators.

In most corp buildings, such a desk would have been manned by a hard-faced troll crammed into a security guard's uniform. Here, though, I encountered an elegantly beautiful young woman wearing an outfit I took to be a turn-of-the-century business suit, in a blue that harmonized perfectly with the lights overhead. She matched the antique ambience of the place almost to a T, the only anachronistic feature being the optical fiber running from the desk to her datajack.

As I approached, she greeted me with a warm smile. The expression didn't seem to reach her eyes, however. In fact, those eyes seemed to glitter in a faintly unnatural manner, and I guessed that my image was being electronically transferred from her modified optics to a database in her security desk.

"Good afternoon," she said politely, "may I help you?"

I shook my head. "Just rubbernecking," I told her, putting on my best tourist's golly-gee smile. "Does this whole building belong to Yamatetsu?"

"That's correct, sir. Just a moment, please." She paused, seeming to glance off into infinity. I figured a call or message must be coming in on her datajack. I started to walk away, but she'd come back to herself. "Sorry, sir," she said, "is there anything else I can help you with?"

Suddenly I was uneasy. It was as though the young woman's silent communication symbolized everything that was going on. I was in the stronghold of my enemy—X—and I felt it, profoundly and disturbingly. But I kept my inane smile in place. "No thanks," I said amiably. "Have a good afternoon." I kept on moving, heading for the down escalator.

"Sir." The voice sounded sharply behind me. Male, and definitely backed by considerable resonant space. Instinctively I glanced back.

One of the elevator doors had opened to reveal three men—troll, ork, and human—in dark green security uni-

forms. All three were armed, although none had yet
drawn his weapon. I picked up my pace and wished for
my Manhunter. A group of sararimen were stepping onto
the escalator. If I could duck in among them, the odds
were reasonable that nobody would start shooting. I
might just get out of this. Just.

"Sir," the troll snapped again. I took two running
steps toward the elevator . . .

And pitched forward, to land in a heap on the carpeted
floor. I tried to move, but my muscles refused to respond. It was like I was a passenger in my own body,
and somebody had turned off the power.

I was face-down, right cheek against the carpet. My
eyes were open, but I couldn't move them, and all I
could see was my right shoulder. I could still feel pain—
specifically, my jaw, knee, and ribs, which had taken
the impact when I'd crumpled—but that was it.

My field of vision shifted, and I knew the sec-guards
had rolled me over. I looked up—totally helpless—into
their faces. The human, small and thin in comparison to
his burly companions, turned to the troll and said, *"Told
you I'd get him."*

The troll grunted. "Finish it," he ordered.

The human pointed his index finger between my eyes.
"Good night," he said quietly.

Down came the curtain, out went the lights, and that
was it.

18

Consciousness returned as suddenly as it had departed,
more like a switch being flicked on than the slow ascent
into wakefulness typical of natural sleep. At the time, of
course, I didn't give a frag *how* consciousness returned,
as long as it did. I'd had no way of knowing what the
security mage—which was what the weaselly human had
to be—was going to do with his spell when he had brought
his finger to bear. He could as easily have been turning
me into a fragging tree as putting me to sleep.

Well, I was no tree. I was awake, and my body seemed to be fully back under my own control. Lot of good it did me at the moment.

I was in the back seat of a luxury car—a Mitsubishi Nightsky, I guessed—pressed between the bulks of two fellow passengers. The chummer to my right was a troll; the guy to my left was human but only marginally smaller than his colleague. Both towered over me, and I felt like a kid in the company of an Urban Brawl team. My minders wore high-fashion business suits, I noticed.

As the car rounded a corner, I "accidentally" swayed back and forth between the two of them. No armor that I could detect, just iron-hard ridges of muscle under the fabric. Natural or augmented? It didn't really matter. I was convinced that either one could have torn me in two without breaking a sweat. Neither responded in any apparent way to my return to consciousness, although I knew they were well aware of it. These boys, in their thousand-nuyen suits, were pros all the way.

Which made me feel better about my situation. Marginally. If my immediate death was the goal, I'd never have regained consciousness. I'd have been reduced to goo and washed down the drain, or transformed into a fragging potted palm to grace some building's roof garden. So I didn't think I needed seriously fear a bullet in the back of the neck in a dark alley, not at once. And as long as I was alive, I had a chance of escaping or otherwise prolonging that condition.

Of course, the prospects for the immediate future still were not too pleasant. Assuming that my current minders were in the employ of X—a logical assumption—then they'd be taking me to someone whose responsibility would be to find out what I knew and who else knew it. Probably in a number of unpleasant ways. Which put escape as the first order of business.

But also totally impossible at the moment. I couldn't move a muscle without one or both of my monolithic minders knowing it. I was unarmed and totally outmatched in hand-to-hand combat. A polarized barrier separated the rear seat, where I was, from the driver in the front seat, so no chance of orchestrating a crash. Not promising.

"Where are we going?" I asked. Predictably, no answer, not even the slightest acknowledgment that I'd spoken.

I checked the side windows. They were partially darkened, which probably meant they were opaque to anyone trying to look in. From the inside, however, I could see out, but not clearly. We were on a wide boulevard flanked with trees. At first I had no clue to our location, but then I saw the rolling fairways of a perfectly manicured golf course. I checked my watch: only about half an hour since I'd entered City Center Building. That told me where we were—cruising northeast on Madison—and gave me a good idea where we were going—the luxury district of Madison Park.

Set on the shore of Lake Washington, Madison Park was one of the most famous—or most notorious—luxury enclaves within the Seattle sprawl. It was like Beaux Arts Village, but even more so, an area of trees, beaches, rolling hills, and a golf course. A fragging golf course! How many hectares does a golf course take up, all the while people in Redmond and Puyallup are scragging each other for a two-square-meter squat in an alley? I'm not a Rational Communist or a Neoanarchist or any other fringe "ist," but sometimes the disparity between the two ends of the socioeconomic scale hits so hard even I can't ignore it.

Obviously, if Redmond squatters are willing to geek each other for a piece of alley, they certainly aren't going to respect a sign that says, "Keep golf carts three meters from green." Equally obviously, since the Madison Park golfers have no need to step around squatters as they stride the fairways, the golf course must have some pretty significant security. In fact, the whole Madison Park district does. When I called it an "enclave," I chose that word on purpose. There wasn't a spike-topped wall, but the boundaries of the region *were* protected. By unobtrusive checkpoints on all the roads leading in, said checkpoints manned by well-armed, -armored, and -paid "private security consultants"—in fact, Madison Park's own private police force and army. Ne'er-do-wells, tourists, rubberneckers, and other personae non gratae are turned back before they can penetrate too far into the sacrosanct region, while uninvited guests who find ways of bypassing the checkpoints are apprehended and dealt with in the most expedient manner. What with the private army, plus very intense enforcement provided by Lone Star, Madison Park has the lowest crime rate in the city, but the highest rate of "suspects shot while trying to escape" or "fatalities while resisting arrest."

As for the houses themselves, well, most of them aren't so much houses as mansions. Usually set in multi-hectare grounds, surrounded by high walls and patrolled by armed guards or guard animals. They say "a man's home is his castle," and the residents of Madison Park take that precept very much to heart.

The Nightsky continued northwest, then swung right. I tried to see the street name, but the signs in Madison Park are so discreet as to be virtually invisible. (I guess the rationale is that if you don't know where you're going, you shouldn't be going there.) All I knew was that we were heading toward the water.

Then we reached our destination. The big car took a sharp left and cruised through a huge gate in an equally huge wall. As soon as the car was through, the gates began to whir shut behind us. I caught a glimpse of a security guard in a black uniform standing at attention as we passed, Heckler & Koch SMG at picture-perfect port-arms.

The car sighed to a stop in front of the house. My human minder looked down at me, and said quietly, "Let's keep this civilized, okay? You're a guest." (Yeah, right.) Then he swung open his door and climbed out, with an economy of motion—grace, even—that belied his huge size. "Please come this way, sir," he suggested.

I slid across the seat, glad to be out from between the two mountains of muscle. Trying to keep it casual, I got out of the car and glanced around.

If I was going to make my bid for freedom, this was *not* the time. My human minder stood three meters away. He had no weapon in his hand, but he looked poised and ready, easily capable of tearing my head off. Even if I'd found a way of disabling or avoiding him, visible weapons were also in the offing. Two more security guards flanked the front door of the house; their SMGs weren't pointed at me—quite—but they could be brought to bear instantly. And then, just to clinch the issue, I felt a looming presence at my back. The troll was out of the car, too. I sighed, discarded even the faintest idea of making a break.

Instead, I looked over the premises. I guessed the grounds to be over ten hectares in area, artistically laid out and reminiscent of an ancient British baronial home—or, at least, of the modern conception thereof. To the left of the house was a tennis court, while to the right, the perfect lawns extended right down to the edge of Lake Washington. A dock of ferroconcrete extended out from the shore, at the end of which was moored a motor yacht, twenty-five meters if it was a centimeter. The place was a potential security nightmare, what with its long shoreline, but I was sure the owner had taken the appropriate precautions.

The house itself matched the grounds. Constructed of what appeared to be rough-hewn gray stone, it was the image of a nineteenth-century manor home, right down to the *faux* turrets and the coat of arms over the blackened-oak front door. I tried to guess the value of the place, but gave up. More than five million nuyen, definitely, but how *much* more?

My human escort gestured politely toward the front door. I nodded in gracious acceptance of the invitation, and started walking. Both business-suited legbreakers took up positions one step back and one step to left and right. Under other circumstances, I might have enjoyed having two such attentive sidemen. Not now, of course. As I climbed the three steps to the front door, the two SMG-wielding sec-guards snapped to attention. I raised an eyebrow in surprise. Exactly what the frag was going on here? This visiting-dignitary drek bothered me.

The door opened as I approached it, and I stepped into an elegant entryway of dark wood, with rich burgundy carpeting. Another black-uniformed sec-guard stood just inside the door, again standing at perfect attention. Two medieval suits of armor flanked the hallway. No sooner had I passed between them, followed by my huge escorts, than a loud electronic beep sounded behind us. When I spun to look, red lights were glowing behind the visors of both suits of armor. The sec-guard at the door hurriedly hit a button, killing the lights and stilling the electronic tone. For a moment I wondered what was going down, then realized the beep had sounded just as my minders had walked between the suits of armor. Weapon-detectors of some kind, no doubt.

"Just a moment, please," the big human said, and stepped in front of me. The troll remained behind. When the human asked me to please follow him, I didn't have much choice.

He led me further down the hallway, then through a door to the right and down a flight of stairs. To the torture chamber in the basement? I wondered. We turned a corner, and I realized I was right in a way.

I stood in the doorway of a large, brightly lit area, filled with heavy equipment that looked both threatening and familiar. It took me a moment to recognize the gear: a Nautilus III circuit over here, a Swim-Ex in the far corner, a couple of massive Ultra Gym units. I was in an exercise room that would put the vast majority of health clubs to shame.

One of the Ultra Gym machines was operating. In the middle of its pumping hydraulic arms and reciprocating cams, I could see a human figure. "Mr. Montgomery, welcome," the figure called out. A strong male voice, as steady as if the owner were ensconced in an easy chair and not exercising his guts out. "Please, come over. I hope you haven't taken offense at the, shall we say, irregular manner of my invitation, but I didn't think you'd accept if I offered it through normal channels."

I walked closer, noting that my two bulky minders remained at the door. Drawing nearer, I could see my "host" a little better. A middle-aged man, but with the physique of a twenty-year-old, probably about my height and build. Short salt-and-pepper hair worn in a conservative, subtly spiked cut that revealed the datajack in his temple. Strong face, with a commanding, aquiline nose and cold eyes. With a shock, I realized I knew him. Not personally, of course, but as a "Mr. Johnson" for whom I'd done some recovery work a year back.

The man must have seen the recognition in my face. He smiled. "Yes, we have met," he said, "but I didn't give you my name at the time, for, er, obvious reasons. It's time to remedy that. I'm Jacques Barnard, Mr. Montgomery. Senior Vice President of Yamatetsu Corporation. I'm currently in charge of our Seattle operations."

He smiled. "I hope you don't think it rude if I don't shake hands, but I'm in the aerobic phase of my workout."

"I know just what you mean," I said levelly.

Barnard chuckled. "I think I'll enjoy our conversation," he remarked. Then his smile grew broader as a thought struck him. "I have two Ultra Gyms," he said. "Perhaps you'd care to join me."

I was about to decline, then thought, what the frag? If I was going to die, I may as well die fit. "Why not?" I sat on the saddle, put my feet on the pedals, and cinched the belt around my waist.

"I'd suggest level three," my host said modestly.

I glanced over at the control panel of Barnard's machine. He was running level eighteen, out of a possible twenty, and his timer was just clicking past ten minutes. I grinned at him and also selected level eighteen. Hell, he was two decades older than me. I grabbed the handgrips and squeezed the trigger.

I'd never used an Ultra Gym before, and within the first ten seconds I swore I never would again. Imagine doing a fast cycle of chest press, biceps curl, shoulder press, lat pulldown, while simultaneously alternating leg press and thigh curl, with a troll drill instructor forcing your limbs into the right motion, then leaving you to deal with the weights yourself. I thought I was going to die. I released the trigger, and the machine grumbled to a stop. Without meeting Barnard's amused gaze, I reset the controls to level three, and squeezed the trigger again. Much better.

"It takes some getting used to," Barnard remarked.

"Yeah, right," I paused, then asked the big question, "Just what is it that you want with me?"

Barnard was silent for a moment, as if getting his thoughts in order. "You did good work for me last year," he said at last. "I appreciated your professionalism and your, shall we say, discretion. I thought perhaps I might have need of your services again in the future, so I . . . well, I decided to follow your subsequent career." He chuckled. "I hope you don't mind having a fan, Mr. Montgomery." Again, his voice was steady, totally unaffected by his exertion. The man was phenomenally fit.

"Go on," I prompted.

"As I said," Barnard continued smoothly, "I followed your career, continuing to be impressed by your abilities. It pleased me that you managed to stay out of the clutches of Lone Star. That would have been such an ignoble end to your career.''

"So you had me watched.''

"Certainly,'' he answered easily. "I was surprised, alarmed and, yes, disappointed when I learned that you were implicated in the murder of Miss Yzerman. Of course, that was when I still believed you might be guilty of the crime.'' I glanced over at him, met his cool half-smile. "That's right, Mr. Montgomery,'' he continued. "I'm now convinced that you're *not* guilty.''

"I don't suppose you'd care to tell Lone Star that?'' I suggested.

He laughed. "If I thought they'd believe me, I might. Besides, my own opinion is based solely on the fact that you seem to be so interested in finding the *real* murderer.''

"How do you know that?''

"Professional interest?'' he said.

"You could call it that.''

He thought about it for a moment. "Do you know what a watcher is?''

I didn't really, but I did remember Greybriar mentioning the word. "Some kind of spirit,'' I answered.

He nodded. "I've had a watcher, er, watching you for the last couple of days. A relatively simple matter, since we've met before and I've had the chance to assense your aura. Although,'' he added with a chuckle, "I did have some difficulty persuading the little fellow to take up the task again after he was chased away by an apparently rather daunting free spirit.''

That had to be Amanda. I was silent for a moment as I pondered the implications. "I didn't realize you were a mage,'' I said at last.

"Oh, I just dabble. More a hobby than anything, though it *is* sometimes an advantage in business.'' Barnard paused, and for almost a minute the only sound was the whirring and hissing of the Ultra Gym machines. Finally, he said, "You seem to have developed an interest in Yamatetsu Corporation. Can you tell me why?''

Now we were down to the serious drek. Everything up

to this point had been simple preliminaries, verbal fore-play. Now we got down to biz. "Curiosity," I said.

Barnard chuckled again. He chuckled very well; it made him sound almost harmless, like someone's friendly uncle.

"Slightly more than that, I'd say," he came back. "You've been looking into Yamatetsu in general, our Integrated System Products division in particular, our SPISES product, relationships between ISP and the military. You even tried to find out more about me personally. Let's see, have I overlooked anything?"

I killed the Ultra Gym, extricated myself from its mechanical guts. If I was going to get ground mentally, I didn't want to be worn down physically as well. "That just about covers it," I told him.

"Not really," he corrected gently. "I recall you also had a rather intense interest in Crashcart and even in something called 2XS. You've been busy. And, oh yes," he said, "one Theresa Montgomery as well, but I assume that's personal and not biz. Your sister, I think?"

"What exactly do you want?" I asked again.

The timer on Barnard's machine beeped, and he released the trigger, climbed out. One of the urbane leg-breakers at the door tossed him a towel, which he draped around his neck. Out of the machine, he stood a centimeter or two shorter than me, but his confident manner made me feel he was taller. "That is exactly my question to you, Mr. Montgomery." Barnard's voice was quiet, without a trace of threat. "What is it that you want? And why are you digging into my business? That makes me very uncomfortable."

"Why is that?" I asked. "Have you got something to hide?"

"Of course we have something to hide." His voice was calm, his words merely a statement of fact. "Show me a successful corporation that doesn't have something to hide. In most cases, as in ours, it won't be something illegal. Why should it be? We generate sufficient revenue through totally lawful means, with no risk of legal consequences.

"But that doesn't mean we don't want to keep our secrets—investment strategies, strategic plans, confidential joint ventures. Trade secrets, products in development, new technologies not yet ready for release. When we discover people—like you—who seem extremely interested in our business, we always wonder why and who hired you to do it. Our competitors, perhaps? Many shadowrunners make a good living from industrial espionage. I have to wonder if you've decided to follow that career path as well.''

"No industrial espionage," I said carefully.

"A personal matter, then?" I didn't answer. He stepped closer to me, and I could feel a sense of cool determination about him. Not direct menace or intimidation, but the impression that I'd better not cross him if I wanted to walk out of here alive.

"Listen to me, Mr. Montgomery," he said. His voice was level, almost casual, but his eyes burned into mine. "I bear you no ill will; quite the opposite, in fact. *As long as* you're not working on something that will be detrimental to my interests. If you are, I strongly suggest you drop the matter. There are always other clients.

"I want you to level with me, tell me what you're working on." He gave me a chilly smile. "Call it a fair exchange for my not taking the easy way out."

I knew exactly what he was talking about. If he suspected that I was making a run on Yamatetsu, the simplest solution would have been to geek me. Problem solved. That simple solution was still all too available to him, of course. Quickly I mentally reviewed what I could tell him, what would satisfy him without giving everything away.

"I'm trying to get out from under," I said at last. "Like you said, Lone Star thinks I flatlined Lolita Yzerman." He nodded, politely interested. "I think she died because she overheard something she shouldn't have." I took a deep breath: *here goes.* "I think she found out something about 2XS." I paused, watching his eyes for a reaction.

There was none. "Yes, 2XS does seem to be a scourge on the street," he remarked casually. "But why your interest in Yamatetsu?"

This was the difficult connection. "I knew a little bit about ISP and SPISES," I went on. "I suspected a connection between the two."

His lips curled in a cold half-smile. "Yes," he said

quietly, "I suppose there *is* a superficial similarity between the technologies. And so, of course, you con-
cluded that the evil, wicked, nasty corporation was
dumping 2XS onto the street to inflate our already excessive profit margin. Is that it?"

I shrugged. "Without the sarcasm, yes."

Barnard shook his head. "We do have an excessive
reputation, don't we?" Then he became serious again.
"Listen, I'll tell you this once. ISP's mandate is to develop and market SPISES booster technology to the military and to other similar markets in North America and
around the world. Do you have any idea how big that
potential market is?"

"Not really," I replied.

"Ballpark figures, in the *billions* of nuyen. And with
no risk. The technology works, and by the time the first
contract's signed, everything will be solidly protected
with patents and registrations through the Corporate
Court in Geneva-Orbital. In comparison, what does a
2XS chip cost? Two hundred nuyen? Three?"

"Five."

He looked mildly surprised. "So? But that's street
price," he went on. "The manufacturer would probably
net about a tenth of that. Fifty nuyen per chip. And how
many chips would one addict be able to slot before burning out? Fifty? No, call it a hundred, although I'm sure
that's a massive exaggeration." I could see where he was
going with his line of logic. "Total net, five thousand
nuyen per addict. Not much return, Mr. Montgomery,
particularly when you factor in the very real risk of legal,
er, *complications.*" He looked pensive. "It makes me
wonder why the manufacturer even bothers.

"No," he said, "I assure you ISP is involved in
SPISES, and SPISES only. That's more than enough to
keep the division totally occupied for the next decade."
He sighed. "Of course, you're not going to believe me
on that. Maybe you'll believe Dr. Skyhill."

"Huh?" I said, or something equally cogent.

Barnard grinned. "Dr. Adrian Skyhill, managing director of Integrated System Products Division, and a top-
notch scientific administrator. I'd like you to meet him
tomorrow. See what it is ISP's *really* working on. I'll
have his secretary call you with the time." He paused,

his smile broadening. "I suggest you bring someone along who understands bioengineering and can ask intelligent questions."

I looked at Barnard steadily. "Why are you doing this?"

He shrugged as he turned away and wiped sweat from his brow. "As I said, I bear you no ill-will, and I recognize and respect your tenacity. You're on the wrong track, but if I don't convince you of that, you'll keep digging into my business. That would be unacceptable, forcing me to take some other kind of action that would be distressing to both of us." He looked back at me, and I saw something else in his eyes. "I like you, Mr. Montgomery, and it's possible that you can help me out again in the future." Barnard glanced at the two suited pros and nodded. I was being dismissed.

But I wasn't quite ready to be dismissed. "One last question, Mr. Barnard."

He glanced at me, obviously annoyed. When he dismissed someone, he expected the person to *go.* "All right, Mr. Montgomery, one last question."

"What's the connection with Crashcart?"

"Officially it's owned by ISP," Barnard answered brusquely. "As such, it's basically autonomous. I know little about it and care less. Is there anything else? No? Then perhaps we'll talk again sometime in the future." He turned away, very pointedly, and headed for a door that presumably led to the changing room. I turned, too, walking slowly toward my minders.

Before Barnard could leave, a phone mounted on the wall beeped stridently. Glancing back over my shoulder, I saw the veep curse and hurry over to pick up the phone. "Barnard," I heard him say, then after a moment, sharply, "What? Damn it, we'll handle security ourselves. Send the Evanston team to ABT *now,* and . . ."

"Mr. Montgomery, it's time to leave." The troll stood beside me, and his voice—even his breathing—drowned out whatever it was Barnard was saying. Trouble in Chicago, apparently, and also apparently none of my business.

"You're right," I told the troll, "time to leave." I followed my bodyguards out, feeling very much like an unarmed knight who, for some reason, had been permitted to walk unscathed from the dragon's lair. I also continued to have the strong sense that more was going on than I understood.

But there was no fragging way I was going to ask Barnard about it.

19

Yamatetsu's ISP Division is located on Creso Road close to the shores of Spanaway Lake in Fort Lewis. Beautiful area: hundreds of hectares of lush evergreen forest, largely untouched by the horrors of what we laughingly call "civilization." Driving into Fort Lewis is like driving back in time, back to the turn of the century and beyond, back to when Seattle was a "city" and not the megalopolis, not the sprawl, it is today.

Creso Road winds down into those woods, leading to a manicured little industrial park. Unlike similar parks elsewhere, or the god-awful Free Enterprise Zones I saw on a visit to Québec, this place seemed almost in harmony with the terrain around it, not just a blight inflicted on the land by people who didn't give a frag. I knew there had to be serious security, but no fences or guard-towers were visible from the road, and the buildings themselves were low-profile, blending into the contours of the land. The only downside was the frequent assault of man-made thunder, the titanic ripping noise of tortured air as UCASAF trainee pilots brought their ESA Stilettos in low over the threshold to play touch-and-go at McChord Air Base.

Jocasta settled herself more comfortably into the passenger seat of her Hyuandai-AMC Harmony. "I feel like I'm on vacation," she remarked gazing around at the scene.

I didn't, but nodded anyway. I appreciated that she trusted me to drive her car, but I missed Quincy's mods. Next to my pseudo-Jackrabbit, any other car seems brain-dead.

After my interview with Barnard, the two suit-clad

minders had driven me back to the Hilton to pick up my car. When they dropped me off, the troll handed me a business card that showed only the name Barnard and an LTG number. "Mr. Barnard instructed me to give you this, in case of . . . contingencies. He trusts you'll have no cause to use it, however." I decided I'd carry it close to my heart like a talisman.

By the time I got home, I found a message on my machine from one Beryl Hollyburn, Dr. Skyhill's executive assistant, confirming that I and my guest had an appointment at ISP the next day—that is, today—at eleven. I immediately called Jocasta. Barnard was right that I'd need someone along who could ask intelligent questions and understand the answers. Jocasta's field wasn't specifically biotech or bioengineering, but she was closer to the mark than I was. Besides, I didn't want to drag someone else in to this.

Hold the phone: What if, as I suspected, our murderous X was part of ISP? Wasn't I leading us both into the killing ground?

Not really, I reasoned (desperately wanting to believe my own argument). Although my confidence had been temporarily shaken yesterday, it still seemed logical that X was at the middle-management level, and that his/her senior management didn't know what was going down. Geeking me and Jocasta at the facility, or in transit to or from the place, would attract too much unwanted attention from within the corp, let alone from outside it.

And to maximize the potential for attention, I'd set up a "dead man's switch" with the information that I already had. I'd written a simple program on my telecom that would, unless I manually keyed in an override, dump everything I knew to three destinations: Jacques Barnard, Mark Kurtz at Lone Star, and the city editor at the *Seattle Intelligencer* datafax. As added protection, I sent Barnard a text-only message explaining what I'd done, and suggesting that he disseminate that information to whoever he thought would benefit from hearing it. Sure, there were ways of defeating that class of precaution, but it was much better than nothing.

The minimal confidence I felt began to slip as we pulled up to the gate. Three fully-armored security guards watched us from various angles, while a fourth removed his helmet and approached the car. Silvered corneas reflected the light as that one looked us over. Then his fingers flew over the keypad of a palm-sized computer that hung on his belt and plugged into his datajack. I could imagine the tiny unit transmitting an image of me downloaded from those cybereyes, and a central machine somewhere comparing that image with an "authorized visitors" file. Everything must have matched up, because it was only seconds before the mirror-eyed sec-guard said, "Welcome to Yamatetsu, Mr. Montgomery. Follow the road to the administration building. Please don't make any improper turns." He didn't complete the thought—"or we'll blow you to hell"—but it hung almost tangibly in the air. "Enjoy your visit," he said—somewhat inappropriately, I thought—and stepped away from the car. The gate silently rolled back, and I drove through.

"Friendly sort," I remarked. Jocasta didn't respond, just kept looking out the window.

The road leading to the administration building was well-marked, leaving no reasonable excuse for straying off course. There were a couple of alternate turnings, leading to outlying buildings, but all such intersections were marked with big glowing No Entry signs in English, Kanji, and interlingual icons. The admin building was almost half a klick from the front gate, which meant the ISP industrial park was bigger than I'd thought.

We pulled up into the lot before the low, windowless building, and I parked in one of the spaces marked Visitors. As I killed the engine, Jocasta finally pulled her gaze away from the view out the window and looked over at me. "I don't like it here," she said quietly. "It feels"—she searched for a word—". . . cold."

I gave her a reassuring smile, though I didn't feel overly reassured myself. "Chill," I said lightly. "It's a corp research facility. Not the most inviting place to spend time." She nodded, but her expression of discomfort didn't change.

I thought about it as we got out and approached the building's front door. I'd heard that magicians can sometimes sense the nature of a location, the emotional equivalent of radioactive background count. Places where there's been suffering or horror would have an especially high count and be greatly disturbing to a mage. This place? While developing their SPISES technology, ISP must have "expended" hundreds of experimental animals, doubtless in unpleasant ways. And later they'd implanted that dehumanizing technology into human subjects. No wonder the place had a nasty, cold feel to it.

The front door soughed open as we approached, revealing to us a reception area that was stylish and almost attractive in a corporate-soulless kind of way. Contemporary furniture, plaques denoting civic awards on the walls, the Yamatetsu logo—a stylized Y—on just about everything. Facing us was the obligatory curved reception desk, with curvaceous receptionist seated behind it. She looked up as we entered, and bathed us in that generic broad, welcoming smile I was coming to know so well. "Welcome to Yamatetsu," she said, but unlike the gate guard, she sounded almost like she meant it. "Mr. Montgomery, and . . . ?" She smiled at Jocasta, waiting.

"And associate," I told her.

Her smile didn't fade one iota. "Of course. Please wait one moment." She touched a key on her desk, and I saw her lips move even though I couldn't hear a sound. Implanted phone, I assumed. I wondered idly how they'd equip next year's model.

Before I was even aware the receptionist had finished, the door beside the reception desk opened and a young elven woman emerged. About my age, short with straight dark hair, she looked like the consummate professional. I recognized her from the telecom message as Beryl Hollyburn, Skyhill's executive assistant. She smiled frostily, didn't offer to shake hands. "Dr. Skyhill will see you now," she said coolly. She turned and went back through the door, assuming without a backward glance that we'd follow.

We followed. Down a typical corp office hallway, brightly lit but sterile. I watched Beryl's rear aspect, but found her walk as lacking in attraction as her manner. Jocasta noticed my scrutiny, and snorted with wry amusement. The elf stopped at a door, tapped on it discreetly. I noticed the plate on the door: no name, just the words "Managing Director." There was a muffled response from inside the room. Beryl swung open the door, stepped out of the way to let us enter.

Enter we did, into a spacious, executive-style office. To the left of the door was a comfortable conversation group consisting of a leather couch and two matching chairs around a marble-topped coffee table. To the right was a large desk and credenza set. The conversation group and the rest of the office were scrupulously tidy, but the desk and credenza were comfortably messy, apparently the preserve of a "hands-on" type of manager. The layout was like a corner office, and though two huge windows appeared to be set into two of the walls, the view from those "windows" definitely wasn't Fort Lewis. An azure-blue sea lapped against a tropical beach while palm trees swayed in a gentle breeze. The illusion was so near-perfect that I almost expected to smell salt mixed with the scent of tropical flowers. Jocasta and I both stood and stared like tourists.

The man seated behind the desk chuckled. "My indulgence," he remarked. "I find it relaxes me." He stood up and came around toward us, extending a large hand. "I'm Adrian Skyhill."

I looked him over as we shook hands. He was human, just slightly taller than me, which put him just under two meters, but his bulk made him seem even taller. He was barrel-chested, with a healthy gut. On a smaller man it might have looked obese, but on Skyhill it looked merely ample. He had a round face, with sandy hair and beard, both kept short. There were laugh-lines around his eyes, and his wide mouth seemed to fall naturally into a smile. I disliked him on sight.

I did my best to conceal that reaction. "Derek Montgomery," I said, matching the pressure of his grip.

"Delighted," he said, releasing my hand and turning to Jocasta. "Ma'am?"

"Call me Jane," Jocasta said coolly. Skyhill took her hand gently, and for a moment I thought he was going to kiss it.

"Then I'm Adrian," Skyhill said. He waved vaguely toward the sofa and chairs. "Please, sit." Jocasta and I settled on the couch, while Skyhill took a chair. "Barnard suggested I meet with you, and Kyoto had no objection," he went on, "so here we are. I can give you an hour''—he favored Jocasta with a smile—''no more, I'm afraid.'' He crossed his legs and sat back. ''What can I do for you?''

Jocasta was about to ask the first of the questions we'd discussed, the one about the exact nature of ISP's research. But something that Skyhill said had caught my attention, and I jumped in instead. ''What you just said makes me wonder about the connection—management-wise—between ISP and Yamatetsu Seattle. Do you report to Jacques Barnard?''

Skyhill paused. ''It's a little complicated,'' he said.

''Try me.'' I told him.

For an instant I could see displeasure on the big man's face, but then his insincere smile returned to cover it. ''Yamatetsu favors a matrix-management scheme,'' he said, ''but that's 'matrix' in the old sense, having nothing to do with computer networks.

''According to our management paradigm, I report both to Barnard here in Seattle and to Senior Executive Vice President Eiji at our central headquarters in Kyoto. This ensures that the ISP Division has some autonomy, but prevents our international mandate from being compromised in the name of local concerns.'' He smiled. ''I'm sure it doesn't make much sense.''

On the contrary, I understood precisely what he was saying. I also knew that Jacques Barnard must hate the setup with a passion. ISP Division, theoretically, was under the umbrella of Yamatetsu Seattle, which meant that Barnard had profit-and-loss responsibility for Skyhill's organization. But Skyhill had somehow found himself a patron—this Eiji—higher up the hierarchy in Kyoto. Eiji had apparently dictated that Skyhill report equally to both Barnard and himself. From Skyhill's earlier comments, it seemed that Eiji had to concur before Skyhill would follow Barnard's direction. It was the classic prescription for management infighting and an ulcer for Jacques Barnard: P and L responsibility but without the unquestioned authority to back it up. No doubt Skyhill was maneuvering for a shot at Barnard's job, and unless Barnard did something to take him down before he made his move, he'd probably get it. Interesting.

But I hid my speculations behind an expression of vague confusion. ''I've never really understood corporate politics," I told him. Then I nodded to Jocasta to go ahead.

"Dr. Skyhill," she began politely, "we understand that the ISP division is concentrating on some kind of electrochemical glandular stimulation. You might call it 'booster technology.' Is that so?"

He nodded. "That's our main thrust at the moment. We call it our Sympathetic-Parasympathetic Integrated Suprarenal Excitation System, or SPISES, for short."

"You did all the preliminary R and D here?" she asked.

"Not really. In fact, we purchased the original technology from a company in the Midwest, whose name I can't mention. Confidentiality agreements and that kind of thing. The tech was in a pretty primitive state when we acquired it, but we invested several tens of millions of nuyen into research and development—all done here in this facility. SPISES is now the premier reaction accelerator and energizer in the world."

"You must have done extensive testing with animals," she remarked.

"Of course," he agreed. "Again, all on-site." He stood and crossed to his desk, picked up a palm-sized remote control unit. His thick fingers touched some keys, and the beach view in one of the office "windows" vanished, to be replaced by a simple line map of the ISP facility. A blinking cursor appeared on the map, moving under Skyhill's control to highlight features as he mentioned them.

"We're here, in the central Administration Building," Skyhill began. "Visitor parking in front here, and down south is the gate you came in. This building contains nothing but offices, meeting rooms, that kind of thing. In the basement is the computer system that serves the entire facility." We nodded obediently. "The other five buildings ring Admin at a distance of fifty to a hundred meters." He smiled beneficently at us. "We wanted to give the workers a sense of space around them, so they wouldn't feel hemmed in, claustrophobic, like people sometimes do in other, less well-designed facilities."

"You've been here from the beginning, Dr. Skyhill?" I interrupted.

"I came aboard six years ago before the corporation

had even bought this land. It was Jay Hawkins, Barnard's predecessor, who hired me.''

Skyhill's voice contained no hint of animosity, but I filed that fact away for future reference. Concealed bitterness over Barnard's receiving the senior veep position that Skyhill had wanted? Perhaps.

Skyhill was continuing with his electronic tour. ''The southernmost building here, Building A, is the animal lab. Next, here, used to be the computer library, before we updated the system and moved it into Admin. Now Building B is our primate lab. Building C up here is biophysics and bioengineering—labs, machine shops, and fabrication facilities. And here's Building D, the experimental clinic and evaluation labs.''

Jocasta pointed to the final outlying building, which was roughly northeast of the main gate. The other buildings all had identifying labels; this one was marked only by the letter E and a trefoil symbol, similar but not identical to the international symbol for radioactivity. ''What's this building, Doctor?'' she asked. ''It's marked biohazard.''

Skyhill chuckled. ''Proud as we are of SPISES, Jane, we're very aware it's just a step along the way. What do you know about viral surgery?''

''Not much,'' she said. ''Why don't you refresh my memory?''

''Certainly, certainly.'' The big man settled himself on the corner of his desk. ''Viral surgery was an idea that first emerged in the 1980s and 1990s''—he grinned hugely—''mostly in science fiction. The technology to make it a reality wouldn't appear for decades. In fact, it's only just maturing now. The central idea is to use viral vectors to insert tailored strands of DNA into certain cells, and to force those cells to incorporate the new genetic material into their own genome.''

''Sounds like genetic engineering,'' I remarked. ''What's new about that?''

Skyhill shot me a quick irritated glance, but covered it with a smile almost before I could notice it. ''Theoretically, it is,'' he went on. ''But in standard genetic engineering, we work either with unicellular subjects— like *E. coli* bacteria modified to secrete human insulin— or with just-fertilized zygotes before the first division.

Now what about true viral surgery?'' He was hitting his stride. I could imagine him strutting around in front of a university biology class, boring his students to death.

"Say you're a diabetic, which means you can't produce enough insulin, an enzyme normally produced by the pancreas. In such a case, your pancreas cells lack the genes to produce the enzyme. If we're limited to genetic engineering, we can create a bacterium that secretes insulin, then inject the insulin into your body daily, and we can make sure that any children you have don't inherit the trait. Not the best answer.

"Using viral surgery techniques, on the other hand, we can take the gene that creates insulin, plug it into a special virus that infects only pancreas cells, and then infect you with that virus. The gene you're missing gets spliced into the genome of the cells that need it, and suddenly you're producing your own supply of insulin. Interesting?''

I had to agree. "Interesting.''

"Then take it one step beyond that. Let's say you want, oh I don't know, let's say thermographic vision, but you don't want surgery. Theoretically, we could virally implant a gene complex that alters the cells in your retina to give you thermographic vision. Or how about faster reactions? Perhaps some virally mediated genetic adjustment to the cells of your adrenals. It's one step beyond SPISES, because there's absolutely no implanted hardware.''

It still sounded like science fiction to me, but Jocasta was nodding as though it made perfect sense. "I assume you've got a containment lab, then,'' she said. "P3 protocol?''

"P5,'' he corrected, grinning. "At least, that's what we call it. It's enhanced-P3 protocol, with added magical precautions. The magic was my idea.''

"Interesting,'' Jocasta said. "But let's get back to SPISES. Is it ready for market?''

"We've already got agreement in principle for our first sale,'' Skyhill gloated. "It's still too expensive for many potential clients, but we're working to get the price down.''

"I know a little about some of the precursors to SPISES,'' Jocasta said smoothly. (She didn't know any more than what I'd been able to remember of Bent's comments, but I was coming to realize she was one hell of a good bulldrekker.) "I understood that they were very, uh, *detrimental* to the subjects."

I expected Skyhill to brush it off, but he nodded slowly. "That has been a problem," he admitted, "and we haven't quite beaten it. Some people are totally unaffected by SPISES—negatively, I mean—while others cannot tolerate it at all. We've had to screen our volunteer subjects very carefully, and make sure we show our clients how to handle the screening as well. Of course, we're trying to fine-tune the technology so anyone can use it."

"What are the contraindications?" Jocasta asked.

"Lack of anaerobic fitness is a big one," Skyhill answered, "and lack of—well, for lack of a better term, mental toughness. Beta resiliency's got to be about four-zero on the Blaydon-Woczici Personality Matrix, if you're familiar with that test."

Again, they could have been talking Elvish for all I understood, but Jocasta seemed to be following it. "Interesting," she repeated. "Any chance we could get a tour?"

20

As a matter of fact, there was, with Skyhill as our guide. Throughout, Jocasta continued talking with the good doctor about subjects totally meaningless to me. So I tuned them out, and concentrated on visual impressions.

Some were disturbing. The bioengineering/biophysics lab, our first stop, meant little to me. I'd seen microelectronics labs before, with their white-robed technicians working micromanipulators while they stare through binocular microscopes, and this one wasn't much different. It was what I saw in the other buildings that was upsetting. In the animal lab, we saw serried rows of cages containing beagles and other experimental subjects and a video of a white mouse, tiny skull trailing optical fibers, attacking and chewing up a huge, fragging house cat. In the primate lab, the soft-eyed capuchin monkeys watched us sadly as we passed.

And finally came the clinic and evaluation lab. The clinic's beds were empty, but Skyhill led us to a glass-fronted control room in the basement that looked out onto a smaller version of the UCAS army's Urban Combat Simulator. We watched while a young woman, wearing only singlet, shorts, and an electronic gizmo strapped to the back of her neck and wired to her datajack, outmaneuvered, outfought, and comprehensively kicked the drek out of four security drones. "Apart from the datajack and SPISES box, she's totally off-the-rack," Skyhill said—needlessly. The woman was wearing so little that the scars from even the cleanest-implanted cyberware would have shown up clearly.

As we left the building, I was glad to return to fresh air. The noontime sun was trying valiantly to break through the clouds, and the verdant woods of Fort Lewis were a soothing balm to my soul. Just what I needed after touring ISP's chamber of horrors.

Skyhill started back toward the admin building. "What about the viral lab?" Jocasta asked.

Skyhill gave that chuckle that had begun to grate on my nerves. "Sorry," he said, "Yamatetsu policy. No visitors in biohazard areas."

"Fair enough," Jocasta said easily. Then, after a moment, she asked, "What's your doctorate in, Adrian? Medicine?"

"I considered it," Skyhill said, apparently pleased to be talking about himself again, "and maybe one day I'll go back for my M.D. No, bioelectronics was my field, although administering a project like this has forced me to branch out considerably."

"How about magical training?" she pressed. "I assume you need to be on top of the magical aspects of research as well."

"Very true. I took a couple of postgrad courses in magical theory and mago-ethics, of course. But it's all academic. I'm a mundane through and through, more's the pity."

When we got back to the admin building, Skyhill shook us off as fast as basic politeness would allow. We'd burned our hour, and more, and he'd discharged whatever duty he owed us. With a last insincere request that we call if we had any more questions, he was gone.

Which was just fine with me. I was happy—no, ecstatic—to see the ISP gate shrinking in the rearview mirror as I swung the Harmony onto Perimeter Road and headed for the I-5.

Jocasta was quiet, thoughtful, as I drove. Finally, I asked, "What do you think?"

"I think I don't like Dr. Adrian Skyhill," she said, and I smiled hearty agreement. "And it's more than just that phony smile."

I could see her struggling to put her impressions into words. "He . . . He just felt wrong." She shook her head in frustration. "I know that's vague, but there was something about his aura. It was . . ." Again she groped for the right word. "It was smooth, untroubled. *Unnaturally* so for so troubled a man."

"You thought he was troubled?"

"Didn't you?" she shot back.

I remembered what he'd said about the political situation with Barnard. I might have described him as driven rather than troubled, but her word wasn't inappropriate. I nodded slowly. "Can you"—my turn to grope for words—"can you do stress management on an aura?"

She laughed at that, not unkindly. "In a way you can," she said. "It's called aura masking. But it's a kind of metamagic, something that only the most powerful mages or shamans can use. And Skyhill's a mundane."

Or so he says, I thought but didn't say. "What was all that about P-whatever containment?" I asked. "Did his story hang together?"

"It hung," she confirmed. "Viral surgery's powerful stuff . . . if it works. But if you hose up somehow, it can be deadly."

"Like how?"

"Like . . . Like you're trying to cure diabetes, the way Skyhill said, but you accidentally come up with a virus that *destroys* the gene that codes for insulin. And then that virus gets out. Anyone infected by the virus loses the ability to make insulin, and instantly becomes a diabetic."

"That can happen?"

"You mean the fragged-up virus?" She nodded. "It's not particularly likely, not with modern techniques. But it can still happen, particularly in the early stages of research. That's what containment labs are for: to make sure nothing dangerous gets out into the world. Labs like that are labeled according to the protocol they use: P1 is about like a hospital operating room, P2 is more secure, and P3 is the most secure. There was a P4 protocol for a while, but new technology made it irrelevant."

"What about Skyhill's P5?" I asked.

She thought for a moment, then chuckled. "I don't want to give him credit for a good idea," she said, "but adding magic to the P3 protocol *is* a good idea."

"Now for the big question. Were they working on anything besides SPISES?"

Jocasta was silent in thought long enough for the Harmony to eat up five klicks of highway. Then she said, "I don't think so, Dirk. We saw pretty much all there was. They weren't manufacturing 2XS chips."

I sighed. I'd come to the same conclusion. Another fragging dead end.

I pulled up outside my Purity doss, climbed out of the car. I checked my watch. Almost fourteen hundred hours, which was when I'd programmed my telecom to dump everything I didn't know to various and assorted destinations unless I told it, "No, no, I'm alive, see?"

Jocasta joined me on the sidewalk, ready to climb into the driver's seat and head off. She smiled at me as she passed.

"Do you want to come up for a drink?" I said on impulse, immediately embarrassed at how clichéd it sounded.

"Why not?" she said lightly.

Then I regretted the invitation all the way up the stairs, but was too abashed to cancel it. I opened the door, and stepped aside for her to enter.

She glanced around, but made no comment, for which I was deeply grateful. She pulled the one chair out from the telecom and sat herself down. Totally at home, or so it seemed.

"It's the maid's year off," I said in a feeble attempt at a joke. "I'll be with you in a moment." I tossed my duster on the bed, then crossed to the telecom, where I quickly pounded the abort code into the keyboard. The machine beeped its acceptance, canceled the scheduled transmission queue, and stashed the information back in hidden and encrypted files. "Just canceling an insurance policy," I told her. "Would you like a drink? I've got whiskey, beer . . ."

"A beer would be fine."

I crouched down to open the miniature fridge I'd installed under the sink. Yes, thank whatever gods there were, I *did* have a couple of beers left. I pulled out two, quickly scrabbled around for the least grimy glasses, and poured the drinks. I handed her one, and sat down on the bed with mine. *"Kampai,"* I said. She echoed the toast with a smile, sipped her drink.

Jocasta looked very out of place here, I found myself thinking. Someone wearing her corporate-style clothes and professional demeanor shouldn't be sitting in a squalid econodoss in the Barrens, drinking cheap beer out of a dirty glass. But here we were. I thought I should say something, start a light conversation, but didn't know how to begin.

Mercifully, Jocasta broke the silence. "You know," she said slowly, "when I was younger I often thought how exciting it would be to run the shadows." She chuckled. "I tried to picture what it would be like to be a famous shadowrunner."

I gestured around to include the doss, the Barrens, everything. "Then you realized you couldn't handle the luxurious lifestyle, right?"

"No, that's not it," she said after a moment. "I realized that I wasn't as tough as I thought—tough mentally, I mean. Definitely not tough enough." She paused again. "Can I be honest?"

I hate that question. The only truthful answer is, No, keep feeding me palatable lies, but I gave the conventional response. "Of course."

"When I first met you," she said slowly, "I didn't like you. The obvious reason was that I thought you'd killed Lolita. But even after I knew you hadn't done it, you made me uncomfortable. It took me a while to realize why. It probably sounds dumb, but you're what I'm not, what I could never be. You scared me, and I don't like being scared.''

"How about now?" I asked. "Do you still fear me?"

She smiled. "Respect, I think is a better word."

Uncomfortable silence again. Where did a conversation go from there?

There was a rap on the door. Convenient escape from social discomfort. I virtually leaped to my feet and crossed toward the door. As I did, I cursed the circumstances that had prevented me from setting up the same Quincy-designed security systems on this door as at my Auburn apartment. The reinforced security chain was set, theoretically preventing the door from opening more than a couple of centimeters, but let's face it, the only space you need is nine millimeters—less if you're using APDS rounds—to make life highly unpleasant for whoever's answering the door. I was just reaching to open the maglock when Jocasta barked, "Don't!"

I turned. She was sitting stiffly, unnaturally still, staring at the door. No, *through* the door, as if she could see what was on the other side and didn't like it one bit. I felt the hair rise on the back of my neck. "What is it?"

"Don't open it," she said. Her voice was low, little more than a whisper, but it crackled with intensity. "Get away from the door."

A sarcastic comment rose to my lips, then died just as quickly. I moved away from the door, never taking my eyes off it, finding my duster by feel and pulling out my gun. I thumbed off the safety. Jocasta was still sitting, frozen. "Jocasta," I said, "you'd better—"

No warning. One moment everything was unnaturally quiet, forebodingly still. The next moment the door ripped from its hinges like it had been hit by a bullet train, hurtling across the room to slam into the opposite wall. Before I could react, a baseball-sized globe of glaring, churning light rocketed in through the empty doorway. When it reached the center of the room, it blossomed into a roaring fireball.

I screamed as the flames washed over me. The concussion was enough to knock me off my feet, smash me back into the wall. Everything went black.

But only for an instant. The wall was still vibrating from my impact when the world came back into focus.

The apartment was a write-off. It looked like a fragging grenade had gone off in it. Furniture smashed to fragments, windows blown out into the street. Small fires were burning everywhere, on the floors, walls, even the ceiling. The reek of seared flesh was in my nostrils. I looked down, found my clothes scorched and smoldering. My exposed skin was red and raw-feeling, already blistering in places. Second-degree burns at the very least.

What was I doing still alive?

No time to think about it now, or I wouldn't be. Two attackers burst into the room, machine pistols at the ready. No doubt they were expecting to pump a couple of rounds into two slabs of cooked meat, just for the sake of completeness. I greeted one with a Manhunter round through the upper lip, exploding what he used for brains out the back of his skull. The second gunman crouched and spun, triggering his weapon as I brought mine to bear. Bullets slammed into the walls around me, and I knew I was dead. Then a bullet tore into the side of his neck, knocking him off balance and his gun off-line, while another shattered his lower jaw. As he fell backward I pumped a round into his throat, and that was it. His death spasm emptied the machine pistol's clip into the ceiling, then the apartment was silent.

No, not silent. I could see hear running footsteps in the hall. I charged across the room, jumping over the bodies, and blasted out the door. A figure was fleeing down the hallway, a small and weaselly elf. The hit-team mage? A good bet. I capped off five rounds after him. He shrieked as they slammed into the wall beside him. At least one round hit him, staggering him and knocking something out of his hand. But then he spun back toward me, gibbering in a language I didn't recognize. I tried to throw myself back into the apartment, but I was too late.

The spell hit me, but it didn't kill me. Instead, it only rang my bell, about the same way as a good, solid punch to the head. I lurched back against the wall, slid slowly to the ground, watched helplessly as two elves ducked around two corners at the end of two hallways, and vanished. I tried to raise my gun to send a farewell gift after them, but the Manhunter suddenly weighed a ton or two. I gave up on it as a bad idea.

Then Jocasta swam into my field of vision. "Are you all right?" she asked urgently.

I nodded, trying to force a dashing, devil-may-care smile onto my face. Judging by her expression, I didn't quite make it. "I'm all right," I told her, and it was only partially a lie. My thought processes were as sluggish as cold soy syrup, but the serious disorientation was passing. I still felt pretty fragging lousy, though.

Much as I'd have liked to, I couldn't just sit there, basking in the attention of Jocasta's concern. Even in the Barrens, a fireball and a firefight are going to attract *someone's* attention. We had to get out of the area.

"Help me up," I told Jocasta. "We've got to move."

We took my car, but Jocasta drove. My sense of both balance and reality were returning slowly, but I didn't yet trust myself behind the wheel. We were silent for the first few minutes, Jocasta concentrating on her driving, while I turned over and over in my hand the item my gunshots had knocked out of the elf-mage's hands. It was a wide bracelet, probably what used to be called a "bracer," made of beaten silver. Set into it was a large black stone that was probably onyx, surrounded by delicate lines and scrollwork graven into the metal. I didn't recognize the symbolism, but it was intricate and seemed arcane. I also found it very disturbing.

The bracer wasn't the only disturbing thing. I thought I'd figured out what had happened in the hallway, why the elf's final spell had only knocked me off my feet instead of geeking me where I stood. Either I hadn't given him the time to put together something more lethal, or he didn't have enough jam left after tossing the fireball to cook me. (Of course, I could be wrong.) But what about the fireball itself?

I looked over at Jocasta. She was as singed as I was, and her clothes were as much the worse for wear. Any other time the considerable expanses of skin showing through burn-holes in those clothes would have been intriguing, but now that flesh looked scorched and inflamed. She was sitting stiffly in the driver's seat, trying to minimize the area of contact with the upholstery.

"What the frag happened back there?" I said at last. "We should have been barbecued. Did you do it?"

"Spell defense," she said, answering my first ques-

tion. "Mages and shamans can protect people near them from the effects of magical attacks." She smiled slightly. "*Partially* protect," she amended.

"So you did it?"

She shook her head. "Not a chance," she said firmly. "I know the theory, but I never learned the practice."

"Could you have done it instinctively?"

She didn't even dignify that with an answer. I was reaching, I knew. The only other possibility I didn't find reassuring: somebody else had protected us. Which meant somebody else was watching us. And, to be honest, the idea was not appealing.

"What's that you're playing with?" Jocasta asked. From the tone of her voice, I figured she found the previous subject as disturbing as I did, and wanted to get off it right fragging now.

"You tell me," I suggested. "The elf mage dropped it when I creased him. Maybe it's some kind of magic drek."

Jocasta took me at my word, pulling over to the side of the road. I handed the bracer over, watched her as she examined it. "It's magical," she said after a long while. "I can feel the power in it. I think it's shamanic."

"Oh?"

"Shamans can throw fireballs, too," she told me. "Don't think otherwise."

I took that to heart. "So what is it?" I pressed.

She was silent for another minute or so. "It's a focus of some kind, I think a power focus. But . . ."

"But what?"

"But there's something strange about it." She said almost apologetically. "It's . . . 'out of true' is the best way I can describe it. Here, take it back, I don't like it."

I took the bracer from her, and she drove on. I noticed we were heading toward north downtown. "Where to?" I asked.

"U-Dub," she said. "We need a place to hide out, right?" I nodded: my Purity doss was certainly, as they say, blown. "Harold can help us. Maybe he can also tell us something about that bauble you picked up."

I grinned over at her. Our minds seemed to be working along parallel lines. Something was telling me that the bracer might be important; apparently Jocasta was hearing the same inner voice. Of course, I wasn't that sure Harold Walks-In-Shadows was a good choice. He might be a drek-hot university professor, but that skill set might not be the one we needed most to keep us alive at the moment.

"Head for Capitol Hill," I told her.

I felt her tense up as much as I saw it. "Why?"

"I've got a contact there. I think he'll be able to help us more."

"I trust Harold," she said. "He'll hide us, and . . ."

I cut her off, but kept my voice gentle. "And in return we'll drag him into the same deep drek we're in," I told her. "The chummer I want to see runs the shadows; that's his biz, that's his life. He knows what to expect, and he knows how to stay alive in my world." I stressed the word "my" slightly. Jocasta flinched slightly, and I knew my point had hit home.

"I appreciate your efforts," I said as sincerely as I could, "and if my chummer can't tell us what this thing is, we'll get it to Harold for his opinion. But we'll do it in a way that won't get him killed. Okay?"

She didn't answer, but she took a right at the next light, and I knew I'd won.

21

The silver bracer caught the afternoon sun as Rodney Greybriar turned it in his hands. "Intriguing," he said. "Quite fascinating." He looked up and smiled at Jocasta. "On first examination, I find I agree with Ms. Yzerman. A power focus, certainly, and one of quite significant power. But, as did Ms. Yzerman—"

"Jocasta," she said.

Greybriar's smile broadened. "As did *Jocasta*, I assensed something peculiar about its aura. Very peculiar indeed."

"That's all?" I asked.

"For the moment," he said calmly. "May I keep this for a while?"

"Yeah, sure," I said. It was strange: I still liked the competent-seeming elf, but he was so urbane that I'd begun to think I was coming up on the short end by comparison. I felt surly, uncultured, while he was the height of civilization and suavity. Was it just his accent or simply because he was an elf? With an effort, I forced these thoughts from my mind. "Can you figure out what it is?" I asked him.

"I'll certainly do what I can," he assured me. He was silent in thought for a moment, then said, "Tell me again what happened in your flat."

I reviewed the attack once more. As I described the fireball again, my numerous burns began to sting despite the painkillers I'd swallowed and the first-aid cream the elf had given us to apply to our scorched skin. When I was finished, he nodded. "Again, Jocasta has to be right," he said. "It was most certainly spell defense that saved your life."

"Could I have done it without being aware of it?" Jocasta asked.

The elf shook his head. "I've assensed your aura," he told her, "and though you do have the potential, you haven't yet progressed far enough along the way of the shaman to control your power sufficiently." Without warning, he raised his voice and called, "Amanda."

The willowy blonde was suddenly standing at his elbow. I saw Jocasta jump at the suddenness of the spirit's arrival, but she quickly controlled her reaction. Amanda bestowed a warm smile on me, then turned to Rodney. "Yes?"

"Amanda," he began, but the spirit already knew what he wanted to say. "Yes, I saved them," she said simply.

"Why?" the elf and I asked simultaneously.

Amanda shrugged. "Shouldn't I have?" she asked innocently.

"I'd just like to know why," Rodney went on.

The spirit shrugged again. "I like him, that's all. It seemed a shame to let him get cooked."

Rodney glanced over at me, his expression somewhat pensive. I wished I knew what he was thinking. "Have you been following him around?" he asked.

Amanda looked abashed, almost like a kid caught

stealing cookies. "Sometimes," she replied, "when I'm not around here."

"Do you mind?" Rodney asked me. "If it disturbs you, I'll ask her to stop."

I found myself wondering if Amanda would cease even if he did ask her. "Free spirit" seemed to have more connotations than I'd thought at first. "She saved our lives," I said. "If she wants to do it again, we're not going to argue."

"So be it." Rodney rubbed his hands together briskly: down to biz. "I assume you need, um, a safe place to stay, correct? Presumably other than a hotel."

I nodded agreement. "I seem to be all out of apartments," I said drily.

As dosses go, it was certainly a few steps up from Purity. Like fifty, maybe. Rodney had given us the magkey to a small two-bedroom place on Capitol Hill just a few blocks away from his own doss. Small by Capitol Hill standards, perhaps, but the whole of my Barrens doss would have fit into the smaller of the two bedrooms. It had a real kitchen, not just a microwave and sink, and the *en suite* bathroom had a bath as well as a shower. The place even had a reasonable view.

"It belongs to two chummers of mine who are currently working overseas," Rodney had told us. "Please, um, do your best to make sure it's in one piece for them when they get back." Then he became more serious. "You contracted me for astral security," he reminded me, "but I haven't installed it yet. Would you prefer I set it up here?"

I thought about that for a moment, then said, "Just give us the bare minimum until I figure out our next move."

He'd nodded at that. "Whatever you say, but I strongly suggest that you, um, just stay in and keep your heads down until you know what that move is going to be."

Good advice. As soon as we arrived, Jocasta and I had tossed for the main bedroom. I lost. So while Jocasta was test-driving the bathtub, I was making what arrangements I could with the telecom.

That was the sole disadvantage to this place, I quickly learned. The telecom wasn't anywhere near the same

league as the units in my own dosses. Which was surprising for a place belonging to shadowrunners, as Rodney had hinted. (Or maybe not so surprising. If they were
"overseas" on a major job, they might well have taken
all their good gear with them, and left a brain-dead
telecom just to take messages until they were back.)

Anyway, I had to make do. I quickly called up my
system in Auburn, which I was surprised to find still on-
line, and downloaded Buddy's fake-out-the-LTG utility.
The new telecom used different hardware from either of
my units, and its capabilities were much more limited,
but I managed to scam together at least a rudimentary
correspondence between the two machines. I couldn't
make outgoing calls from this apartment with the same
guarantee of secrecy, but at least any calls incoming to
my Auburn system would be transferred to this telecom
without anyone knowing about the switch. Be thankful
for small favors.

I'd just finished defrauding the telephone company and
was checking out the liquor cabinet—remarkably well-
stocked—when the newly gimmicked telecom beeped.
Beeped twice, to indicate that the call was originally directed to my Auburn number. I hesitated. I was feeling
edgy—understandable, I think, after somebody tries to
cook you. The strong possibility also existed that the
caller might be the same person who had hired the killers, checking to see if I was in any condition to answer
the phone.

So I didn't answer it, not personally. I hit the key to
trigger my sound-only, synthesized-voice outgoing message. "This is one-two-oh-six, eight-seven, six-six-oh-
three. Please leave a message."

A hard-lined male face filled the screen. Mid-forties,
with iron-gray hair and a jaw like a shovel. Dark eyes,
small and piggy, and his voice sounded like twenty klicks
of bad road. "Pick up the phone, Montgomery," he
grated. "I know you just linked into this number."

I felt cold—Quincy had assured me it would be impossible to detect the switch I'd made—and then angry,
which was probably just reaction to the fear. I hit a key,
picking up the line but making sure my video pickup was
disengaged. "And who the frag are you?" I snarled back.

"Captain Scott Keith, Drug Enforcement Division."

I was glad my video was off: I'm sure my face went white and my eyes bugged out. Scott Keith and DED—pronounced "dead," of course—I knew of, fortunately, only by reputation. DED was a semiautonomous division of Lone Star, composed mainly of ex-members of the old UCAS Drug Enforcement Agency, or DEA. Over the last decades, the DEA, and later the DED, had changed their focus from strictly drugs to drugs and illicit chips, but nobody had bothered to change the name. Scott Keith had clawed and backstabbed his way to near the top of the DED hierarchy, earning a reputation worthy of a robber baron crossed with a corp hit man. Under his guidance, DED had racked up a phenomenal record against BTL distributors and dealers, but at the cost of even more flagrant infringement of civilians' civil rights than the Lone Star norm—and that was saying something.

So I'm quite willing to admit it. It frightened the drek out of me that Scott Keith was glaring out of the telecom and that he knew I'd just pulled some kind of trick with it. Not that I had any quarrel with DED, of course. I'm not a chip dealer or user, and so they have no official interest in me. But if Keith could dig me up, even to this degree, what about the other departments of the Star, the ones that would just love to see my hide nailed to the barn? On that topic, even if Keith had sources of information to which the rest of the Star wasn't privy, there was nothing to stop him from passing on what he knew to others in the organization. Things were suddenly a whole lot more dangerous for me. Just what I needed.

Of course, I couldn't let on to Keith that I was shaking in my boots. "So what do you want?" I growled.

I didn't expect what came next. "Lone Star's got trouble," Scott Keith said. "That means I got trouble." He grinned nastily. "And that means *you* got trouble, Montgomery. Unless we can come to some kind of arrangement."

All my subconscious signals were screaming "Setup!" but I couldn't afford the risk of breaking the line. "What kind of arrangement?" I asked.

"Like, you help me, I help you."

"Forget it, Keith," I told him flatly. I wasn't reaching for the Disconnect key, but I hoped the tone of my voice would make him think I was. I wanted to see how serious he was about this ''arrangement.''

''Hold it,'' he snapped. ''Don't disconnect. You don't hear me out, you're dumber than I thought.''

''Talk away,'' I said after a moment.

''I got word you're digging for drek on Yamatetsu.''

That shot my eyebrows up into my hairline, but I managed to keep my voice level. ''Maybe.''

''So are we. Don't ask me why, cause I fragging-A won't tell you.''

''I couldn't give two frags why you're looking,'' I lied to him harshly. I could *guess* why Keith was interested in Yamatetsu, I realized after a moment's thought. Somebody in DED, maybe Keith himself, had made the connection between SPISES booster tech and 2XS. ''Keep talking,'' I told him.

''We got shut down,'' he almost shouted. For the first time his anger wasn't directed at me, and I rather enjoyed watching the way he ground his teeth. ''I got told to drop the investigation.''

''Oh?'' I said, amused. ''And who pulled the plug?''

''Veep, Enforcement,'' he answered. ''Corbeau, the slot.''

Very interesting. Mariane Corbeau, Lone Star's Vice President, Enforcement, for Seattle, had the reputation of being one of those totally incorruptible types. Of course, some people use an air of incorruptibility as a bargaining chip to jack their price way up. Apparently this was true in Corbeau's case; it certainly seemed that Yamatetsu, maybe in the person of Jacques Barnard, had purchased a veep.

Or did that make any sense? I wondered, remembering the tricky political infighting at Yamatetsu. ''Go on,'' I told Keith, more to give myself time to think than anything.

''I think she sold out,'' he snorted, echoing my own thoughts. ''Ever since she got back onto full duty, she's been acting strange.''

Again, that caught my attention. And as it did, I was struck by a particularly nasty thought. ''Echo that,'' I snapped. ''You said, 'back on full duty.' She was away?''

''Fragging car crash, she almost died.'' From his expression, I gathered he was less than overjoyed at her survival. Was Scott Keith angling for a veep corner office?

Of course that wasn't relevant right now. "When was this?" I asked.

"Couple months back," he answered. Then his eyes narrowed. "Why do you care about that?"

"Idle curiosity," I lied. "Go on, you were going to offer me a deal."

"Yeah, a deal." His smile was highly unpleasant. "*I* can't dig into Yamatetsu. So *you* dig. You dig up some dirt, especially something that smears Corbeau, and maybe I'll get the rest of the force off your back." He chuckled nastily. "Like, maybe I'll tell them you died. Or maybe I'll show them the evidence showing you *weren't* the one geeked the Yzerman bimbo."

"And if I say frag you?"

He shrugged and tried to make his face look ingenuous—a downright impossibility. "I know a lot about you the other departments don't, Montgomery," he answered predictably. "Like the doss you got in the Barrens and that fancy corp-broad you're running around with—the dead girl's sister, yet. It's simply my duty to pass what I know on to my colleagues, right?"

It was reassuring to know Keith wasn't as close on my ass as he thought, otherwise he'd have known my Barrens crash-pad had been turned into a pizza oven. But I couldn't deny he knew enough about my actions to give the rest of the Star a major assist in tracking me down. "So you want me to just dig into Yamatetsu?" I asked him.

"No," he shot back, "I want you to dig *real deep*. Find the fragging bodies, Montgomery." He paused, and I saw him smile widely as a new idea occurred to him. "Let's make this like a game," he said, "and what's a game without a time limit, huh? If you don't dig up some drek in—what do you say, Montgomery?—three days? Yeah, that sounds good. If you don't dig up some real heavy drek in three days, I'm going to have to do my duty, I can't deny it any longer. Doesn't that sound like a good game? So," he went on, "are you going to play my little game?"

Fragging sadistic slot, I thought. But I kept my voice

as casual as I could. ''Why not? I've got nothing better
to do. Give me a number where I can reach you.''

He grinned, showing his soykaf-stained teeth. A local
LTG number appeared on the bottom of the screen, and
I saved it to chip. ''You get anything, you tell it to the
nice machine,'' Keith instructed. ''See you, Montgomery.'' He raised his watch to the video pickup so its face
filled my screen. ''Clock's running.''

I slammed the Disconnect key almost hard enough to
break the keyboard. Fragging slot. Scott Keith was everything bad about the Lone Star organization all rolled
up into one loathsome body. I knew what he was hoping.
He was hoping I'd charge right into the jaws of Yamatetsu
in a mad attempt to get the Star off my butt. Or, to use
a different metaphor, he was hoping I'd walk into the
killing ground, while he stood safely back and watched
who geeked me. Then he'd follow up on that lead, because an investigation into my murder was no longer a
direct run against Yamatetsu.

Of course, his bets were covered both ways. If I managed to survive and actually came up with something
useful, he'd use it to back-stab Mariane Corbeau and ease
his way into her spot. And then what would he do? Clear
my name of Lolly's death and tell the rest of Enforcement
to forget about Dirk Montgomery? Not a fragging chance:
he'd use everything he knew and anything more he
learned to hunt me down, just to cover up the fact that
his ouster of Corbeau was premeditated. Just fragging
wonderful. Never trust a man with two first names.

22

So it was back to Buddy's. Since I'd got off the phone
with Scott Keith, Esquire, a nasty idea had been buzzing
around in the back of my brain. Actually, several ideas,
all of them more or less unpleasant. The thought process
went something like this. Incorruptible Mariane Corbeau, Veep Enforcement at Lone Star, had done something dumb with her car, and ended up scragged pretty

bad. Soon after she came back to full duty, she was busy forcing Keith and DED off an investigation into Yamatetsu, Obvious conclusion: she'd been bought.

Not-so-obvious conclusion: Yamatetsu had some other kind of hold over her. Yamatetsu . . . or some part, division, or subsidiary thereof. Like Crashcart Medical Services Corporation, owned by the semi-autonomous Integrated System Products Division, perhaps? Crashcart, the outfit that had put something unpleasant into the cyber-replacement shoulder received by the late, lamented Daniel Waters. "Kill the Yamatetsu investigation, Corbeau, or we'll turn off the 2XS circuit in your cyber arm." It made a hideous kind of sense.

Provided that Corbeau was picked up after her MVA by Crashcart, and provided that some kind of cyberware prosthesis was involved. Otherwise down comes the logical structure. Unfortunately, that's not the kind of info that can be dug out easily, what with medical ethics—and the fear of malpractice suits—and everything. Crashcart and DocWagon records are even more sacrosanct, if possible, than the personal files stored in hospital medical-record departments. Definitely not available for the asking.

Hence my visit to Buddy. She opened the apartment door at my first knock, and wordlessly led me into the living room. Everything seemed just as it was last time I'd been there, except that Buddy seemed to have even less interest in housecleaning than ever. She said nothing until she'd seated herself comfortably in lotus position. Then she looked up into my face. "What this time?"

"Crashcart," I told her. "Client records first, then if the person I'm interested in *is* a client, I want to see her medical records."

She chewed that over for a moment. "Tough. Very tough."

"Don't you have a back door there?"

Her expression softened almost imperceptibly, the closest I was going to get to a smile at this phase of her cycle. "Maybe. *Still* tough. Why?" I just smiled and shook my head. She looked sour again, both with me for not telling her and with herself for asking such an unprofessional question. "All right," she groused at last. "Who?"

"Mariane Corbeau. Veep at Lone Star."

Buddy didn't show the slightest reaction. One target was just the same as another. "Got her SIN?"

"She neglected to give it to me."

Buddy looked sour again, and I wondered what it would be like to have "unpredictable mentation"—a phrase I'd once heard a shrink use—like she did. From her reactions, I sometimes wondered if her questions and comments were not really under her conscious control, and were as surprising—and sometimes disruptive—to her as they were to me. That had to be one of the most terrifying situations imaginable, I decided. How did Buddy put up with it?

While all this was going through my mind, Buddy was reviewing my request. "Okay," she said at last. "Standard rate."

I nodded, and bent to pick up the crown-of-thorns inductance headset.

"No." Buddy's voice was sharp. I stopped, the rig halfway to my head. "No," she said more quietly. "Tough run. No hitchers."

"I've got to come along, Buddy." I kept my voice low and reasonable the way I might if I was talking to an unpredictable dog. "I don't know exactly what I'm looking for or what's important. I won't know till I see it. I've got to ride along."

"Slows down my reaction," she said. Her voice was more petulant than angry now, and I figured I could win this one.

"It's important, Buddy," I told her, making my voice the epitome of earnest sincerity. "I've got to ride along." Then I added, "Double rate?"

She looked troubled, and I wondered if I was pushing over the wrong thing. She was the expert, after all. If she didn't agree this time, I wouldn't push it again.

Then Buddy suddenly nodded. "Double rate. Okay." From her expression I could see she didn't like it. Neither did my credstick, but I knew it would be better if I could see things first-hand.

The inductance rig felt almost familiar as she tightened the straps. *Uncomfortably* familiar, I thought, as I remembered the last time I'd worn it. The craving for the false reality of the 2XS chip had faded, but images from the experience still kept coming back in dreams. I sat down—on the floor this time—and nodded to Buddy. "Ready to roll," I told her.

She balanced her Excalibur deck across her knees, then began tapping the keys.

Again, that moment of blindness, then the electron skies of the Matrix burst into my consciousness. I thought I remembered its beauty, but saw at once how pale and inadequate was memory when it came to capturing an experience like this. I heard myself gasp aloud with the power of it all.

As the first time, we plummeted from the ebony sky toward the glowing network of the "ground" below, plunged into one of the glowing data "pipes" that crisscrossed the landscape. The sense of speed was overwhelming, and I wanted to cry out with exaltation.

Almost too soon, we burst from the pipe into a different corner of the Matrix from the one we'd visited before. A huge icon faced us. Not a gleaming gold star this time, but a cross, each of its four arms an identical cube, glowing a reassuring green. The regularity of the icon and its soothing color made me feel at peace.

"Crashcart Medical Services Corp," Buddy told me needlessly.

We approached slowly. As we drew nearer to the icon, its true size—if "true" has any meaning in the Matrix—became apparent. It loomed over us like a corporate skyraker. And it kept expanding, or perhaps we were shrinking. Finally we stood at its base, about equivalent in scale to two ants gazing up at an apartment block.

We were within touching distance of the green structure now, and for the first time I became aware of a faint hum in my ears. It took me a moment to place it, then I remembered the sound of a powerful electrical substation. Not the hum of motors or moving parts, but the sound of power itself. I almost thought I could smell the slight tang of ozone in the air.

With her slender hand, Buddy's icon reached out toward the green wall. As her fingers approached, the color of the wall shifted from a rich and comforting tone to a green that was harsh and virulent. The hum increased in volume and pitch. Buddy drew back her hand quickly, as though in pain. "Heavy duty," she grouched. "You sure this is important?"

I didn't bother answering. She—we—examined the featureless wall for a few moments. Then both of Buddy's hands moved into my field of view. One held a small box with a dial on it, something like a doctor's diagnostic instrument. The dial showed no markings and no obvious sensor through which the device could gather information about the world. But then I remembered that this "device" didn't exist, in any real sense. It was merely a symbol, as the whole Matrix was a symbol, of some kind of program that Buddy was running on her cyberdeck.

She held the little device up in her left hand, while she ran her right palm over the wall in front of us. She didn't touch the glowing green surface, but brought her hand so close that the color change I'd noticed before became even more pronounced. Using her hand as a sensor, Buddy's icon seemed to be scanning an area of wall about two meters high and twice that wide. Sometimes the needle on the meter would twitch; when it did, the color change on the wall remained permanent, not fading back to its normal hue.

Buddy seemed to be working totally at random, with no logical sequence or plan that I could discern. She was also, out of necessity, standing very close to the wall, making it impossible for me to see if the areas of permanent color change followed any kind of pattern.

For several minutes she worked, and I was much too engrossed—and, let's face it, scared—to interrupt her. Finally, though, she grunted and stepped back from the wall. The small device was suddenly gone from her hand. She put her/our hands on her/our hips and examined her handiwork.

A shape stood out, bright, glaring green, against the darker hue of the wall. A door, it looked like. The lines weren't continuous, and in some places were wider and more intense than in others, but Buddy seemed satisfied. "Not as bad as I thought," she remarked.

"Don't be too hasty," I told her, "we're not in yet," but she just snorted.

The door swung open at our approach. As we stepped over the threshold, I felt an instant of biting cold, and the smell of ozone was suddenly more intense. But then we went on through.

Through, into an image from a paranoid's nightmare. We stood in a corridor, a hospital corridor, judging from the traffic of gown-clad doctors and starched-looking nurses hurrying past us in both directions. But the walls, floor, and ceiling of the corridor were mirrors. In every direction—left, right, above *and* below—reflections receded off into infinity. We seemed to be suspended in the midst of a lattice, a moving lattice of figures, that extended without end all around us. The mirror surfaces weren't perfect, I noticed after a moment; they had a slight silver sheen to them that made it possible to determine exactly where the walls were. Otherwise I think we'd have been totally disoriented, unaware of direction, dependent entirely on feel—"navigating by braille," a phrase I'd once heard—to find our way about.

The doctors and nurses seemed totally oblivious of our presence. Buddy had to step back hastily to get out of the way of one onrushing doctor, but in avoiding her we almost got clipped by a nurse so intent on his own destination that I think he'd have gladly walked over us. Buddy cursed viciously under her breath. In the nearest mirror-wall, I saw an infinity of Buddy-icons wave a hand over her body, as if to erase an image. As the hand passed, I saw that Buddy's image had changed. No longer the gorgeous young woman in her evening dress, she now looked like a middle-aged and very imperious doctor, wearing the same white gowns as all the other doctors around us.

The change was astounding. It was as if we'd suddenly been rendered visible. A large nurse who would have stomped us into the floor suddenly dodged aside, bobbing his head in greeting and perhaps respect. In infinite reflection, I saw Buddy's altered head nod in satisfaction.

"What now?" I whispered.

"Don't fragging whisper," Buddy snapped, at normal volume. "They can't hear us, we're not talking here."

I let the philosophical ramifications of that one slide on by. "What now?" I repeated.

Buddy was silent for a moment, then decisively strode off down the hallway. The traffic flowed around us, rather than trying to walk through us. Apparently the system had accepted that we belonged here.

The hallway was long, with many turns and many branches. Unmarked doors, their color slightly grayer than the silver of the walls, lined the corridor. I figured we'd walked maybe half a klick when the corridor opened out into a kind of central lobby, with other corridors leading off in all directions. A mirror-finish desk that I guessed to be a nurse's station stood in the center, staffed by several officious-looking, white-suited staff.

Buddy strode right up to the desk. "Records?" she demanded, in a voice that wasn't hers.

A staffer looked up at her. For the first time, I noticed the figure's eyes glowed with an unpleasant silver sheen. "What department?" he asked.

"Intensive care," I whispered.

"ICU," Buddy answered.

The staffer pointed down a hallway to our right. For an instant the floor of that hallway glowed a faint red. Buddy nodded and turned away.

"Wait," the staffer snapped. We turned back. The staffer's silver eyes had narrowed suspiciously. "Let's see your authorization."

With unnatural speed, Buddy's right hand lashed out, clutching a scalpel with a blade that glowed the red of a CO_2 laser. Even though the blade was no more than two centimeters long, it severed the staffer's head as smoothly as a katana. The staffer's body slumped back in his chair, while his head bounced off the surface of the desk. Then both body and head dissolved. As calmly as if she'd just swatted a bug, Buddy strode down the hallway the dead staffer had indicated.

That was when I really wanted to have some control over the icon's body. Specifically, I wanted to look around to see if anyone had taken undue notice of the cavalier way Buddy had dispatched the staffer. But Buddy was in control, and she either didn't care or else knew how much or how little attention would be paid. Apparently, judging by the figures that *did* enter our field of vision, no one was paying any attention whatsoever.

This corridor was different from the one we'd initially entered. Less crowded, for one thing, with more doors in both walls. These doors had a faint green tinge to them.

"Time for biz," Buddy muttered, more to herself, I

think, than to me. She waved a hand over her body again and her reflected image returned to its normal form. Immediately, she had to step out of the way of an oncoming doctor who apparently couldn't see us. "Wiz," she murmured.

Quickly we moved along the hallway, dodging traffic, with Buddy laying a palm against each door as we passed it. The surface of the door would flare to brightness at her touch, but none had the power I'd sensed in the outside wall. After maybe a dozen doors, Buddy grunted with satisfaction. "Corbeau, right?" she asked.

"You got it."

She pushed on the door in front of us, and it swung open. From the ambience of the hallway, this would probably have been the entrance to a semi-private or private ward, had we been in a real hospital. We were in the Matrix, though, and nothing is ever what you expect. The room was much larger than it should have been, judging by the spacing of the hallway's doors; old-style filing cabinets took up virtually every square meter of available space. A white-clad figure was searching through a file drawer, but looked up as we entered. Apparently this one could see us. The figure's silver eyes flashed brilliant red as it took a step toward us.

With the speed of thought, Buddy threw something, a small sphere of silver light, at the figure. The sphere burst, expanding into a gleaming net that wrapped itself around the figure's limbs. Before the trapped figure could respond, Buddy hurled herself across the intervening space, and drove a glowing hypodermic into the struggling figure's arm. It fell limp at once, but didn't dissolve.

"We've got to work fast," Buddy muttered. She pulled open the nearest file drawer. Instead of the hard-copy records that would have matched the imagery of this place, the drawer was filled with a swirling cloud of alphanumeric characters. Without hesitation, Buddy shoved her arms up to the elbows into the cloud.

As before, glowing text suddenly resolved before my eyes, scrolling past so rapidly that it became merely a blur. This time I didn't interfere, though, just let Buddy handle it as she knew best.

It didn't take long. After only a few seconds, the madly

scrolling text stopped. Centered atop my visual field was
the name CORBEAU, MARIANE T. "Can we download
this?" I asked.

"No," Buddy snapped.

So I concentrated on reading as fast as I could. It
seemed that in late June, Ms. Corbeau had done something ill-advised on I-5 at night and wrapped her new
toy, a twin-turbo Porsche 999, around a lighting stan-
chion. As I'd suspected, Ms. Corbeau had recently
switched her personal medical coverage from DocWagon
Super-Platinum to Crashcart Executive Diamond. Corbeau had been whisked away by a trauma response team
to Crashcart's central clinic. After she was stabilized,
unrecoverable tissue—in this case, a leg—was excised.
When the ICU technicians were confident that she
wouldn't croak, Corbeau was transferred to another department for reconstructive work, authorized by J. Carter
and K. Mobasa, supervising physicians D. Horbein, X.
Marthass, P. Dempsey, and A. Kobayashi.

And that's where the record ended. She was out of ICU
by the first week of July, file transferred and closed. Frag
it.

"That what you wanted?" Buddy asked.

"For starters," I told her. "Her file was transferred.
I want to know where to, and then I want to scan that
file."

She snorted again, apparently really angry this time.
"This ain't enough?" she demanded harshly.

I hesitated. Somebody loses a leg, they get it replaced—at least if they can afford it, which Mariane Corbeau definitely could. I'd confirmed most of my nasty
suspicions: Corbeau *had* been worked on by Crashcart,
and she *did* get a cyber replacement. But I still didn't
know for sure that the cyberware they'd plugged into her
body was anything out of the ordinary. That final connection was still missing. Whether or not I would have
proof by looking further into the records of her stay in
the clinic all depended on how detailed were the files.
There might be nothing of any use or interest, other than
a graphic medical description of someone who survived
having a leg torn off in a car crash. But, there just *might*
be something. I couldn't turn aside from that chance.

"We've got to go further," I told her.

I thought Buddy was going to protest, but she didn't. Instead she just pulled her hands out of the swirling bits of data and slammed the file drawer. Without a glance at the figure still lying motionless in the corner, we walked out of the room and back into the hallway.

I expected Buddy to return to the "nurses' station" for more information. Instead, she strode along the hall in the other direction. She seemed to know where we were going, so I didn't interrupt. We turned left, left again, then left a third time. If this had been what we normally think of as reality, the corridor we were in now would have intersected the hall we'd been in previously. But geometry was apparently as arbitrary as everything else in the Matrix.

The hallway had changed, too. It was wider, the doors fewer and further between. There was almost no traffic here, just an occasional white-clad nurse scurrying by. Archived records, I assumed. Buddy again went through the procedure of touching each door as we passed it. This time it was a longer process. We'd walked for more than a kilometer, I figured, and checked eighty or so doors before she found what she was looking for. Without a word—she was still angry with me, I guessed—she pushed open the door and stepped through.

They were on us instantly: three hulking figures the size of trolls. Their garb was the familiar nondescript white, but their bodies immediately identified these figures as different from anything we'd see so far. Instead of normal flesh, these were creations of angular shining metal, as though their entire bodies were cyber. Their faces were hideous, intersecting planes of mirror-polished chrome, out of which red eyes burned like hot coals. They fell on us as soon as we stepped through the door or, more precisely, they fell on Buddy, the only one of us who had a body. Fingers like knives slashed into the flesh of Buddy's icon, but the plain blossomed in *my* mind. It was as though I were being torn apart.

With the speed of a chipped fencer, Buddy danced back. Her scalpel was in her hand, its tiny blade looking ludicrous in comparison to the razor-sharp fingers of the opposition. She feinted at one, then slipped a lightning-fast stab under the guard of another as it moved in. The scalpel bit deep, and with a teeth-aching screech the chrome figure dissolved. Buddy tried to recover from her thrust in time to block a raking attack from the third figure, but she was a millisecond too slow. Fingers like five gleaming daggers tore into her left shoulder. We screamed simultaneously, Buddy and I, a terrible harmony of pain. Through a red haze of agony, I saw Buddy's left arm fall to the ground, then pixilate and dissolve.

She staggered back to give herself time. But not if the two gleaming attackers had anything to say about it. Closing with her, their fingers made feinting motions toward Buddy's face and belly.

We weren't going to win this one. "Jack us out!" I screamed.

A large red button sprung into existence before our eyes. Buddy reached up to stab it with her other hand.

The silver monsters were too quick. Before she could touch the button, both had lunged in, burying their hands in her/our gut. Agony again exploded within me.

"Dirk!" I heard Buddy screech, despairingly. Then nothingness surrounded me.

An instant of transition, then I was back in my own body, lying on Buddy's floor, the inductance rig digging into my scalp. My heart was beating wildly, irregularly, but I could feel it beginning to slow and its rhythm becoming steady once more. The memory of agony washing through my body was strong, but the actual pain was gone. I pulled the inductance rig from my head and rolled over.

Buddy.

She was crumpled, face-down, over the deck. I crawled over to her, moaning deep in my throat. I unfolded her body gently, lay her back on the floor, set her precious deck aside. I felt for a pulse at throat and wrist, jammed my ear against her chest. Nothing.

Though I knew it was futile, I used what CPR I could remember, until I was drained and panting, soaked with sweat.

Nothing.

Carefully, I picked her up. Her body was childlike in my arms as I carried her out of the apartment, down the elevator. In the lobby, the security guard stepped forward with an offer of help. I turned cold eyes on him, and he stepped back. I put her in my car, accelerated recklessly out into traffic. Even as I searched my memory for the nearest trauma clinic, I knew it was useless. Buddy was gone. The intrusion countermeasures of the Crashcart system had killed her.

I had killed her.

23

Buddy's death was on my hands, on my conscience. I tried to explain that to Jocasta.

As I'd expected, the trauma clinic could do nothing for her. The black ice guarding the Crashcart system had set up a lethal biofeedback in Buddy's central nervous system, basically shutting down her breathing and stopping her heart. No one could have done anything.

As for me, I'd looked on the medusa and lived. The ice had tried to do the same job on me and had damn near succeeded—hence the palpitation and arrhythmia when I'd come back to myself. If not for the inductance rig, I'd have been hosed, too. I could never have withstood the intensity of the attack except that the rig made the interface with the Matrix indirect. That killer computer code had tried to stop my heart just the way it did Buddy's, but the most it succeeded in doing was to slot up its rhythm. Buddy was, of course, running through her datajack, giving the ice direct access to her brain. When she failed to jack out in time, she didn't have a chance.

And it was my fault.

Oh, sure, Jocasta made all the appropriate noises. "She was a professional, she knew the risks," and all that drek. Yeah, she'd known the risks. And she'd wanted to call it quits after we found our first file. I was the one who pushed her into going the next step—against her better judgment. To make it even worse, her death had been for nothing. I hadn't gotten what I wanted, hadn't caught even a glimpse of Mariane Corbeau's file. I knew no more than if we'd jacked out after that first file.

* * *

No, wait, that wasn't quite true. There'd been no killer ice on the first file. Only the second file, the one presumably dealing with the nature of Corbeau's cyber replacement, was loaded with serious ice. That told me something right there.

I suppose it was possible that it was pure coincidence that Crashcart would so heavily protect that kind of file or maybe it was just standard procedure. But neither possibility seemed really feasible. Some decker—maybe it was even Buddy—had once told me that no system designer loads ice except where it's really needed because it slows down system-response time too much. That could only mean that Crashcart was pretty touchy about unauthorized eyes seeing Corbeau's restoration record.

If Buddy's death was the price for that bit of information, it was one hell of a price to pay. Lolita, Naomi, and now Buddy. How many more? How many more friends was I going to kill?

Then I pushed that self-pitying drek out of my mind. I couldn't afford to become a basket case over such thoughts, not with X or maybe Scott Keith so ready to relieve me of the burden of my existence. And with me gone, who would even the score with the killer or killers? No matter how much I hurt inside, I had to keep on top of things.

It was time to review what I knew—or thought I knew. I figured I'd confirmed my suspicion that Corbeau's decision to pull Keith off Yamatetsu wasn't a case of typical corruption. Yamatetsu, through its wholly owned subsidiary Crashcart, had installed 2XS or something very much like it in Corbeau's new leg. They'd then used that additional circuitry as a lever, either threatening to turn it off or simply by playing on the debilitation effect of 2XS. I didn't know which, but it didn't much matter. Corbeau had buckled, and Yamatetsu was safe. They thought.

So what was Yamatetsu/Crashcart's real goal in all of this? Not just a cheap-and-dirty field test of their SPISES technology, as Bent and I had discussed. If that was all, they probably wouldn't have chosen such high-profile subjects as Corbeau and Daniel Waters. No, the way it looked, they had something much bigger in mind.

They must have set things up so that people in power would volunteer themselves freely into Yamatetsu clinics—hence the vigor of Crashcart's marketing thrust. And then they just sat back and waited for the movers and shakers to get fragged up so that as many powerful people as possible could be loaded with twisted circuitry. (Or maybe they *didn't* wait. I was suddenly wondering exactly how Corbeau's car happened to veer off the road. A sniper's rifle bullet into a tire, perhaps?)

This was serious fragging drek. I'd been thinking conspiracies before, but these new possibilities dwarfed my initial hunches. Frightening or not, though, my theory hung together too well; I couldn't punch holes into any of its logic. I figured I'd finally got it chipped. (But wasn't that what I'd said a day ago?)

All right, so what was the next step?

Got me, chummer, I was *way* out of my depth, and too scared to think straight. I needed help.

One of the advantages of the dossing arrangement was that Jocasta was around at moments like this. After trying to cheer me up over Buddy's death, she'd drifted away to give me the time to wrestle my demons. At the moment she was reading the telecom screen. When I looked over her shoulder, I saw it was something called the *Neo-Anarchist's Guide to North America*. Sounded like pleasant light reading to me.

"Got a couple of ticks?" I asked.

She flagged her spot, and smiled at me. "Ready to talk?"

I talked, all right. I talked her through everything: Scott Keith's disturbing phone call, the assault on Crashcart's system, what little I had learned about Mariane Corbeau. Mainly, though, I concentrated on my logical construct: The Yamatetsu Plan, reconstructed by one Derek Montgomery, Esquire.

Jocasta was a good listener. Her rare question was always to the point, and from the look on her face she often seemed one step ahead of my narrative on the logical connections. When I was done, she pursed her lips into a silent whistle. "I thought private investigators investigate divorce cases," she said with a sly smile, "not corporate plans to take over a fragging city. Today Seattle, tomorrow the world."

"That's what it sounds like, doesn't it?"

Her smile died suddenly. "Yes, it does," she said slowly. "And that bothers me. It's too . . . too . . ."

"*Manga?*" I suggested, naming the blood-and-guts style of Japanese adult comic books that had survived, almost unchanged, into the current decade.

"Too *manga,*" she agreed. "Too overblown, with no logic behind it. The facts are there," she added hastily to cut off my objection, "and they do hang together the way you described them. But I can't see what Yamatetsu gets out of it."

"Maybe they want to take over the government of Seattle," I suggested.

She shook her head. "Corps don't want to take the place of government," she said. "After the Chaos, the corps had the chance to *become* governments. With most standard civilian governments in ruins, the corps could have just walked in and taken over. But they didn't."

"Why not?"

"Too much responsibility," she said with a smile. "You become the government, you've got to handle the drek governments have to handle. Social programs, maintaining the infrastructure . . . negotiating contracts with the garbage collection company, for god's sake. Too much work. Remember, corps are officially extraterritorial. To a great extent they can do whatever the frag they want, particularly one as big as Yamatetsu. They prefer to remain being the power behind the thrones, so to speak." She shook her head again. "The costs outweigh the benefits. We're missing something here."

"Missing what?" I demanded. "They *did* drop drek into Daniel Waters, and it sure as frag looks like they did the same thing to Corbeau."

"I know. I just don't think it's a power grab."

"Then why?"

She thought about that for a moment. "Protection, maybe?" she said quietly. "Or maybe pragmatism. Corbeau's good to have on your side in case you have to deflect Lone Star's attention. Waters is good in case you have to deflect *public* attention." She shrugged. "I don't really know. I just think we're missing something."

"So where do we go from here?" I asked after a pause. "What's the next step?"

"Well," she said slowly, "I think . . ."

I never did hear what she thought. At that instant, there was a knock on the door, and simultaneously a figure blinked into existence in front of us. Fair-haired and willowy, it was Amanda. "Don't worry," she said with a smile. "It's Rodney at the door. Do you want me to let him in?"

"I'll do it," I said hurriedly, jumping to my feet. The apartment had a security system almost good enough to rival the one I had in Auburn. I used it to scope the hallway outside the front door. Yes, it was Rodney, and he was alone.

"Told you," Amanda's voice whispered directly into my ear, even though her body was standing across the room with Jocasta.

I opened the door, beckoned Rodney in, and locked up behind him.

"I trust I'm not interrupting," he said by way of greeting. "I probably should have called first, but I don't particularly like phones."

"No, you're not interrupting anything," I told him. "What's going down?"

"Well, this." He reached into the small synthleather carry-bag slung over one shoulder, pulled out the silver bracer I'd given him. I noticed he wasn't touching it with his bare hand; instead, he was holding it in a fine, silky cloth that seemed to glimmer with its own faint light. I didn't think I liked this. "I found out what I could. More than I cared to, actually."

Jocasta joined us quickly. She reached out as if to take the silver band from Rodney, then seemed to think better of it and dropped her hand. "What is it?" she asked quietly.

"May I sit down first?" the elf inquired. "I'm quite exhausted. And could I trouble you for a drink?"

"Tea?" I suggested.

"Gin," he shot back.

It was a couple of minutes before we were all settled down around the apartment's low coffee table. Greybriar's face *did* look a little pale, and his eyes somewhat sunken as though he was running on reserves. The first sip of gin seemed to revive him, however. He set the bracer, still partially wrapped in the gauzy cloth, in the center of the table.

"It's shamanic, as we suspected," he began, "but I was unable to sense any connection between it and any of the conventional totems to which shamans dedicate themselves. There *is* a connection, though, and a very strong one at that, but it's to an entity that's shows nothing I am familiar with."

I glanced over at Jocasta, who was nodding slowly. I remembered how she'd described it—"a power focus, but 'out of true.'" Rodney was saying exactly the same thing, but using different words. "So you don't know what it is," I said.

"I *didn't,*" Rodney corrected, "not at first. But I discussed it with some others, specifically people who follow the way of the shaman and who know more about such matters. The person who was the most help was a chap called Man-of-Many-Names. He seemed to recognize it the moment he assensed it." The elf frowned a little. "He didn't seem to want to tell me about it, either."

"But you convinced him," Jocasta said.

"Eventually," Greybriar admitted. "He talked about something that didn't mean that much to me—insect totems. Honestly, I didn't think these were such things." He looked questioningly at Jocasta, but she just shrugged. "In any case, Many-Names described this as a 'totem-specific power focus'—something else I didn't know existed—bonded to the totem figure Wasp."

I raised an eyebrow. "That's it?"

"Well, he also suggested I not trifle with it myself."

"Is that why you're so tired?" Jocasta asked. "You *did* 'trifle' with it, didn't you?"

The elf flashed an embarrassed smile. "I've always been a curious soul," he confessed. "I tried to explore the nature of its bond to its totem figure. On the astral plane, this *thing*"—he pointed at the bracer—"has more power than I have ever seen poured into *anything*. Trying to examine it was like, well, trying to examine a tornado with your bare hands. I have to admit that the effort drained me more than I would have expected."

"Did you learn anything else?" Jocasta asked.

"Not really, no," Rodney conceded. "Other than the fact that I did not want to spend any more time with it than I had to."

"So you brought it here," I said. "But what does it all mean?"

"Actually, I haven't the foggiest idea," the elf said. "Does it have to mean anything in the bigger scheme of things? Perhaps the shaman sent to, um, erase you just happens to be a twisted bugger who follows Wasp. From what Many-Names said, shamans who follow insect totems are nasty bleeders, perhaps just the kind who'd relish hit-for-credit wetwork."

I nodded slowly. Intellectually, that was a possibility, but it didn't sit well with my gut. Paranoia really seemed to be getting the better of me, but that might not be such a bad thing anymore. "Maybe," I said. "Thanks for the help, I appreciate it."

"You're more than welcome," he said. " It seems . . ."

"Contact!" The voice was Amanda's, the word one that had been drummed into us throughout Lone Star training. "Contact" means bad drek going down *right fragging now.* Without even thinking I rolled aside, reaching automatically for where my pistol would be if I'd been wearing my duster.

Something tore through the air, just where my skull had been an instant before. I rolled again, kept on rolling. As I did, I caught a quick impression of a hideous figure, bipedal but definitely neither human nor metahuman. It seemed to have appeared out of nowhere, squatting obscenely on the couch where I'd been sitting. It opened a mouth filled with needle teeth, and screamed. I didn't see any more as I all-foured it across the floor to where I'd left my Manhunter. Behind me I heard gunshots—a light pistol, probably Jocasta's Colt—but I didn't waste time looking. I'd be no good to her until I had that gun in my hand. Plus, I knew she was as much of a survivor as I was, despite all her fears to the contrary.

I grabbed the duster off the chair, dragged it to the floor. I rolled again, in case someone/thing was drawing a bead on my back, hauled out the gun as I did so, and came up into a combat crouch. The *thing* whatever it was, was advancing on Jocasta, while she fired round after round from her small Colt into its expanse of chest. Rodney, looking even more pale and drawn, was declaiming something in a weird language—something that sounded like, "In hoc signo, vincavi ad munditia"—and a harsh, brittle glow was building around his right hand. Amanda was nowhere in sight.

I brought the heavy Manhunter to bear, sighting it in on where the creature's ear would be had it been a man. For an instant I allowed myself to notice its grotesque appearance. It was tall, angular, with long limbs that seemed jointed wrong—or perhaps they had an additional joint. Its head was deformed, bulbous, dominated by two huge, multi-faceted eyes colored the yellow-white of pus. Spines and things that could be antennae sprouted from above those eyes, while the skull narrowed until its lower half was all mouth. The thing opened its mouth to shriek again, and I saw a tongue—short, black, and pointed—lashing around within its maw. As the creature reached for Jocasta with thin hands that had only three fingers each, each tipped with a claw as long as my thumb, she responded by pumping another round full into its chest. I heard the bullet strike home—a *crack* like breaking plastic—and saw fragments scatter from the point of impact. The thing had a shell, I realized with horror, or something more like an exoskeleton—natural armor.

Of course, I didn't take the time right then to catalog all those impressions. Analysis came later; at the moment I was just recording all sensory impressions, like a camera would. My gun came to bear, the ruby spot of my sighting laser settling on the side of the thing's misshapen head. I pulled the trigger again and again, riding the punishing recoil, keeping the barrel on line. In the confines of the apartment, the booming concussions of the Manhunter were like physical blows to my ears.

The monstrosity was inhumanly fast. The flare of my sighting laser must have given it the split instant it needed to react. Instead of drilling into the center of its skull, my first round smashed a chunk off the back of the creature's head as it ducked forward. A hideous wound, but apparently not mortal. My follow-up shots plowed into the jutting shoulder the thing had raised to screen its head. The heavy rounds pulverized the creature's exoskeleton, splattering green-black slime onto the carpet, but I knew that neither I nor Jocasta had placed a killing shot yet. Her Colt was clicking empty, and I was down half a clip. How the frag would you kill this thing? A particularly relevant question, considering that I seemed to have attracted its attention and it was turning my way. I burned the rest of the clip into its torso as it crouched to spring. My fire chewed great holes into its natural armor, but didn't seem to slot up anything critical. I looked behind me for some kind of cover. Nothing.

"Rodney! Do it!" It was Jocasta's voice, but the thought was mine.

Out of the corner of my eye, I saw the curly-haired elf complete his preparations. He stabbed his right hand out toward the horror, yelled something that sounded like *"Esse!"* I felt more than saw something burst from his extended finger, barely visible like a shockwave in still air. It hurtled across the room, slammed into the monster . . .

With an impact like a speeding car. The thing was smashed from its feet, and I heard the crunch as its chest and head were staved in. It reeled back into the wall, spouting black goo from a dozen wounds. Screeched once, a despairing, bubbling noise, then collapsed to the floor.

Jocasta shoved her gun into her belt, dashed across the room to Rodney. The elf had dropped to his knees, his skin ashen, face slack with exhaustion, his body soaked with perspiration. He raised his head as Jocasta steadied him, but I didn't think he could bring his eyes to focus on her face. "Is it dead?" he asked in a hollow voice. I looked back at what was left of the creature to make sure.

And that was the only reason I saw the air shimmer as another one of the things took shape in the corner. "Jocasta!" I yelled. As she spun in horror, I ejected the empty clip from my Manhunter, slammed another one into place without taking my eyes off the new visitor. It was between us and the windows. I'd locked the door, which meant I'd have to unlock it before we could escape that way, and I didn't think the thing would give us that time. There was no useful cover. Throwing the last spell had obviously trashed Rodney out but good. And our bullets didn't seem to do more than slot the thing off.

The creature was advancing slowly on Jocasta and Rodney—cautiously, as though it wasn't quite sure which of the two had geeked its fellow. "Get away from them, you lousy fragger!" I yelled, bringing my gun up fast.

The monster turned my way, took two terrifyingly fast

steps across the room toward me. And that's when I pumped three rounds into its left eye.

The sheer impact of the bullets snapped its head back. The multifaceted eye itself burst in a spray of crystalline fragments and caustic liquid. It screamed its agony to the sky, its arms flailing wildly, and I burned the rest of my clip into its belly just for good measure. It screamed again.

But it didn't fall. I couldn't believe it: three rounds through its eye into its braincase—assuming the head was where it kept its brain—another twelve into its guts at point-blank range. Anything normal would be busy expiring messily. It screamed a third time, and I swore I could feel the force of its will as it struggled to control its pain. It turned its single remaining eye on me, and took another step forward.

I spun away, dropping my empty Manhunter, picked up a chair and swung it at the creature like a club. It blocked the swing with an arm, a move that would have cost a human a broken wrist, but seemed not to hurt it at all. Then it tore the weapon from my grip with its other hand, hurling it against the wall. I stepped back, although I knew in my gut there was nowhere to go. It swung at me with its claw-tipped hand, and missed wildly—probably lack of depth perception because of missing an eye, but I was sure it wouldn't make the same mistake twice. I ducked away again, looking for something—*anything* to hide behind. Nothing. I knew it was maneuvering me into a corner, but I couldn't do anything about it.

"Get out of here," I shouted to Jocasta and Rodney. If this thing was going to rip my guts out, there was no reason it should cost them their lives, too. "*Go, frag you!*"

Of course they didn't. Jocasta was firing into its back, though I don't know what good she thought her little Colt could do if my fragging Manhunter didn't drop it. Rodney, the idiot, was trying to put together another spell, muttering to himself in Latin, though he knew the effort would probably kill him. Drekheads! The *thing* raised a clawed hand to tear me in two.

The blow never fell. Instead, the thing spun, slashing wildly at the empty air and screaming in frustration and

anger. Had Rodney got his spell off? No, the elf was still muttering, although now he was also gaping at the monster's gyrations. Good old Jocasta was still peppering it with bullets, with predictably minimal effect. What the frag was going on?

"Get out of here!" Not my voice. This time it was Amanda's. For an instant, I saw her shadowy image locked in hand-to-claw combat with the *thing*. She lashed out an insubstantial arm, landing a blow to the creature's chest. I was amazed to see the monster's exoskeleton buckle as though struck by a battleaxe. The thing struck back, its claws passing through Amanda's body with no effect. No, I was wrong, there *had* been an effect. No wound in the normal sense, but her appearance was changed. She looked less human; the lines of her body were altering, becoming more angular, as though . . . My mind rebelled at the conclusion I was drawing. The thing's claws tore through her transparent body again. She cried out once more, and now her voice was very alien: wind howling down a deserted alleyway would have sounded more human. The words, however, were clear as a bell: "Get out of here."

I ran to Jocasta, grabbed her arm. She was still staring at the combat, at what Amanda was metamorphosing into. I had to shake her to get her attention. But then she was back in the real world. We grabbed Rodney by the shoulders and literally dragged him out of the apartment. As we pounded down the hallway, I heard a hollow, breathy voice sound in my ear. "Goodbye."

24

"He's taking it hard." Jocasta sat down on Rodney's couch, rubbed her eyes with her fist, like a tired child.

I nodded. It wasn't until we were downstairs and out of the building, on the way to the car, that the elf brought himself far enough back from the edge of exhaustion to fully realize what was going down. He fought like a wildman, trying to break free of our grip, desperate to charge back into the apartment. Back into the fray, to save Amanda. I had to physically restrain him, then shove him into the hatchback of the Jackrabbit, while Jocasta drove us out of there. Fast. All the way back to his doss I heard him weeping in the back, calling over and over, "Amanda." I knew she'd never answer.

When we got back to his apartment, we put him to bed. Just like that, just like a little kid. Jocasta had a couple of Lethe™ sleeping pills in her purse, and she got the elf to take them, though it was probably more like forcing them down his throat. Now, at least, he was resting more or less peacefully.

"I think I know what really torments him," Jocasta said softly. "Left to herself, Amanda would have been immortal. Spirits never die, they just get wiser and more powerful. She could have lived forever. Instead she threw it all away so that he could live. That's a hell of a weight on his soul." She was silent for a good minute, wrestling with her own thoughts. I left her to them. Finally, she said, "I think he loved her."

My first reaction was to scoff. How could a man love a spirit? I wanted to say. But then it occurred to me that it was, to a great extent, exactly what we *do* fall in love with. In most cases, the spirit—or the soul, if you want to call it that—is housed in a flesh body. But whoever said that was a necessary condition? Rodney Greybriar had behaved as though he considered Amanda something of a pest. Did I believe him, or was he like the schoolboy who says, 'What, love *her?*' about the girl whose picture he hangs in his locker? Methinks the elf doth protest too much.

I shook my head. I was scragged to the bone. Maybe that's why I was thinking about things like love and soul and even a misquote from Shakespeare. Not my usual behavior pattern. I sighed.

Jocasta broke into my thoughts. "Where do we go from here?"

"I don't know," I said. "Maybe nowhere." She looked at me, her eyes steady. I was tired, and when I'm tired I think out loud. Sometimes that's when I do my *best* thinking, when the mental watchdog that edits out "politically incorrect" thoughts is dozing in a corner.

"You were right earlier," I went on. "Private inves-

tigators usually *do* handle divorce cases. I have. I've also
helped people recover lost items, tracked people who've
skipped on various obligations, and bailed people out of
office politics gone bad.'' Jocasta smiled a little sadly at
that; she'd caught the allusion to Lolly. ''That's what I'm
good at. That's my level. I'm a little guy, Jocasta. I've
never thought any different. We're all little guys—you,
me, just about everyone I've ever met. We don't play in
the big leagues.

''Frag, Jocasta, the biggest conspiracy I ever investi-
gated—if you could even call it that—involved a grand
total of seven orks running a con racket.'' I knew I was
babbling, but that didn't mean I could stop. ''The way I
keep score, if I can make a positive difference for *one
person*—like, stop him getting geeked—I figure I've won.
You know what I'm saying?''

She nodded. ''I know.''

''*This* drek, it's about as far out of that scale as . . .
as . . .'' I couldn't think of a suitable analogy, and had
to be satisfied with waving my arms eloquently. ''The
way I feel now is that it's time to leave the heavy plays
to the heavy hitters, you know? Like, stay with the small
drek, the stuff where I can make a difference. The stuff
I know.'' I sighed. ''I think maybe . . . Maybe what I
should do is just track down my sister. Leave DED and
Yamatetsu to frag each other blind. And Theresa and I,
we'll just get the hell out of Seattle, once and for all.
Start over somewhere like Atlanta maybe, where nobody
knows us. Or, I don't know, maybe slip the border into
one of the Native American Nations. What do *you*
think?''

She was silent for a long time. Her eyes searched my
face. At last she said, ''Are you asking me if I approve?''

I thought about that, then answered truthfully, ''I guess
so.''

She nodded. Again a long pause. ''You know, I've always thought stories and movies and trideo have done us
a disservice with the fiction that *one* person can change
the world. You know what I mean: Slade the Sniper brings
down an entire government. Neil the Ork Barbarian
single-handedly repels the invasion.''

She smiled at the idea. ''But that's not the way it really
works. In the real world Lone Star would toss Slade in

jail for civil insurrection, and fifty big guys would beat Neil's skull in. Some things are much too big for one person. The way changes happen is the way *you* work, Derek. A lot of little people work on the stuff they can change, where they can make a difference. Individually it doesn't seem to matter, but it all adds up.''

She chuckled self-deprecatingly. ''Now you've got me talking philosophically. But I still think that if you go up against something that's too big for you and you get killed, then the world's lost out. Because you won't be down there in the trenches any more, making a difference for the people you've helped in the past. You know what I mean?'' I nodded, and she chuckled again. ''Who knows? Maybe when you decide to slip the border, I'll come along.'' She looked at her watch. ''It's later than I thought.''

I checked my own watch, saw it was past 2200 hours. I'd have put it at about 1900. Time flies when you're getting the drek kicked out of you.

I don't remember whose idea it was, or whether it was just one of those times when two minds share the same thought without a word being spoken. Whatever. Jocasta and I shared the single bed in Rodney's spare bedroom. It was what we both needed: to put aside the trauma of the last couple of days, to lose ourselves in the sensations of physical love. There was tenderness and warmth, and at last there was deep, refreshing sleep.

I woke at about two in the morning. Through a break in the clouds, the moon was beaming in through the partially polarized window. Jocasta's head was on my shoulder, her arm resting loosely across my chest. In the moonlight her face was still and untroubled. I could easily picture the child she'd been, the solitary girl whose ''invisible friend'' had once spoken to her. I felt a slight ache in my heart as I gazed at her. Not love; love doesn't happen like that. But tenderness, definitely. I wondered if she'd been even vaguely serious about skipping Seattle. I hoped so: I could use a friend.

For maybe a quarter-hour I stared at the ceiling. My body needed more sleep, but my mind wouldn't relax. I *had* made the decision to bug out. It wasn't one of those logical decisions where you weigh the pros and the cons,

and then say categorically, "I select option A." It was
more a case of recognizing that some part of your mind
has already been persuaded by emotional factors, and
knowing that logic wouldn't change the feeling in your
heart.

So be it. Accept the decision. What would be the first
step to bringing it into reality? Obviously, find Theresa.
But how?

I let my mind drift, not directing it at all, but letting
my subconscious bring up on my internal screen whatever it wanted to show me. As I slipped down, at last,
back toward sleep, I replayed my two calls to the Brotherhood, my search through the other clinics, my request
to Naomi to check the records for any mention of my
sister. From there I switched to the news of Naomi's
death. And from there—I could see the morbid trend
building—to my last Matrix run with Buddy. A less-than-
logical transition—isn't it wonderful what the drowsing
mind can do?—and I was reviewing the preliminary report on Mariane Corbeau's accident.

And suddenly I was awake, my whole body tingling. I
had a connection, and I knew what I had to do next. As
gently as possible, I disengaged myself from Jocasta's
arm, put a pillow under her head to replace the support
of my shoulder. I dressed quickly, then scrawled a note
explaining where I was going. Then I slipped out of the
apartment and into the night.

The Puyallup chapterhouse of the Universal Brotherhood turned out to be in what used to be a medical-dental
building. Another heritage building, like Greybriar's
apartment. The restoration work was beautiful, down to
the neon-illuminated caduceus above the front door. In
keeping with the Heritage Committee rules, the signs
identifying the building as a Brotherhood chapterhouse
were relegated to the lawn on either side of the door
("Unleash Your Inner Abilities!" "Building A Better Tomorrow").

I drove by it slowly, scoping the area. At three-
something in the morning, there was almost no traffic on
the streets, and no movement in or around the building.
Few lights were burning, and I was sure that the front
doors were locked (even though you'd think building a

better tomorrow would be a round-the-clock concern).
Like the Redmond operation, the entry to the soup
kitchen and clinic appeared to be off the back alley. *Un*-
like the Redmond chapterhouse, the Puyallup building
was in the middle of the block, which meant that prospective patients had to make their way along fifty meters
of darkened alleyway to reach their destination. This entrance was open for business.

So this was where Fitz the troll had taken Theresa when
she crashed. I could picture my sister's hulking benefactor parking his stolen car beside the dumpster just inside
the alley, then carrying her to the clinic door, her skinny
body looking like a child's in his arms.

I parked the car two blocks away, slipped back like a
wraith through the night and took up position. Crouching
in the shadow of another dumpster in another fragging
alley. Watching around the corner to keep an eye on the
clinic door.

I was here because of that final connection I'd made,
staring at the moonwashed ceiling. The piece of data buried in the Crashcart file on Mariane Corbeau had brought
me here. As I lay in bed, I'd been able to read the closing
entries of that file as clearly as if they'd actually been
displayed as on-screen text. Suddenly, I noticed what I
hadn't paid attention to the first time I'd seen the file.
The name, or I should say the significance of that name.
"Authorized by Drs. J. Carter and K. Mobasa, supervising physicians Drs. D. Horbein, X. Marthass, P. Dempsey, and A. Kobayashi." *P. Dempsey,* Dr. Phyllis
Dempsey, newly hired supervisor of the Brotherhood's
Puyallup clinic, successor to one Dr. Boris Chernekhov.

Coincidence? Perhaps, but I just didn't fragging buy
it.

Assume Dr. Dempsey was somehow dirty. It cleared
up a couple of issues. I meant Fitz the troll *had* brought
Theresa here, just like he'd said. No more figuring why
he might have lied or where he could have gotten the
Brotherhood nurse's name-tag to support that lie. And
what about Fitz's death, the murder the Prowlers blamed
me for? The troll had liked Theresa; all the Prowlers had
thought Teri was "stone." Odds are, he'd gone back the
next day to see how his friend was doing. He'd asked the
wrong questions in the wrong manner—trolls aren't re-

nowned for their subtlety—and got his throat ripped out for it.

It looked like it was time to have another talk with Dr. Dempsey, a very intense talk. When we'd spoken on the phone, she'd mentioned going back on afternoon shift. She'd also said something about reading some "four A.M. shift report." Add to this fact that health-care clinics generally run twelve-hour shifts. Conclusion: Dempsey's afternoon shift was probably 1600 to 0400 in the morning. Which meant she'd be getting off duty in—I checked my watch—about two minutes. Would the people coming off shift stay in the building? Doubtful: they'd most certainly want to get home. And would they leave through the front of the building, necessitating unlocking the doors? Again, doubtful: they'd leave by the alley route. Which I was keeping staked out.

If anything was going to happen, it would happen soon. I checked my watched again. 0402.

Bingo! The door into the alley opened. In the wash of light, I saw five figures emerge, heard the chatter of good-nights offered to those inside. Then the group broke up. Okay, the gods were on my side. Three figures were heading the other way, down the alley from me. Two were coming my way. One large figure—a big man or an ork, I guessed—and one slighter, but almost as tall. Dr. Phyllis Dempsey, with friend/bodyguard. I ducked further into the shadow of the dumpster, pulled my Manhunter from its holster.

The two figures approached. Side by side, no conversation. The guy with her was a human, and from the way he glanced side to side, I knew he was a bodyguard. But his night vision would still be pretty lousy after the brightness of the clinic. Even with enhanced optics, he'd be at a disadvantage for a second or two, and that's all I needed.

Time! The two figures drew level with me. My legs were coiled under me like springs. Now I straightened them, hurled myself right at the taller of the two figures. Crashed the mass of my pistol into the side of his head behind his ear. As he started to fold, I pistoned my other fist, weighted by a chunk of cement, into the back of his neck. He went down bonelessly, without making a sound.

It had all happened so fast that Dempsey had time to

do nothing more than start to turn toward me. Then I grabbed her arm, dragged her almost off her feet, and slammed her into the alley wall. I stuck the Manhunter muzzle into her face and triggered the sighting laser. I saw her pupils contract to pinpoints, knew she was effectively blinded for the moment.

"Let's talk," I hissed at her.

Her chest was rising and falling fast, and I could see the gleam of her white teeth against black skin. I thought she was panting, her lips drawn back in a rictus of fear. But then I realized she was laughing, and that profoundly scared me. I moved back a step, keeping my gun leveled on her face and the laser playing over her eyes.

"Well, good evening, Mr. Montgomery," she said quietly, a tone of truly disturbing amusement in her voice. What the frag did she find so funny? "And just what is it I can do for you tonight?"

Even though, by all objective judgments, I had the drop on her, I was staring to feel like it was me who was at the disadvantage. I was in deep drek again, probably even deeper than I suspected. And I didn't know why, or how. But I wasn't going to show her how I felt, so I kept my voice harsh and forceful. "I want my sister, you scag," I told her. "Where the frag is she?"

Dempsey chuckled, a quiet and horrid noise in that dark alley. "Oh, she's safe, Derek Montgomery," she said. "Safer than most people in the sprawl." She grinned. "Safer than you, for instance. And soon to be safer still, in one way of looking at things."

"What are you talking about?" I demanded.

"If you're lucky, you'll find out eventually." Her smile, obscene in the shifting, reflected laser light, made the phrase sound like a threat. No, not a threat, a baleful prediction.

Again the sense washed over me that she was in control, that she was playing with me. I tightened my grip on the pistol. "Where is she?" I snarled.

"Somewhere where you won't get to her."

"Where?" I demanded again. She just laughed quietly. Fear and disgust merged, churning, in my belly, and then burst into flames of anger. I snapped my pistol forward, rapping the barrel hard against her forehead, hard enough to break the skin. The impact should have been staggeringly painful, enough to stun virtually anyone, and rack most people with nausea. Although the crack of metal against bone was loud in the deserted alley, she gave no indication that it had hurt her in the slightest. Her smile was unchanged, her tiny-pupiled eyes fixed on mine. *"Where?"* I repeated.

She remained silent. I contemplated hitting her again, harder. But the fear of seeing her untouched by even a more solid blow was enough to stop me. "A troll brought her here," I said instead.

"Of course. He came back the next day asking too many questions, sadly for him."

"You'd sent her elsewhere."

"Of course," Dempsey repeated.

I wanted to sigh with relief. There'd always been the fear, so deep-seated that I couldn't admit it even to myself, that Theresa was dead. Something seemed to shift in the depths of Dempsey's eyes, a hint of more profound amusement, and I was convinced she knew what was going on in my mind.

"Where did you send her?" I was almost shouting by this time, regardless of our proximity to the clinic, the very real danger of being overheard. *"Where?"*

Now she laughed. Full-throated peals of laughter. "But you *know,* Derek," she said through her mirth. "You've been there. It's in Fort Lewis. The ISP facility. Good old Building E."

Oh, Jesus fragging Christ . . . So, that was where ISP obtained their experimental subjects for SPISES, from the city's free clinics. And that was why David Sutcliffe had wanted Patrick geeked when he asked about his missing woman: she'd probably already been shipped to Fort Lewis. Oh, Jesus, Theresa . . .

My focus had slipped for an instant, and Dempsey took advantage of it. She hurled herself forward with such inhuman speed I hardly saw her move. Her left hand lashed out and grabbed my gun wrist, forcing the Manhunter off-line to the right of her head. The laser beamed into the darkness beyond her ear. Her right hand grabbed the side of my neck, her long-nailed fingers digging into my flesh. The woman's strength was unbelievable, horrible. I couldn't fight her. My gun arm was immobilized as effectively as if it was locked in a vice, and her right

hand was slowly dragging my neck and head down toward her face. I could see her white teeth, opened wide,
as if she would sink them into my throat. A fragging
vampire?

I couldn't move my right arm. I could pivot the gun,
but not enough. She tightened her grip, and I could feel
the small bones of my wrist shifting. Through the agony
I knew I had a couple of seconds before she broke my
wrist, then ripped out my throat.

My left hand was still free. I fired a couple of short
jabs into the side of her head, but our bodies were too
close for me to get any leverage, and my fist felt like I'd
slugged the dumpster. I brought a knee up hard, aiming
for the soft parts of her—sure, it's not as effective as
against a guy, but a solid blow to the groin will bring a
woman to her knees. But she'd shifted her leg, and my
knee drove into a rock-hard thigh muscle. She laughed,
and dragged my head closer to her mouth. Her eyes were
still staring into mine.

I reached around with my left hand, drove my fingers
into those eyes. She screeched. With all my strength I
pulled, forcing her head back. Then I threw my full
weight into her, driving her backward—one step, two—
into the alley wall. (Son of a slitch, it worked. Strong
she may have been, but she still had only the mass of an
elf woman.) The back of her head smashed into the wall,
with a nasty crack of bone. She screamed again, and I
drove my left shoulder harder into her throat.

Then *I* screamed as her teeth sank into my shoulder—
ice-cold pain turning to fire. I pulled away, felt her teeth
tear free of my flesh.

My laser targeting spot was on the wall, right beside
her ear; the light reflected onto her temple. I pulled the
trigger.

The Manhunter roared and kicked. The bullet smashed
fragments from the wall, lacerating my face, then ricocheted off to slam into the side of Dempsey's head. Her
grip on my wrist and neck tightened spasmodically, then
released. I dragged myself away, stumbled a step back.

She was still alive, barely, which just shouldn't have
been the case. Part of her skull was literally blown away,
but she was still standing. Her rolling eyes, now looking

far from human, fixed on me, and she moved forward.
Her voice was a hideous, bubbling thing.

I fired again. Again and again. Kept firing after she
was down, until my clip was empty. Resisted the impulse
to slam in a new magazine and cap *it* off as well. Then I
turned and fled down the alleyway like the devil was behind me. And I wasn't completely sure it wasn't.

25

My left shoulder felt like pure pluperfect hell. Even
the analgesic salve Jocasta had slathered on didn't take
away all the pain, and the flesh seemed to have swollen
up around the dressing she'd attached. The wound itself
burned, the familiar pain of lacerated flesh, but deeper
in the shoulder was a dull throbbing that seemed synchronized with my heartbeat. When we'd got back to
Rodney's apartment, the sensation had been isolated in
the shoulder. But now pain and weakness seemed to be
spreading down the left arm.

Jocasta knelt on the couch beside me. A well-stocked
medkit lay on the coffee table, and an optical fiber led
from the unit to a watch-sized sensor array that Jocasta
held against my shoulder. "Some kind of venom, I
think," she said, consulting the medkit's readout. "It
suggests a broad-spectrum antidote patch."

"I'd trust its judgment over mine," I said. "Go
ahead."

"What *was* she?" Jocasta said as she removed the protective covering from the slap patch and positioned it on
my back near the wound.

I shrugged. It was about 0500 by the time I got back.
With the trip being a combination of slow driving and
frequent stops for fits of the shakes, I'd had plenty of
time to think. My first reaction after the attack was to
believe that Dempsey had been some kind of poison-
fanged, unnaturally strong monster. Now I realized that
had to be mainly my fear talking.

Her strength? Cyberware, pure and simple. Not every

replacement limb has to look like chrome. The fact that she took a bullet to the head and didn't geek? It sometimes works that way. Wound shock—or lack thereof—just isn't predictable. One guy will take a bullet in the hand and die of shock. Someone else can absorb a few dozen rounds and keep bopping for minutes before his brain admits he's dead.

And her poison bite—if it really was toxin and not just bad dental hygiene? I've seen street muscle with razors for fingernails and knives in their forearms. Come to think of it, I was surprised not to have heard of poison-filled fangs—probably with carbide steel tips—before now.

"I don't know what she was," I said. "All I know is she took my sister and gave her to Yamatetsu. The *fragger.*" The pain was fading from my shoulder as the antidote patch did its work. Thank the gods for modern medicine. I jumped up from the couch; I felt the need to pace.

Jocasta watched me calmly. I knew she understood what I was going through, for she'd just lost her own sister, but my anger and my pain were more immediate. They burned and they churned and they writhed in my belly. I had to do something.

"What are you planning to do?" Jocasta's voice was calm, soothing—the last thing I wanted at the moment.

"Take them down," I growled. "Get my sister back."

"How?"

I rounded on her. "I don't *know* how."

"Then let's talk about it," she said quietly. "I want to help you, Derek. I *will* help you. But I need to know how." I didn't want to accept the logic in her words, but I had to. Reluctantly, I sat down beside her.

"So, then," she said with a reassuring smile, "let's figure out what we've got to do."

One thing was obvious as soon as we got to talking about it. If we wanted to get anywhere near Yamatetsu's ISP facility, we needed more bodies and serious muscle—or muscle-replacement.

The key word was "serious." Like anyone who works the streets and the shadows, I knew several dozen people who styled themselves shadowrunners. Strictly speaking,

I guess they were. But gradations exist among shadow-runners just as they do among, say professional riggers. The vast majority of riggers are perfectly capable of cruising a truck down a highway without hitting any-thing—or at least not too often. But then there are the guys who can blaze a panzer down a winding canyon at night, dodging incoming missiles, while simultaneously engaging the attacking helicopters with the tank's main gun. Despite what you see on the trid, the latter are few and far between.

Same with the heavy-hitter type of shadowrunner. He or she's one in a thousand—maybe even rarer—and as much like the run-of-the-mill street muscle as a bogie is to a lap poodle. I met one bona fide, top-drawer shadow-runner once—a samurai who called himself Hangfire—in a semi-social situation, and that was enough for me. I thank whatever gods there are that I've never had to face off against one.

But now such heavy-hitters were exactly what I had to find. Hiring standard-issue runners isn't difficult: you go to the right kind of bar and pass the word that you need such-and-such talent for such-and-such assignment. Then just weed through the applicants until you find what you need. But the varsity doesn't hang out in bars, nor do they accept just any job. And they almost always work through intermediaries.

Which was why I phoned Anwar. Much as I dislike the little weasel, his network of contacts is wider than mine will ever be. I laid out a rough description of the job and the level of talent I was after, leaving out the corp name, of course. "I figure I need two, maybe three, really good guns," I told him. "I'll supply a decker"—I was thinking of Rosebud, whose rates were reasonable—"and a mage." Rodney of course. "But I need muscle."

I could see the little nuyen signs light up behind An-war's dark eyes. This was going to be a big contract, which meant he'd pocket a big commission. "Yeah, sure, sure," he said. "Sure, I know some a'the people you want. You want smart, too, huh, not just tough? Race a problem?" I shook my head. "Then there's Easter out of Detroit—troll, real good rep. Or Ripper out of At-lanta—dwarf merc, one of the hardest. Or maybe . . ."

I cut him off. "Think local," I told him. "I need them tonight if possible."

"Oh, *rush* job," Anwar bleated, and the nuyen signs got brighter. "Yeah, you want . . ." He pulled up, and his eyes narrowed. "You *can* pay, huh?" he said suspiciously. "Big players want big credit."

I nodded. Jocasta and I had already gone through this. I could scratch together maybe seventy-K nuyen, basically by putting a lien on everything I owned or ever would—not too much of a problem, since I fully intended to skip as soon as I had Theresa—and Jocasta had promised to make up any difference. (She hadn't said why, and I knew enough about gift horses not to ask.) "I can pay," I told the weasel.

"Yeah, okay. You want local, there's a group calls itself the Wrecking Crew. Two samurai, a combat mage, and a decker."

"I just need the muscle," I told Anwar. "I'll supply mage and decker."

Anwar shook his head. "No go," he said. "The Crew always work together. No exceptions: you get one, you get 'em all."

Four heavy-hitter shadowrunners would blow my budget to hell and gone. "Who else?" I asked.

He shrugged in his weaselly way. "Nobody, if you want 'em tonight."

I ground my teeth. "What's their going rate?"

The fixer looked at me as if I'd asked him his favorite sex position. "You make an offer, they decide if they want it," he snapped. I knew that was the usual protocol, but I'd been hoping for a clue so as not to waste more time than necessary on negotiation.

I muted the phone and turned to Jocasta, who'd been watching silently from the couch. "Four of them. Twenty each?"

She thought about that for a moment, then suggested, "Make it thirty."

I hesitated. That made a total of one hundred twenty thousand nuyen—my seventy plus fifty from Jocasta. "Are you sure?"

"Make it thirty," she said firmly.

I turned back to the phone, brought Anwar back from

electronic limbo. "Okay," I said, "one-twenty total; they pay your cut."

The weasel's face showed no reaction; Anwar would be one hell of a good poker player. "I'll pass your offer on," he said noncommittally. "And the job?"

"Get ready to receive," I told him. When he was ready, I pumped a short briefing file down the phone line. The file contained everything Jocasta and I knew, remembered, or could reconstruct about the ISP facility, plus a description of the mission. Even though protocol in deals like this forbade the fixer from scanning any communication from prospective client to the operatives, I'd taken the precaution of loading a read-only single-scan virus into the file. This virus made sure the file could only be opened once and that any attempts to copy it or remove the viral protection would immediately delete it. Paranoid maybe, but paranoia was starting to seem like the price for staying alive.

The weasel accepted the file, then cut the connection. Pushing myself away from the telecom, I sat back and tried to relax. Nothing to do now but wait.

We didn't have long. A blessing, because tension was eating away at my gut. When the phone beeped, I damn near wiped out a few pieces of furniture getting to it fast. I hit the receiver key. "Yeah?" I barked into the pickup.

The face on the screen wasn't familiar, but it could only be one person. Handsome in a hard kind of way, he had a long face with a large jaw, short hair, and a mouth you could describe as either determined or cruel, depending on your mood. His eyes were gray, with a slight silver glint that hinted at modifications. His manner may have been even more distinctive. It had none of the swaggering machismo, the feral edge, that most runner wannabes take on as a mantle of their profession. His was more the air of a high-ranking military officer so confident of himself and his skills that he had no need for posturing. You either took him seriously or you didn't. In the latter case you'd probably die, but it probably wouldn't really matter to him one way or the other.

"Mr. Johnson?" he said quietly.

My brain stuttered for a moment. Why would Anwar

have set me up with a Johnson? I was the one doing the hiring, which, I suddenly realized, made *me* the Johnson.

"Yes," I said finally.

"You can call me Argent."

"Thanks for getting back to me so fast," I said.

"I've discussed your offer with my team," he went on, as if I hadn't spoken, "and shown them your briefing file. We've decided to accept your contract." I stifled a sigh of relief. "Your intermediary said you wanted to go tonight. That true?"

I nodded. "It's important that we go fast."

"If that's the way you want to play it," the samurai said equably, "I suggest we meet at eighteen hundred for a tactical briefing. Do you have a secure location?" I nodded, gave him the address of Rodney's apartment.

"Agreed," Argent said. "Hawk and I will be there at eighteen."

And that was it. I'd hired myself a shadow team.

Rodney had emerged from the bedroom while Jocasta and I were waiting for the Wrecking Crew's call. He looked like hell—complexion pale, eyes sunken, the whole trip. I didn't know if it was burnout from tossing spells or grief over Amanda's death, and it didn't seem the right time to ask. He didn't say much to either Jocasta or me until after the call. That's when he told us, "I'm coming along tonight."

"It's not your fight, Rodney," I said quietly.

He stared at me, a strange look in his eyes. "Maybe it is," he said. For the first time since I'd met him, he looked dangerous. I remembered the killer spell that had ripped the *thing* apart, and nodded quickly.

"Your call," I said. "If you're sure you're up for it."

"I'm up for it," he said. I was in no position to argue.

I passed the time until 1800 hours in the most constructive ways I could think of. First, I went over and over in my mind the guided tour that Skyhill had given us of the ISP facility, concentrating on things like the lay of the land, logical positions for guards, and other tactical considerations. Then I got back on the horn to Anwar. I wanted whatever background he could offer on the shadow team that called themselves the Wrecking Crew.

Very impressive brag sheets these guys had. Argent,

the leader, had learned his skills in Fuchi's corporate
army, with three seasons' worth of Desert Wars under
his belt. Definitely a tough customer. One very disturbing note in his record caught my attention, however, and
wouldn't let it go. Argent had two cyberarms. Now that
wasn't so unusual in itself, particularly after three Desert
War tours of duty. I think I'd have been more surprised
to learn that he'd come through *without* losing some of
his body parts. No, what I found so disturbing was that
the cyberarms were voluntary replacements. Translation:
Argent had chosen to have this perfectly functional meat
arms lopped off and replaced with metal. What the frag
kind of person would make such a decision? What would
go through your mind as you told the surgeon, "Go
ahead, cut'em off"? Scary.

Argent's second-in-command was an Amerindian
named Hawk. He was also a combat shaman, a rarity in
the sprawl. According to Anwar's data, Hawk was an
Eagle shaman who'd served a full tour of duty with the
Sioux Special Forces—that's right, the infamous Wild-
cats—in the magically active Spiritwalker unit, then resigned his commission to go solo. One very tough
hombre, this Hawk.

Then there was Toshi, another razorguy. His background was more like that of most of the runners I knew,
but more so. Raised on the street, ran with the gangs,
metalled himself up, and carved out a solid rep—the usual
thing.

Rounding out the team was Peg the decker. Another
interesting case. Thanks to a bike crash when she was
sixteen, Peg was a high quadriplegic. The trauma to the
spinal cord was so severe and so high up that even
cyberware couldn't help. You need motor nerves to com-
municate with cyberlimbs, and she didn't have any functional ones left. Peg could handle a datajack, though, and
she took to the Matrix as the only world where her in-
juries weren't a disadvantage. In the ten years since, she'd
built up a track record that included jobs on every continent, though she never left her room in the San Fran-
cisco clinic that was home. For the past three years, Peg
was the only decker the other members of the Wrecking
Crew would ever work with.

Interesting reading, and very reassuring. I was getting

good people for my money. My confidence increased: we had a good chance of pulling this one off.

So, I passed the time by planning and by reading. But mainly by worrying myself sick.

At 1800 on the nose, I heard the roar of heavy-bike engines in the street. Three, I thought: Argent, Hawk, and Toshi. A logical procedure would be for Argent and Hawk to attend the meet, while the other samurai patrolled outside, just in case it was some kind of setup.

A knock sounded on the door. Rodney closed his eyes, seemed to slip into a kind of trance for a couple of seconds. Then he roused himself and told me, "It's them." I nodded, and he opened the door.

Argent was the first one in. A big man, even bigger than I'd guessed from his image on the phone screen. Despite my intention to keep my eyes on his face, my gaze was drawn down to his angular metal hands. Not the shining chrome that most would-be street monsters select, but a matte black finish that made the hands look even more lethal—evil, even—than I'd have thought possible. My gaze slipped back to his face, searched his cold eyes for some clue to his personality. But his expression was unreadable.

Behind Argent was an Amerindian, surprisingly slender-faced and ascetically handsome, but with a muscular body that rivaled Argent's in size. This had to be Hawk, the combat shaman. Both runners wore standard "business suits," form-fitting black garments that showed the characteristic ridging of armor plates under the surface. Neither had any visible weapons, but I knew they had to have hold-outs concealed somewhere.

Argent scanned the room coolly, Hawk standing a meter back and to his right. Perfect interlocking fields of fire for right-handers. Then the big razorguy nodded to me. "Good evening, Mr. Johnson," he said, gesturing to the phone. "I'd like Peg to join us, if that's all right with you." At a nod from me, the samurai crossed to the phone, punched in a code. The screen remained blank, but a female voice sounded from the speaker, "I'm on-line, Argent."

Argent then settled himself on the couch, while Hawk leaned casually against the wall near the door. Their ap-

parent casualness didn't fool me. I knew they were both
hair-triggered and ready for anything.

"Okay," the samurai said quietly, "let's go over the
situation again. It's a straightforward penetration and lift-
out. Site: a corp research facility. Subject: one female
human. No other constraints or requirements. Right?"

"Just one," I told him. "The three of us will be going
with you."

Argent's cold eyes flicked over me, Jocasta, and Rodney. "You didn't say anything about tourists," he said
after a moment.

Before I could answer, Hawk spoke. His voice was
slow and deep, even deeper than his size might have implied. "The elf's a hermetic mage, Argent," he said. He
fixed Rodney with a curious gaze. "Initiate?" Rodney
nodded. "The woman's magically active, but at a low
and uncontrolled level. Class her as an adept, maybe.
And Mr. Johnson . . ." He looked me over, grinned with
dry humor. "Mr. Johnson's mundane, but he has a serious mad on, and is ready to kick ass and take names.
Not your standard tourists."

Argent shrugged, seeming disinclined to dispute the
Amerindian's assessment. "Fine," he said after a moment's thought. "You come." He changed the subject
abruptly. "I sent Peg in to get more background on the
site. Specifically, guard assignments and security provi-
sions." He tossed a chip my way. "Here's the tactical
database she put together. I want you three to scan it—
and commit it to memory—by twenty-three hundred. We
move at twenty-four."

I nodded agreement. Argent was the pro, and I was
quite willing to leave tactical matters in his metallic
hands.

"We'll supply you with weapons," the big man went
on. I started to speak, but he cut me off. "I *know* you've
got your own ordnance. But if you use ours, I'll know it's
going to work." He turned to the shaman. "Hawk, why
don't you have a talk with your *colleague?*"

Rodney and the Amerindian adjourned to the kitchen,
and I could faintly hear them discussing things like spells,
grades of initiation, degrees of drain, and other drek that
could just as well have been Greek to me. Argent looked
as though he had simply turned himself off. His eyes

remained open and idly scanning the room, but he seemed to have withdrawn inward. For the briefest moment I considered trying to strike up a conversation, then rejected the idea.

Instead, I took the chip the big samurai had given me and slotted it into the phone, called up the text onto the screen. Peg had been busy. Somehow she'd managed to discover that the regular security detachment guarding the ISP facility numbered twenty-five, and she'd even listed them by fragging name. Times of shift-change were given, and even historical records on when senior officers had conducted surprise inspections. Then she'd gone on to itemize the site's electronic security—a depressingly long list that included everything from standard motion sensors around the perimeter to vibration/pressure units near the individual buildings. Still, the decker's comments stated that she foresaw no problem disabling those systems when she ran so-called "Matrix overwatch." I wished I could share her confidence.

The most disturbing item on the tactical database, though, was the news that ISP used "parabiologicals" as part of their security regime. In other words, they had Awakened critters as watchdogs: a couple of hell hounds, to be precise. Just peachy fragging keen. Hell hounds were basically good little doggies who could spit flame and reduce a militant troll to hamburger in under a minute. I wondered how Argent and crew planned to deal with these pets.

After the security aspects, the tac database went into issues of timing and "disposition of assets"—basically, estimates of time for penetration, total mission duration, fall-back points, meeting locations, and various contingency plans in case the whole thing hosed up. There was even an estimate of our chances of success: 90 percent, with a confidence interval of plus or minus 4 percent. (Now, where those figures came from, I couldn't even guess. But they were presented in such an authoritative style that I dared not take issue.) All in all, it was a piece of work almost military in its precision. Considering the background of the team leader, of course, that shouldn't have come as a surprise.

After a while, Rodney returned from his conference with Hawk, and he and Jocasta joined me at the terminal.

Despite the complexity and high data content of Peg's tac database, there were few enough things that we really had to remember. Basically, two major rules. Listen to the Wrecking Crew, and if they said to do something, do it *now,* no questions asked. And, if things went to hell, meet at the perimeter directly opposite the main gate. Peg would have the alarms disabled and enough computer-mediated chaos to make sure the security guards were heavily involved elsewhere.

Though I had expected the time to crawl by, midnight came almost too soon. The relative silence of the street was ripped by a heavy bike gunning its engine.

"Time to go," Argent said, rising to his feet with the silent grace of a hunting cat.

"How do we travel?" I asked. "I've got a car, but it's a two-seater."

"You and you"—the samurai pointed to Jocasta and Rodney—"take the car. Mr. Johnson rides with us."

The Wrecking Crew rode bikes that perfectly fitted their style and their business: fast and almost brutally powerful. Hawk and Argent rode Harley hogs—"combat bikes," Hawk had called them with a grin. Seated astride a Honda Viking was Toshi, the second samurai, a tall, edgy-looking elf of Japanese extraction. The bike looked faster than the others, but higher-strung, probably matching his personality.

"Gear check when we hit Fort Lewis," Argent announced. "Mr. Johnson, you ride with me." I nodded. "Follow us," he told Jocasta, who was driving my car, with Rodney in the passenger sat. "And keep up," he said. He twisted his throttle, and the big engine blasted like a heavy machine gun. "Okay, Mr. Johnson, mount up."

I swung a leg over, settled myself on the rear of the saddle. Argent's shoulders were like a huge wall in front of me. I placed my feet on the pegs and grabbed the handles. "Okay," I said.

He grabbed a handful of throttle, and we were away. The scream of the bike echoed off the buildings around us, redoubled as the others took off after us. The night air was cool, rushing against my face. Argent laid the heavy bike way over to negotiate the turn onto Twenty-

third Avenue East. From there it was a straight shot south
toward Madison, and he just rolled the throttle on. The
other two bikes pulled up beside and slightly behind us,
a vee-formation of hurtling metal.

Toshi grinned at me, his smile feral in the street lights.
Slipping his feet off the pegs, he let the metal toe-caps
of his boots drag, kicking sparks from the road surface.
I risked a glance over my shoulder. Jocasta and Rodney
in the Jackrabbit were close behind, our group forming
a tight little convoy as we screamed south toward Fort
Lewis.

26

We pulled off the road into a wooded area about a klick
away from the ISP facility. While the Wrecking Crew
were killing their bike engines, Jocasta was carefully
driving my Jackrabbit as deep into the trees as she could
get. I swung myself off Argent's Harley, my muscles
complaining a little from riding pillion for almost an
hour.

"Weapons check," Argent said quietly. "Let's see
what you've got, Mr. Johnson." I pulled out my Manhunter, made sure the safety was on, and handed it to
him. The big samurai quickly checked the action, then
flipped it around so that he held the barrel and then passed
it back to me. "Good condition," he acknowledged.
"Okay, you keep that." He turned to the other samurai.
"Toshi, a Roomsweeper for Mr. Johnson."

The edgy-looking samurai had opened the "trunk" of
his Viking, the storage area under the saddle. From its
recesses he pulled out a short-barreled shotgun, tossed it
to me. I quickly checked the weapon over, trying to be
as efficient and businesslike as Argent. The Remington
Roomsweeper seemed new, its action like silk, having
been used just enough for the parts to work in properly.
I checked the tubular magazine under the barrel—six
shells—then glanced up, about to ask for more ammo.
Argent had anticipated me. I took the box he offered,

checked the shells: double-ought cubic pellets, suitable for the biggest game. I stuffed the pockets of my duster with a dozen extra rounds, and adjusted the Roomsweeper's strap so it hung comfortably at my hip. It was a good weapon combination—the shotgun for "suppressing" a room in a hurry, the Manhunter for targets requiring accuracy over firepower.

"*Daisho*," I remarked to Argent, naming the traditional long sword/short sword combination of the Japanese samurai. He grinned slightly in appreciation. I felt edgy but ready: locked in, cranked up, out on the pointy end and ready to rock and roll.

While I'd been checking my equipment, Toshi and Hawk—the latter now wearing a knife as long as my forearm on his hip—had been gearing up Jocasta and Rodney. I saw they were both packing silenced Uzi III SMGs. Good choice, I thought: highly lethal, but simple enough for people not extensively trained in small arms. As a matter of course I checked out the Crew as well. Argent had twin Ingram smartguns holstered on his hips, and four grenades on a bandolier across his chest. Toshi cradled a Heckler & Koch HK227S, and wore an Ares Viper flechette pistol on his hip. In addition to his knife, Hawk carried an AK-98 assault rifle, although the profusion of fetishes on his belt and bandoliers hinted that he wouldn't be depending exclusively on mundane firepower if we hit resistance.

Argent touched me on the shoulder. "One last thing," he said. "It's stupid to take any chances." In his hand was a standard two-color pack of camo paint. He dipped two fingers into the pigment and quickly smeared my face. He streaked dark pigment over my cheek bones, forehead, jawline, and nose, then swiped the lighter tone in the hollows of both cheeks, under my eyebrows, and under my chin. It seemed like a rather desultory job. Shouldn't the paint be applied thicker? I wondered. But then I looked at Jocasta, who was getting the same minimalist treatment from Hawk. The dark paint was applied to the high points of the face, the places that generally look lighter, while the light paint was applied to the shadowed areas. It had the effect of removing all sense of depth, of relief, from the face, making it surprisingly difficult to recognize it *as* a face. These guys knew what they were doing.

Then an interesting thought struck me. "What about thermographic vision?" I said. "Paint won't make any difference there."

The big samurai nodded. "There's some debate on that," he said quietly. "Toshi, he's got what he calls his 'cool suit.' Chemical cool-packs under his armor to lower his body temperature. Though I think it just slows him down." The smaller razorguy shot Argent a sour look. "I prefer these," the leader went on, touching the grenades hanging from his bandolier. "Thermo grenades. They kick out more heat than light, so they're more dazzling to thermographic vision than normal vision."

He turned aside brusquely—interview over—and strapped a miniature phone onto his wrist, slipped the wireless earpiece into his ear. He raised the wrist unit to his mouth and spoke softly, "Peg, point one." Of course I didn't hear the response.

Point one. According to the tactical plan, that meant we had ten minutes to get to our penetration point. Then Peg would start her electronic violation of ISP's security systems. A minute or two later we'd go over the fence, and the game would be on.

Toshi tossed me something: a pair of night-vision goggles. I was familiar with the technology from my days at the Star, so I had no problem slipping them on and adjusting them properly. When I turned them on, they made the nighttime forest look almost day-bright. Disconcerting at first were the slight graininess and faint persistence of light-colored objects, which led to a smearing effect when I moved my head, but I knew from experience I'd soon stop noticing. Toshi was fitting a similar set onto Jocasta, but Rodney waved away the unit offered by Hawk. Presumably his elven eyes made such technological intervention irrelevant.

Argent raised a clenched fist and we moved out, slipping like wraiths through the woods. Or, more correctly, the Wrecking Crew did. The two samurai made about as much sound as a small woodland animal—in other words, not much—while Hawk's movement was utterly silent. He might have been no more than a holographic projection for all he disturbed the foliage. In comparison, the rest of us moved like a herd of moose.

It took us almost the whole ten minutes to get to point two, a spot just outside the perimeter nearest to building E, the containment lab. The cloud cover was total, and under the trees the night was as dark as the inside of a sack. Without the night goggles, I'd have been blind. The compound on the other side of the four-meter-high fence was in darkness as well; not a single light showed. That told us one thing: ISP's security contingent were either depending on thermographic vision or night scopes or else on beings that could see in the dark.

As soon as we reached the fence, Hawk settled himself down on his knees. His eyes closed, and his breathing slowed until it was almost imperceptible. After maybe a minute he shook himself, as though just waking up, and rose to his feet again. "No spirits or elementals on patrol," he whispered. "There *are* two hell hounds, but I don't think they spotted me. The buildings are all warded, and have magical barriers up. The barrier on building E is *very* powerful."

"Could you break it?" Argent asked.

"Maybe," the big Amerindian answered after a moment. "But I wouldn't want to have to try. I wouldn't be good for much afterward."

The leader accepted that with a nod. He raised his wrist phone, was about to speak.

"We've got company coming," Rodney said quietly. Everybody else was facing the ISP compound; Rodney had his back to the fence, and was scanning the jungle. He pointed back along our tracks. "Fifty meters," he said.

So fast I didn't even see him move, Argent was by the elf's side. Both Ingrams were out and tracking in the direction Rodney had indicated. "Security?"

The mage shook his head. "I don't think so."

"Armed?"

Rodney nodded to Argent's question. "Yes, very much like us."

The big samurai gritted his teeth in anger. I could see that he didn't appreciate complications. "Okay, fade," he whispered to the rest of us, "and hold fire until we get a positive visual ident."

His two colleagues took him at his word. When he said "fade," they faded; in fact, they vanished. I hunkered down behind a small bush near Jocasta. Rodney didn't move, but just stood there murmuring in Latin, all the while seeming to dissolve into the background. Every time I took my eyes off him, it was more difficult to reacquire his image. I shook my head. Mages.

There was a rustling in the underbrush ahead. I could see a black-clad figure approaching. It wore a sophisticated suit of body armor, complete with helmet, whose style was disturbingly familiar. I'd seen armor like that; I'd *worn* armor like that. The figure's hands were empty, and he moved upright with little concern for concealment. The figure reached up and removed its helmet. My night goggles made it difficult to pick out subtle details, but I recognized that ugly face.

I stood up from behind my sheltering bush. "Keith, you drekhead!" I hissed. "What the *frag* are you doing here?"

As if my movement had been a signal, six bright red sighting-laser spots appeared over Scott Keith's face and on the torso of his Lone Star Active Response Team armor. (*Six spots?* I wondered. Then I realized Argent had both his Ingrams on line.)

Scott Keith blinked, and turned away from the lasers' dazzle. "Okay, okay," he whispered, "I know you're not alone. Neither am I."

Hawk's voice sounded calmly from beside me, even though I knew his meat body was ten meters away. "Just what is going on, Mr. Johnson?"

Keith's nasty smile broadened at that. If we hadn't been in the middle of a fragging forest at night he'd probably have guffawed. " 'Mr. Johnson'? We're certainly moving up in the world, aren't we?"

I took a step toward him, showing my empty hands as two targeting spots bloomed on my own chest. "Get down and we'll talk about it," I hissed.

We crouched face to face in the underbrush. His body was rank from sweating in the full combat armor, his breath reeked of alcohol and onions. The miserable slot had taken a couple of belts—dutch courage, probably—before coming here.

"What the frag are you doing here, Keith?" I snarled into his face. "I'm doing what you wanted," I lied, "getting the dirt on Yamatetsu. You trying to hose it up for me?"

"Now *there's* an idea," he said in mock surprise. "Wish I'd thought of that myself. No, Montgomery—oh, oh yes, *Mr. Johnson*—I'm only here to make sure you go through with it and don't sell out to the scum."

"How did you know it was tonight?" I demanded.

Keith's unpleasant smile grew even wider. I struggled not to flinch away from his breath. "Oh, a friend of yours told me you were hiring muscle," he said casually. "He even told me who, isn't that nice? So of course I knew what you were up to." He hesitated, then said mock-solicitously, "Read-only single-scan viruses don't cut it anymore. Thought I should tell you that."

I kept my face expressionless—I think—but my thoughts were racing. *Anwar, you fragging weasel. Sell me out to the fragging DED, huh?* I filed that away under unfinished business, and forced my mind back to the present. "Okay, Keith," I said, "you had the whole thing chipped. But you're here now, and you've got, what, four . . . ?"

"Five."

"You've got *five* troopers backing you. I've got my runners. What do we do now? Shoot it out right here, and let the survivors—if there *are* any—go over the fence? Just what the frag do you have in mind, chummer?"

He shrugged casually, as though thinking it through for the first time. I knew he had something in mind, though. "I think we'll just tag along with you guys," he said. "We'll guard your backs." He turned away so fast that he didn't see my one-fingered salute.

Predictably, Argent didn't like the arrangement one bit. Hawk liked it less, and Toshi was on the point of unilaterally deciding to geek Keith and his troopers—and frag Mr. Johnson's opinion in the matter. Finally, however, the fact that we had a deal—and the righteous anger engendered by the fact that I'd got fragged by my fixer—settled the matter. We'd go in, and the DED boys could come along. But at the first sign of *anything* untoward, it was major hosing time.

I didn't like the game any better than Argent, but at least I understood enough about Keith's situation to feel a little more confident. Scott Keith was out on a very slender limb, bringing a full five-person squad of DED troopers along. If things did get hosed, and the Yama-tetsu guards took even one trooper—dead *or* alive—Keith would be up for the chop, big time. Even the best-trained DED hitters couldn't be confident of taking down the Wrecking Crew without losses and without a whole drek-load of noise, so the chances of this whole thing being a setup were very slim. It had to be that Keith was con-vinced that the night's expedition would supply him with enough dirt to bring down Mariane Corbeau and take her job, because that—apart from an in-and-out that didn't trigger any alerts—was the only outcome that wouldn't slot up his Lone Star career but good.

So that's how we ended up crouching outside the pe-rimeter, the six members of my group, plus Scott Keith and his black-armored troopers with their H&K MP5s. Argent had called in a somewhat-belated point two, and Peg had begun to slot with the electronic security. After a few minutes, the metal-armed samurai nodded, and we started the penetration.

I'd been wondering how Argent intended to go over the fence. It was heavy chain-link, about four meters high and topped with three strands of cutwire. The whole thing was mounted on its supporting pillars with ceramic re-sistors, so I knew it was carrying juice. And *consider-able* juice, judging from the size of the resistors. I couldn't think of any easy ways over that didn't involve either equipment we lacked or magic.

As it turned out, null perspiration. Argent murmured something into his wrist phone, then announced in a whisper, "Fence is down."

Toshi leaped forward, a pair of bolt-cutters in his hands. The samurai's enhanced strength and speed made short work of the fence as he cut a slightly larger-than-man-sized "gate" into the chain links. He tossed the cutters to Hawk, then dived through the hole he'd made. He came up in a combat crouch, his SMG scanning the area for targets.

"Move," Argent snapped. "One minute."

One by one we passed through the hole in the fence. Me and my shadow team first, followed by Keith and his troopers. As soon as the last black-armored figure was through, Toshi closed the gap in the fence, using what looked to me like metal twist-ties to hold the wire in place. The instant he was done, Argent whispered into his phone, "Okay, Peg." The twist-ties, or whatever they were, sparked blue for an instant, and I knew the electric fence was live again.

We moved across the landscape grounds toward building E. Toshi and Argent, probably chipped to the max, advanced in flickering dashes, broken by moments of total immobility as they scanned around them. Although they seemed to be paying no attention to one another, I noticed their "dash-and-cover" moves were perfectly synchronized to let them leap-frog across the terrain, always covering each other. Hawk moved behind them, cautiously searching the area with senses both mundane and arcane. Then it was me, Jocasta, and Rodney. We all had our weapons out, and those two looked almost as tense as I felt. Fanning out behind us were Keith and his troopers. They were pros, too, moving in a slower version of Argent and Toshi's advance, keeping a 360-degree watch.

Hawk and Rodney spotted the incoming trouble almost simultaneously—the elf shouting, "Uh-oh!" while the big Amerindian barked a more communicative "Contact!" The things leaped at us out of the dark, suddenly appearing in my goggles' field of vision. *Big* dogs, the color of the night itself, standing almost a meter at the shoulder. Gaping jaws displayed oversized teeth. Their speed was terrifying. As one lunged toward Toshi, it made a harsh, grunting noise, its mouth loosing a tongue of flame that went a good meter. If the chipped samurai hadn't hurled himself backward, the flame would have washed over him. Even while dodging the flame, Toshi still managed to trigger a short burst from his silenced SMG. My goggles let me see that every round hit, but the hound seemed undaunted.

That was when Hawk stepped forward. Right into the jaws of the attacking hell hounds, it looked like. I was sure he was meat. But the two dogs slammed on the brakes, virtually froze in their tracks. I could see their eyes, blood red against their black pelts, fixed on him. They stood stiff-legged, and their hackles bristled wildly. One whimpered softly. Then Hawk pistoned his arms up and out, threw back his head as if screaming to the sky even though he made no sound. As one, those two doggies tucked their tails between their legs, turned and bolted, disappearing almost instantly into the darkness.

Only when they were well and truly gone did Hawk break his pose, returning to a combat crouch. We moved forward again, the shaman near the front. Though he was keeping up, his movements seemed tired. I mused on that as we advanced. Basically, my only knowledge of high-powered magic came from trideo dramas, in which mages can toss killer spells all day and still have the energy to jam their love interest all night. I was starting to learn that reality was somewhat different.

I also noticed something else important about this encounter. Not one of the DED troopers or any of the Crew had capped off any rounds at the hell hounds. Only Toshi had fired, which was understandable because one of the dogs had him labeled as a midnight snack. That reassured me that the level of discipline was high. Other than the fear of taking a round in the back from Keith and friends, my fear about having the five troopers along was that they would immediately open up with all the ordnance they had at the slightest provocation, blowing everything to hell. I still had enough to worry about, but one less thing was definitely a blessing.

We reached building E with no further incident. Like all the other buildings on the ISP site, it had neither windows nor lights. It also showed the "concrete block-house" style of architecture of all the structures we'd seen during our guided tour. The ferroconcrete-composite walls were angled at almost forty-five degrees, and the corners were slightly rounded to offer no salients. It was almost as if the architects had designed with defense in mind. I was sure those walls could withstand a couple of shots from a panzer's main gun.

The door followed the same mindset: reinforced metal, with flanges all the way around to reinforce it. The keypad for the maglock was protected by a screen of translucent black macroplast, with a smaller keypad mounted above. A lock protecting the lock: just fragging great.

Argent whispered into his wrist phone, "Point three, Peg. Can you get the lock?" He paused for a moment, then the macroplast screen hissed back. "No," he told the decker in response to some question, "you've freed the main lock, but the door's still secured." Another second of silence, then he frowned and said, "Local, got you." He beckoned Toshi forward. "Do it, *omae*," he instructed.

Toshi brushed his hair back from his forehead, and for the first time I saw the datajack in his temple. Samurai *and* decker? My respect for the irritable elf went up a couple of notches. He pulled a length of optical fiber from a belt pouch, snugged a jack into the socket in his head, and attached a couple of adhesive leads to the keypad enclosure. His eyes rolled back in his head as he started his work.

"Come on, come on," a whispered voice sounded in my ears. It took a moment to realize the voice was my own.

The lock keypad issued a soft beep. Toshi pulled the jack out of his head, rolled up the fibers and stuffed them back into his belt pouch. He glanced questioningly at Argent, received a nod in reply, then punched a single key on the pad. The door hissed back, and light washed out.

Show time. There were three sec-guards in the entryway, armed and armored. They turned toward us as the door opened, weapons coming up and mouths gaping open, and there was no time for subtlety. Argent dropped two with head-shots from his silenced Ingrams, Toshi blew the third's throat out with his H&K. The loudest sound in the entire exchange was the clatter as the armor-clad bodies hit the floor. If I hadn't figured it before, I knew now that I was in *way* out of my depth. We all crowded into the entryway, and Toshi hit the key to close the door behind us. Jocasta and I slipped off our night goggles, while Keith and his troopers flipped up the active visors of their helmets.

The only door out of the place was right ahead of us. While waiting back at Rodney's apartment, Jocasta had sketched for us how she thought a P3+ —style containment would have to be laid out. According to that schematic, the door ahead would lead us into the administrative area. From there we could move into the changing rooms, where people put on the protective suits they needed to wear in the lab proper. Beyond that would be the lab itself, isolated from the outside environment by, at the very least, a double-doored airlock arrangement, but more likely by a kind of autoclave that sterilized everything passing in or out. There'd also be the physical plant that handled support matters such as oxygen supply for the sealed lab.

In other words, we'd probably encounter a certain amount of office-building style hallways and offices behind the door, making the tactical situation very tricky. Any turn of the corridor could conceal armed guards, while someone in a room could theoretically burn a clip of ammo into us, aiming by sound alone, right *through* the construction-plastic walls or doors. Not a pleasant prospect.

Hawk closed his eyes again, stilled his breathing. After a few seconds, he re-emerged from his trance-like state, a frown on his face.

"Well?" Argent whispered.

"Another barrier, very powerful," the shaman said, his voice troubled. "I don't know if I can break it."

Argent's lips formed a thin line. "Don't try." He turned his cold eyes on me. "I don't like this," he said.

Well, hell, neither did I. But according to the late, unlamented Dr. Dempsey, my sister was somewhere in here. Then I remembered what Skyhill had said about "added magical precautions," and I relaxed an iota. "It's part of the containment lab," I told him.

From their expressions, I didn't think that either Argent or Hawk really bought that. But pro is pro, and I could see them both decide to live with it. In response to Argent's hand signal, Toshi moved forward and checked the door. He nodded, and rapidly swung open the door, which was decorated with disgusting sprays of blood and tissue.

Something was very wrong. I'd expected office-style hallways, industrial-gray carpeted floors, construction-plastic walls. I didn't see any of those. We were looking into what seemed to be a big stairwell, with a spiral staircase leading down. No, not a *stair*well; it was a helical rampway, more than two meters wide, that led downward. Walls, floor, and ramp looked to be made from a kind of ferroconcrete, but colored a kind of faint beige rather than the conventional gray. And the surface wasn't smooth, but slightly rippled. The light level was low, about that of dusk but redder than sunlight. The air that rolled out through that door was warm, redolent with a strange odor. The scent triggered memories of breweries, but it wasn't quite like that. Ruby-red aiming dots drifted over the far walls as tense fingers touched triggers. Then, after a second or two, they vanished, telling me the weapon-owners had controlled their reactions.

Argent looked over my way, raised his eyebrows questioningly. I shrugged in reply, pointed forward with my empty left hand. He shook his head, a grim half-smile on his face, and politely gestured, "After you."

Great. Wordless though it had been, our conversation had been direct and to the point. I tightened my grip on my Roomsweeper, and cautiously moved forward through the doorway. The moment I stepped onto the gray surface, I knew at once it wasn't ferroconcrete. The floor was slightly soft, giving a minuscule amount under my boots. On impulse, I crouched down to touch it. It felt warm, slightly less than body temperature, like the cooling flesh of a corpse. Hastily I snatched my hand back. I didn't like this at all.

I glanced back at Argent, but his expression hadn't changed. I shifted my gaze to Jocasta, and could see her fear, her concern. That reinforced my flagging will. I stepped onto the spiral ramp.

The ramp was bounded by a guardrail, but it was unnaturally high, reaching to about shoulder-level rather than to the waist. It would still be at least partially effective at keeping me from pitching off the ramp, but it simply didn't match the way most people would have designed it. I leaned over that too-high rail, and looked down. The spiral ramp descended two and a half turns— about twenty meters—into the red-tinged darkness. There was no movement, nothing at all untoward. But that strange, vaguely biological smell kept catching in the back of my throat, triggering all sorts of mental warnings.

I beckoned to the others, and they joined me. I looked questioningly at Argent and pointed downward. After a moment's thought he nodded. He and Toshi took the lead. It was almost as if I'd made it through some rite of passage, and the pros were now willing to walk point again. Jocasta was beside me as I started down, the pressure of her shoulder comforting. We exchanged grins—patently fake—and moved on.

The ramp disgorged us into a large, square chamber about fifteen meters on a side. Floors, walls, and five-meter-high ceiling were the same slightly resilient beige-colored material as the ramp. The light was even more reddish, coming from translucent hemispheres, about thirty centimeters in diameter, set into the walls at about knee level. They reminded me disgustingly of glowing blood-blisters, and the low-angled light cast our shadows—elongated, warped, and horrible—up onto the walls and ceilings. The biological smell—yeast, that's what it reminded me of—was even stronger now.

There were two doors on opposite sides of the chamber, leading north and south. Argent, his modified optics picking up the red tinge of the light until they looked like the eyes of the attacking hell hounds, glanced at Hawk. The shaman spoke up immediately, "I don't like this. Astral barriers on both doors."

"Which is the stronger?" the samurai asked. Without hesitation, Hawk pointed to the north door. Argent turned his lurid eyes on me. "Well, Mr. Johnson," he asked, "any bright ideas?"

I knew what was going through his mind. He and his crew had been hired for a standard lift-out, which this no longer resembled even faintly. His first inclination was to bail, to bug out and take his team with him, leaving me and the rest to rot. The only thing holding him back was his professionalism. He *had* accepted my contract—verbally only, of course, because shadow agreements never make it to paper—but that was binding enough. (If he didn't believe that this was as much a surprise to me as to him, he'd have geeked me on the spot.) So now he was offering me a graceful way of releasing him and his people from the contract, with no ill will or loss of face on either side. All I had to do was say we were hosed, and he'd lead us back out of there, doing everything in his power to make sure we all made it safely to the outside world.

But that wasn't what I was after. I was here for a reason, and no matter how much it freaked me, I was going ahead. I looked him squarely in the eye. "Head north," I said. "People go to more trouble to protect the important stuff."

Argent's eyes were cold and steady, and I could see that he was weighing my decision—and perhaps my life. As he held my gaze for several seconds, I heard the pounding of my own heartbeat in my ears, sweat pricking my brow. But then he nodded curtly. "We head north," he whispered.

Toshi did the door again, swung it back even faster this time. Argent took a quick look through the doorway, then hurtled across it in a diving roll. I heard the muffled drumming of his silenced Ingrams. Before I could even react, Hawk and Toshi were through the door—the former breaking left, the latter right—and all I could do was follow.

The room beyond was even darker than the ramp chamber, the floor softer, the joints between walls and floor or ceiling more rounded. I noticed those features with only part of my mind. My major attention was on the moving figures. Two massive, bipedal things were near the center of the room. I recognized them immediately: they were the same monsters that had attacked us in Capitol Hill. One was staggering under the concentrated fire of the Wrecking Crew. Even as I charged into the room, I saw the ugly thing collapse, its head a shattered ruin. I swung my Roomsweeper around to target the second creature, which was advancing toward Argent, but held off the trigger at the last moment. It was very probable that our penetration of the lab had been undetected to this point, so why add to our problems by blazing away with an unsilenced shotgun?

It didn't seem to be necessary anyway. The three shadowrunners had switched their aim to the new threat, and the sheer impact of the hail of lead was driving the horror back. Silenced spits sounded from beside me. I turned to see Rodney crouching, squeezing off short, precisely targeted bursts from his Uzi. The elf's face was like stone, and I could literally feel the tension in his body. (Of course, I thought after a moment, it was these things that killed Amanda.) The creature, gouting black ooze from a dozen massive wounds, gave a bubbling cry and crashed to the ground.

Another figure was beside me: Scott Keith, his normally florid face pale in contrast to his black armor. "What the frag was that?" he asked in a hushed voice.

I felt my lips draw back from my teeth in a savage grin. "Welcome to Yamatetsu, chummer," I hissed.

I looked around the room. It was large, maybe thirty meters long by half that wide, but the dim reddish light made it hard to judge dimensions. I guessed the ceiling height at considerably more than twice my own height. There were shapes lying against the walls; I counted an even dozen of them. Human-sized shapes, reclining as though asleep. The nearest was five or six meters away. I started to walk slowly toward it. An iron-hard hand fell on my shoulder—Toshi's hand—but I shook it off. The samurai shrugged.

From the corner of my eye I saw the movement, down at the other end of the long room. A human-scale figure, not another hulking monstrosity. Instinctively I turned toward it, my gun coming up, but too late. I saw the muzzle plume of a large-bore weapon; the report seemed diminished, as if the walls were anechoic.

There was nothing diminished about the impact as the bullet hit me on the left side of my chest. My armored duster stopped the round, spread its kinetic energy over a wider area, but it was still like taking a wild pitch in the ribs. I was sure I felt a rib crack, or maybe two, and the pain was like a knife in my side. All my muscles down that side seemed to convulse in reaction, jerking me further around and taking my gun offline. It was all I could do not to cry out from the agony.

Before that gun could blaze a second time, I saw Hawk bring his AK-98 to his shoulder, trigger off three single rounds. I heard a cry from the other end of the room, and the big weapon sent a shot into the ceiling as the figure pitched backward. The two chipped samurai flashed forward, and I followed as fast as I could . . . pulling up short the moment I was near enough to get a good look at the first prone figure.

Long, slender limbs, blonde hair. Face peaceful in what looked to be sleep. It was Theresa.

27

Hawk and Rodney knelt by the motionless body of my sister, conversing in quiet tones. I stood behind them, concentrating all my willpower on not hopping from foot to foot in impatience. Jocasta had her hand on my shoulder, probably in an attempt to calm me. Though I appreciated her solicitude, I didn't *want* to be calm just then. It was my sister, frag it. The others were fanned out around the room prepared for any other unpleasant surprises—*expecting* them, in fact: the two gunshots from the other end of the room hadn't been silenced. Scott Keith kept glancing my way, but didn't come over to say anything, for which I was thankful. He was probably still wondering what he'd gotten himself into.

After what seemed like an hour but was probably only a few minutes, Hawk looked up. His handsome face was troubled. "What?" I demanded.

"She's comatose," the Amerindian said. "Probably has been for more than twenty-four hours. And there's something else." He held up something that looked like a sickly yellow umbilical cord.

That was the first mental impression I got, and I only realized how appropriate it was when Rodney carefully rolled Theresa over onto her back. She was wearing shorts and a singlet, and that disgusting cord vanished up under her top. The elf pulled up her singlet to bare Theresa's stomach, and I could see the *thing* spread out into a grotesque parody of a placenta, which was somehow attached to her skin. The flesh around the fist-sized attachment was reddened, and I thought I could see blood vessels, an abnormal concentration of them, under the skin. I tracked the yellow cord with my eyes, realized that it merged with the soft material of the wall. Slowly I reached out to touch it, drew back my finger at the last moment. Nausea churned in my belly, and bile rose in my throat. I wanted to turn away, but forced myself to

keep looking. "What . . . ?" was as far as I got before
my voice gave out.

It was Rodney who answered. "I'm not exactly sure,"
he said quietly. "The connection"—he indicated the umbilical—"is active, but I can only guess what it might be
doing."

"Guess, then," I said sully.

"It's feeding her," Hawk replied. "Keeping her
alive."

"There's more," Rodney said, though he seemed re-
luctant. "Something is very wrong with her aura. I don't
really know . . ."

Hawk's powerful voice overrode him. "There are other
presences in her aura," the shaman said. "As though
other elements have been incorporated into it."

"Elements?" I asked. "What elements?"

"They have auras in their own right," Hawk said. I
could see, despite his monolithic control, that he was
disturbed. No fragging joke. "Auras of astral creatures.
Like she is the host to astral parasites." He trailed off.

"There's more," I snapped. *"Tell* me."

"The auras are like . . . I've assensed them before."

"Like *what?"*

"Like those." Hawk pointed at the shattered bodies
of our monstrous assailants.

"You know what they are?" In answer to my question,
he nodded slowly, unwillingly. "What the frag *are*
they?"

He hesitated, then seemed to make a decision. "Insect
spirits," he said quietly. "I thought they were of the
Wasp totem, but *this"*—he indicated the umbilical—
"changes things. Another form of Wasp, maybe." He
shrugged his shoulders.

Too much, too fast. I wanted to withdraw, tell the
world "time out." I felt myself begin to sag. This mental
shock, so soon after the physical shocks of Dempsey's
attack and the bullet in the ribs, made me want to curl
up and forget everything. But then I heard Rodney's voice
softly chanting something in Latin. I glanced over at him,
saw his eyes steady on me, and I felt relief flood through
my body. My mind cleared, and I felt as rested and ready
for action as if I'd just slept for eight hours. Even the
massive bruising and the putative broken ribs on my left

side didn't hurt as much. The elf smiled faintly and stopped his chanting, looked back at my sister.

I took a deep breath. The fear and the tension were still there, but I felt able to cope with them now. "So," I said, "astral parasites. What can you do about them?"

"Nothing here," Hawk replied at once. "I believe it might be possible to do something, under the right circumstances. The first problem is to free her . . ."

"Without harming her," Rodney added, "or killing her."

I looked at the umbilical cord, nodded, and averted my eyes. The sight still sickened me. "Okay," I told them, "do what you can."

When nothing else had jumped out and tried to eat us or gun us down, the others had spread out even further around the large chamber. Toshi was just returning from the far end, carrying something. It seemed virtually weightless, judging by how little it slowed down the samurai's movements, but I recognized it as a body even before the elf dumped it unceremoniously at my feet. "Know him?" he asked.

I was about to make a smart-mouth answer, but froze. I *did* know him: not personally, but from a picture in a computer file. It was David Sutcliffe. "Old home week," I muttered.

Toshi fixed me with a sharp stare, waited for me to enlighten him further. When I didn't, he shrugged and turned away. "Big double doors at the end down there," he told Argent. "Where now?"

Argent came over to join me, pitched his voice for my ears alone. "Where to, Mr. Johnson?" he said, but I heard no sarcasm. "She's the target, right?" I knew what he was really saying. Our deal had been for a lift-out, the rescue of my sister. Anything beyond that was beyond the scope of our contract, and Argent had the right to pull his team out—bringing us out with them if we so wished—if he felt it was too heavy. That was something I had to know to make sensible decisions from here on in, and I appreciated his keeping it confidential. Jocasta and Rodney weren't a problem, but it was something I'd rather not have Scott Keith hear.

I nodded my thanks. It wasn't a tough choice: I had what I wanted. "How's it going?" I asked Hawk. He and Rodney were doing something inexplicable with a couple of fetishes. The shaman's big killing knife was out, and in the ruddy light its blade looked to be already wet with blood, but I forced that from my mind.

"It's going," he said without looking up. "Couple minutes."

I nodded again. I raised my voice a little and said, "We're pulling out when Hawk's done. Call it in, Argent." The big samurai nodded, started whispering into his wrist phone.

As I'd expected, Scott Keith was in my face in a moment. "What the frag's this, pulling out?" he demanded. Like many people I've known, he was covering up his own fear with anger. "You haven't got the dirt yet."

I made a gesture encompassing the soft-walled chamber. "Then what's this?" I asked quietly. I pointed to the dead creatures. "What are those?" I indicated Theresa. "Or that? Why don't you take some pictures, and get the hell out with your life, you drekhead? Or stay if you want, it doesn't matter to me." I pointed at Theresa again. "Looks like there's a vacancy opening up." And then I turned away from him, leaving him sputtering and blustering.

Hawk and Rodney were just finishing with Theresa; Jocasta—ever the scientist—was watching over their shoulders. Hawk was using his big knife, but as delicately as a scalpel. The umbilical cord came away from my sister's belly in a spray of blood and liquid that wasn't blood. Rodney pressed a slap patch into place over the raw flesh that had been exposed, while the shaman touched the end of the umbilical, which instantly burst into flame and shriveled. Theresa stirred and moaned— a heart-rending sound—but didn't awaken.

The big Amerindian picked her up, and she looked like a child in his arms. "What about the others?" he asked me.

I looked around the room. There were another eleven figures, presumably in the same state as my sister. Could we just leave them here, to whatever god-awful fate to which all this was a prelude? If not, what else could we do? There were enough people, if you included the DED troopers, to carry them all, but that meant all but one of us would be loaded down with a body if we had to fight

our way out. There was more to it than that. I checked
my watch: it had taken Hawk and Rodney almost ten
minutes of intense work to free Theresa from the umbilical. Assume they'd get better with practice, so call it an
average of eight minutes. That meant it would take *one
and a half hours* to free them all. I couldn't believe that
we'd be left to our own devices for even a quarter that
long.

I glanced at Jocasta. Her eyes were on my face, and I
knew that she knew what I was going through. Hawk,
too: his dark eyes were full of empathy. I wanted someone else to tell me what to do—to tell me the *right* thing
to do—but this was my call.

The choice was between saving Theresa and ourselves
by bailing now or possibly killing everyone by staying
around. Put that way, it was clear that I could make only
one decision—still not easy, but clear. Sometimes you've
got to grab the little victories when you can. "We move
out," I said aloud.

Scott Keith was about to say something, but I just
flipped him the finger. The DED officer reached for his
sidearm, but a targeting laser from Toshi's H&K, centered on that fat man's nose, dissuaded him from making
an issue of it. Toshi didn't seem to like me much, but he
liked Keith a lot less, and was obviously itching for an
excuse to geek him. That seemed like sufficient insurance
to me. I turned my back on Keith.

Hawk passed Theresa's unconscious body to Argent.
The big samurai slung her over his shoulder, but seemed
unaffected by the additional weight. "Out the way we
came," the leader of the Wrecking Crew said.

I turned, cast one last, long look around the chamber.
Eleven comatose figures, each one quite probably host to
astral parasites. And I was leaving them here. I knew I'd
be seeing a lot of this place in my dreams.

And that was when the screaming and the shooting
started. I spun.

Three of the hulking monstrosities—"insect spirits,"
Hawk called them—were suddenly among the DED
troopers. There'd been no warning. The creatures seemed
to appear out of thin air just as they had in the Capitol
Hill apartment.

The troopers were fast and well-trained, I'll give them

that. They spun, rolled aside, sprayed bullets into the twisted figures. But the attackers were even faster. DED troopers became dead troopers. I saw a monster lash out with its clawed arm, tear the spine from an armored trooper, then break the back of another with a back-swing. One of the things seemed to explode under the concentrated fire of a half-dozen SMGs, but the other two seemed little damaged. The troopers were trying to withdraw, to put some safe distance between themselves and those rending claws. If they could extend, they could pump fire into the things with no risk to themselves. But the monsters wouldn't *let* them extend. They kept pressing forward, moving with inhuman speed, seeming not to feel the dozens of rounds slamming into their bodies.

I had my Roomsweeper up, and was looking for a chance to use it. But the things were too closely engaged with the troopers for me to risk a shotgun blast into the melee. The troopers might be working with Scott Keith, but that wasn't—quite—enough reason to waste them.

Toshi and Argent didn't have the same problem. Their smartguns pumped short, precise bursts of fire into the creatures whenever an opening presented itself. A second monster collapsed in a heap, its head literally blown to pieces. The odds didn't look good. Three troopers were down—most definitely dead—while a fourth stared, screaming, at the mangled ruin of her left arm. That mean one fully effective trooper left, plus Keith—count him as one-half—plus my team.

The remaining trooper backed off fast, still pumping shots into the creature. Then his MP-5 clicked empty. He ejected the empty magazine, slammed another into place. In that second, the monster leaped. It reached out with both hands, grabbed the trooper's head, lifted him clear of the ground. The man's agonized scream broke off in mid-ululation as his skull ruptured.

The under-barrel mount of Hawk's AK-98 spat flame. A mini-grenade slammed through the exoskeleton of the creature's chest, detonated an instant later. The monster's torso literally exploded, spraying black fluids and tissue for meters in all directions. Fragments of natural armor lacerated the final, dying trooper, and she collapsed. The air reeked of cordite, blood, and more disgusting odors.

"More of them!" Rodney screamed, pointing at the

door through which we'd entered the chamber. The knee-level lighting in the ramp chamber cast hideously distorted shadows onto the ceiling and into the room. Despite the angular distortion, I knew what they were: more of the insect spirits—or whatever—at least four of them.

I turned, looked at the big double doors at the far end of the room. We were down to the Wrecking Crew, Jocasta, Rodney, and me, plus Scott Keith. Against four more of the things? We didn't have a chance. I pointed at the doors, yelled, "This way!"

Argent, still carrying Theresa, was by my side before I even saw him move. "We're being herded," he hissed.

The same thought had occurred to me. If the things only wanted us dead, why hadn't they simply materialized or manifested or whatever among us the way the first three had? "We don't have much choice, do we?" I said. Argent shook his head.

We moved. The things were advancing much slower than they might have, adding to the impression we were being forced along this path. Hawk and Argent did what they could to slow them down some more by laying grenades in the doorway to set up a curtain of fire and fragments.

Toshi led the way to the other end of the room. The double doors were huge, taking up half the width of the room and extending almost to the ceiling. The doors themselves were made of metal, apparently designed to slide back at the touch of a button mounted on the wall nearby. I wondered just what the hell these massive doors were built to accommodate . . .

Hawk and Argent's rear-guard action was having some effect but not enough. The first two of the creatures were already into the room, advancing slowly toward us. The two shadowrunners were pounding fire into them, but the monsters weren't ready to drop yet. The two men backed rapidly toward us, still firing.

"What's in there?" I asked Rodney.

He shook his head uneasily. "There's a major astral barrier," he said, "and the background count is enormous. I can't see a thing beyond this door."

"Do it, Toshi," Argent barked. I didn't like this at all, but we had absolutely no choice in the matter. I clutched the grip of my Roomsweeper tighter.

Toshi punched the button on the wall. The big double doors started to open with a hiss. While Argent covered our backs, Toshi and Hawk spun into the opening, darted through it. "Clear," the elf samurai snapped a moment later.

"Go," Argent ordered.

We didn't need a second invitation. Rodney, Jocasta, and I slipped through the still-opening doors. Scott Keith was close behind us. His presence was an unpleasant distraction, but there wasn't anything I could do about it at the moment.

We were in some kind of hall, actually more like a tunnel. As I picked up the details, my fear and disgust grew within me. The tunnel was oval in shape, about eight meters wide and half that high. It continued ahead of us for maybe ten meters, then turned to the left, masking from view whatever lay beyond. The inner surface gave under my feet, giving me the disturbing impression that I was walking on flesh. In color it was the same sickly yellow as the umbilical cord that had been attached to Theresa. In fact, in my imagination it was almost as if we'd somehow been reduced to the size of mosquitos and were *inside* that umbilical. My stomach churned, and I wanted to puke. Thankfully, the image passed, as did the nausea; but the fear still remained.

Toshi had found another button, a duplicate of the first, set into the soft wall beside the door. "Argent," he called.

The steel-armed samurai triggered final bursts from both Ingrams, then ducked through the door. Toshi hit the button, and the doors hissed shut again. As soon as they'd closed, Toshi fired a short burst into the panel where the button was mounted. Sparks flew as the electronics shorted out.

From the other side of the doors, I heard a harsh shriek of anger. Had one of those creatures tried the button, found the system was disabled? How intelligent *were* those things? Something heavy slammed into the metal doors.

"Hawk, can you seal them?" Argent said.

The shaman stepped forward, examined the doors. He set his assault rifle down at his feet, then pulled one of the many fetishes from his belt. Clutching the bone-and-

feather item between his clenched fists, he began to sing
quietly under his breath. The melody, what there was of
it, seemed to tell of wilderness and solitude. As I watched
in fascination, the shaman's face changed its appearance.
His already aquiline nose extended, hooking further down
until it resembled a beak. His eyes grew larger, became
more piercing, and his skin took on the color and texture
of golden feathers. For an instant, I realized, I was looking at the face of Eagle. The line where the two halves
of the door met was limned in faint electric-blue light,
and I smelt the tang of ozone in the air.

When I glanced back at Hawk, his song was complete
and his face had returned to normal. It was as if the
transition had been only in my imagination. He took a
deep, cleansing breath, and bent over to retrieve his
weapon.

"Hawk!" Rodney yelled.

28

The big shaman looked up, threw himself backward.
An instant too late. The insect spirit that had shimmered
into existence above his head lashed out with a clawed
arm, tearing through the shoulder and chest of Hawk's
body armor. Blood sprayed, and Hawk gasped with pain.
The thing landed lightly, poised itself to spring on the
wounded shaman. I raised my Roomsweeper, but Hawk
was between me and the monster. Targeting lasers flashed
over Hawk's back as the others sought a clear line of fire.
The thing lunged.

But Hawk reacted an instant faster. First he ducked
low, under its sweeping claws. Then he came up, holding
his broad-bladed knife in both hands. With a grunt of
effort, he drove the knife with all his strength into the
belly of the monster, wrenching the hilt upward to tear
through its exoskeleton. The thing squealed deafeningly
and flailed with its arms, its claws leaving score-marks
in Hawk's back armor, but not penetrating. The big man
thrust upward again, and the monster fell backward, bub-

bling and gouting black ichor. The instant the sight-lines were clear, Toshi sprayed a long burst into the dying thing, shredding its head and torso.

Hawk staggered back. He was covered in blood and ichor, the pain and exhaustion graven deep into the lines of his face. Jocasta rushed to him, tore away his chest armor, and pressed a field dressing against his ripped shoulder. His face tightened with agony even as he nodded his thanks. Again he was singing faintly. Perhaps his magic could help him more than Jocasta's medkit.

I turned to Rodney, pointed at the dead creature. "Could it have come through the door?" I asked.

The elf mage closed his eyes for a moment, then shook his head. "Impossible. The astral barrier's still in place," he said. The look on his face told me we'd reached the same conclusion: the thing had already been on our side of the door when we came through it and the creature had probably not been alone.

Jocasta was still busy tending to Hawk, but everyone else seemed to be waiting for me. Maybe the disgusting appearance of the tunnel had put off the two samurai. Or maybe they were waiting for the "Mr. Johnson" who'd gotten them into this to take point for once. Much as the thought terrified me, I couldn't blame them.

I strode forward, past Scott Keith, who was looking around like a trapped rat. I slapped him hard on the shoulder. "Glad you came along, huh?" His answer was both irrelevant and unprintable. I tightened my grip on the Roomsweeper's stock, and took the lead down the tunnel.

The floor grew even softer underfoot as I approached the turn. No more of the red light-globes. The tunnel walls themselves seemed to glow with a putrid yellow light. Phosphorescence of some kind, I wondered, or something even more unpleasant? The air was warm and damp—I could feel my sodden clothes sticking to my skin—and the yeast-like smell was strong, almost choking. I glanced over my shoulder. Yes, the others were following me, but cautiously and a couple of meters back.

Just as cautiously I followed the turn in the tunnel, scanning the way ahead with my shotgun barrel. Nothing there. The others were hanging back, waiting for me to reconnoiter. I beckoned them up, and moved forward slowly.

Another turn ahead, this one sharper. I peered around it, *carefully.*

Ahead of me the tunnel opened up into another chamber, a smaller version of the one where we'd found Theresa, illuminated by the now-familiar red globes. It looked empty. I signaled "all clear" and edged forward.

The floor was firmer here, with more the resilience of turf than of flesh. The chamber was, I guessed, about ten meters on a side. I scanned it, the Roomsweeper barrel tracking with my gaze. I'd been right that it was empty. I turned back to wave the others on.

"Derek Montgomery." The voice was familiar and came from within the chamber. I spun back.

I knew that barrel-chested figure, the close-cropped sandy hair and beard. A moment before no one had been there—I swear to it—but now Adrian Skyhill was standing in front of me, hands on his hips and a big drek-eating grin on his face.

Instinctively I ducked aside, brought the Roomsweeper to bear—*anything* down here was an enemy—and squeezed the trigger. The shotgun roared, kicking brutally in my hand.

The shot was accurate, but the pellets never reached Skyhill. Instead they sparked off some kind of curved, invisible barrier in front of him, spraying off wildly in all directions. I pumped another round into the chamber, but didn't pull the trigger.

The shadowrunners were beside me in an instant. Rodney's and Jocasta's lasers showed up clearly on his dark business suit, now studded with evil-looking fetishes, but they didn't fire.

Skyhill's smile broadened, but his face had something terribly strange about it. At first I thought it was because of the shadows cast by the weird lighting, but then I realized it was more than that. When I looked directly at Skyhill, his face looked normal. When I moved my eyes slightly, so that I was viewing him out of my peripheral vision, his face was alien, hideous. His eyes were enlarged and looked multifaceted, and where his mouth should have been was an array of serrated mandibles, knife-edged slicers, and other mouth parts. Look back at him directly, and all was as normal. I remembered the way Hawk's face had changed when he was magically sealing the doors. Was I seeing the face of Skyhill's totem? Hawk had mentioned the Wasp totem. Didn't that imply there were Wasp shamans?

Skyhill looked to my left, at Argent, who was still carrying Theresa over one shoulder. The insect shaman's smile faded a little. "I see you found your sister," he said. "Oh well, we'll soon return her to where she was. It seems a shame to deny her after she's made it this far."

My forearm ached from my death-grip on the Roomsweeper. Suddenly, sickening, I thought I knew what he was implying. "You *infected* her," I screamed. "You infected my sister with astral parasites."

Skyhill looked puzzled. "Oh, I understand what you mean," he said after a moment. "Those aren't 'astral parasites.' They're immature Ichneuman Wasp spirits."

"I don't care what the frag they are!" I bellowed at him. "Get them out of her!"

The big man looked honestly surprised. "Why would I wish to do that?" he said. "They'll be mature soon, Then one of them will possess your sister, and she'll *belong*. Forever."

"Like *you* belong?" I demanded sarcastically.

He shook his head sadly; sarcasm was lost on him. "Belonging will not be mine for some time," he said morosely. "There's so much more for me to do before I can accept that gift."

"I'll kill you!"

"You'll try," Skyhill said calmly, "and you'll fail."

I pumped another shot at him. Again, the double-ought pellets spattered away harmlessly. Why hadn't the shadowrunners fired? Were they under some kind of magical control? Or did they merely understand the futility of it better than I did?

"I can offer you the same belonging," the insect shaman said, totally unconcerned that I'd just tried again to blow him in two. "You're strong-willed enough. The merge might be good."

I lowered the Roomsweeper's barrel, shook my head as dull amazement grew within me. "*This* is what you were hiding all along," I said quietly. "You've got nothing to do with 2XS at all."

"Of *course* we do," Skyhill said, with what might almost have been offended pride. "It's our technology. We developed it specifically."

"*Why?*" I was way out of my depth, again.

Skyhill shrugged. "Money, influence. But those are secondary. You know how destructive long-term 2XS use is?" I nodded. "If someone has the strength to survive it—like your sister—they are perfect candidates for belonging. They'll be strong enough to act as hosts for the immature spirits, and when it comes time for their own possession, the chances are excellent that the merge will be good. They'll retain their own physical form, but gain the powers of the Ichneuman Wasp spirit—the truest form of belonging. Don't you understand?" he went on earnestly. "We can't offer belonging to just anyone, we have to seek out the best candidates. I found the perfect way in 2XS."

I stared at him. "You destroy people with 2XS," I said, "and the ones you don't destroy, you bring here and destroy *this* way." I hooked a thumb back at Theresa. "*You motherfragger!*"

Skyhill looked hurt. "Unfortunately you don't understand," he muttered, more to himself than to us. "Unfortunate."

And then he began to sing, a high-pitched keening song, with buzzing overtones. It pierced my mind, infiltrated my thought processes. I was confused. Why was I pointing my weapon at Skyhill? I wondered. It was the big fragger to my left who was trying to kidnap my sister. Wasn't it he who caused all this trouble in the first place? I snarled in anger as I started to turn toward Argent.

But then, suddenly and shockingly, I felt Rodney Greybriar's eyes on me, steady and concerned. I felt the presence and the strength of his personality pass through my mind like a brisk wind, blowing away all traces of the abnormal thoughts I'd been thinking a moment ago as if they were so much dust. My snarl became a scream of rage, of horror at what Skyhill had almost done to my mind. The Roomsweeper came up, and roared. I jacked another round into place, pulled the trigger again.

This time the two samurai joined their fire with mine, but with no better success. Spent bullets whined about

the chamber as they ricocheted off Skyhill's arcane shield.
The insect shaman was singing again.

"Tactical cover," Hawk snapped. And then the big
Amerindian collapsed bonelessly to the ground.

Skyhill stopped his whirring song. With a frown, he
sank down into lotus position, and closed his eyes. The
shadowrunners checked their fire.

I rounded on Argent. "What the *frag's* going on?"

The samurai bounced a single shot off Skyhill's magical shield before answering. "Hawk's going for him on
the astral," he answered calmly. "When the enemy's
barriers go down—which they will—we gut him."

I saw Rodney's face light up in a smile. "More hands
make light work," he remarked casually. Then he, too,
crumpled to the ground.

Toshi scanned the chamber all around us for unwel-
come guests, while every second or so Argent capped off
a round at the unconscious Skyhill.

It was over quickly, and I wished I'd been able to see
it and understand it. Skyhill suddenly screamed, and one
of the fetishes he wore on his clothes burst into flame,
blossomed into a fireball like the one that had almost
toasted me in Purity. I turned aside, shielding my face
with my arm.

But it wasn't necessary. The flame expanded, but only
so far, as if constrained by an invisible hemisphere, some
invisible bell jar, surrounding Skyhill. The same arcane
shield that had kept our bullets out now served to keep
the fireball in.

In an instant the fireball was gone. Argent triggered a
burst into the slumped figure of Skyhill, but it wasn't
necessary. The insect shaman was scorched meat, sullen
flames still licking here and there over his body. Greasy
smoke and the reek of burned flesh filled the air.

Hawk and Rodney stirred, climbed slowly to their feet.
They looked tired, and both were bleeding from nicks
and cuts that hadn't been present before. If someone's
wounded in a fight on the astral plane, I wondered, do
those wounds transfer themselves to his physical body?
It seemed that they must.

"Are you all right?" I asked. Both nodded their heads,
but didn't say a word. Their satisfied smiles said all that
was needed.

"Where now, Mr. Johnson?" Argent asked softly. "Back the way we came?"

Fragging good question. Skyhill or no Skyhill, we still had the four—or more—insect warriors left behind us, and the chamber we were in had only one exit: the tunnel through which we'd entered. Dead end.

Rodney saved me from answering. "Why don't we go through there?" he suggested lightly.

I looked to where he was pointing—at the featureless wall opposite the tunnel entrance. For an instant I wondered if he was joking, but then he closed his eyes and murmured some Latin words under his breath. My image of the wall began to shimmer, as if I were looking through flame or heat haze. When it steadied again, I saw an opening, another tunnel identical to the first. I kept my voice and expression casual as I responded, "Why don't we?"

I resumed my position of point. Not that I really wanted to, but I figured it was still my duty . . . if that word meant anything. My thoughts and emotions tumbled chaotically. I felt split. Part of me wanted to sit down and think, deal with the consequences of what Sky-hill had said. Another part wanted to bury the whole crock of drek so deep in my subconscious that it would never again see the light of day. At the moment, of course, the latter was the most logical course of action. Survive now, think later sounded the best deal to me. I advanced slowly down the tunnel.

One turning, two. Then Argent's metal touch on my shoulder stopped me. "Don't rush it," he whispered. "Something I need to know first." He raised his wrist phone to his mouth and murmured, "Peg, track in on my signal. Got it? Okay, where the frag are we?" I couldn't hear the decker's answer, of course, but I did see the samurai's brief smile.

He closed the phone and said, "Want to guess?" I shook my head. "We're about fifteen meters below ground level, about a hundred meters southwest of the first ramp. That means we're almost directly below the admin building."

That was good news. I figured our chances of getting out of here in one piece had just gone up a couple of notches. Why excavate directly under another building if you're not going to install some connection to the surface?

I pressed on, shotgun at the ready. Another turn. I was mentally exhausted, and physically drek-kicked. What the frag was it with all these tunnels anyway? I wondered. Nobody in their right mind would design this way. But then I remembered who/what we were dealing with. Insect spirits or insect totems or whatever they were, would have—by definition, I suppose—thought processes that only vaguely resembled those of humans or metahumans. And if Skyhill was any example of how proximity to those creatures could totally slot up your thinking, I figured I'd best discard all ideas about the way things should or should not be laid out. If I wanted to live to tell about it, that is.

Another fragging turn, but this time with darkness all around it. I ducked back, taking a moment to slip on the night goggles and snug them into place. Then I sneaked a peek around the turn again.

Still darkness. There was nothing there. I stepped cautiously out from the wall, advanced one step, then another.

A faint flash of light ahead of me. Without thinking, I threw myself to the side, fast but not quite fast enough. The bolt of mystical energy crackled and roared out of the darkness, a stream of blue-white fire. If I hadn't moved, the raging core of that bolt would have torn through my chest. As it was, the fainter, less-energetic margin of the beam washed over my left arm.

That was enough. I screamed as a white-hot blowtorch of pain blossomed through my body. My arm was on fire, in flames, but I wasn't sure whether it was the flesh itself or just my clothing. I fell to the ground, smothering the flames with my body. Darkness washed over me, tried to engulf me, but I forced it back with an Olympian effort of will. My vision swam and blurred, my thoughts flowed sluggishly like synth-vodka fresh from an extra-cold freezer. The agony in my left arm was still excruciating, but it was as though I were experiencing it from a distance. As if I was both hurting and watching somebody else hurt. Wound shock, I knew, potentially fatal if not treated.

But none of my companions had any time to tend to

me. They were too busy fighting for their lives. In the
position where I lay, the floor seemed to be at an angle
of about thirty degrees, making the whole scene look
even more confusing than it already was. But I simply
couldn't find the energy to roll over and bring the world
upright.

The chamber ahead was lit now with the standard
blood-red light, punctuated by muzzle flashes, grenade
bursts, and arcs of magical energy. It was more than
bright enough for me to see what a part of my mind had
been anticipating all along.

The Queen.

About five meters long, she was a distorted shape the
unclean white of a maggot. Huge, segmented lower body,
again like a maggot or a grub. Seeming to sprout from
the fore end of the pustulant mass was something that
looked like the torso of a woman, and two small, possibly vestigial, limbs angled out and back where the two
parts joined.

But no, I realized, with a jolt of horror that penetrated
the mental fuzziness of wound shock, that wasn't the right
way round at all. The white lower body sprouted from
the woman's form—not the other way round—from her
abdomen. Those two jutting limbs were actually the
woman's legs, spread wide—probably dislocated from
their sockets—by the mass of the bloated abdomen.

She was lying prone, arching her upper body back,
holding herself up with one arm. Her lips were drawn
back from her teeth in what could have been either a
smile or a snarl. She'd once been beautiful, I saw. But
now her long blonde hair was missing in patches, and
seemed to have the texture of straw. Her honey-colored
skin was discolored here and there to pus-beige, and
looked bloated and blistered. Her eyes were larger than
normal, and their dozens of facets reflected spears of
lights.

The shadowrunners were in the mouth of the tunnel
around me, spraying automatic fire into the monstrosity.
The bullets glanced from her body in whining ricochets.
The rounds seemed to actually bounce off the Queen's
body, rather than reflecting off an invisible shield as they
did with Skyhill. Jocasta and Rodney were there, triggering short, ripping bursts from their Uzis. Even Scott

Keith was there, emptying his MP-5 into the distorted form.

With her free arm, the Queen reached out toward us. Another coruscating bolt of blue lashed out. It took Keith full in the chest, turned the DED officer into a human torch. Even for someone I hated, it was a frag of a way to go.

Hawk dropped his assault rifle, tore another fetish from his belt, and began his song of the clean, open sky. A shimmering aura of power built around him, then burst outward toward the bloated Queen. It struck, and for a moment I saw the shaman's power and hers strive against each other in a sparking, crackling curtain of sheer energy. From another angle, a force of another kind slammed into the Queen, and I knew Rodney was also doing what he could.

But then the Queen's blue lightning cracked forth again. Even with his chipped reflexes, Toshi couldn't evade it. The blue arc smashed into his chest, burst out through his back. For an instant he stood transfixed by it, screaming, then his body burst into flame and crumpled to the ground.

I had to do something to help my friends. But what? Their guns had been ineffective. How could I expect mine to harm that obscenity? Frag, I wasn't even sure if I could move.

Out the corner of my eye I saw a shimmering as something took shape in the tunnel behind us. And I learned that I *could* move if I really had to. Pain washed through me as I rolled over, and it took everything I had to keep from fainting so I could bring up my Roomsweeper.

There were two of them, two of the insect spirit warriors that I now seemed to know so well. I squeezed the trigger. The recoil conducted up my right arm and into my body, triggering another burst of pain in my left arm and a scream through clenched teeth. I put the Roomsweeper's pistol grip against my shoulder and worked the pump one-handed. Then I brought the barrel up again and blasted another load of double-ought shot into the lead creature's chest. I screamed again, in exaltation this time, as I saw the colossal damage done by the shotgun blast. Once more I worked the pump, and again pulled the trigger. *"Die, you fraggers!"* Whose voice was that? An instant later I realized it was my own.

By that time Argent had turned, his Ingrams spitting death into the oncoming horrors. The first one, the one I'd already ruined, collapsed, and I put another blast into the second. I grabbed the pump again, but there was no resistance behind it. The tubular magazine was empty, and no way I could re-load.

It didn't matter anyway. Argent bent over, dumping Theresa unceremoniously to the ground as he picked up the AK-98 that Hawk had discarded. Firing from the hip he drove two minigrenades into the insect warrior. Detonating almost simultaneously, the grenades blew the monster to fragments.

Harsh blue light reflected off the walls, and my ears were filled with the horrible crackle of the Queen's magic. I rolled over, too exhausted to even scream from the pain in my left arm.

Hawk was the target this time. The blue arc struck him, but didn't immolate him. Instead the light hissed and spat, licking over his body like St. Elmo's fire. For a second or two the display continued, then the light faded.

The big Amerindian sagged, his face gray and haggard. He tried to take up his song again, but his voice was cracked and hoarse, and he gave up after a couple of notes. He staggered and dropped to his knees.

In the background, I saw Rodney launch another spell. Barely visible, like a shockwave, it flashed across the space and slammed into the Queen. The impact was tremendous, rocking the hideous creature back. What was left of her hair flew, and some was torn from her scalp. He'd hurt her this time.

But Rodney was almost as scragged as Hawk. I saw that if he tried to do that again, it'd kill him.

Rodney looked over at me and our eyes met. Suddenly, with terrible certainty, I knew what he was going to do. "No, Rodney," I tried to yell, but my voice came out as a croak.

The elf darted over and snatched the shaman's broadbladed knife from its belt sheath. Rodney moved so fast the Amerindian didn't have time to react, but I saw comprehension in Hawk's sunken, pain-racked eyes. "Walk with beauty," he said, his voice almost a whisper.

"He who walks with beauty has no need of fear," the elf mage replied. It sounded like a ritual response. "Have you got enough left?"

The shaman nodded. "I've got enough."

The elf darted forward, straight at the Queen. Blue light crackled out, licked over the mage's body. His clothes were aflame, but he continued his mad rush. With a scream of defiance, perhaps even triumph, he flung himself onto the human upper body of the Queen. Even as she tore him in two with her clawed hands, he drove the knife deep into the chest between her withered breasts.

The Queen flailed and screeched. She reached to grab the hilt of the knife and drag it forth.

Hawk took up his song again. A proud, sad melody. I knew it was the last song he'd ever sing. He raised his arms in an invocation and pointed to the writhing Queen.

Flame—white, cleansing flame—washed over her. As the flame consumed her, the fire's roar also swallowed up the sound of her screeching. The light of his final spell reflected in Hawk's eyes. Then he pitched forward and was still.

Silence. I felt a touch on my shoulder, knew it was Jocasta. I tried to roll over, look up into her face, but I didn't have the strength. It felt as though someone was lifting me, then darkness opened before me like a pit, and I tumbled in.

Epilogue

Consciousness didn't return easily. I pursued it, sometimes drawings near to my quarry, but not quite catching it. There were dreams, dreams of white lights and sharp smells, of pain and nausea. Flashes of memory followed by immeasurable spans of blissful forgetfulness. People visited me, I think, but I wasn't sure whether they were real or only more dreams. Maybe I talked to them or maybe I dreamed that, too.

I don't know how long this pseudo-death went on before I finally opened my eyes and was able to assign words to what I saw. A white tile ceiling, fluorescent light fixtures. Smells in the air that meant hospital.

I looked around. Yep, hospital bed, in a private hospital room. (Who was paying for it? I wondered briefly before discarding that worry as meaningless. Being alive was all that mattered.)

I was lying on my back, my right forearm attached by a soft strap to the side rail of the bed. It was obviously so that I couldn't roll over and accidentally pull out the IV needle and various sensor electrodes inserted into my wrist. My left arm . . .

I closed my eyes, took a calming breath, before looking over at my left arm. Wasted effort, I couldn't see it anyway. The whole left side of my upper torso was concealed from my view by a sheet over a kind of frame. I felt sick.

After a few moments, a few more deep breaths, I tried to inventory my bodily sensations. Basically status normal, except for my left arm. There I was feeling small, random shooting pains in my fingers and forearm. I tried to flex my fingers, but felt nothing whatsoever. Tried to move the whole arm. Still nothing. The sheet over the frame didn't move; nothing moved against my left side.

Phantom pain is what they call it. When you've lost a

limb, your nervous system never really accepts the fact. You keep feeling nagging aches and pains in the limb that doesn't exist any more. Phantom pain. I let my head fall back on the pillow.

I heard the door open, heard two people approach, but didn't look up. A woman cleared her throat. Jocasta? No, the sound wasn't right. I didn't bother to look.

Finally, a man's voice said cheerily, "Well, Mr. Johnson, how are we feeling today?"

A nurse, it had to be. Just as cops are the only people who say "exited," nurses are the only people who say "how are *we* today?" I neglected to give the standard answer, "I think *we're* pretty lousy," but I did look up.

I'd got it right in one. Young, trim-looking nurse, wearing a standard off-white coverall. Beside him stood someone who was undeniably a doctor: in her late forties, with serious face and even more serious manner. So this is how they break the news now, I found myself thinking. A demented medical version of "good cop/bad cop."

"Good morning, Mr. Johnson," the doctor said. Her voice was serious enough to make her face and manner seem flippant by comparison. "I'm Dr. Judith Zebiak, and I've been handling your case for the past two weeks."

"Cut the snow, Doctor," I said sharply. "You had to take it off, didn't you?" She looked at me blankly. "My arm," I amplified.

She hesitated, then I saw her come to a decision. "Normally we'd wait a little longer," she said drily, "but since you insist . . ." She stepped to my bedside.

I turned my face away, closed my eyes—I'd asked, but I wasn't sure I wanted to know, not *this* brutally—and I heard her whisk away the sheet. But of course there was nothing to be gained by denying reality. Sticking their heads in the sand hadn't saved ostriches from extinction. I forced my eyes open, turned my head slowly.

My arm was there, still attached to me. I felt a cold rush of relief throughout my body, so intense I think I almost fainted again. The tight fist of tension loosened in my stomach. I wanted to cry.

My arm lay there, palm-up on the bed. The skin was a little pale, but that was a small price to pay. I'd thought for sure it was history.

I tried to move my fingers. Nothing happened. The "phantom pain" was still there. Drugs, maybe? Some kind of neural blocker to prevent me from moving and damaging the arm while it was still healing? I looked up at Dr. Zebiak and asked, "When can I move it?"

"Usually I'd say another week," she said, "but this *is* a special case. And if you insist . . ."

"I do," I assured her.

She shrugged. She withdrew something from her pocket that looked like a small electrical probe. Some kind of medical instrument, I assumed. She bent over my left wrist, brought the instrument close to the skin.

And fragged if she didn't flip open a tiny access port and insert the probe. She pushed a button on the tip.

My arm *buzzed*. Sensation rushed back. I could feel the cool sheet under my skin, the weight of my arm on the bed. There was a strange, somehow unnatural feeling in the wrist. The doctor withdrew the probe, closed the access port, and the unnatural feeling went away.

My stomach churned. I thought I was going to be sick.

Zebiak must have seen the distress in my face. She hurried to the foot of the bed, lifted up a little device the size of a palm-top computer, examined the screen. "What's the matter?" she asked me.

I couldn't speak, I couldn't force the words out. I just pointed at the arm.

She nodded, still not understanding. "Yes," she said, "it's the model you requested, I assure you. Later, when you're adapted, we'll work on matching skin tone and follicle density—"

"But I *didn't* . . ." I managed to gasp. "What the frag happened to me?"

Her stern expression softened a little, and she whispered into the tiny computer. I wasn't supposed to hear, I suppose, but I picked up the words "retrograde amnesia." Then she was talking to me, but quietly, maybe even kindly. "Memory sometimes take a while to come back, Mr. Johnson. Do you want me to fill you in?" I nodded dumbly. "You were unconscious when you were transferred from Seattle General, of course," she said, "but—"

I cut her off again. "Where am I now?"

She blinked. "Harborview. Where else?"

Where else? I lay back, closed my eyes. "Sorry," I said. "Please go on."

"You were unconscious when you arrived, but Mr. Barnard's instructions were clear." Mr. Jacques Barnard. I decided not to interrupt her again. I'd figure it all out later. "He said you'd specified the Wiremaster CDA-15 with enhanced strength, and also that you'd requested being kept under electrosleep throughout the entire first stages of the procedure." She looked a little troubled at that, but went on, "Not a common request, but the department head approved it, so we went ahead on that basis. We continued the process of excising the unrecoverable flesh, and . . ."

I raised a hand—my meat hand—to stop her. I did *not* want to hear any more about how they'd chopped off my ruined left arm, which is what she was talking about. "So Barnard is paying for all this?" I asked.

"Of course," she said, giving me more to think on later. "He left you this." She tossed an envelope on the bed.

"Thanks," I said. "And thanks for clearing me up. I think things are starting to come back," I lied. Then I paused. I had another important question, but wasn't sure if I wanted to hear the answer. "Did . . ." I trailed off, tried again. "Did anyone visit me while, while . . ."

Dr. Judith Zebiak smiled, and her face didn't crack after all. "Ms. Josie Eisenstein spent several days here," she told me. "She asked me to tell you she would have been here today, but that your, er, mutual friend needed her assistance. There's a message from Ms. Eisenstein in the envelope as well. I'll leave you to read it." She hesitated. "Would you like me to turn off the arm, or will you be careful?"

"I'll be careful," I assured her.

As soon as she and the nurse had left, I tore open the envelope, pulled out the contents. On top was a handwritten note from Jocasta—sorry, from Josie Eisenstein. I read that first. It was just a couple of lines.

"Glad you're back in the land of the living. Sorry I couldn't be there on the big day: slight reversal with Theresa. Don't worry. Prognosis favorable, but a long process. See you soon—J."

I folded the note, returned it to the envelope. Prog-

nosis favorable—guess I couldn't hope for anything better. And *everything's* a long process. Now that I knew
Jocasta was still going to be around, I was glad she wasn't
here at the moment. I still had too many things to sort
through and to slot into the right spaces.

I took the other two pieces of paper from the envelope,
presumably the message from Jacques Barnard. It wasn't
the note I'd expected, however. The first sheet was a
laser-printed statement of a bank account in the name of
one D.M. Johnson, itemizing the disbursement of
120,000 nuyen to Demolition Man Building Services Inc.
for "services rendered," plus an additional 30,000 nuyen for "miscellaneous expenses." Apparently Barnard
had paid off the Wrecking Crew—that was, Argent, Peg,
and the estates of Hawk and Toshi—in full, plus bonus.

The second piece was a hard-copy transcript of a Lone
Star death report for one Derek Montgomery, of no fixed
address, no current SIN. According to the report, I'd
died in a failed assault against the Yamatetsu ISP division
in Fort Lewis, burned virtually beyond recognition by
one of the company's hell hounds (authorization permit
number etcetera etcetera drek etcetera), final ident verification through dental records (partial) and gene typing
(inferred), confidence level 99.91 percent.

I very carefully folded the papers and returned them
to the envelope. So I was dead; at least, the odds were
about a thousand to one that I was, and that was good
enough for me. It certainly would be for Lone Star. I was
out from under, off the hook, choose the cliché. My debt
to the Wrecking Crew was paid, and I could be confident
that, unless I did something real stupid, the Star would
never again be on my tail. You could say I had one more
debt outstanding—the one to Anwar, concerning the way
he'd sold me out to Scott Keith—but whether or not it
was ever collected was entirely my decision. A very significant gift, particularly when you added in the cost of
a new arm plus private treatment at Harborview. Thank
you, Mr. Barnard.

But of course, corps don't give gifts; they make investments. One day soon, Barnard would come around to ask
me for something in return. In services, or out of my
hide, depending on his needs of the moment.

Or maybe not. I understood now that Barnard had sent

me to Skyhill in the first place in the hope that I'd bring down his rival or that said rival would geek me and Barnard would catch him at it. Well, I'd brought down Skyhill all right, which probably meant that the ISP division, with its profitable SPISES deal and possibly 2XS thrown in, too, would fall under Barnard's control. Maybe all this was his idea of fair payment for services rendered. I'd probably never know for sure until I got that phone call from Madison Park or maybe directly from Yamatetsu International in Kyoto.

I looked over at my new arm. Lying there on the sheet it sure looked real. I raised it to my face, ran the new fingers over my skin. It felt real, too. All the sensations were just as before.

I'd lost my arm; it had been burned away beneath the rolling ground of Fort Lewis. But they'd replaced it.

What about my self-image, my world view—why the frag not use the word?—my *soul?* I'd lost something there, too, but *it* could never be replaced. My belief— my cocky, self-centered, drek-for-brains belief—that I was in control: of myself and of the world around me. *That* was gone forever.

Theresa always saw things clearer than I did. I realized that now for the first time. She saw how dark and inimical the world could be, and she accepted the truth of that. That was why she couldn't cope, why she'd turned to simsense chips, to BTL, finally to 2XS.

And me? I'd *thought* I could cope. Thought I could handle it. But my "coping mechanisms" were all types of denial, ways of avoiding having to deal with the truth. Alcohol, my "knight-in-shining-armor" posturing, most of all my facile judgments of people like my sister. I'd always believed—deep down—that I was better than her, more competent to deal with the world. Lying here, with my new arm humming softly to itself as it performed some self-diagnostic, I knew that belief for the drek that it was.

Patrick Bambra? You and I were very alike, my friend, even though I couldn't, or wouldn't, see it. We each had our romantic illusions. The only difference was that I hid mine better.

And Jocasta Yzerman. You'd probably never fully understand what I was going through. You were more like

Theresa. You could look at the world honestly, face its darkness undismayed because you know who you are. Me? Maybe I'll be able to say that someday. But until I can, I think we'll be living in different worlds.

So where would I go from here? I felt the overwhelming craving for what I'd experienced when the signal from the 2XS chip went trickling into my brain—the confidence that everything was in control. Wasn't that confidence just an electronically reinforced macrocosm of the great lie I'd always told myself? That the world was something I could confront and understand, and that eventually I'd have everything chipped? *There* was the real attraction of 2XS, I understood for the first time: it was for people who weren't as good as I was at lying to themselves.

So, what now? Well, I had to get myself physically healthy, that was the first order of business. And then I had to do what I could for Theresa. Maybe we *would* slip the border into some other, less complicated environment (or was belief in such a possibility just another lie?). Maybe Jocasta would come with us, maybe not. Only time would tell.

But that was all in the future. For now I had the time to remember. And the time to mourn. Lolly and Buddy. Amanda, who threw away eternity to save the lives of some mortals. Hawk and Rodney, whose sacrifices were just as real. And part of myself.

I interlinked the fingers of my right and left hands— old grasping new.

And I tried to sleep.

MAGICAL REALMS

☐ **KING OF THE SCEPTER'D ISLE—A Fantasy Novel by Michael Greatex Coney.** Fang, the most courageous of the Gnomes, joins forces with King Arthur and the beautiful Dedo Nyneve to manipulate history in a final confrontation of wills and worlds. "Spirited, zestful . . . truly magical." —*Booklist* (450426—$4.50)

☐ **SUNDER, ECLIPSE AND SEED—A Fantasy Novel by Elyse Guttenberg.** Even as Calyx struggles with her new-found power of prophecy, her skills are tested when the evil Edishu seeks to conquer Calyx and her people through their own dreams. (450469—$4.95)

☐ **WIZARD'S MOLE—A Fantasy Novel by Brad Strickland.** Can the politics of magic and the magic of advertising defeat the Great Dark One's bid for ultimate power? (450566—$4.50)

☐ **MOONWISE by Greer Ilene Gilman.** It was Ariane and Sylvie's own creation, a wondrous imaginary realm—until the power of magic became terrifyingly real. (450949—$4.95)

☐ **THE LAST UNICORN by Peter S. Beagle.** One of the most beloved tales in the annals of fantasy—the spellbinding saga of a creature out of legend on a quest beyond time. (450523—$6.95)

WORLDS OF WONDER

☐ **BARROW by John Deakins.** In a town hidden on the planes of Elsewhen, where mortals are either reborn or driven mad, no one wants to be a pawn of the Gods. (450043—$3.95)

☐ **WIZARD WAR CHRONICLES: LORDS OF THE SWORD by Hugh Cook.** Drake Douay fled from his insane master, a maker of swords. But in a world torn by endless wars, a land riven in half by a wizard powered trench of fire, an inexperienced youth would be hard-pressed to stay alive. (450655—$3.99)

☐ **THE HISTORICAL ILLUMINATUS CHRONICLES, Vol. I: THE EARTH WILL SHAKE by Robert Anton Wilson.** The Illuminati were members of an international conspiracy—and their secret war against the dark would transform the future of the world! "The ultimate conspiracy ... the biggest sci-fi cult novel to come along since *Dune*."—The Village Voice (450868—$4.95)

☐ **THE HISTORICAL ILLUMINATUS CHRONICLES, Vol. 2: THE WIDOW'S SON by Robert Anton Wilson.** In 1772, Sigismundo Celline, a young exiled Neapolitan aristocrat, is caught up in the intrigues of England's and France's most dangerous forces, and he is about to find out that his own survival and the future of the world revolve around one question: What is the true identity of the widow's son? (450779—$4.99)

Prices slightly higher in Canada.

If you and/or a friend would like to receive the *ROC Advance*, a bimonthly newsletter featuring all the newest and hottest ROC books and authors, on a complimentary basis, please fill out this form and return it to:

ROC Books/Penguin USA
375 Hudson Street
New York, NY 10014

Your Address
Name _____
Street _____ Apt. # _____
City _____ State _____ Zip _____

Friend's Address
Name _____
Street _____ Apt. # _____
City _____ State _____ Zip _____